T0103441

THE LAST LETTER FROM LONDON

Pam Lecky is an Irish historical fiction author. Having been an avid reader of historical and crime fiction from a young age, it was inevitable that her books would be a combination of the two. Pam lives in North County Dublin with her husband and three children. She can be contacted through social media or by visiting her website www.pamlecky.com.

By the same author:

Her Secret War
Her Last Betrayal

THE
LAST
LETTER
FROM
LONDON

PAM LECKY

avon.

Published by AVON
A division of HarperCollins*Publishers*
1 London Bridge Street
London SE1 9GF

www.harpercollins.co.uk

HarperCollins*Publishers*
Macken House, 39/40 Mayor Street Upper,
Dublin 1, D01 C9W8
Ireland

A Paperback Original 2023

1

First published in Great Britain by HarperCollins*Publishers* 2023

Copyright © Pam Lecky 2023

Pam Lecky asserts the moral right to be identified as the author of this work.

A catalogue copy of this book is available from the British Library.

ISBN: 978-0-00-855830-7

This novel is entirely a work of fiction. The names, characters and incidents portrayed in it are the work of the author's imagination. Any resemblance to actual persons, living or dead, events or localities is entirely coincidental.

Typeset in Bembo Std by Palimpsest Book Production Ltd, Falkirk, Stirlingshire

Printed and Bound in the UK using 100% Renewable Electricity at CPI Group (UK) Ltd

All rights reserved. No part of this text may be reproduced, transmitted, down-loaded, decompiled, reverse engineered, or stored in or introduced into any information storage and retrieval system, in any form or by any means, whether electronic or mechanical, without the express written permission of the publishers.

This book is produced from independently certified FSC™ paper to ensure responsible forest management.

For more information visit: www.harpercollins.co.uk/green

Dedicated to Conor, my husband,
with thanks for your love and support.

None of this would be possible without you.

1

12th March 1944, Tony Anderson's Flat, Paddington, London

Sarah woke up slowly, luxuriating in her drowsiness, reluctant to let the day intrude and break the spell of her slumber. As she yawned, she stretched her legs down into the cooler part of the bed. She wriggled her toes and was about to doze off again when a footstep close-by brought her fully awake. Sarah opened one eye and couldn't believe it. Tony was up, half-dressed, and looking mightily pleased with the world.

'Morning, sleepy-head,' he said, leaning down to ruffle her hair before he stepped over to the window. Whistling under his breath, he opened the curtains and flipped the blackout blind up before peering out.

'Hey!' Sarah exclaimed, turning away. 'The sun's right in my eyes.'

'It's a fine morning, Irish. Would be a shame to waste it. Up you get.'

Sarah glanced at the alarm clock and groaned. 'And it will still be a fine morning in an hour or so. Come back to bed,' she said. 'It's far too early.'

Tony grinned. 'As tempting as that invitation is, no can do.' Then he quirked his mouth in that cute way he had. 'Some of us have work to do.'

The grumble left her mouth before she could stop it. 'Not today, surely. It's Sunday,' she said, wiggling into a sitting position. 'I thought we'd have the day together. I haven't seen you in weeks.'

'Sorry,' he said, looking slightly sheepish. 'I have a desk groaning under the weight of files I need to read. I'm always behind with my paperwork.' He grimaced. 'Not my favourite part of the job. If I don't clear it today, I'll be behind all week.'

'But can't it wait? Even a couple of hours?'

'Madam, don't you know there is a war on?' he exclaimed, throwing her a cocky look over his shoulder.

He uses that mantra far too often, Sarah thought, her good mood slipping. She whipped the pillow, which still bore the imprint of his head, from the bed beside her and chucked it at him.

Tony side-stepped easily and laughed. 'You'll have to do better than that, sweetheart.'

'Be thankful it wasn't something more solid,' she muttered.

His ridiculous workload was becoming all too frequent an issue. When he had returned from his stint in France, she had been overjoyed, thinking they would get to know each other better. But all too often, Tony would disappear for days or weeks on end, his new posting invariably the reason. During his absences there was no communication from him, something she found just as frustrating as the time demands of his job. However, she was reluctant to bring it up and spoil the mood this morning – especially as she'd already been up half the night ruminating over those very grievances. Not that it was Tony's fault; his role demanded total commitment. She understood that only too well. Besides, everyone was under strain, with no end to the war in sight. She, too, had moments when her thoughts turned bleak. Everyone tried to keep positive, but behind closed doors, Sarah suspected most people succumbed to gloom every so often. Even Tony, who was usually very upbeat. Just last night, as she had stared into the darkness, Tony had tossed and turned in the bed beside her, clearly also troubled by something.

'You were very restless during the night. Bad dreams again?' she asked.

'I don't recall. My mind's busy with work, that's all. Sorry if I disturbed you,' he replied, still looking out the window.

But she wasn't convinced. Sarah could sense the barrier, the warning: 'don't probe'. Ever since his return from France, she had noticed his sleep was disturbed. However, whenever she queried it, he brushed her off. Why would he not confide in her? It was the same when she asked about his childhood and his family. He would brush her off with a flippant comment and change the subject.

Not that her own childhood had been wonderful; far from it. A drunk and abusive father who had terrified them all, and a mother worn down by poverty and fear, subject to their father's violence on the flimsiest of excuses. Sarah's own bruises were long gone, but some scars remained; the mental ones. Perhaps something similar had

3

happened to Tony. But such things seemed impossible for men to open up about.

Tony picked a clean shirt from the wardrobe and put it on. Sarah watched him continue to dress. She would usually take pleasure in the sight, but today it irked her because it meant her plans were in tatters. Her hopes of having lunch somewhere, a walk in Hyde Park, maybe a drink later before they had to go their separate ways, were dashed. Once again, she could not compete with the demands of US Navy Intelligence.

'I thought . . . I hoped when you returned from France, we would get to spend more time together,' she said. It sounded petty, even to her own ears, but she couldn't help the comment escaping her lips.

'So did I, hun, but this new post is tough,' he said. 'I still need to prove I can handle the responsibility. Not everyone thinks I deserved the position.'

Sarah could empathise. Her own promotion within MI5 was recent and had ruffled many feathers – mainly those of her male colleagues – so she felt a similar pressure. Most of the time, she was able to ignore the snide, often discriminatory remarks, but there were days when they hit home. Her job was difficult enough. Not everyone understood how a working-class Irish girl had ended up working for MI5. She, too, marvelled at how her life had changed so rapidly since coming to England. But she never regretted her decision to leave Ireland and her old life behind.

'Tony, I know you are under pressure, but if you keep this up, they'll expect you to work this hard all the time. Besides, you have nothing to prove.' Tony just shrugged, then turned to the mirror to fix his tie. 'You more than earned the post, Tony. After what you went through in France with the SOE—'

Tony frowned into the mirror. 'I wasn't the only one, Sarah. Plus, I was lucky enough to get out alive. Many didn't.'

'I know,' she replied, suddenly feeling rotten. Tony hadn't told her much about his eighteen months behind enemy lines, but she knew it had left its mark on him. The SOE stories bouncing around MI5 had been toe-curling, adding to her anxiety. Tales of capture, torture, and death. The Nazis showed no mercy. They had torn up the Geneva Convention without a second thought. To them, prisoners of war were purely a source of slave labour. As a result, she had spent the time he was away worried sick she wouldn't see him again. This was part of the reason she had knuckled down so hard in her own work. If she was tired at the end of the day, the oblivion of sleep kept the bad thoughts and dreams at bay. But not always.

It wasn't only Tony that haunted her sleep these days. She often dreamt of her sister, Maura, who had died only feet away from her when their house had collapsed in a German bomb attack in Dublin in 1941. That night was a watershed in her life. In the blink of an eye, she'd had to throw off her old life of innocence and she had become a woman bent on revenge, no matter where that would take her. Paul, too – her fiancé for so brief a time – often featured in her dreams. A Nazi torpedo had brought her hopes and dreams about life with Paul to an end when his ship was sunk on its way to America, where he was to complete his RAF training. It had been devastating, not least because he had been her last link to Dublin and her former life. For months, she had struggled to come to terms with the loss. And then there was Da, who had betrayed them all, delusional till the end, content only to die as a martyr for the IRA cause on a lonely hillside in South Wales.

Tony gave her an apologetic look as he sat down on the edge of the bed, bringing her back to the present. 'Penny for your thoughts, Irish,' he said. 'Look, I'm sorry about today, honestly. But there's a lot going on. Things are heating up. Damn!' He ran his fingers through his hair. 'I wish I could confide in you more.'

'There's not much either of us can do about that. However, I am aware of what's happening down south, Tony. Operation Fortitude?' Tony nodded. 'And I know how much is riding on it working. How many lives may be saved if our plans work. I don't have sufficient clearance to be privy to all the details, but plans are progressing at an astonishing rate. Our workload has increased dramatically since Christmas.'

'It's vital it succeeds, Sarah; it could be the beginning of the end,' he said. 'Unfortunately, I will be tied up in it. Don't be too surprised if I disappear without warning. But I'll make it up to you when I return, I promise.'

The demands this war were putting on their relationship were huge, but like everyone else, the personal sacrifices were necessary. Sarah smiled sadly. 'I'm going to hold you to that, mister!'

Tony reached out and gently tucked a strand of hair behind her ear. 'As if I could refuse you anything. How about dinner on Tuesday to make up for today?'

'I can't. *I* will be away,' she replied.

'Oh! Where?'

'Can't say. Sorry.'

He raised a brow at that. 'Work related, I assume.'

'Of course.'

'Dangerous?'

'Unlikely,' she answered with a shake of her head.

Tony frowned at her. 'I'd rather hear a definitive no from you.'

Sarah reached for his hand and curled her fingers through his. 'That is sweet of you, but I must remind you I do have some experience under my belt. I'll be alright.'

'Hmm, well, I suppose I'll have to trust that Jason isn't sending you into a difficult or risky situation. Am I allowed to ask if you are going alone?'

'I am. Jason says I'm ready. Actually, I'm looking forward to it. They are trusting me with a very important task and I'm keen to prove myself. We have an operation underway which, if successful, could change the course of the war.'

Tony quirked a brow. 'Interesting! I've heard rumours.' He put up his hand. 'Yes, I know you can't tell me any more, so I won't pry.'

Sarah was grateful that he understood. 'I am tired of transcribing tapped phone conversations and steaming open post. Who'd have thought some of our public figures could lead such grubby lives?' Sarah wrinkled her nose. 'The seedy side of the business is hard to stomach. I hope I'm done with the menial stuff at last.'

'But it's safe work,' he said.

'Ah, Tony. Safe is dull.'

'Dull! Good Lord, you have faced more danger than most. Are you forgetting about Winchester or Fishguard? You almost got yourself killed on both occasions. I don't think anyone would blame me for being concerned. Sometimes I think you are a magnet for trouble.'

A little too close to the truth, but not something she would ever admit. 'Nonsense! It was a close-run thing, I'll admit, but sure you came to my rescue when it mattered.' Tony gave her a wry look. 'Besides, it's all part of the job. As it is for you.'

'Ye-es, but—'

'Don't you dare say "I'm a man, it's different" because it isn't, really.'

'Of course, it's different. I have Navy training and years of experience. You're a civilian, plucked out of a dangerous situation, and thrown into the deep end. Everleigh has been reckless and not only with you. Far too many MI5 operatives are civilians, in my opinion.'

A niggle of annoyance made her frown, even though he was probably right. Many of the newest recruits were friends of agents from college or their previous jobs. Although they were often clever people, they lacked – as she did – military training. Most of them had to learn on the job, but that was the nature of war. Danger and risk were part of life now; you just had to accept it.

'But it's needs must, Tony. Everleigh must draw on the resources available to him. Alright, I will admit I was lucky in Winchester, but I also kept my wits about me and that's why they wanted me.'

Tony sighed. 'I'm not trying to belittle your achievements, Sarah. God knows I have first-hand experience of your pluck and quick thinking. But it's hard not to worry that something bad might happen to you and I won't be there to help.'

'Just because I'm a woman and not a soldier or sailor? Come on, Tony. Women are capable of all kinds of things, given the chance. The war has proved that over and over. Besides, they *have* given me some instruction.'

'Now, Irish, you know as well as I do that you can face all sorts of situations out in the field. A few hours down in the shooting range isn't enough.'

'There's been more than that since my promotion. In fact, last week . . . Well, I suppose I shouldn't really say what they were teaching me.' Tony looked alarmed at this, and she patted his hand. 'Anyway, don't forget all you have taught me.'

'Frankly, I was shocked I had to, although I hope you never have to use any self-defence. But the fact is, MI5 should have given you that training, not me.'

'Perhaps, but you may console yourself. It has already come in handy,' she said, only to be alarmed to see the colour leave his face.

'*What?*'

Now she would have to tell him. That would teach her to let her tongue run away with her. 'I had to use what you taught me in a . . . situation that arose.'

'On the job?'

'Actually, no. Look, I'm not sure I should tell you. Gladys would kill me.'

Confusion now replaced the alarm on Tony's face. 'Gladys? I don't understand.'

'Very well, I'll tell you, but under no circumstances are you to say anything to Glad,' she replied. 'She got herself into a scrape and she is extremely embarrassed about it.'

Tony shook his head and sighed. 'Well, that sounds like Glad, alright. Now, out with it!'

'Well, it all started, just after you left on your last trip away. I came home from work one evening and found Gladys sobbing her heart out. Eventually, she admitted she was in trouble and she showed me this letter she had received.'

'Was it a threat of some kind?' he asked.

'In a way. It was a proposal of marriage.'

'Good Lord!' Tony exclaimed, then frowned. 'And it was a problem. Why? Didn't she like the guy?'

'Well, that's just it. She barely knew him. This fellow, Alfie Smyth, was a regular on her bus route. Gladys being Gladys was friendly to him – you know how she loves a bit of banter – and unfortunately, the man got the wrong idea and things escalated very quickly. He started to follow her home, which, of course, terrified her. However, she said nothing to me or Judith and tried to sort it out herself by confronting him and telling him to leave her alone, which didn't work.'

'Poor old Glad!'

'Yes, so I had to help her.'

'I have a horrible feeling you decided to tackle this Alfie chap yourself,' Tony said.

'Not quite. I pulled in a favour from Ewan Galbraith. Do you remember him? I'm sure I told you about us working together.'

'Yes, I do. He's Special Branch, isn't he?'

'Yes. He advised the best course of action was for both of us to visit Alfie and well . . . discourage him from pestering Glad. Unfortunately, on the day, Ewan was delayed, and I decided to go ahead on my own.'

Tony groaned and shut his eyes as if in pain. 'Dear God, Sarah, what were you thinking?'

'I don't regret it, Tony. In fact, I'm proud that I handled the situation satisfactorily. I disarmed Alfie and the icing on the cake was that I introduced Ewan and Judith, who are now an item.'

'Whoa, whoa, whoa there! What do you mean, *disarmed Alfie*?'

'You don't need to yell! When I told Mr Smyth that Gladys wanted nothing to do with him, he didn't take it very well. He went for me with a bread knife.' Tony put his head in his hands so she quickly continued. 'Thanks to your training, I was able to knock it out of his hand and I kicked him in the groin for good measure. That did the trick!'

Tony stared at her, in shock. 'You can hardly blame me for worrying about you!' he said, looking put out, which was a bit sweet.

'And I worry about you, too. But please, let's not argue about it. We have so little time together.'

Tony's answering glance was difficult to read and for a moment she thought he was going to say something, then he seemed to change his mind. Instead, he drew her hand to his lips and kissed her fingertips, sending a shiver down her spine. Then his gaze deepened, and a wicked smile appeared as he glanced at the clock.

'I suppose I am running a little early. Perhaps we do have some time before I need to leave . . .'

2

A sudden hush settled over the platform. Sarah watched as the German POWs marched past, heads held high. They were a ragged bunch up close, not quite what you would expect from the propaganda films coming out of the Reich. However, the locals stood back against the station wall as the group filed past towards the exit. Their shock at seeing the German uniforms was evident in their horrified expressions. One young mother grabbed her child's hand and pulled him into the ticket office, from where she peered out through the door. Perhaps it was understandable, the desire to protect the innocent from the ghastly reality, Sarah thought. But at this stage of the war, surely everyone had been touched by it in some way, even the smallest of children.

But Sarah knew today was different for the people of Comrie. This group of POWs were the first German prisoners to be sent here. The prison camp to which they were bound had only held Italian prisoners up until now; men who were so low risk they helped on the neighbouring farms and were on friendly terms with most of the locals.

These prisoners were different; these were hard-core Nazis.

Lieutenant Pike, who was the officer in charge of the prisoner transport, had told her they were all fanatics, which was why they were going to Cultybraggan. Only recently, the camp had been designated to hold the staunchest fascists; the most dangerous.

Cultybraggan Camp was Sarah's destination, too.

Up to this point in her career in MI5, Sarah had only encountered fifth columnists with Nazi leanings. Now, it was unsettling to see native Germans on British soil. Men like the Luftwaffe pilot who had killed her sister Maura and destroyed her home back in Dublin. Or perhaps U-boat crewmen who might have been responsible for setting off the torpedo which sank her fiancé Paul's ship, mid-Atlantic. How could she bear to look at them and feel . . . well, nothing? What a surprise! Had her experiences over the last few years softened her resolve, or was she now simply weary of it all? When she had left Ireland, it was to seek revenge. Nothing else had mattered. And here was the perfect opportunity. All she had to do was grab a rifle from one of the Tommies and pull the trigger. She was an excellent shot, although she had only ever used a gun once in the field and that was to wing an assassin. However, she still cringed at the memory of shooting Clara Mazet; Sarah was no killer. Besides, taking down one Hitler fanatic would not bring Maura or Paul back . . . If only she could be confident her endeavours were making a difference and helping to end the war. There had been days, recently, when she had doubted it. Today, however, might change all of that. Her assignment was risky, the dangers unknown, but she would be in control.

As she looked at the prisoners, all Sarah felt was curiosity. What was it about national socialism that turned decent human beings into killing machines? As one youngster passed, she reckoned he was no more than sixteen; another example of a brainwashed Hitler Youth sent to the frontline. Was it possible that he, too, was full of zeal and cruelty? *God help him, he's only a child.* He caught her gaze for a moment, and much to her surprise, she saw his chin tremble as he turned away. Did he fear what lay ahead or was it the knowledge he had let Hitler down by getting caught?

Outside the train station, the POWs were ordered to line up by their escorting guards. They stood to attention, completely rigid, their faces masking whatever emotions churned beneath the surface. Yet Sarah was sure their hearts must be full of dread. What awaited them? Did they fear the conditions of the camp would mirror those at home in the Fatherland? The rumours she had heard about German and Japanese camps were blood curdling. Intelligence was scant, but she had heard of people being worked and starved to death, roped into the Nazi war machine. There was even talk of death camps and mass murder. Sarah found it difficult to comprehend that people had the capacity for such cruelty and yet, she had to admit, the past few years had shown her people were capable of almost any depravity if pushed to their limit. As a result, she now rarely trusted anyone until they had proven themselves; a far cry from the Sarah Gillespie who had first left Ireland to seek refuge with her relatives in Hampshire. Her aunt and uncle had welcomed her into their home and their life, her cousins Martin and Judith had become close, and Sarah was ever thankful for that. And even though there had been low points in her life since, she knew she could always rely on them.

It had taken two days to get here, and the last leg of her journey had been on the special train for the transport of prisoners; an arrangement made by MI5's man in Edinburgh. For most of the trip, Sarah had been in the company of Lieutenant Pike. He had informed her they had captured the majority of the prisoners only the week before. Half the men were Kriegsmarine U-boat crew, the others were Fallschirmjäger, members of the parachute branch of the Luftwaffe. Two, however, were Waffen-SS officers, easy to pick out with their black uniforms, giving them a more sinister appearance than their compatriots. Maybe that was what had spooked the young mother on the platform.

As Sarah's eyes travelled down the line, the signs of battle were clear. One or two of the men had arms in slings or had bandaged wounds and some of their uniforms were dirty or torn. But it was the expression in their eyes that gave her pause. It spoke of horror and death, a look she had seen before in the faces of Allied personnel, home on leave in London. The more seasoned were easy to spot when out and about in the clubs at night. Invariably, it was the forced gaiety or excessive drinking that gave them away. She could identify the cause, empathise even, but without experiencing war up close, it was difficult to understand its effects fully. But she did wonder what horrors greeted them in their dreams at night.

Lieutenant Pike shouted out orders to his men in readiness for the march ahead, then joined Sarah where she stood by the side of the road.

'Are you sure you want to walk to the camp with us, Miss Gillespie? I'm sure I could arrange some form of local transport. It is a good thirty-minute march' – he paused, looking up at the sky – 'and the weather may close in before we reach Cultybraggan.'

'No, Lieutenant, thank you. I'd prefer the walk. I have been sitting in trains for the last two days,' she replied, as they fell into step behind the column of prisoners.

'As you wish, miss.'

As she matched the rhythm of the march, she knew a good brisk walk in the cold would help clear her mind for the task ahead.

They crossed over a bridge, the swollen river pounding over the rocks underneath, and soon they were out on the flatter terrain of the river valley, leaving Comrie behind. It was a vast landscape, magnificent in its bleakness. In the distance to the south, snow-capped peaks rose into the ever-darkening metal-grey sky. Snow-covered fields lay to either side, with deep drifts marking the edge of the roadway. It was almost dusk and it was much colder than it had been in Edinburgh without the tempering effect of the sea. The cold air was bracing, almost enjoyable, but Sarah was not looking forward to retracing the journey to Comrie when it would be pitch dark.

As she walked along, Sarah realised she hadn't thought about Da for a while. She hadn't visited his grave in Cardiff since his funeral, either. It was still too raw; what he had done. Sarah could never forgive his betrayal and she partially blamed him for her sister's horrible death, buried beneath the rubble of their home. If only he had come back that night when the bombs were falling on North Strand. He could have taken them to safety. But he was too busy pretending to have perished in the attack so he could escape to England to head up an IRA cell. She and Tony had hunted him down eventually, but not before he had helped many fifth columnists and Abwehr agents travel into and out of Wales undetected. His death, at Tony's hands, still haunted her nightmares. But she did not blame Tony. Her father had known he was dying and had goaded Tony into shooting him so he could become a martyr for the Irish Republican movement. Da's logic had always been warped.

Suddenly, one prisoner burst into song, tentatively at first, but soon his compatriots joined in, their voices swelling with confidence. Pike, walking by her side, exchanged a quick glance with Sarah, a brow raised. But she just shrugged. It was disquieting, certainly, to hear their native tongue, but it gave her an excuse not to make small talk with the lieutenant. Her mind was too full of the task ahead and the consequences should she fail. Sarah could sense Pike was curious about her and what she might want at the camp. But he had been canny enough not to enquire. However, even if she wanted, she was in no position to enlighten him. The knowledge she held was so sensitive, so dangerous, that it brought her out in a sweat even thinking about it.

Despite now being an experienced MI5 officer, she didn't know what to expect when she got to Cultybraggan.

She still could not believe that they had assigned her this task. Colonel Everleigh, the head of MI5's B1A unit, and the man who had originally recruited her, had caught her totally off-guard when he had summoned her, along with her immediate boss, Jason White, to his office a few days earlier. When he had informed her of her task, she was sure she had gaped at him in disbelief. However, once she had gotten over the initial surprise, excitement had taken over. At last an assignment to test her abilities, and her courage. Best of all, it was a job that could have a real impact on the outcome of the war.

For the past year and a half, she had been kept busy, mostly based in London and the Home Counties, undertaking surveillance work. Much of it had been tedious stuff, listening to the bugged conversations or reading the intercepted mail of suspected fifth columnists. However, her discovery of an MP with Nazi sympathies had earned her a promotion. And now, Everleigh was entrusting her with her most important job yet. It was slightly terrifying. What was worse, she could not divulge the nature of it to anyone, not even Tony.

Pike interrupted Sarah's thoughts, pointing across the fields. 'There it is, miss.'

The road ahead forked, and down to the right, she could make out the curved roofs of Nissen huts and several watchtowers along the perimeter. There was no backing out now.

Once through the security checks at the gate of the encampment, Sarah bade farewell to Lieutenant Pike and watched as his group marched away into the distance. A young soldier introduced himself and asked her to follow him to the camp adjutant's hut. As they went deeper into the encampment, Sarah was struck by the neatness of the rows upon rows of Nissen huts, most of which were occupied, to judge by the level of noise. The facility was divided up into various compounds, each with its own open space, which she assumed was for exercise. As she passed one such area, she saw two men huddled together, smoking. They stared at Sarah through the barbed wire fence. Unnerved, she fixed her gaze straight ahead and increased her pace.

'If you wait here, miss, Captain Hartfield will be with you shortly,' the soldier said, stopping before a hut and opening the door.

'Thank you,' she replied and stepped inside.

A paraffin heater in the corner was a pleasant sight, and Sarah warmed her hands for several minutes while she scanned the room. Other than some shelves, a filing cabinet, a desk, and two chairs, the space was spartan and not particularly welcoming. Grim, in fact.

Sarah wandered over to the window and gazed out. It really was a desolate place. For a brief moment, she thought about the young German she had made eye contact with at the station. How would he fare in this place? *Not that it's my concern. God knows what atrocities he has committed in the Führer's name.* Sarah gave herself a mental shake. *I have enough on my plate without worrying about adolescent Nazis.*

From the little she had seen so far, Cultybraggan was substantial, and she wondered how many prisoners it contained. Colonel Everleigh had given her only the sketchiest of details. It was, after all, irrelevant to her task. A sudden shout drew her attention to the far side of the road, but she had to strain to see what was causing the commotion. She was relieved to see that it was merely a group of prisoners playing football in one of the large open spaces. That was one way to keep warm on such a bitterly cold afternoon.

Then Sarah spotted a tall, thin, grey-haired man in uniform approaching the hut. He walked with a swagger and was barking out orders to a harassed-looking junior officer, who was doing his best to keep pace. It was probably Captain Hartfield. Sarah scooted across to the nearest chair and sat down just before the door opened and the two men entered.

'Miss . . . eh, Gillespie, is it?' Hartfield said, holding out his hand as he drew near.

'Yes, sir, that's correct.'

'Captain Hartfield. And this is Lieutenant Browning, my deputy.' They shook hands, and then the captain sat behind the desk and took off his cap. His lieutenant remained standing.

'Well, well, MI5. We are honoured indeed,' Hartfield said with a humourless laugh. Not sure how to take this, Sarah merely nodded. 'So, you have come to look after our little problem?' he asked.

'I hope so, sir.'

'Excellent. Dashed awkward for us, you know. Can't have a woman like that in the camp. Causes all kinds of difficulty, isn't that so, Browning? Not least where to put her.' The lieutenant nodded vigorously.

'I can imagine,' Sarah replied somewhat dryly.

'Yes, well, I assume you will take her away with you?' the captain asked.

'Well, sir, that depends on whether she is willing to co-operate.'

21

Hartfield scowled. 'She can't stay here! It is out of the question. We were happy to facilitate the police and MI5, but this can only be a temporary – very temporary – arrangement.'

Sarah smiled. 'I will do my best, sir. Have you been able to get any information from her?'

'Not one iota. I don't have the time or the training for that sort of interrogation either. All we know is she walked into the police station in Perth and announced she was a German spy but wanted to work for the Allies. Highly suspect, if you ask me.'

'How did she get to Perth, sir?' Sarah asked. 'We had been tipped off that she was on her way to Britain and that she was likely to be dropped off on the Scottish coast, but where she was headed after that, we didn't know.'

'Well, I've no idea, young lady. Again, I suggest that is something for you to discover.' Hartfield frowned across at her. 'You do know what you are doing, I hope? To be frank, I was expecting them to send a man.'

Sarah bit down on the retort she wished to make. 'I have been trained, sir.' No need to tell him it had consisted of a hurried two hours of interrogation training last week.

'Best get on with it, then, Miss Gillespie. Browning will show you the way.'

3

14th March 1944, Cultybraggan POW Camp, Perthshire

Sarah glanced in the hut's window while Browning unlocked the door. The sight of a diminutive and elegantly clad woman in a stylish, light-blue coat was not what Sarah had expected. Right away, she had to ditch the image of a frumpy fräulein that had formed in her head as she had travelled up from London. Had her aversion to double agents coloured her view? Of course, you never could spot a spy based on looks alone. It was often the plainest, most inconspicuous people who turned out to be the slipperiest of agents. And the most effective.

But above all, Sarah had a deep-seated mistrust of those who switched sides so easily. When Everleigh had told her she was to be the handler for a potential double agent, the idea had troubled her. It was only when he had explained the importance of the role envisaged for the woman that she had agreed. A major deception was underway, and MI5 was using a raft of double agents to send a mix of true and false information to German handlers, hoping to convince them that a potential invasion of Europe would be centred on Calais. As such, their stable of double agents was key. Crucial, in fact. And Sarah would play an important role as a conduit for the information flying back and forth.

Pushing down her distaste, she nodded to Browning as she passed him into the hut. Browning handed her the key and Sarah locked the door after him then shoved the key into her pocket. Then she turned and quickly sized up the woman seated at the table in the centre of the room. Perfectly dressed and groomed, the woman was very serene for someone in her tenuous position. As Sarah walked over to join her at the table, she was acutely aware that Adeline Vernier was scrutinising *her*. Sarah sat down, determined not to be intimidated.

'Good afternoon,' Vernier greeted her with only a hint of an accent. 'I hope you are here to free me from this place.'

Sarah detected a touch of arrogance in her tone, but also a flicker of uncertainty in the woman's eyes. *Ah, not so composed, then.* It wouldn't be surprising; after all, her future rested in Sarah's hands. But there was something perturbing about the spy's gaze too; her dark brown eyes were alight with intelligence, or was it cunning? Laughter lines, only visible up close, suggested Vernier was older than Sarah's initial guess of early twenties. Vernier blew out her cigarette smoke through ruby red lips as she held Sarah's gaze, and Sarah thought she would not look out of place in a West End nightclub.

'Welcome to Scotland, Fräulein Vernier. My name is Sarah Gillespie.'

Adeline wrinkled her nose and shook the dark curls that framed her face. 'Oh, no, no! There is some mistake. I am French, *not* German.' She smiled. 'The Nazis believe me to be on their side, but it was only a subterfuge on my part to get here. I have come all this way to help you.'

Sarah wondered if she was supposed to applaud this little rehearsed speech and did her best not to smile. Instead, she cleared her throat. 'Most magnanimous of you, *Mademoiselle* Vernier.'

Vernier's gaze faltered. Perhaps she had not expected sarcasm? After a moment, she recovered. 'Can you explain why I have been brought to this awful place and treated like a common criminal?' Vernier waved a hand in the air and gave an exaggerated shudder. 'And as for that stupid captain with his silly questions, he has made me most *angry*. The man would not *listen* to me.'

'They are not used to female detainees here, mademoiselle.'

'It shows. If this is how you treat your friends, I hate to think what your enemies in this camp are going through.' Vernier leaned forward, her expression fierce. 'The facilities and the food are *trés mal*. Not fit for humans.'

Sarah found herself echoing Tony's mantra. 'There is a war on, mademoiselle!'

'Indeed, but it is no excuse to lower one's standards, Miss Gillespie. I would warn you not to drink what they claim is coffee.' Vernier's hand went to her throat. 'I dread to think what they are using as a substitute.'

Sarah felt some sympathy. The cuisine in a POW camp was unlikely to suit a French palate. However, she sensed this woman was trying to put her on the back foot. Something they had warned her about during her training.

Sarah kept her voice even and firm, remembering her instructions. Obviously, she needed to lay down a marker or this woman would ride rough-shod over her.

'My apologies, mademoiselle, if you feel you have not been treated appropriately. However, we know very little about you. Any *spy* who lands in Britain is treated with suspicion until such time as we find out their true intent.' She let that sink in for a moment. 'Of course, we have become adept at this. No spy entering this country is free for long, I can assure you.'

A tinkling laugh was Vernier's response. 'Ah, you think I am dangerous. How droll!'

Sarah ignored this. 'As to when you will leave here and where you will go next, that is down to me.'

Vernier's eyes narrowed as she once again scanned Sarah's face. 'Is that so? How interesting. Perhaps you could tell me who you are, exactly.'

'I work for military intelligence. I have been sent here to ascertain who you are and what you want.' Sarah showed Adeline her identification card.

The Frenchwoman read it carefully, then regarded her with amusement. 'You look far too young for such a role. How much experience do you have?'

Sarah bit the inside of her lip. Best to ignore the baiting. After all, she was more than aware of her own inadequacies; she didn't need a snooty Frenchwoman to guess at them.

'Enough to do my job well,' Sarah replied. 'Now, shall we get down to business? Do *you* have any identification with you? I need to establish exactly who you are before we can discuss anything further.'

'But of course,' was the smooth reply. Adeline reached

down and pulled out a sheaf of papers from her handbag. She pushed these across the table, a challenge in her eye.

Sarah unfolded the top page only to be confronted by characters she did not recognise. 'I'm sorry, what is this?' she asked, holding it up.

Adeline blew out an impressive smoke ring above her head. 'That is my Russian birth certificate; April 1916, if you need to know. The 20th, if you feel inclined to help me celebrate.'

Sarah frowned. 'I don't understand, mademoiselle; a minute ago you said you were French.'

'I am; at least I consider myself French; it is where I grew up. However, I was born in Russia. My family had to leave when I was a baby. As my mother was a White Russian, life became somewhat difficult after the revolution, and they could not stay. My father was French, so we settled near Bordeaux, close to his family. I moved to Paris when I was nineteen.'

'I see. So, do you speak Russian?'

'Yes, of course! I learned it at my mother's knee. I am also fluent in English and French, and have a smattering of German and Italian.' Sarah was impressed, if not a little envious of the woman's aptitude for languages. Adeline smiled across at her, much too sweetly. 'Would that be useful to you?'

'I imagine so,' Sarah replied, keeping her tone cool. 'May I ask how you came to learn German?'

Adeline shifted in her seat, a shadow of a frown forming on her brow. 'I visited Berlin several times before the war. My editor sent me there to cover the rallies. I am a journalist, you see, Miss Gillespie; a rather good and experienced

27

one, too. It was at one of those rallies that I was approached by an Abwehr agent who suggested I might like to spy for the Reich. He offered to send me to England and set me up with a job. In fact, I was offered a lot of money, too, but I refused, for I did not like what I saw of the regime. I think you will agree that time has proved my instincts to have been correct.'

'Indeed. However, how do I know that isn't exactly what you *are* doing here; spying for Germany?'

'Tut-tut, Miss Gillespie, that is hardly a polite question.'

'And yet I must ask it,' Sarah said, equally saccharine.

Adeline shrugged and continued to smoke.

Sarah sat back in her chair and surveyed the spy for several seconds in silence, mostly to see if she could rattle her composure. But Adeline merely smiled back at her. *This woman knows a thing or two! Who has trained her?* Sarah wondered. How was she to root out the truth? Was the woman really here to help, or was she up to mischief?

'I am as I say,' Adeline said eventually, and to Sarah's surprise, gently.

'Very well, mademoiselle, let us assume you are *not* spying for the enemy.'

'*Merci!*'

'When you arrived at the police station in Perth, you declared you wished to become a double agent and work for the Allies. Is this correct?'

'This is true, yes. I will be most useful,' Adeline answered with an impatient shimmy of her slender shoulders.

'Then you must convince me your motivation is genuine,' Sarah said.

'And if I do not?'

'There are countless options to be considered. You have already admitted you are a spy, mademoiselle.'

Vernier looked confused. 'But I only pretend to work for the Germans—'

'That's as may be. However, the authorities would be within their rights to consider execution, deportation . . .'

Sarah could have sworn Vernier blanched. 'Ah! This I would not like at all.' Adeline gnawed at her lip, focusing hard on Sarah. 'And my fate is in your hands?'

'For now, yes.' Sarah took out a pen and paper from her bag. 'Perhaps you would like to tell me your history? It will help me make my decision.'

Mademoiselle Vernier stubbed out her cigarette. 'Very well. As I said, the Abwehr were keen to recruit me, but I did not like what was happening in Germany. I returned to Paris shortly afterwards. You can imagine my dismay when the Germans followed a couple of years later.'

'Indeed. What did you do then? Did you stay in Paris?' Sarah asked.

'Of course I did. I had an excellent job at a newspaper, so I kept my head down for I had no wish to draw attention to myself . . . Well, as it happened, I had a problem.'

'Oh? And what was that?' Sarah enquired.

Adeline studied her nails and Sarah realised she was gathering her thoughts. Was she trying to come up with some kind of story? On her guard, Sarah waited.

Eventually, Adeline lifted her gaze back to Sarah. To Sarah's surprise, her expression was glum. 'Nikolay, my Russian boyfriend, was stuck in Paris once the Germans arrived and he was hiding in my flat. I could not risk his being caught, for both our sakes.' Adeline paused, a flicker of sadness crossing her features.

Sarah wondered where this was going. How was this man relevant?

'Let me assure you, Miss Gillespie, my Nikolay does not like all the hiding. He desperately wants to get back to Russia to fight alongside his countrymen. But if the SS find him, they will shoot him on the spot. I had to protect him.'

Sarah looked up from her notes. 'That is unfortunate, however, he is not my concern, mademoiselle.' Adeline reacted instantly with a scowl, but Sarah continued: 'So what changed? Why did you agree to spy for Germany, after all?'

'Ah! It was a clever plan of mine. If they trusted me to spy and would send me to England, I might be able to get Nikolay out as well. You must understand I hate the Nazis and what they are doing. I have lived in an occupied city, Miss Gillespie. It is not . . . pleasant. The things I have seen. They are brutes! Friends . . . people I knew in Paris . . . some have disappeared. Any link to the Resistance is pounced on. Betrayal is everywhere. You can trust no one.' Suddenly, Adeline thumped the table with her fist, her eyes burning with emotion. 'It is vile, what this war has done. France must be free again. I will not rest until it is so.' Then she sat back, breathing hard, and with shaking hands, she lit another cigarette and inhaled deeply.

Sarah was uneasy. That was quite an outburst. But were the woman's reasons for switching sides genuine? Sarah had to stay focused. If MI5 were to recruit this woman, they had to be sure of her. 'Tell me about your German handler, please, and what training they gave you.'

'SS–Obergruppenführer Stefan Haas recruited me.' Adeline gave a mirthless laugh. 'A bastard and a clever one, too. He questioned me for days in Paris before he would agree to use me. Then he insisted I go back to Berlin for training. I was nervous about that, of course, but I had no choice. Once I had finished my training, they sent me to Lisbon. That is where Haas is based. From there, they put me on a ship, then a U-boat, and days later I arrived here.'

Sarah's blood ran cold. This information put the woman across the table in a whole new light. To be recruited by the notorious Haas meant this woman was either highly dangerous or a naïve fool. Haas was well known to the secret service. Head of German intelligence and an SS officer, he orchestrated their activities throughout Europe from the German embassy in Lisbon. It was speculated that he was keen to prove himself having taken over when the Abwehr was abolished by Hitler only months before. Haas's organisation, the Reichssicherheitshauptamt, had a reputation for cruelty that was unsurpassed. There were rumours that MI6 had attempted to assassinate him on several occasions, but the man was far too wily to be caught.

'What kind of preparation did they give you?' Sarah asked.

'Similar to most spies, I would guess.'

Why was she prevaricating? Sarah stopped writing and looked up. 'Please, I need more detail.'

'Very well. They taught me how to use a special invisible ink so that I could write letters with hidden messages when I was safely in Britain. They trained me to use a radio and they were insistent that I learn to identify different Allied uniforms so that I could report back on troop movements.'

'And ciphers?'

31

'Yes, of course,' Adeline snapped.

'And what is your call-sign?'

'Anya. Now, we are wasting time, Miss Gillespie. Is this not enough for you? I tell you; I can help, but I must communicate with my German contact here soon or he will be suspicious. He is expecting me. If I do not show up, all will be lost. He will tell Haas I didn't arrive or will assume I have been captured.'

'Herr Pfeiffer?'

Adeline's eyes popped. 'Why, yes! How do you know of him?'

'He works for us, mademoiselle,' Sarah said.

'But . . .'

'Every agent the Germans have sent here has been turned and is working for us. Your wireless message, informing him of your arrival, was passed on to us so that we could form a welcoming committee.'

Adeline sat up straight. 'But this is marvellous. How clever you British are! And how droll! I am liking this English sense of humour.'

'Thank you. Let me assure you that if you had not handed yourself in, we would have found you eventually.' Sarah flicked a glance down at her notes. 'I must be honest with you. As it stands, I still need to be convinced that we can trust you.'

Mademoiselle Vernier grimaced. 'What must I do? Sign my name in *blood*? This is foolish!'

'And yet here is the fact you must consider, mademoiselle. If I feel you are not trustworthy, you may be deported, or worse, as I have said already. So, are you willing to put your life at risk? What we will ask of you will not be easy. Spying is a dangerous game; being a double agent takes it to quite a different level.'

'Yes! Yes, I understand all of this. I am a woman of the world.' Vernier's throat worked for several seconds before she spoke again, her tone more moderate. 'I ask you, woman to woman, to help me. You must trust me. I am in an impossible situation. The man I love is trapped in France, his life in danger. You may think I should not have agreed to work for the Germans, but my intention was always to betray them. From the inside. It is perfect. Don't you see?' Adeline stretched her hand out across the table. 'You *must* believe me.'

Sarah stared at Adeline's hand, tempted to give the woman the reassurance she wanted. Perhaps they should give her a chance to prove herself? Vernier was certainly passionate. Maybe they could harness that. Above all, this was a chance for Sarah to prove her worth to MI5, and she desperately wanted to be part of any operation that might bring an end to the war, no matter how dangerous it might be.

'Very well. I will take you back to London with me, mademoiselle, but I cannot promise anything. Those senior to me will make the final decision and they may not be willing to take a gamble on you.'

'Oh, thank you, Miss Gillespie, thank you.' Adeline beamed at her. 'However, I do have one stipulation.'

Taken aback, Sarah could only gape at the other woman.

'It is but a simple thing. I will only work for you if you British promise to get my Nikolay safely out of France.'

4

Sarah was shown into Colonel Everleigh's office only to find her immediate boss, Jason White, already there. It was a relief to see him. Having worked for him for the last two years, they had a solid relationship, and she could always be sure of his support. For some reason, he had taken her under his wing, determined to make her the best possible agent she could be. And she was grateful. Although at least twenty years her senior, he was always approachable and had been particularly kind to her after the death of her father.

The colonel, however, was a very different sort of man. Old school army, with black slicked-back hair, piercing blue eyes and a hook nose; his appearance was striking. Always self-assured, he had an unerring ability to read one's mind, with the result that Sarah often felt as though she was before a headmaster when summoned to his office.

And now, here she was, having to face both men and explain her decision regarding Adeline Vernier. She had been anxious about this meeting since departing Scotland with the spy in tow. However, there was no turning back. And, unfortunately, a day in Adeline's company had done little to reassure Sarah that her decision was the right one. Adeline was a strange mixture of childish charm one minute and cunning the next. However, Sarah was more than keen to prove herself worthy of Everleigh's trust. But she knew he would not be ecstatic about Vernier's stipulation that her boyfriend be rescued from occupied France.

As Sarah concluded her summary of Vernier's interrogation, she twisted her fingers in her lap, waiting on tenterhooks for both men's reaction. Jason raised a brow but made no comment.

As she had expected, Everleigh gazed at her as if she were mad. 'She wants us to *what*?'

'I know, sir, but what could I say? It was easier to agree at the time and I thought perhaps it would be possible to smuggle this boyfriend of hers out of France . . . in due course.'

'And how would we manage that, pray?' the colonel asked with a scowl.

Sarah felt the colour rush into her face. He was right. It was ludicrous. Jason threw her an amused glance, which didn't help much.

'I thought the Resistance might help with that,' she said, watching nervously as Everleigh rose and paced the floor. She hurried on: 'Besides, the adjutant wanted rid of her. He had no facilities for female prisoners. If I had not taken her, she would have been handed back to the Scottish police and ended up God knows where. I didn't want to risk that because if she didn't contact Pfeiffer here, and then Haas in Lisbon, within the allotted time, Haas would suspect British Intelligence had caught her. I thought it best to err on the side of caution.'

'Of course you had to take her on, Sarah. Letting her loose was out of the question,' Jason said, his eyes following their boss as he paced.

The colonel harrumphed before sitting down again. 'I suppose I cannot argue with your logic, Sarah. And, as you say, Jason, best we keep the woman under our control. The last thing we need is for her to contact fifth columnists and get up to mischief, particularly now with our plans so far advanced.' With a sigh, he glanced down at Sarah's written report. 'She was recruited by Haas, directly? That is a bit of a coup for us. Perhaps she can give us some intelligence about his operations?'

'Their training methods, certainly, sir,' Sarah replied. 'She has described those to me in some detail. I must say, for her to come here and offer her services to us actually makes her rather brave.'

'Or someone to be wary of?' Jason asked with a raised brow. 'Too good to be true?'

Inwardly, Sarah groaned. He was right. Had her own naïvety brought her to the wrong decision regarding the spy?

'We must trust Sarah's judgement, Jason, for she has interviewed the woman and is satisfied she is legitimate.' Everleigh said this with a nod to Sarah.

Oh, God, Sarah thought, *no pressure then!* 'Unfortunately, sir, most of her dealings with Haas were in Paris,' she said.

'She was only a few hours in Lisbon, en route to here, so cannot give us any information about his headquarters or agents based in Portugal.'

The colonel grimaced. 'That's a pity. The man is a nasty piece of work. It is said he shot one of his officers for disobeying an order. No court-martial, no justice whatsoever. Just pulled out his pistol and shot him in the head in front of his staff.'

'Good heavens!' Sarah exclaimed. 'I didn't realise he was that bad.'

'Mad and bad, as are most of those at the top. The Abwehr, at least, had some decent men in it, which, ironically, led to its demise. This organisation is far more worrying. Most of 'em are hard-core Nazis,' Everleigh replied. 'It is a shame she can't give us more information on Lisbon, though, as it is now the centre of espionage in Europe. Ensure we do get as much out of her as we can.' His gaze flicked between Sarah and Jason. 'The most important question is, can we trust the woman?'

'Sir, I believe she is sincere in wanting to help the Allies, though I suspect she is a little unpredictable.' The colonel grimaced, and Sarah rushed on. 'However, more of her history came out during our journey down from Edinburgh. She hasn't had an easy life and I do think she will need to be watched closely, but surely, sir, we cannot pass up this opportunity. Haas trusts her. She is a tricky character to read, but I am certain her abhorrence of the Nazi regime, and her desire to see France free once more, is sincere. She is more than willing to work for us.'

'Just the small matter of her boyfriend's extraction from occupied France!' Everleigh exclaimed.

'Well, yes, sir, I'm afraid so,' she replied.

Everleigh sighed. 'We need her, of course. Operations Bodyguard and Fortitude are essential if we are to land successfully in France where and when the Nazis least expect it. As you know, we already have a network of double agents who are drip-feeding the Nazis the information they request, along with the false information we want them to act upon. So far, they appear to be falling for it. Our fictional US 4th Army up in Edinburgh has them worried, according to the wires.'

'That's marvellous, sir,' Sarah replied. 'I assume the ruse is to make them believe an invasion of Norway is planned?'

'Precisely! The more troops the Germans keep in Norway, the fewer are stationed in France to greet our boys when they do drop by.'

'How long must we keep this deception up?'

'For as long as it takes, Sarah,' Jason said. 'Pfeiffer's fake network of agents, supposedly feeding him intelligence for the Germans, now stands at twenty-five. He has invented every last one of them. Quite ingenious, really. That was why it was important to find this "real" agent that Haas was sending over before she might blow the entire operation. Pfeiffer's imaginary chain of agents is set up all over the country and Haas, so far, appears to be swallowing every little nugget of information Pfeiffer sends him.'

Sarah weighed this up. 'But she could still cause us problems. If she finds out Pfeiffer's agents aren't real, for instance, and lets Haas know.'

'Well, you must ensure she doesn't. She must never meet Pfeiffer, face to face,' Jason said.

Controlling anything about Adeline would likely test Sarah to the limit, and her own inexperience could spell disaster. For the greater good, perhaps she shouldn't take on Adeline. 'Would it not be safer to stick to using these fake agents as they are already well established and trusted by Haas?' she asked with a great deal of reluctance.

'Ah, but we can use Adeline Vernier to our advantage. As you said, Sarah, Haas knows her and sent her here with a specific task, no doubt. He ensures he strikes terror into his recruits so there is less chance of them betraying him.'

'Adeline is certainly terrified of him,' Sarah confirmed.

'Good. He will be well aware of that and trust her as a result. And if Pfeiffer verifies her information, Haas will think he has set up the perfect spy network here,' the colonel said.

It was brilliant, of course, but also highly risky, Sarah thought. Perhaps too risky.

'Indeed, he will, sir,' Jason replied. 'We must use every means at our disposal, including controlled leaks.'

'A thousand little lies are far more effective than one gigantic lie, which could be easily disproved. It is vital we keep the deception flowing,' Everleigh said. 'The XX Committee is clever enough to divulge only what is necessary to the different groups involved in this operation. No one team knows everything. And I think you will agree, after our little escapade with that traitor Evans in Wales, that is the best way to work. The next few months will be vital in hoodwinking Jerry. However, I cannot foresee an incursion into France before the summer.'

'Surely, the Germans will expect the same,' Sarah said.

'Undoubtedly, but the Channel conditions are rarely ideal. Even in summer, they can be treacherous. Thankfully, that is not my decision. Now, we best set this woman up quickly.'

Everleigh glanced down at the file, then regarded Jason with one raised brow. 'I see we have given her the code name *Honey*, Jason. I assume, after reading Sarah's report, that someone is being ironic.'

'Yes, sir. The boys always like to have their little jokes,' he replied with a wink at Sarah.

Sarah smiled back. Adeline was far from sweet.

However, the colonel sniffed his disapproval. 'Hmm.' Then he turned to Sarah. 'What is Haas expecting from her?'

'The arrangement is that she writes to him in Lisbon, pretending he is her uncle. The letters will be full of family news, but she will use invisible ink to impart the secret messages. Adeline says he is most eager to know about troop movements, particularly in the south.'

The colonel chuckled. 'I bet he is! We will oblige, certainly. Just not the real ones.' He leaned back in his chair. 'I only wish her communications were by radio; those we could monitor easily. I fear she may sneak something into those letters that we don't want divulged. Any idea what language she will use?'

'The letters will be in French, the secret messages also, as Adeline has only basic German and Haas has only a smattering of English. That is what she has already agreed with Haas. To change the arrangement might draw suspicion.' Sarah gnawed at her lip. 'I'm sorry, sir, but I can't speak or read French. I won't know what she is saying in those letters.'

Everleigh's brows snapped together. 'Well, that's far from ideal.'

'Yes, sir, but don't worry. My French is pretty good,' Jason said. 'If Sarah brings me the letters before posting, I can check them.'

'That's fine, Jason, but what about the secret messages?' the colonel asked. 'What is she using to write them, Sarah?'

'Pyramidon, sir. As far as I understand the process, Haas must use heat on the letter for the message to become visible.'

'Then we can't expose the secret notes to check them before the letters are sent. If the message is visible, Haas will know straight away that someone else has handled and read the letter,' Jason said.

'I don't like it. How can we be sure she is sending what we tell her?' Everleigh asked Jason.

'We can't, sir,' Jason replied with a shake of his head.

Everleigh ran a hand over his brow and Sarah felt a rush of affection for him. He was exhausted, his skin grey from lack of sleep. The man was run ragged, as the department was extremely short on resources and yet the demands on MI5 increased daily. On top of this, he had to handle the political pressures from his superiors.

'Sir, I am sure I can manage Vernier. I will do my best to build up a rapport. If she trusts me, hopefully she will pass on only what I tell her,' Sarah said.

'Well, we will know soon enough when we intercept Haas's messages to Berlin. That will close the loop. However, she could still do damage and we won't be able to stop her. That first message will be a risky but necessary test,' the colonel said.

Jason cleared his throat and stood. 'Sorry, sir, I have a meeting and need to go.' He turned to Sarah. 'I'll see you in the morning, Sarah. Best of luck settling her in.'

Once Jason had quit the room, Sarah was eager to know more. 'Can we do that, sir?' she asked, amazed. 'Break the Nazi codes?'

Suddenly Everleigh's cheeks pinched, and Sarah suspected he had let that piece of information slip unintentionally. 'Eh, yes, we have broken their codes. But that information must not leave this office, Sarah. Is that understood?'

'Yes, sir, of course. But that is fantastic. That gives us such an advantage.'

Everleigh held up his hand. 'And that is why it cannot become common knowledge.'

'I understand, sir.'

The colonel relaxed back into his seat. 'How is that rascal Anderson, by the way?'

'Very well, sir, and settling into his new role.'

The colonel tapped the file open before him. 'Excellent. Now, back to more mundane matters. What shall we do with Vernier? She will need a job of some sort. Any ideas?'

'Well, she is an experienced journalist, and her English is excellent. Would it be possible to get her a position with a London newspaper?'

'Yes,' Everleigh rubbed his chin, 'that should not pose a difficulty. I know a few of the chaps over at *The Gazette*. In fact, that would be most useful. We've had the idea of getting the papers to run personal ads that will give credence to our fake army divisions scattered around the country. We could set her up to run those.'

'Such as marriage announcements?' Sarah asked, intrigued.

'Yes, that sort of thing. We know the Germans are picking up our newspapers abroad. Every little lie helps weave our deceit.'

'That's very clever. What about accommodation for her, sir?'

'By chance, we have a vacant flat near Paddington Station, looked after by one of our retired agents. My secretary, Miss Abernathy, will give you the details. I chose it as it is not too far from where you live. I think I'd feel more comfortable if you supervised this woman closely.'

'That sounds perfect, sir.'

'Excellent,' Everleigh said, closing over the file with a flick of his wrist. 'I'll have a quick chat with her before you leave. Set her straight on a few matters, eh?'

'Yes, sir. She might take the news better coming from you.'

'I'll make no commitment regarding this Russian chap, you understand. And neither should you. Keep dangling it before her as a possibility.'

'Very good, sir,' Sarah replied, but with a sinking heart. Stringing Adeline out would be tiresome and unlikely to work for long.

The colonel rose. 'Settle Vernier in today. I'll have Miss Abernathy contact Heinrich Pfeiffer immediately. He'll notify Haas that she has arrived safely and that will set the wheels in motion. Then make sure she writes that first letter to Haas and run it past Jason before you post it. Haas won't be expecting it to contain intelligence, only to confirm that she has set herself up and is ready to spy. So for God's sake, do your best to ensure that it is all she tells him. I will watch your progress with interest.'

'Thank you, sir,' she answered, as they shook hands. Just what she needed: the pressure of knowing Everleigh was monitoring her! Though it was probably to be expected. The next few months and this operation were so vital for the Allies. However, how she was to ensure Adeline toed the line, she wasn't quite sure.

The colonel grinned back at her. 'If she proves trust-worthy, we can start feeding her some interesting titbits to get those German tastebuds tingling,' he said as he ushered her out the door.

5

16th March 1944, Sale Place, Paddington, London

It was late afternoon when Sarah and Adeline turned the corner into Sale Place. For most of the journey from St. James's Street, Sarah's charge had remained silent. Sarah assumed Adeline was still digesting her conversation with the colonel; a conversation she had not been privy to, but she could easily guess the gist of it. Everleigh could intimidate when he put his mind to it. No doubt he would have been determined to quell any false hopes cherished by Adeline that they could rescue her boyfriend easily. Sarah hoped he hadn't completely quashed Adeline's expectations, as it would make her life so much more difficult. Sarah sneaked a look at her companion, but she was giving nothing away. Reluctant to broach the topic with her, for fear of opening those volatile French floodgates, Sarah focused on finding the right house.

All of a sudden, Adeline sighed and came to a stop,

dropping her case to the ground. 'Are we nearly there, please? I am exhausted.'

'Yes, I promise; this is the street. I'm sure it's only a little further along.'

Adeline's answering glance spoke volumes, but she picked up her case and waved Sarah onward. Scanning the door numbers, Sarah strode ahead. Halfway down, she found the address provided by Miss Abernathy. She almost groaned aloud. The sight of the narrow terraced house did little to improve her mood. Victorian, Sarah reckoned by the style of it, and the brick façade was filthy, as were most of the other houses on the street. Not surprisingly, a look of aversion crossed Adeline's features as she drew level and stood staring up at the house. Sarah had to admit the three-storey building didn't look welcoming, particularly as its neighbour was a bombed-out shell with a pile of rubble visible above the hoarding which surrounded it. A criss-cross of wooden beams supported the gable wall of the building Adeline would call home for the months ahead.

'This is where I am to live?' Adeline turned to her, slowly shaking her head. '*C'est impossible!*'

'I am sure it is fine,' Sarah muttered, before lifting the door knocker. *Please God, let it be better inside.*

Adeline dropped her suitcase to the ground before pulling out her cigarettes from her coat pocket. As she lit one, her gaze roamed up and down the street. When it came back to rest on Sarah, it was a mix of dismay and disbelief.

More worrying, Sarah's knock remained unanswered. After several more minutes, Adeline broke into a smile and waved towards the door. 'Perhaps no one is home? This is good. I would prefer a hotel.'

Sarah smothered a retort and knocked once more. 'This is the right address, and the landlord will be expecting us.'

At last, her knock was answered and an elderly man with straggly grey hair and a watery gaze peered out at them. 'Miss Gillespie?' he asked, his eyes flitting between them.

'Yes, sir, I'm Miss Gillespie. Nice to meet you. Are you Mr Cartwright?' Sarah asked, stepping forward.

'That's right. I, eh, look after the place for the firm. Retired now, I am.'

Adeline drowned out Sarah's reply. 'How wonderful! A concierge, like I had in Paris.' She brushed past Sarah and held her hand out to Cartwright. 'I am Mademoiselle Vernier,' she said in a regal tone. Mr Cartwright shook her hand and waved her through, but his expression, when his gaze met Sarah's, was one of puzzlement.

'Mademoiselle Vernier is French,' Sarah said as she shook his hand, hoping this would explain Adeline's imperious behaviour.

'Ah, I see, a Frenchie.' But Sarah caught him rolling his eyes as he closed the door.

As Sarah became accustomed to the dimness of the hallway, her dismay returned. Adeline stood halfway down, stiff with what Sarah guessed was distaste, but to be fair, it wasn't a homely place. The corridor smelled of damp wood and overcooked vegetables and it was disquieting to see the large crack in the wall, which bordered the bombed-out site next door.

'It would appear you had a lucky escape,' Sarah remarked, nodding towards it.

'Oh, aye; nasty business. Damn Jerries! They got Paddington Station the same night.'

'When was that, Mr Cartwright?'

'April '41. Won't forget it in a hurry, I can tell you. Luckily, me and the missus, God rest her soul, made the shelter in time.' Cartwright shuddered. 'Heard the blighters doing their worst, though, all bloody night. Glad to see we are giving them a taste of their own medicine now. That'll teach them to tangle with us.' His expression turned grim as he eyed the wall. 'I wish they'd clean up the mess next door, though. Bloody kids are always going in there and messing about. I keep running them off. It ain't right. They go in there trying to find anything of value to sell down at the pawn brokers. Little blighters would swipe the cigarette out of your very hand, they would. I've complained to the Council several times, you know. And the local bobby, but he says unless he catches them in the act, there ain't nothing he can do 'bout it.'

Sarah made sympathetic noises, but she sensed Adeline was growing impatient. 'I hope it is sorted out for you soon. Perhaps we could see the flat now, Mr Cartwright?'

The landlord waved towards the stairs. 'Right you are! Up to the first floor, ladies. I've saved the best flat for you, miss.'

Adeline looked sceptical, but headed up, leaving Cartwright no choice but to pick up her case and follow. Sarah brought up the rear, smiling despite herself. Adeline was a ticket!

Much to Sarah's relief, the flat was a pleasant surprise. It comprised a large kitchen cum sitting room, a bedroom overlooking the back garden, and a tiny bathroom further down the landing. Everywhere was bright and airy, and looked as if it had been recently painted. Even Adeline appeared surprised.

'I've left some basic supplies for you, as instructed,' Cartwright said, nodding towards the kitchen area. Then he placed two sets of keys down on the table at the window. 'I'll get that going for you,' he said, heading for the fireplace. Seconds later, he had lit a rolled-up news-paper, and the kindling sparked. 'There now, mind you keep that going. Will be cold tonight. Any questions, my flat is on the ground floor. Just knock on the door at the back of the hall.' He grinned at Adeline, who nodded back, unsmiling. Cartwright sent Sarah another puzzled look before moving towards the door. 'Well, I'll leave you to settle in then.'

'Thank you, Mr Cartwright,' Sarah called after him.

'What a funny little man!' Adeline said as soon as the door closed.

'I'm sure he's very nice. Please don't forget this is his home. I'd guess he has been through a lot, so try to be kind to him, please,' Sarah said. The last thing she needed was a litany of complaints about Adeline's rudeness, directed at either her or Jason.

Adeline must have guessed her thoughts, for she grinned. 'I am nice to *everyone*.' Adeline ran her hand along the top of the mantlepiece before holding it up to Sarah. 'I am astonished; it is clean!'

'Yes, I must admit the flat is a pleasant surprise, consid-ering the condition of the rest of the building. But this will suit you perfectly. It's not too far from the Tube station, which will be handy for getting around.'

'If you say so,' Adeline answered, staring out the window. 'But London is so different to my home. I think I will be lonely here.'

Sarah was surprised. She hadn't expected to hear Adeline wallowing in self-pity. So much for the resilient and independent image she had been projecting since Scotland. Sarah was finding that she often had to readjust her assessment of her charge. Adeline might come across as shallow at times, but Sarah suspected it was a ploy to keep people at bay. Could she blame her? Faced with similar circumstances, would she not also create a protective layer? However, it also meant that Sarah could not be sure what lurked beneath the surface. Duplicity took many forms, and until such time as she figured out the woman's true character, she needed to be on her guard.

'Come now, you won't be lonely for long, Adeline. You will start work shortly and I'm sure you will make friends there. And I live reasonably near and will pop by when I can.' Sarah scooped up one set of keys and popped them into her coat pocket. Adeline's gaze followed her actions, but she made no comment.

'So, will this do, Adeline?' Sarah asked.

'Do I have a choice?'

'Sorry. Not really.'

'This is not what I envisaged. My flat in Paris is much larger, and the furniture is stylish and of my choosing. And as for the view, why, it is superb. Notre-Dame is so beautiful.' Adeline's hands fluttered, but then suddenly she closed her eyes and sighed. 'Oh, I don't know what to think. I am so weary.' She dropped onto the sofa and leaned her head back to gaze up at the ceiling. 'It will do until Nikolay joins me. Then we will need something bigger.'

'Eh, hold on a minute. You told *me* he wanted to join his comrades in Russia.'

Adeline threw her a sharp glance. 'Eventually, yes, of course he does, but I must be sure he is well. I *must* see him before he returns to his homeland.'

'Colonel Everleigh explained how this works, Adeline. Do not pretend otherwise. We are employing you, not your boyfriend. Besides, it will take some time to get him out of France. You must be patient.'

Adeline sat up straight, frowning fiercely at her. 'You and your boss assured me you can get him out.'

'No, no! You have misunderstood. The colonel would not have said that and neither did I. However, we *will* do our best to extract him.'

'That is not the same, not enough. I only agreed to work for you based on Nikolay being freed. I need more than vague promises. You have to get him out as quickly as possible.'

Sarah sat down at the table. How could she placate Adeline without committing herself? 'You must be reasonable, Adeline. It is no easy thing to spirit someone out of Nazi occupied territory. It will take time and planning. Don't you see? If you prove your allegiance to us, it will help your boyfriend's case. Colonel Everleigh will be more likely to prioritise his escape. MI5 cannot get him out alone, you must realise that. We must rely on other . . . agencies . . . to do it for us.'

'Piff! I do not like these excuses. I think you try to trick me.'

'No one is trying to trick you. I promise I will do my best to keep the pressure up, but you must help by co-operating. And no better time than the present. Before I go, I need you to write that letter to Haas and I can post it on my way home.'

'Really? Now? I'm exhausted. You do not trust me to do it later?' Adeline asked. Sarah gave her a hard stare and eventually Adeline muttered, 'You English are sneaky. This is no way to treat someone who is going to help you win this war.'

'I'm not English, Adeline; I'm Irish.'

'Oh!' Adeline shrugged. 'I'm sure it's the same thing.'

'I assure you, it is *not*.'

'I do not care,' Adeline replied. Sarah glared back at her, and finally Adeline looked away. 'Very well, I will write it.'

'A short note will suffice,' Sarah snapped and immediately felt bad. She couldn't let Adeline get under her skin so easily. How would she feel in Adeline's shoes? In a strange country with no friends, her boyfriend trapped in France and her about to embark on a career of duping the Nazis: would she be as brave? Still, could she be sure that there was more to this woman than the veneer of selfish socialite? Could she really trust her? They could never be true friends; they were too different. There was a sharpness to Adeline that Sarah found unsettling. However, it was up to her to ensure their relationship was a productive one. So, in a more moderate tone, she continued. 'Did Haas give you a specific code to include in your first communication?'

Adeline sighed heavily as she rose. 'Yes, yes.' She pointed at her case sitting inside the door where Cartwright had dropped it. 'I will need my things.'

To keep the peace, Sarah bit her lip and fetched the case. She placed it on the table with deliberate gentleness and sat back down.

Adeline flashed her a smile, then clicked open the latches and rummaged through her clothes. She pulled out a small black bag and emptied the contents onto the table, which comprised a bundle of toothpicks, a jar of painkillers and a pad of writing paper.

Sarah picked up the bottle of pills. 'Pyramidon,' she read.

'Why, yes. Do you not know of it? It makes an excellent invisible ink solution.'

'Of course I am aware of it, but as a painkiller only. I didn't know it was used as an invisible ink. However, I'm no expert in that particular field.'

Adeline looked surprised at her admission, then smiled. 'Well, until Haas's people showed me, I did not know about it either. Perhaps you could fetch me a glass of water? I need to dissolve two pills to make the writing solution.'

'Certainly,' Sarah replied and went over to the sink. As she turned back with the glass of water, she caught a flash of red as Adeline shoved something back into her case, under some clothes. It had looked like a book.

Now, what is she up to? I can't turn my back on her for a minute!

'Here you are.' Sarah handed the glass to Adeline and watched her drop two tablets into the water.

Adeline pulled out the other chair and sat down. After a minute, the solution in the glass was ready. 'I must write the secret message first,' Adeline explained. 'Then the paper must dry before I write the visible one, in the other direction.' Adeline picked up a toothpick and dipped it into the ink solution. 'I cannot risk the ink running or I will have to start again.'

'What language will the message be in?' Sarah asked to see if Adeline had been telling the truth before. She had to be alert for inconsistencies.

'French, of course,' Adeline said with an impatient sigh. 'Hurry, please, tell me what you wish me to say.' Adeline sat poised with her toothpick.

'Have you memorised your codes? Do you not need to consult something?'

'No, no. I have them in my head.'

Sarah suspected she was lying, but to challenge her at this moment might not be the cleverest move. 'Very well. Tell Haas you have arrived safely, and that Pfeiffer has set you up with a job and a place to stay. That should suffice. How are you supposed to sign off?'

'With my code name,' Adeline snapped. 'Now, can I do this please?'

Sarah waved her hand for the other woman to continue and contemplated her in silence. She had no way of checking what Adeline was writing, even if she could read French. The toothpick left a damp impression on the paper, two lines of indecipherable marks. Adeline's message was short, that much she could see. Hopefully, there was no hidden code in there to set alarm bells ringing with Haas.

'Would you like me to read it out to you?'

'No, that won't be necessary,' Sarah replied.

Adeline looked surprised, then blew on the page before waving it about. 'We must wait now. I dare not write the ink message until the paper is fully dry.' Adeline blew on the page once more and then tilted the paper as she examined it. 'I cannot put it close to the fire to dry it as the heat would make the message visible.'

'Don't worry, I understand. I can stay; I'm in no hurry,' Sarah said. 'Why don't I make some tea while we wait?'

Adeline looked horrified. 'There is no coffee?'

'I'll check,' Sarah replied, then rummaged around the shelves. 'Sorry, no. It's hard to get, so I'm not surprised.'

'Very well, I will suffer the tea,' Adeline replied with a shudder, looking extremely put out.

6

They drank their tea in silence, and after about ten minutes, Adeline showed the page to Sarah. There was no trace of the message.

'Clever, *n'est-ce pas*? This rough paper is best to use as it does not stretch when wet.'

'Did the Germans give it to you?'

'Yes, of course. If I were to use different paper, Haas would be suspicious. Now, I will write the letter to my *dear* uncle.' She cocked a brow at Sarah. 'This will also be in French. Will that be an issue? Will this get through your postal service?'

Sarah nodded. 'It should do.' Sarah almost smiled when she noticed Adeline's subtle shake of her head. The spy knew well that all post was checked and, in her case as she was a double agent and therefore under suspicion, MI5 would ensure that all her incoming and outgoing post was read thoroughly.

When the letter was finished, Adeline folded it, put it into an envelope addressed to Haas's alias in Lisbon, and handed it over to Sarah. 'Now I prove myself to you, yes?'

Sarah tucked the letter into her handbag but couldn't help herself saying, 'Time will tell, Adeline.'

Vernier lit a cigarette and smiled across at her. 'You are very suspicious. I'm thinking I do not like *you* very much, Sarah Gillespie.'

Her frankness was a little alarming, but Sarah respected her for it. 'We do not need to be bosom pals, mademoiselle. Just work together.' Sarah stood and patted her bag. 'I'll get some stamps and post this on my way home.'

The Frenchwoman shrugged, then smiled up at her, distrust plain to see. It was as if Adeline had had the last word, despite saying nothing at all.

Sarah had mixed feelings as she walked away from Adeline's flat into the growing dusk. Dealing with the spy made her irritable as well as uneasy; the woman was so difficult to read. Without doubt, Adeline was temperamental and prickly, but perhaps it was an act to keep Sarah guessing about her true intent? How was she to break down the barrier? Her gut was telling her she had to gain the woman's confidence if this was to work, no matter how uncomfortable that was. Showing sympathy regarding the boyfriend might be a good move. But would Adeline see through such an attempt? She had never met anyone like Adeline before. Sarah was on the back foot and didn't like it.

This assignment for Colonel Everleigh was her most important so far, but so much hinged on Adeline's co-operation and loyalty. Like the other double agents,

Adeline was a small but critical cog in the Allies' deception plan to make the Germans believe Calais would be the landing point of choice. Failure was not an option because when the Allies eventually landed in France, it was vital that the location and the date were a complete surprise to the Nazis. MI5 was already laying the groundwork for that through the double-cross system, and hopefully, Sarah and Adeline's contribution would help secure success. But could MI5 trust the Frenchwoman not to betray the system? The very idea sent a shiver down Sarah's spine. She had seen at first hand the consequences of deception, and she had learned how duplicitous people could be when driven by idealism or money.

Two years before, a German mole in MI5, who she and Anderson had trusted implicitly, had almost single-handedly destroyed the entire intelligence network in South Wales by defecting in the middle of an operation. What would be the consequences for her if Adeline proved to be as duplicitous? It was a heavy responsibility to shoulder, particularly when Sarah was reluctant to share her anxiety with any of her colleagues, not wishing to appear incapable. So, who could she go to for advice? Certainly not the colonel. The problem was, she couldn't say much to Jason, either. He had already stuck his neck out for her. She could not run to him with every issue she encountered.

Sarah didn't go to the post office, as she had promised Adeline she would, but instead made straight for a Lyons Corner House she had spotted earlier. Once settled at a table, Sarah pulled out the letter to Haas and gazed at it in frustration. Not for the first time, Sarah regretted her poor education at the hands of the nuns back in Dublin.

If only she could have learned French. Thankfully, the visible part of the letter was brief. Out of curiosity, Sarah tilted the page to catch the light, but she could see no trace of the invisible ink. It was marvellous how well it worked. If not for the fact that she had watched Adeline write the secret message, she might have doubted it existed at all.

Taking her time, she transcribed the message onto her notepad for Jason to translate first thing in the morning. They had to be sure there was no obvious warning to Haas contained within it. Also, she needed to keep a record of the language and tone Adeline used in communicating with Haas in case it had to be checked later. If only there was some way to ensure the spy wasn't deceiving them. The French text, either visible or invisible, might include a code word, or a seemingly innocent phrase, which could warn Haas that something was amiss with his newest agent.

On that less than happy thought, Sarah finished her tea and left, now eager to get home before it was dark. She picked up her pace as she headed along the busy streets towards the flat and her mood lifted as she drew closer. For two years now, she had shared it with her cousin Judith, and her friend Gladys, her old comrade from Supermarine. It was more than home, really; it was a sanctuary, and she treasured her friendships with the girls above all else. When work was difficult, it was always good to relax with them, or as often as not, be dragged out to a local hostelry or dancehall, which helped her forget, even if only briefly, when the bad memories threatened to overwhelm her. Their friendship had helped her through Tony's long absence as well. Now, the bond between them had strengthened, for over the last few years they had been through much together: heartache, loss, and even the death of friends fighting overseas.

Most of all, their camaraderie soothed the pain she still felt over Maura's death. She often reflected on how much her life had changed since those relatively peaceful days down in Hampshire, when all she had had to worry about was accuracy in her assignments. Those precious few weeks when she had first arrived in England, she had felt safe in her uncle's household. To add to her happiness, she obtained a job she loved, tracing drawings for Spitfire planes. At the time, it seemed the perfect way to get revenge on the Nazis for the loss of her sister and the destruction of her home.

Still, as Gladys often commented, Hursley had been a dull enough place for young women freshly out in the world. All Gladys had ever wanted was to come to London and 'live a little'. When Sarah had declared that she was heading to the capital to take up a new job, Gladys had been insistent she accompany her. It hadn't been an easy decision for Sarah to leave her family, but she knew there would be few opportunities to avenge her sister's murder if she stayed in Hampshire. The intervening time had offered ample chances to inflict damage on the German Reich's plans, and, of course, through her work, she had met the love of her life, Tony.

7

16th March 1944, Paddington, London

Twenty minutes later, Sarah turned her key in the latch, thankful to be home and out of the cold. Three days of travelling had taken its toll, and all she wanted was an early night. Then, hopefully, she could face Adeline in the morning with renewed purpose. However, as she stood on the threshold of the flat, she could hear raised voices within. Slightly baffled, she closed the door behind her and realised the commotion was coming from the kitchen. As she drew closer, Sarah recognised the male voice was Martin, her cousin, and her heart soared. So absorbed in the problems with Adeline, she had forgotten that he was due to stay with them for a couple of weeks while he attended a training course in the city.

Sarah dropped her bag in the hall and rushed into the kitchen, only to find Martin and Gladys glaring at each other over the kitchen table. The atmosphere was strained and the tell-tale signs of anger coloured Gladys's cheeks. Martin was rigid in his seat, huffing. Sarah hesitated in the doorway and cleared her throat. Two pairs of angry eyes swivelled round to look at her. Gladys's expression closed while Martin sprang to his feet. Seconds later, he enveloped Sarah in a hug and kissed her soundly on both cheeks.

'You're a sight for sore eyes, cousin,' he said, holding her at arm's length.

'It's good to see you, too,' she replied. Sarah glanced at Gladys, who rolled her eyes, her lips a grim line of disapproval. As Sarah's gaze returned to her cousin, she was aware of Gladys springing up, scooping the empty teacups from the table, and taking them to the sink.

'When did you arrive?' Sarah asked him.

'About an hour ago. Gladys, here, has been keeping me company.' Sarah did not miss the undercurrent in his tone. A snort from Gladys, over at the sink, was the only acknowledgement of his words. Gladys rinsed out the cups with a thoroughness that almost made Sarah wince. She feared they might have to drink out of saucers for the foreseeable.

At last Gladys turned around, nose in the air. 'I'm off. I'm on the evening shift,' she declared as she brushed past Sarah and escaped out the door. Martin's dagger gaze followed her.

Sarah knew Martin and Gladys had never been friendly, but the angry mood she had sensed on entering the kitchen puzzled her. It was rare to see him so het up.

'What was all that about?'

'Only a difference of opinion.' He sniffed loudly, pulled out his chair, and sat back down. 'We don't see eye to eye on most things, you know that; never have.'

Sarah wasn't fooled. This was different. It had been a shouting match. 'Oh, I do know! But you've only been here five minutes and you've already had an almighty row? I don't understand.'

'It was nothing. A misunderstanding. Probably my fault,' he mumbled.

'It didn't sound like nothing; you were yelling at each other. Oh, Martin, tell me.' He hunched his shoulders, his lips pursed. She pushed: 'I'll get it out of Glad, you know. It might be best to tell me your side of it.'

Martin's face creased into a grimace, and he lowered his voice, his gaze flicking towards the doorway. 'She was telling me what happened with that Alfie chap. I was shocked, to be honest. She considers the entire episode hilarious now. I don't understand the girl. Why, it could have been a tragic outcome. And why did she have to involve you in her mess?'

'She's my friend, Martin. I had to help,' Sarah replied.

'Hmm, that girl needs to grow up. She lurches from scrape to scrape. If I thought you or Judith took such risks—'

'Oh no, you didn't tell her off!' Sarah almost laughed. That would be a red rag for Gladys.

Martin pinched his lips before answering. 'I merely advised her to be more sensible. God knows who she is dealing with on those buses as a conductress. She, however, told me to mind my own business.'

Sarah could see why, but thought it best not to say so. 'Martin, she's not stupid, you know. She is a happy-go-lucky person but Gladys has been a clippie long enough to know what's what.' Martin just grunted. 'Besides, you shouldn't worry about her. She grew up with older brothers and knows how to look after herself.'

'I can imagine.' He sniffed. 'That tongue of hers is sharp for sure. Cut a man in two, I dare say.' Martin scowled.

'Martin, you will be here for a few weeks, on and off. I am pleading with you to—'

'What?' he huffed.

'Show some restraint: be the bigger person. I know you two don't get on, but the rest of us want some peace and quiet when we are at home.'

'Alright! I'll stay out of her way, but I'm telling you, that girl is far too flighty; always has been. Have you ever had a serious conversation with her? I very much doubt it!'

'I'm sure you mean well, and I can understand your pride is a wee bit hurt, but I know Gladys far better than you. She is a good egg with a strong independent streak. And she has needed it, I can tell you, after what she has been through in the past. Now, let's say no more on the subject. Is there any tea left in that pot?'

Martin was too busy glowering at the door to answer at first. He turned back to her at last. 'Oh, yes, there should be.' He took off his glasses, cleaning them with his hand-kerchief. Something he usually did to hide discomfort.

A change of subject was required. 'Did Judith arrive home safely? Your mother and father must be delighted to have her back home for a week,' she said, pouring out her tea. 'She's been looking forward to the break for ages.'

Martin grinned. 'You can imagine the fuss. Mother has been saving rations for weeks in anticipation. I hope Judith has a good appetite. Mother intends to fatten her up.'

Sarah smiled. 'Well, it was lucky that she had that leave coming. It would have been a wee bit cramped here with all of us if she hadn't.'

'I would have been happy to sleep on the sofa,' Martin said with a sniff. 'But yes, it wouldn't have been ideal.'

'Well, I'm delighted you will be staying. We have some catching up to do. I've missed our chats. It will be like old times,' Sarah said.

'Yes. Maybe you can show me some of the sights? Treat your old cousin to a night in the pub? That sort of thing.'

'Absolutely! I'd love to. We could go to the West End and see a play or a show.'

'Even better,' he replied. Then Martin popped his glasses back on and looked at her over the rim. 'Tell me, truthfully; how is Judith doing? She doesn't say much in her letters. Sadly, we're not as close as we once were, and I can't help worrying about her. It seems there is a sadness in her eyes sometimes, or am I imagining it?'

'No. I've caught that expression a few times as well. But there's no need to worry, honestly, and I will always look out for her, you know that.' He nodded. 'Such a shame you think you have grown apart. I doubt it's true, Martin. Though the distance to Hampshire doesn't help with travel so regulated and tiresome.'

'I suppose you're right. Maybe, when this blasted war is over, we will see more of each other. Has there been anyone in her life since that fiasco with her boss? What a rotten bounder he turned out to be.'

Martin didn't know the entire story about Gerald, Judith's old boss and, for a while, her lover, but knew enough to know it had had a terrible impact on Judith's confidence.

'Yes, an awful man and thankfully now virtually forgotten. But don't worry that she's become a hermit. Judith has gone out on plenty of dates, but the poor chaps don't last long. I think she's afraid of getting hurt again.' It was clear Judith hadn't told him about Ewan yet, but Sarah wasn't concerned. Judith would tell her brother about him when she was ready.

'Can't blame her after what she went through with that snake,' Martin continued, lacing his fingers.

'I hope you never told your parents,' Sarah said. 'The fact Gerald was married would have crushed them.'

'Of course, I never said a word. After all, you both told me about him in confidence. No, they are too set in their ways and would never understand. Mother, in particular, is so religious.' He tilted his head and grinned at her. 'And how are you?'

'Fine.'

'Hmm, you look done-in to me.'

'That's only because I had to travel a lot this week. I'm busy though, which is a good thing. Keeps *me* out of mischief. How are Aunty Alice and Uncle Tom?'

'All well. Though Mother really misses you girls. I know Judith will never come back to live in Hursley, but I don't suppose there is any chance of you returning to Supermarine?'

Sarah shook her head. 'I've too much on here. Besides, they have promoted me. I'll be sticking with this job until the end of the war. After that,' she shrugged, 'heaven knows.' Martin looked doubtful, and she continued. 'You know how it is. This work means I'm helping the war effort in a real way.'

'Supermarine *is* part of the war effort,' he replied, looking put out. It was a sore point with Martin that he couldn't enlist because of his poor eyesight, and even though his draughtsmanship was considered exceptional, he still longed to serve on the frontline.

'Yes, of course it is. But this work I'm doing is more hands-on, if you know what I mean?'

With a sniff, Martin folded his arms. 'I guess I do. And I suppose a certain US naval officer, stationed back in London, might have something to do with you staying here, too?'

Sarah waggled her head and laughed. 'Tony is a factor, of course. It is wonderful that he is safely back from France, but he has a new role, which involves a lot of travel around the country. I don't see as much of him as I'd like.'

'That's a pity, but he's a good lad. I'm glad you have someone like him in your life.' Then he broke into a grin. 'Saves me having to look out for you all the time.'

'Huh! As if you ever had to.' Sarah sipped her tea and gazed at her cousin. Something was up, she could sense it, but she knew from experience that he was always reluctant to open up about personal stuff. Still, it was worth a try.

'And how about you? Is there anyone special at the moment?' she asked. As far as she was aware, his last girl-friend had been Ruth, and that had ended tragically for everyone.

Martin gave a shrug. 'I'm too busy for any of that malarkey.'

'But what about the Hursley Players? Surely, you have time for them. Are there no nice young ladies in the cast this year?'

Again, he shrugged. 'No one of interest. Besides, I have this training course and it's going to take up a lot of my time, on and off, for the next few months. It's likely I will have to bow out of their next project altogether.'

'Oh, no. That would be a shame, Martin. You're such a talented actor.'

'Thank you, but if I'm successful in my exams, there could be a promotion in it. I daren't jeopardise that.'

'That's wonderful! Uncle Tom will be so proud of you. I'm sure you will do absolutely fine. You're an experienced draughtsman at this stage. You could probably give the course.'

Sarah was pleased to see the effect of her words as Martin straightened up and a smile replaced his sad expression. 'It would be nice to get some recognition at Supermarine. I'm seven years in the company now,' he said.

'Of course you will. They wouldn't have sent you on the course if they didn't think you'd succeed.'

'Sarah, I'm off,' Gladys shouted from the hallway, and the front door slammed shut. Martin winced.

Sarah threw him a sympathetic look. 'Don't worry about her. Honestly, she will be fine. That nasty incident is all behind her. Now, why don't you put on the radio, and we can listen to some music? It's been a long day.'

'Sure,' he replied, and headed for the sitting room. Minutes later, the strains of a Benny Goodman song came through.

Sarah took her cup to the sink and rinsed it out. Lost in thought, she stared out the window. It wasn't like Gladys to be in a snit. Certainly, she had a short temper, but usually she was quick to smile and make up, too. If she got a chance, she'd try to sound Gladys out in the morning. Taking up a cloth, she quickly dried off the cups on the drainer.

With a sigh, she pulled her thoughts back to the present. *Everything seems upside down today*, she thought as she flipped the light switch and followed the music to the sitting room. If only Tony were around for a chat and a comforting hug.

8

The next day, Sarah sat and waited as Jason read Adeline's letter to SS-Obergruppenführer Haas. When he handed it back to her, it was with a smile.

'All good,' he said. 'Nothing suspicious about it. Nothing obvious, anyway.'

Sarah peered at the page. 'But what does it say, sir?'

Jason took the letter back. 'Dearest Uncle, I hope this finds you and my aunt in good health. My journey to England was uneventful, except that I was sea-sick for most of the crossing. Now, I am settling in here in London and have found a nice flat. Hopefully, I will find work soon. Missing you all very much. I will write when I have more news, Yours, etc.'

'It sounds innocent enough,' Sarah said, rising from her chair. 'I'll post it on my way to her flat. But . . . I wonder if I might have a word, sir?'

'Oh, yes?'

Sarah sat back down. 'Well, after the colonel's story about Haas and how he uses fear to ensure loyalty, I'm concerned about Adeline and her true motivation.'

'I can understand that, Sarah, but we have no intelligence to suggest she is lying to us.'

'But so much is at stake. She is a strange creature, sir. I can't help thinking she is hiding something. What if she causes trouble for us? Her obsession with getting her boyfriend out of France could be an issue. I don't wish to lie to her, but I think we need to give her some hope. Otherwise, I don't think she will co-operate, or worse, she will expose our operation to Haas.'

'So, you fear she isn't a double agent at all.' Sarah nodded. 'That is the risk we must take, and at the moment, we have little choice. As for the situation with the boyfriend, all you can do is promise her we will do our best.'

'But is that realistic, sir? Could we get him out?'

Jason rubbed at his chin. 'Honestly? I doubt it. His best hope is to stay in hiding and that our chaps liberate France in the next couple of months. If the Nazis should catch him, he's history.'

'Of course, I understand. I will do all I can to keep her optimistic and reasonably content,' Sarah replied.

'Good. Keep a close eye on her and what she sends, if possible. I'm happy to translate for you if required.'

With a nod, Sarah got to her feet. 'Yes, please, sir. Not every letter, but it would put my mind at ease if we did random checks. I wish we could check the invisible text as well.'

'Not possible before we send the letters without giving ourselves away, though,' he replied. 'However, if we intercept

Haas's radio messages to Berlin, and they contain our false information, it will give us the reassurance we need.'

'But until we intercept those, we cannot be sure, sir.'

Jason shrugged. 'There is little certainty in our business. You are right to be on your guard. You have great instincts, Sarah, which is why we promoted you.'

'Thank you, sir,' she said. In other words, he expected her to take on the responsibility, whether the operation be a failure or a success. It was both daunting and exhilarating. But she knew she could only do her best.

As she stood to leave, Jason delved into the pile of papers on his desk. 'Hold on. Ah! Here it is.' Jason held up a note. 'This is the name of Everleigh's contact at *The Gazette*. He is one of the senior editors and will expect you. Might as well bring her over there this morning.'

'Mr McKensie,' Sarah read out from the note. 'Do you know him?'

Jason shook his head. 'Don't worry, he should be fine. He's an old friend of the colonel and Everleigh has spoken to him directly, explaining what we would like her to do. It's all set up. You only need to bring her to the offices and introduce her.'

Sarah pulled on her coat. 'That shouldn't be a problem. So, when do you want Adeline to send the next message?'

'Let's give it a few days as Haas won't expect her to have gathered information just yet. Get her settled into the job at *The Gazette* and we can take it from there.' Jason tilted his head and gave her a smile. 'You still look worried.'

Sarah looked down at the letter in her hand, then frowned at her boss. 'Do you think her message contains a code word? When I asked her about it, she said it did and that

77

she had memorised them. But you can only remember so many, surely?'

Jason shrugged. 'It's hard to know. Of course, sometimes, it's what is left out that is key.'

'What do you mean?'

'The code might simply be a missing full stop.' Jason grinned. 'You could always insist she tell you . . .'

With a quirk of her lips, Sarah laughed. 'Like she'd tell me! Still, it would be good to know.'

'The Jerries use various methods with different agents, hoping to elude us. Vernier may have memorised a list of words, as she claims, or she could be using a set text.'

'That's not very reassuring, sir,' Sarah said. 'And what if Adeline does not let me see Haas's replies? I assume we are intercepting her post?'

'Of course, but if they are working with an agreed text, that won't help us much.'

Sarah made a face. 'But she must realise we would check, sir.'

'Of course she does. Mademoiselle Vernier is anything but stupid. Cheer up, Sarah! Those Nazis like to keep us on our toes, but I have every faith in you,' he replied.

Sarah left his office, less than comforted by his parting words.

Half an hour on the Underground brought Sarah and Adeline to Fleet Street and the offices of *The Gazette*. Throughout the journey, and much to Sarah's surprise, Adeline appeared nervous, constantly straightening the silk scarf around her neck. Instead of climbing the flight of steps to enter, Adeline stood gazing up at the building. It was an imposing structure; red-bricked and five storeys high, with a forbidding arched entrance. The sandbags, piled up on either side of the door, did not soften the impression. A large sign proclaiming *The Gazette* stretched across the width of the offices, below the windows of the second floor. What was inside was more likely what was worrying Adeline and Sarah could understand her anxiety, recalling the first time she had stood outside MI5, a naïve girl with no idea how bizarrely her life was about to change.

Sarah patted Adeline's arm. 'You will be fine; you have nothing to worry about. With your experience, they will be glad to have you working for them.' Sarah's biggest fear was that Adeline would take umbrage over something and be difficult. Everleigh would be cross if the woman upset his editor friend. That was the kind of embarrassing situation Sarah wished to avoid, but she could hardly urge the woman to put on a charm offensive as Adeline would likely produce the exact opposite.

'I hope you are right,' Adeline replied in a strained voice. 'I'm ready. Let us go in.'

A porter brought them up in the lift to the top floor, then along a corridor that echoed with the clacking of typewriters and snatches of conversations coming from the various rooms down its length. At the end, he stopped before a door marked 'Mr E McKensie'. He tapped lightly and opened the door before stepping back to let them through.

Mr McKensie's office was at the front of the building, a large bright room with mahogany furniture and several chairs in an arc before an ancient and well-used desk. The man behind it looked up as they entered and beamed across the room. To be more precise, he beamed at Adeline. Amused at the effect her companion was having already, Sarah made the introductions. McKensie's admiring gaze swept up and down Adeline with only a cursory flicker directed at Sarah. But Sarah had to admit that Adeline looked well today in her tailored navy suit, crisp white blouse with a contrasting scarf in red and blue. Perfectly groomed, Adeline was the epitome of French style and sophistication. To be fair, it was difficult not to admire her. However, Adeline's new boss couldn't have been more of a contrast with receding blond hair, and grey eyes in a round face. It was also clear he had a penchant for the better things in life, revealed by a stomach barely contained by his shirt. Could this really be an acquaintance of the colonel? Sarah suspected he had to be a friend from his club rather than his army days.

McKensie came around his desk at surprising speed for a man of his girth, waving them towards the chairs.

'Mademoiselle Vernier, what a pleasure to meet you at last!' he gushed, standing over her. McKensie grabbed her hand and held it for several moments as he openly admired her. Adeline almost purred. Sarah had to make do with a limp handshake when he could drag himself away. Doing her best to hide her smile, Sarah sat down beside the woman of the moment. It looked like Adeline had landed, cat like, on her feet.

McKensie leaned back against the desk. 'Well now, isn't this just grand? Our readers will be delighted. A touch of French sophistication for our house and home articles.'

Adeline threw Sarah a wary glance before she replied. 'Most of my journalism has been of the investigative kind, monsieur. Politics and world affairs.'

McKensie waved a hand. 'No need to worry about

80

that sort of thing. No, no, what we need are pieces our lady readers will devour. French fashion and style, music, theatre . . .' He trailed off, taking in Adeline's frown.

'Perhaps,' she said a tad frostily, 'your readers might wish to know what it is like to live under Nazi rule.'

His smile died. 'We wish to keep morale high, Mademoiselle Vernier, not plunge our readers into despair.'

Sarah hurriedly broke the awkward silence that followed. 'I'm sure Adeline will be happy to provide a whole range of articles for you, Mr McKensie. And, she has kindly agreed to help us out with those special notices we would like printed.'

McKensie's gaze swung around and rested on Sarah. 'Yes, very well. I agreed all of that with Everleigh.'

'Perfect, and thank you, sir.' Sarah rose. 'I'm sure you would like to get settled in, Adeline.' She touched her shoulder as she passed in what she hoped was a reassuring gesture. 'I will call on you tomorrow evening to see how you are getting on.'

Adeline pursed her lips and did not respond, however, there was a decided twinkle in her eye as she turned away. Sarah had little doubt that McKensie would be wound around Adeline's little finger before the day was out.

9

Sarah had taken extra care with her appearance, even blagging a pair of silk stockings from Gladys. No doubt her friend would exact a heavy price, but it was worth it to feel the luxury of stockings against her skin. Tony was in for a surprise. That afternoon she had had her hair cut short, making it far more manageable, her childhood curls reappearing. Judith had said it made her look more sophisticated. Even Gladys had approved.

Sarah's gaze swept around the hotel bar as a mixture of excitement and anticipation bubbled up inside her. Tony had said to meet at eight; it was now fifteen minutes past. The bar was as busy as ever, The Savoy being a magnet for those wishing to escape the realities of war. It was a beautiful room, and one of her favourite spots in London and not only because it was her and Tony's meeting place of choice. There was always a buzz, and you never knew who you might spy sipping cocktails at the bar. On a previous visit, she had spotted Churchill in one of the darkened corners with a group of his cronies. Funnily enough, it was also a notorious drinking spot for many of London's foreign agents, and a hotbed of gossip.

As she waited for Tony to appear, her thoughts drifted to Adeline. Was she sitting alone in her flat tonight thinking about her Nikolay stranded in Paris? The woman was isolated to a degree, knowing so few people in London; was there not an onus on Sarah, as her handler, to help her build a life? She wasn't really sure that was part of her remit. Would any of the male handlers worry about such things? Probably not. Normally, Sarah was happy-go-lucky and eager to make new friends, but there was something about Adeline that held her back.

It was clear that the Frenchwoman preferred male company. In the presence of men, she would turn on the charm; it was as if someone had flipped a switch within her. The only exception appeared to be poor Mr Cartwright, Sarah thought with a smile. Perhaps Adeline had learned that behaviour to survive in occupied France. And who was she to judge another woman's strategy for survival? So, what was really holding her back from befriending the woman? Perhaps it was merely a reluctance to mix business and pleasure. But no; that was lame. She needed to make more of an effort. London could be a hostile place for a newcomer if you were on your own. She had been so lucky in having Judith here already when she first arrived, and of course, having Gladys in tow helped enormously.

However, it wasn't only the mercurial Adeline who was making Sarah restless tonight. She was on tenterhooks as she waited for Tony. They had been a couple for two years now, the longest she had ever walked out with anyone. But their busy lives kept them apart. If there were moments when she wished things could change, she did her best to dismiss them because she had no control; the war dictated everything. While Tony had been in France, she had worried about him constantly, each day wondering if today was the day that would bring bad news or the dreaded telegram. Even now that he was back in London, she often succumbed to gloomy thoughts. But there was nothing unique about her worries. Sarah was sure that every woman with a man in active service had similar fears.

Maybe it was the war dragging on for so long, making it impossible to make plans for their future together that was really niggling away at her. What form that future would take was intriguing to think about. Some would say the future was for dreamers only while the war continued, but it was only human nature to daydream about what might be when the guns finally fell silent. And when it did end, would they still be together? Would they stay in England or go to America? Tony never spoke of his aspirations. He was firmly centred in the present, and always turned the subject when she tried to bring it up. At times, she wondered why Tony avoided the topic. Was it really because of the war, living day to day with the fear it might be your last, or was it a more fundamental desire to avoid commitment?

It had only been a week since she had last seen Tony, but she missed him more than usual. Surely, at this stage, she should be used to Tony's long absences, but if anything, it was getting harder. Luckily, work kept her busy, but it was in the evenings, sometimes even when she was out on the town with the girls, that her thoughts strayed to him, and she wondered where he was and if he was safe. And, more importantly, when she would be in his arms again. She missed the physical closeness. It scared her, sometimes, how much she needed him in her life, particularly as she considered herself an independent woman, but losing loved ones had happened far too frequently in the past, leaving her vulnerable to fear.

Her mind wandered. She missed Maura enormously. And Ma, well . . . she had always been a bit distant, but Sarah realised that was down to the physical abuse she had suffered at the hands of their father. As children, their mother's elusiveness had bewildered them. As a result, they had tended to seek comfort in each other's company. Then Ma had died young, and Sarah had to assume the role of mother. Protector too, as Da's fists flew far too often in their direction. Losing Maura had felt like she had lost a part of herself.

And just as she was coming to terms with Maura's loss, she had lost Paul in that German U–boat attack. For months after Paul's death, she had struggled, almost afraid to care for anyone ever again. Then along had come Tony; big, brash, challenging, and fun. Their experiences in Wales, on the trail of her miscreant of a father, had brought them together. At first, it had been purely seeking comfort in intimacy, but it wasn't long before she realised her feelings for him were deepening. The only uncertainty in her mind was Tony's reticence to share his emotions. However, so far, they had survived many separations, and it was foolish to fret; the vagaries of fate and war would dictate the future no matter what their wishes might be.

Sarah darted a look at her watch again. Eight-twenty. Tony *was* late. Could he have been delayed? It wouldn't be the first time, but he invariably sent a message if he couldn't make it. With surprise, she glanced down to see her glass was almost empty. She'd have to slow down, or she would be on her ear by the time Tony arrived.

It was then she spotted a GI on the other side of the bar trying to catch her eye. Sarah knew with the least encouragement he would be at her side, chatting her up. Why could a girl not sit at a bar alone and have a drink in peace? She averted her gaze and took another swig of gin.

'Taken to drink, Irish?' a familiar voice behind her said.

'Tony!' She swung around, delighted, and hopped off the bar stool. And not for the first time, she marvelled at how like Gary Cooper he looked, with his brown eyes always so full of mischief.

Tony stooped down and embraced her, grazing his lips against her cheek. 'Did you think I had abandoned you?' he asked, before sitting down on the bar stool next to hers.

With a sniff and a slowly arched brow, she tried her best to look disdainful, but it didn't last long, and she broke into a grin. 'Not at all.'

As Tony looked at her, his eyes widened. He reached out and stroked the back of her neck, his fingers winding around the silky curls. 'Wow! I love your hair like this. Very cute.'

Sarah felt the colour rush into her cheeks, but she was pleased he liked it. 'Thank you. It's a big change.'

'It suits you,' he replied with a grin. Then he nodded to her glass. 'Do you want a top-up?' Sarah shook her head and Tony beckoned the barman over. 'Scotch on the rocks, please.'

'When did you get back to London?' she asked.

'About an hour ago. Sorry, I was delayed and missed my train. Then I had to stop off at the office and drop off some papers.' He grabbed her hand and squeezed it. 'What a week! I've missed you.' Then he sighed, letting go of her hand. It was then Sarah noticed how tired he looked, with dark shadows under his eyes.

'I've missed you, too,' she said. 'Was it a difficult trip?'

'Not really. It went quite well, but you know what it's like. I've told you before the kinda guys I deal with, Army and Navy, all jostling for position.' He broke into a chuckle. 'They are worse than politicians. Full of self-importance, trying to outdo each other to get noticed. Sometimes I wonder if we are all on the same damn side. Sorry, I know we normally avoid work talk.'

'No, it's OK. I understand,' she replied, patting his hand. 'If it helps to talk about it, go ahead.'

'Nah, I'd rather talk about you,' he replied. The barman left Tony's drink on the counter. Tony scooped it up and clinked her near-empty glass. 'Don't we have your solo mission to celebrate? I'm delighted to see you have survived intact!'

'How could you doubt it?' she asked, trying to act indignant. However, the reminder of Adeline's existence made her scowl. 'It may well turn out to be a poisoned chalice.' Concern crossed his features, and she regretted her words. Didn't he have enough to deal with without her worries as well? 'It's nothing,' she reassured him. 'Just a tiresome person I must work closely with for a while. It's fine, really.'

'Whatever you want, hun, but you know you can always talk to me if things are—'

'Yeah, I know. And I appreciate it, but there are things I can't tell you.'

'Sarah, come on; you can trust me,' he said. 'I should think, if push came to shove, I'm still an honorary member of MI5.'

'Perhaps. Everleigh certainly misses you.'

Tony shook his head. 'I doubt it, sweetheart. My joining SOE didn't go down well, if you recall.'

'That's long forgotten. He was asking after you only the other day and he would no doubt have you back in a heartbeat.'

'I always knew he was a man of discernment.' Tony laughed as she rolled her eyes.

'Enough work talk,' she said. 'Of much more importance, are we going on that holiday to Devon or not?' They had made tentative arrangements on the Sunday morning before he'd had to dash off.

Tony sipped his drink before answering, and her heart dropped. He was stalling. 'Sarah, it might not be workable for a while.' His voice lowered, and he leaned closer. 'It's impossible for me to commit to anything right now with the stuff that's going on.'

Sarah knew he was referring to the Allied plans to invade France, but a public bar was not the place to discuss it. 'Oh, that affects me, too. Actually, it's unlikely I will be able to take leave either.'

He looked relieved at her words. But she was merely saving face. The invasion plans had been common knowledge in the upper echelons of the intelligence services for months. So why had he been so keen before? His backtracking left her unsettled. What had changed? Had Tony agreed to the holiday last week just to fob her off?

10

It was Saturday lunchtime at last. It didn't help that Sarah's head hurt. A lot. She hated to admit it, but she was hungover after her night out with Tony. As usual, they had gone back to Tony's flat, where she had spent the night. Soon, she was smiling at the memory. It was a welcome distraction from the transcripts of recorded conversations she had been poring over all morning. A job she had hoped she had seen the back of, but with the shortage of staff, a stack of files had somehow ended up on her desk, courtesy of Jason's secretary. A woman no one dared challenge. However, Sarah's reverie was interrupted a few minutes later when Jason stuck his head around her door.

'Glad I caught you,' he said, stepping into the room. 'Here you are.' Jason handed her two pieces of paper. 'The first page is the personal notices we want to go into *The Gazette*. Tell Adeline to give this to the editor on Monday. He will be expecting it. I've included the dates with them. Hopefully, these will give credence to our fake army units. The other is a letter we need sent to Lisbon. Get Honey to write this message to Haas this afternoon.'

'So quickly?' Sarah asked, reading through the details. 'I thought you said he wouldn't be expecting information just yet?'

'I thought so too, but I've just been informed we need to step things up.' He pointed to the page. 'Those troop movements should get Haas interested. But it must go into the post this evening.'

'Fake manoeuvres?'

'Yes, of course,' he replied with a broad smile. 'Our ghost battalions have been busy.'

Sarah frowned. 'But, sir, how would she have come across this information? Won't it seem a bit too soon?'

'We don't have a choice. This has come directly from the XX Committee this morning so you will need to come up with explanations yourself or with the agent. It's part of the job. Didn't you realise?' His frown spoke volumes.

Sarah hurried to reassure him. 'Oh, yes, of course, sir. I'll think of something.'

'It must be plausible,' he replied.

'Don't worry, I have a few ideas already,' she lied.

Gradually, to her relief, his expression cleared. 'Good. I'm off. See you Monday,' he said before disappearing out the door with a cheery wave.

Sarah sat back down. Damn! She should have expected it would be down to her to come up with believable stories to cover Adeline's activities and intelligence gathering. She had been too busy thinking about Tony these last few days and not her job. Her blunder, just now, would have Jason worrying about her competency.

For several minutes, she pondered likely scenarios in which Adeline could have come across the information. After a few deep breaths, Sarah calmed down. *I must be logical.* So, how would a young woman, newly arrived in London, gain this kind of intelligence? A trip to the south coast seemed the most obvious explanation, but in this weather and with the current travel restrictions, that didn't seem feasible. Would the Germans check such details to verify the information? A cycling break in the middle of March? Surely not! No, that was ludicrous; no one would believe that. So, how would Adeline most likely travel to the coast? By train was the obvious answer, but one had to have a good reason to travel. Was she overthinking this? Would Adeline need to impart that level of detail to Haas? Hopefully, in the interests of brevity, they could leave it out, but she would need to emphasise to Adeline that the back story would be important in case Haas became suspicious.

Then it dawned on her. Adeline didn't have to *travel* down to the coast at all. She could say she was at Victoria Station and spotted some troops with insignia she didn't recognise from her training in Berlin. To learn more, she engineered bumping into one of the GIs who told her where they were going and the battalion to which he belonged. If anything, this story would raise Adeline in Haas's estimation and hopefully, give credence to her future messages as well.

Sarah's heart pounded as the enormity of the job hit her. This was a huge responsibility. At times it scared her how much rested on the success of their deceptions. It would take only the smallest mistake and the whole web of lies could unravel. If Jerry discovered the existence of the fake network of agents MI5 had set up, the summer landings would be in jeopardy. She *had* to ensure that Adeline did as she was bid. She pocketed the instructions for Adeline, her muzzy head gradually clearing. It must be the adrenaline, she surmised as she headed down the stairs. It was a relief too, for she had a feeling Adeline would take advantage of any weakness she might show. Then a sudden and horrible thought brought her to a standstill. Could Adeline be dangerous? She hadn't really considered the possibility before. Was the Frenchwoman proficient in more than spying? Assassination, perhaps? Adeline's Nazi boss certainly was. With such disconcerting thoughts floating around in her mind, Sarah stepped out onto St. James's Street and shivered, pulling her collar up against the biting wind and driving rain.

Although the rain had ceased by the time Sarah reached Sale Place, the street was almost deserted as she rounded the corner. As she side-stepped yet another puddle, something caught her eye and she recognised the figure some yards ahead of her. She'd know that blue coat anywhere; it was Adeline. To Sarah's dismay, the spy paused half way down the road at the post-box, drew a letter from her bag, and posted it. *Oh no*, Sarah thought, *what is she up to? Who is she writing to?* Sarah's stomach plummeted with dread. Might the spy write to Haas, unbeknownst to her? How treacherous! And then a worse thought; perhaps it wasn't the first letter Adeline had posted. *Crikey!* Jason would have something to say about that! But, no, she needed to keep calm. She was letting her imagination run away with her. It might be an innocent letter to a relative or friend. Either way, she berated herself for not keeping a closer eye on Adeline.

As Sarah watched, Adeline scurried across the road, pulled out her keys and entered the front door of Mr Cartwright's house. Sarah stalled. She needed to think. How was she to handle this? If she came on too strong, Adeline was bound to be upset and might refuse to co-operate. Sarah could not jeopardise the letter going out today. Jason had been adamant that the timing was crucial so that another agent's lie could corroborate Adeline's tiny lie. However, Sarah could not ignore what she had witnessed. She would have to question Adeline as to what was in that letter and who it was for. But it would be wise to wait until Adeline had written the next secret message before she brought it up. She would have to be smart in her handling of this. Adeline was a clever woman and had made it plain she didn't trust Sarah. There was some consolation in that, as Sarah didn't have to feel any guilt about distrusting her, either. *Oh, but it is tricky work. Well, no one had said the job would be easy*, Sarah thought. With a frustrated sigh, she crossed the road and entered the building.

There was no sign of Mr Cartwright, so she continued up the stairs to Adeline's flat. Adeline answered her knock and ushered her in. 'I have only just arrived in from work. Please put the kettle on and we will have some coffee.'

Sarah gasped when she saw the glass jar of American coffee in Adeline's hand when she turned around. 'Where on earth did you get that?' she asked. Folgers was almost impossible to get. All they had back in the flat was that awful chicory rubbish. 'I've only ever seen GIs with that.'

Adeline merely smiled. 'A friend gave it to me as a welcome gift.'

Intrigued, Sarah lit the gas and placed the kettle on the ring. 'Was it McKensie? He certainly appeared very taken with you.'

Adeline removed her hat, a secret smile lingering on her lips. 'Men like him are easy to manage.'

'And the work?'

Adeline struck a match, bent down, and lit the fire. 'Far too simple. Such silly stuff he wants me to write.' She glanced up at Sarah and shook her head. 'But soon enough, he will assign me proper articles.'

Sarah laughed. 'I don't doubt it. You'll be running the place in no time.'

Adeline frowned. 'Running the place – what does this mean?'

'You will be in charge.'

A tinkling laugh was Adeline's response as she sat back on her hunkers, blowing at the base of the fire. Then she tut-tutted. 'This wood is damp. I will complain to the concierge. He is a strange man, Sarah. I do not like him. Someone else would be better.'

'Adeline, he owns this house. I'm afraid you are stuck with him. Anyway, I thought he was alright. He seems friendly and helpful to me.' Sarah poured the boiling water into the cups and stirred. 'Trust me, I've had worse landlords and landladies. Some were absolute horrors. Here, drink this while it's hot. Do you want milk?' Sarah asked, placing the cups on the table.

A look of horror crossed the spy's face. 'Why do you destroy good coffee with milk? Horrible stuff!'

'I guess I'll drink it black, then,' Sarah replied, sitting down. She lifted the cup and sniffed the glorious aroma of the coffee, savouring the scent and anticipating the wonderful taste. The last time she had drunk proper coffee was back in Dublin in '39, in Bewley's Café.

Adeline remained standing, frowning at the smoking fire before throwing her hands up. 'Hopeless! The wood is wet.'

'Give it a minute. Come on, drink your coffee,' Sarah said. 'And tell me all about *The Gazette*.'

'There is nothing to say.' Adeline rolled her eyes heavenward. 'The articles I can write in my sleep. Most of the time I am trying to avoid the attentions of that McKensie man. The other women tell me he has a terrible reputation.'

'Oh no! How horrible! I once had to work for someone like that. Did he not give you the coffee, then?'

'Perhaps he did, or perhaps it was someone else,' Adeline replied, looking smug.

Always so coy, Sarah thought, fighting sudden irritation. 'Well, I'm sorry if he is a pest, but it is important that we keep him happy.' Sarah pulled a sheet of paper from her bag. 'We'd like these notices to appear in the newspaper over the next couple of days. McKensie is expecting this, so it shouldn't be an issue.'

Adeline barely glanced at the page. 'Yes, this is easy. But I don't understand why you want to put these silly notices in the paper.'

Sarah scrambled for an answer. She couldn't tell her the real reason; that the units mentioned were made up. 'Oh, these contain codes for our operatives overseas.' Once she had said it, she immediately regretted her words. Perhaps that was what they really were! She only had Jason's word that their purpose was to convince the Nazis that the fake Allied units were real. She almost laughed aloud: life was becoming a little too complicated!

Adeline, however, seemed to accept what she said. 'How clever,' was her reply.

'It all helps, Adeline.'

The spy's expression shut down. She took a sip of her coffee, then trained a fierce glance on Sarah. 'I help you, but where is Nikolay? Do you British keep your promises or not?'

'As I told you the other day, these things take time. You must be patient.'

They drank their coffee in silence, Sarah mulling over the trickiness of asking her to write another secret letter when Adeline's thoughts were firmly fixed on her boyfriend and the possible duplicity of the British secret service. In Adeline's position, Sarah knew she would feel the same. Still, there was no room for sympathy. This was a job.

'There is something else,' Sarah ventured after a few moments.

With a sigh, Adeline sat back in her chair and stared across the table at her. Her expression was not encouraging. 'Well?'

'We need another letter sent to Haas.'

'Today?'

'Yes. I will post it on my way home.'

'Another one so soon?' Adeline asked.

'Yes. I'm sorry, but I have no control over the timing of these things,' Sarah said. She took the second sheet from her bag. 'Here is what you need to send.'

Without a word, Adeline went into the bedroom, returning minutes later with paper and her equipment.

Sarah brought her a glass of water and watched as the pills dissolved. Reluctant to disturb Adeline as she worked, Sarah sat down in the fireside chair and listened to the scratching of the toothpick on the page.

'This must dry now,' Adeline said after a few minutes. 'What shall I write in the covering letter?'

'A simple note should suffice. Something about the new job, perhaps?'

When the invisible message had dried out and disappeared, Adeline asked, 'Why are you telling Haas about these troop movements? Is it not dangerous for him to know these things?'

Again, Sarah couldn't tell her the truth. It was safer Adeline didn't know which information she was sending was false, and which was true.

'If we send him intelligence he can verify as true, then he is more likely to believe the false reports as well.'

'Ah, I see. Very ingenious. But I suspect you will keep me in the dark as much as Haas,' Adeline replied.

Far too smart, Sarah thought. It was pointless to prevaricate. 'Does it matter?'

Adeline just smiled and drained her cup. Then she tapped the letter. 'I don't recall Haas mentioning these regiments.'

Darn! Sarah hadn't anticipated that.

'Well, he probably doesn't know them all; how could he?' she replied. 'They are newly formed US units and only recently arrived here.'

Adeline pondered this for a few moments, then gave a

knowing look. 'I think you British are playing games.' Then she shrugged. 'But if it helps end this war, I do not care.' Adeline began to write the visible message. When she was finished, she placed it in an envelope and addressed it. 'There; it is done.'

'Thank you,' Sarah said, taking the letter and slipping it into her bag. She sat down at the table opposite Adeline. 'Look, I'm sorry I must ask this, but on my way here, I saw you post a letter. Who were you writing to?'

The colour drained from the spy's face, and to Sarah's horror, she burst into tears. Momentarily speechless, Sarah could only stare at her. Adeline tried to speak between sobs, but she was incoherent. What could cause her to lose control so completely?

Sarah's heart filled with sympathy, and she moved her chair beside her. 'Tell me what's wrong, Adeline,' she said gently. For a moment she wavered, then touched her shoulder. 'I'm sorry; I didn't mean to upset you.'

'It was . . . it was to my Resistance friend who is hiding Nikolay. I beg her to pass my letters on to him. But she never replies. I do not know how he is, and I cannot bear to be without him.' Adeline dropped her head onto her arms and sobbed.

How ghastly! She must be desperate for news, Sarah thought, but this would have to be checked out. She would have to tip off the boys based at the sorting office. It would be easy enough to check if Adeline was telling the truth, as they were already monitoring Adeline's post. In the meantime, however, she would have to take Adeline's word that the letter was for Nikolay.

'Oh, Adeline, I'm sorry. I know it must be hard for you.

100

Look, I promise I will talk to my boss again and see if there has been any progress. Please don't fall into despair.'

Adeline's response was muffled, her head still buried.

'I'm sorry; what did you say?' Sarah asked.

'I hate this place and I'm so lonely here without Nikolay. I worry about him all the time. What if they catch him? They will shoot him; I know it. I need him here. How else can I be sure he is safe?' Adeline asked, tears streaming down her face.

'Of course. I understand. All we can do is hope and pray. And I know it must be lonely, but you must give yourself time to settle in. I'm sure you will make friends soon enough.'

'No, it is impossible!'

Sarah took in her distraught expression and melted. 'As a matter of fact, my friend Gladys has a birthday next week. We all plan to go out next Saturday night to a club to celebrate. Why don't you come along? It would be good for you to get out and socialise. Meet new people.'

To Sarah's surprise, Adeline's chin wobbled. 'Hmm, yes, perhaps that would be nice,' Adeline replied with a watery smile. 'Thank you, Sarah.'

11

25th March 1944, The Embassy Club, Old Bond Street, London

Sarah stood at the entrance to The Embassy Club, stamping her feet to stop her toes turning to ice in her thin dancing shoes. With an impatient sigh, she pulled back the sleeve of her coat once more to peek at her watch. Quarter-past. Where on earth was Adeline? She could not be lost, as Sarah had given her written directions when she had visited her during the week.

Another group of revellers headed inside. Sarah thought of her friends in the nice warm club and grumbled under her breath. Maybe Adeline had changed her mind about meeting up. *I'll give her five more minutes, then I'm joining the others.* Some young women strolled up, one of them giving Sarah a sympathetic look as she passed close by. *Cheeky madam; she thinks I've been stood-up*, Sarah thought, her mood darkening even further.

When they had arrived earlier, Gladys had hurried inside,

hoping some of her fellow clippies were already there. Martin had followed her, looking slightly bemused. For the entire journey to Old Bond Street, Gladys had been in top form, laughing and joking with Tony and teasing Martin without mercy. Sarah was reassured to see her in such good form again.

'You'll freeze to death if you wait out here for your friend,' Tony said when Sarah had stalled outside the main entrance. 'Come on in with me. I'm sure she will be here soon.'

'But she doesn't know any of you. It would be very intimidating for her to go in on her own.'

'How old is she? Fourteen?' His tone was sceptical.

'No, of course not,' Sarah replied, surprised at his impatience. 'But I'd like to think someone would do me the courtesy of waiting and making proper introductions.'

Tony shook his head. 'You are too sweet for your own good, Irish. Who is this woman, anyway? You've told me next to nothing about her.'

Sarah had suspected he was curious about Adeline from the first time she had mentioned her earlier in the week, but she couldn't tell him the woman was a double agent. She had to prevaricate. 'I met her through a mutual friend, that's all,' she replied airily. 'Adeline has recently made it out from France and is finding it all a bit lonely. I felt sorry for her. It will take her a while to settle down and make friends. Please, try to be nice to her.'

'Of course,' he said. 'Am I not always nice to ladies?'

'Well, don't be *too* nice,' she replied with a frown.

'I can't win!' Tony threw his hands up, but grinned, too.

'OK, I'll be on my best behaviour. I will charm the birds from the trees. She will fall under my spell—'

'Alright, alright, stop! Now you're just being silly,' she replied.

'Me silly? Never.'

'Oh, go on in! And Tony, try to get one of those nice booths, will you? They are much more comfortable, and you are far less likely to end up with your drink in your lap. You know how close some of those tables are to the dancefloor.'

'Yes, honey. I'll do my best,' he replied with a salute, before disappearing into the entrance hall, preventing her from giving him the almighty scold the cheeky sod deserved.

Sarah heard a blast of music, chatter, and laughter as the inner door of the club opened and Tony was admitted. It only made her more impatient to join the others. Saturday night was always crazy at The Embassy; so crazy, in fact, that it was impossible to dance properly. All you could do was shuffle around the floor. It was certainly intimate. Perhaps that was why it was so popular.

It was bitterly cold. Sarah needed to distract herself, to think about something else. At least work was going well. Jason had told her he was very pleased with how things were working out with Adeline already. Apparently, a listening station had decoded a message from Haas to Berlin, outlining the troop details Adeline had sent him. Sarah was relieved to hear it. All week she had worried about what exactly the spy had written in invisible ink. *This job wasn't for the faint-hearted!*

Deep in thought, Sarah didn't notice the figure approach along the blacked-out street. As a result, she jumped when she felt a hand on her arm and Adeline's face loomed out of the darkness.

'Lord! Adeline, you frightened me. Everything alright?'

'Yes, of course. What an odd-looking place,' she remarked, peering at the shop fronts on either side of the entrance to the club.

'Don't judge it from the outside. We come here a lot. It's fun, and the music is always good. Just one thing before we go inside.'

'Yes?'

'Obviously, we can't say what your actual job is. If anyone asks, say you are a journalist—'

'Which is true,' Adeline said with a frown.

'Yes, but you mustn't say anything about your other work.'

'Of course not. I'm not a fool.'

'Sorry, I wasn't implying you were,' Sarah replied. Adeline gave her a knowing look, then shrugged. 'Come on, let's get inside. The others are already here,' Sarah said, linking her arm.

Once they had checked in their coats and pushed through the crowds in the lobby, Sarah dragged Adeline behind her as she negotiated the tables and passing dancers, searching for the familiar faces of her friends. It took several minutes to find the others seated at a table at the far end of the dancefloor. Thankfully, Tony had been successful in getting one of the comfy booths. As they approached, Tony and Martin were engrossed in conversation and Gladys was sipping a drink, a cocktail by the look of it, and chatting nine to the dozen with one of her clippie friends, Muriel.

'Here we are,' Sarah announced, to get everyone's attention. She nudged Adeline ahead of her. 'Everyone, this is my friend Adeline, newly arrived from Paris. Adeline, this is Gladys, my friend, flatmate, and birthday girl. That's my cousin Martin, and my boyfriend Tony. Gladys, you might introduce your friends from work?' Gladys nodded while Tony and Martin jumped to their feet and shook hands with Adeline.

'Do squash in beside me,' Gladys shouted above the music to Adeline, 'so I can introduce these reprobates I work with!' Gladys then treated Martin to a dark scowl. 'Go on, Martin, you shift yourself.'

Martin hurriedly stepped back and let Adeline slide past and take his vacated seat. As he walked around the booth behind Gladys, he threw Sarah an annoyed glance, but Sarah just smiled back at him. Once Adeline was settled, Sarah sat next to Tony, opposite Gladys and Adeline. Martin sat on the other side of her, throwing the odd glare in Gladys's direction. Sarah hoped Martin and Gladys hadn't been arguing in here, of all places. So much for thinking matters had been resolved between them.

'Everything OK?' Tony asked Sarah, his gaze sliding over to Adeline.

'Yes, fine.' Sarah couldn't help herself. 'What do you think of her?'

'Very glamorous, but then French women generally are.'

Sarah remembered his old girlfriend, Clara, who had worked in the Free French headquarters but had turned out to be a Vichy spy. A stunning blonde with a nasty streak. 'Is that why you find them so irresistible?'

'What? Oh, I see. You are trying to be funny, Irish,

referring to poor old Clara, I suppose. That was ages ago, now.' He stared off into the distance, a wistful expression on his face, which she knew was deliberate to annoy her. With a sigh, he said: 'I wonder if she is still in prison.'

'I certainly hope she is.' She couldn't resist and gave him a mock indignant look. 'Don't tell me you still pine for her?'

'All the time; how did you guess?' he replied. 'So, what part of France is your friend from?'

'Bordeaux, originally. Actually, she's Russian by birth, but her family left there when she was very young. However, she considers herself French.'

Tony raised a brow. 'How interesting. So, is she your "poisoned chalice"? What is she doing working for MI5?'

Sarah flinched. She'd forgotten their previous conversation. 'I didn't say she *was*.'

'Then how do you know her?' he asked.

'She works for *The Gazette* but has been helping with some translation work for us. Jason introduced us at the office one day and we got talking.' It was the first thing that came into Sarah's head. She hoped he would buy it and stop asking questions because she hated lying to him.

Tony's expression held doubt, but he nodded. 'I see. Good for her. Alrighty, do you want your usual?' Sarah nodded, relieved at the change of subject. 'Any idea what Adeline drinks?' he asked.

'I've no idea. Best ask her.'

Tony stood and leaned across to interrupt Gladys in full flight. By Adeline's expression, she wasn't understanding much of what Gladys was saying, anyway. Tony addressed Adeline in French, and she beamed up at him.

Soon the pair were nattering away like old pals. Then, with a nod, Tony straightened up and headed off towards the bar. Sarah could not fail to notice Adeline's gaze followed him.

An hour later, and Sarah was feeling mellow. The evening was going well with everyone in excellent humour. Gladys was in flying form and thoroughly enjoying her birthday outing if the screams of laughter coming from her group on the far side of the table were anything to go by. It was good to see her friend so happy. Almost back to normal, except she wasn't. Sarah's instinct told her that something still wasn't quite right. But what could she do? The girl refused to talk about whatever was bothering her. She wondered if Alfie was still on her mind, and felt disappointed that Gladys hadn't confided in her. They had shared so much of life's knocks over the years. And surely Sarah had proven how good a friend she was by sorting out the issue with Alfie Smyth in the first place?

A big band number ended, and soon Adeline and her dance partner approached the table. In fact, she had been up on the floor dancing for almost the entire evening. The couple stopped close to Sarah.

'Thank you,' Adeline said, turning to her partner. 'These are my friends. You may go now.'

The young officer's face fell at the dismissal. He was clearly smitten. 'Perhaps you would care to dance again later?' he asked.

Sarah cringed at his pleading tone and worse, Adeline blinked at him as if he were crazy. 'No, no, we are done.' The poor fellow walked away, crushed.

'You are conquering all around you this evening, Adeline,' Sarah couldn't help but remark.

'Pooh! These men are mere children.' Adeline's face hardened. 'They cannot compete with my Nikolay,' she said, tossing her head as she sat down.

Sarah had no answer to that and was a trifle annoyed. Every conversation they had ended up being about Nikolay. Her curiosity about the man, however, was piqued, and she wondered what he was like. Clearly, Adeline adored him to risk so much to gain his freedom. Would Sarah be brave enough to do the same for Tony? Would he do the same for her?

The next thing she knew, Martin slid into Tony's empty seat and nudged her with his elbow. 'How about being nice to your poor old cousin?' He nodded towards the crowded floor as the band started up again. 'Take a spin around the floor with me? Go on!'

'I'm honoured,' she replied, looking down her nose at him. 'I've hardly seen you all evening. That last girl you danced with looked very taken with you.'

Martin grinned and shoved his glasses up his nose. 'Yes, she was rather nice. A Wren, no less. Unfortunately, she had to leave as she has an early start in the morning.'

'That's a shame,' she replied.

'Can't win 'em all. Come on, it's been years since we danced together. Let's show 'em how it's done.'

Laughing, Sarah stood. 'Well, if you put it like that. Lead on!'

'Where are you two off to?' Tony asked, arriving back at their table with a handful of drinks.

Sarah swung Martin's hand up. 'To show the peasants how to execute the jitterbug with flair.'

110

Tony smiled, shaking his head. 'Off you go. I believe I have trained you well. Just try not to injure anyone.'

'He's a cheeky sod, your boyfriend,' Martin said to her as they walked away. Sarah turned to Martin to reply, only to see, over his shoulder, Adeline patting the seat beside her and beckoning to Tony to join her.

Sarah had always enjoyed dancing with Martin and hadn't realised how much she had missed it. Since joining MI5, they had seen very little of each other. His job at Supermarine kept him down in Hursley and days off for her were few and far between. Whenever possible, she spent her free time with Tony, if he was in London. Sarah and Judith did travel down to Hursley each Christmas, but those brief visits left insufficient time for catching up with Martin. And though they kept up some correspondence, that wasn't the same. She felt guilty; after all, he had been so kind to her when she had first arrived in England, without family and without hope. Martin's friendship had helped her overcome her grief, and she loved him dearly, considering him the brother she had never had.

As ever, Martin danced with extraordinary enthusiasm and by the end of the set, Sarah was struggling to catch her breath. Several times, they had been close enough to see over to their booth and each time, Sarah saw that Adeline and Tony were still sitting beside each other. In fact, they had their heads together and appeared to be thoroughly enjoying an in-depth conversation. Of course, the club was noisy. One had to either shout or speak directly into someone's ear to be heard. Still. Did they have to be that close? What could they be talking about? Then it struck her. Tony

111

was fluent in French from his time with SOE in Normandy. It must be nice for Adeline to have someone to talk to in her native language. That would be it. But Sarah caught a glance from Martin, his brows raised. He had noticed it too. No. Surely, this was foolish, she berated herself. *Tony loves me, and I can trust him.* Unfortunately, at that moment, she saw him throw his head back and guffaw, Adeline's hand on his arm. Clearly, he was finding Adeline entertaining company. Sarah looked away, irritation simmering inside her.

Maybe I can trust Tony, but the real question is, can I trust Adeline?

It was almost two in the morning when the group finally exited the club and walked out onto the street. Gladys's work friends headed home after hugs and kisses and general nonsense, while Gladys clung to Sarah's arm, bleary eyed, and the worse for wear.

'Best we get a taxi,' Sarah said to Martin, who was eyeing Gladys with distaste. 'She can't walk home in this state. Be a dear and nab one, will you?'

'It won't be easy,' he said, staring at the milling revellers around them. 'Everyone else has the same idea.'

'Show a bit of leg, Martin,' slurred Gladys. 'Usually works a treat for me.'

With a shake of his head and a grunt, Martin walked a little further down the street and out of sight. Sarah hoped he could hail a taxi quickly. Gladys really did not look well. Hopefully, they could get home before she threw up or passed out. She turned to Tony to say good night, but he was still chatting away to Adeline in French. Sarah cleared her throat to get his attention.

When he looked up, he said: 'Adeline and I will share a taxi; Sale Place is close to my flat. I don't think it would be safe for her to travel alone at this hour.'

That's hardly necessary, Sarah thought, as the little green monster took hold, but she didn't say it aloud. *I'll not give Adeline the satisfaction.* She had hoped that Tony would accompany them to the flat and then they could travel onwards to his place. Just the two of them. Now, that plan was in ruins.

Anyone observing their party tonight would have assumed Tony and Adeline were old friends, nattering away for the latter half of the evening. Initially pleased that Tony was making an effort to befriend Adeline, Sarah soon regretted her friendly impulse, particularly when the pair headed off onto the dancefloor for half an hour. Sarah thought that would be the end of it, but on their return, they sat down beside each other again and continued to converse. The club was too noisy for Sarah to hear what they were talking about, but the few snatches she heard were in French. Was that deliberate on Adeline's part to keep Sarah at arm's length? Sarah couldn't help the tendrils of jealousy creeping into her head. *So much for pining after Nikolay!*

Tony walked over to her with a smile, seemingly oblivious to her disquiet. Sarah stiffened as he stooped down and planted a kiss on her cheek. Adeline looked on, her eyes brimming with . . . Sarah wasn't sure what, but she suspected Adeline was laughing at her.

'Thanks for inviting me tonight, Sarah. I have enjoyed myself far more than I expected,' Adeline almost purred.

'You're welcome,' was Sarah's curt reply as she turned to Tony, expecting another kiss or a hug to say good night.

However, a casual wave was all she received. Now thoroughly annoyed, Sarah could only watch Tony and Adeline walk away in the opposite direction.

Sarah's thoughts ran dark as she waited for Martin to secure a cab, Gladys leaning heavily against her . . .

That's what you get for trying to be nice, you stupid idiot! That will teach you to mix work and pleasure.

12

29th March 1944, Sale Place, Paddington, London

Much to her surprise, as Sarah put the key in the latch at Sale Place, the door swung open, forcing her to take a step back. In the doorway, Mr Cartwright stood in his coat and hat, frowning at her as if he didn't quite recall who she was.

'Good evening, Mr Cartwright,' Sarah said. 'How are you?'

The landlord frowned, and she realised he was trying to recall who she was. How odd! Was he a little senile? 'Very good . . . you're with the eh, firm, aren't you? A friend of Mademoiselle Vernier?'

'That's correct, sir. Sarah Gillespie.' She nodded towards the stairs. 'I'm dropping by to check in on her. To see if she has everything she needs.'

'Sorry, but you're out of luck. I saw her go out about an hour ago. All dolled-up as usual. Leads the life of Reilly, that one, if you ask me,' he replied, stepping through and closing the door behind him. 'I'm off for a pint if you fancy joining me?'

'No, no, thank you,' Sarah said, taken aback. Then she felt bad as his face fell. Perhaps he was lonely. But she had other plans, and they didn't involve sitting in a smoky pub with a near stranger. Sarah continued: 'I have another call to make this evening. Perhaps another time?'

With a sniff, Mr Cartwright turned away. 'Suit yourself.'

Sarah watched him walk off. She glanced up at Adeline's window, reflecting on Cartwright's comment. How interesting, she thought. By the sounds of it, Adeline wasn't one for sitting home alone, pining, after all. Sarah couldn't help wondering where she could be. Should she be concerned that Adeline was leading a life she knew nothing about? What if she was up to mischief? Jason would be livid with Sarah if she missed something important. But the problem was, she had no evidence. As she stood in the porch, her heart pounded. Dare she? Adeline was out. It was the perfect opportunity to check the flat. A quick scan of the road reassured her. No sign of Cartwright or Adeline. Sarah slipped the key in the lock, checked over her shoulder once more, then raced up the stairs.

All was neat and tidy. Right! What was she looking for? She mooched about, pulling out drawers and rifling through the few books she could find, and all the while her hands shook, her senses on high alert. Nothing. Now, where could Adeline hide a radio set? They weren't exactly small items. Sarah went into the bedroom and checked the inside of the wardrobe, then the top. Again, nothing. Under the bed was clear, too. Sarah felt foolish. Still, it had to be done. At least there was nothing obvious to set off alarm bells. Except, of course, that letter the other day. Was she reading too much into too little?

It was risky to stay any longer. If Adeline returned and found her here, it would be difficult to explain. Sarah locked up and headed back outside. But as she made her way to Tony's, her irritation would not lift. Had Adeline's distress been genuine that day she had broken down, or had she been manipulating her? Looking for sympathy? Perhaps it had all been an act to distract Sarah from something else. But what could Adeline be up to? The worst plausible answer was that Adeline was really working for Haas and was in contact with other German agents, secretly based in Britain. What fools they would look if that were the case. That would jeopardise everything MI5 had been working on. Operations Fortitude and Bodyguard would lie in tatters. *Oh God,* Sarah thought, *that's all I'd need.* Well, right now, she didn't know where Adeline was, so there was little she could do. She needed to give this some thought overnight and tackle Adeline tomorrow.

A ten-minute walk brought Sarah to Tony's maisonette, which was above a corner newsagent's shop. The owner of the shop gave her a cheery wave as she passed. Sarah paused and smiled back at Mr Emsley before heading to the side door, which led to the upstairs flats. Normally, she wouldn't call on Tony unexpectedly, not least because he was rarely at home – when he had to work late, he often slept in his office – however, they hadn't spoken since Saturday. Had he been called away suddenly? The trouble was she longed to see him, even though she was still peeved with him. Tony's overly solicitous attention to Adeline on Saturday

117

night at the club had annoyed her. He didn't have to be quite *that* friendly, even if Adeline had been more than encouraging.

Typically, when Tony was in town, he haunted their flat. Judith often complained, half-joking, that she was constantly falling over his long legs. But even Gladys had commented on his recent absence. A little disappointed but not too concerned, Sarah had figured he was busy with work. Although she didn't know exactly what his new role entailed, other than it related to US naval intelligence operations in Britain, it stood to reason there would be enormous demands on his time. Plans for an invasion of France by the Allies in the summer were ramping up, which would affect all of them in the coming months. The volume of MI5's so-called leaked intelligence had soared. It was likely Adeline, and all the other double agents, would be busy in the months ahead. That was her reason for calling on Adeline this evening: another tempting scrap of information to dangle before Haas needed to wing its way to Lisbon. Jason had wanted a letter to be written, and then posted in the morning, detailing a fictitious camp at Dover, which was full of US troops preparing for 'something big'.

As she neared the top of the stairs, Sarah could hear voices coming from Tony's flat. Then a burst of laughter. Female laughter. Perplexed, she stood on the landing, staring at the door as horrible ideas wound their way into her head. Surely there was an innocent explanation for him entertaining a woman in his flat at this hour of the evening. It must be a colleague. Taking a deep breath, she rang the bell.

Tony wore a startled expression as he opened the door. 'Irish! I wasn't expecting you.' With a smile, he clutched her hand and dragged her over the threshold before drawing her into an embrace. Tony planted a kiss on her nose and all her worries vanished in an instant. Sarah almost laughed out loud. It must have been a radio she had heard.

'Good evening, Sarah.' Sarah stiffened, instantly recognising Adeline's voice. She tilted her head and looked past Tony in astonishment. The woman was standing in the doorway of the sitting room, looking rather smug and at home. *What on earth? Not a radio, then.*

'Don't worry, I was about to leave,' Adeline purred, pulling on her coat, then her gloves. 'I'll leave you two lovebirds alone.'

'There's no need to dash off, Adeline,' Tony said. 'Stay for a drink.'

Sarah had to restrain the urge to kick him in the shin. Instead, she pulled out of his arms and smiled back at Adeline. 'Yes, do,' she uttered. But it sounded insincere, even to her.

Adeline treated her to a knowing smile. 'No, no, I must go.' She swept past them towards the front door, a tantalising waft of perfume following in her wake. Expensive perfume, if Sarah wasn't mistaken. The type she couldn't afford on her salary.

Tony jumped forward and opened the door for Adeline. 'Thanks again for the book. It was mighty good of you to drop by with it. I promise I will look after it.'

Adeline waved her hand. 'Take your time; I'm in no hurry to read it again.' Her gaze swept over Sarah. 'Goodbye.'

'Good night, Adeline,' Sarah said somewhat pointedly. 'Oh, before you go; I called to Sale Place a short while ago, to give you this.' Adeline turned around with a sigh, and a flash of annoyance in her eyes. Sarah was tempted to scold her, but of course she could not do so in front of Tony without giving away their true relationship. Instead, she pulled the sheet of Jason's instructions from her bag. 'Sorry about the short notice, but it's some urgent translation work for Jason. The same procedure as usual. He would appreciate if it could be completed by the morning.'

'The morning? Really?' Adeline said, making a show of looking at her wristwatch. 'It is getting late.'

Sarah glared at her. 'Isn't it just? I was surprised not to find you at home.'

'You are *too* funny. I am not a hermit, Sarah. Was it not you who told me to get out and meet people?' Sarah didn't trust herself to respond but held the page out towards her. Adeline glanced at it as if it were a snake. 'Oh, very well; I'll do my best.' Then Adeline took the page, folded it, and shoved it into her bag. 'Good night, Tony, and thanks for *your* hospitality,' Adeline gushed, flashing doleful eyes at Tony, her hand lingering on his forearm just a little too long. 'Enjoy the book,' she said as she floated out the door.

Sarah heard the front door close as she stalked into the sitting room, absolutely seething. She recognised flirting when she saw it. *How dare she!* Making a play for Tony right in front of her! And that on top of her contemptuous attitude to her work. At their next meeting, she would have to lay down the law, set boundaries. Perhaps the woman's working conditions were a little too comfortable. Come to think of it, how was she able to afford such luxuries as perfume? Despite all her anti-Nazi rhetoric, Adeline seemed happy enough to accept their money. She could suggest to Jason that she be moved to a hostel instead, preferably one for vagrants.

Tony followed her. 'What was all that about? I thought you two were friends. You weren't very nice to her.'

'And you appear to be the exact opposite,' Sarah snapped, spinning around to confront him.

Tony stalled in the doorway; eyebrows drawn together. 'Hey, Irish. Stop right there! What the hell are you getting at?' He folded his arms and continued to glare at her.

'I thought it was obvious or do I have to spell it out?' she asked, incredulous, her own temper rising. But that was good. It pushed down her hurt and disappointment.

Tony nodded slowly. 'Perhaps you do, missy. Because I don't like what you are implying.'

'I haven't heard from you all week and then I find you alone with *her* in your flat. You only met her for the first time on Saturday. And here she is, acting like she was your long-lost . . .' She didn't dare say lover, which was the word that had popped into her head. Despite the urge to lash out, she needed to rein it in. After a deep breath, she said: 'What am I supposed to think?'

'My God, Sarah; nothing!'

'Did you invite her here? Has she been here before?'

Something akin to guilt flickered in his eyes. 'She stopped off for a nightcap on Saturday night.'

'You invited her in?'

'It was the polite thing to do.'

Sarah stared at him, open-mouthed. 'At two in the morning?'

'Yeah! And why not? I don't know what you are getting so het up about. It's my home. I can entertain anyone I want here. I wasn't aware I had to run it past you first,' he said quietly, but she wasn't fooled; there was a defensive edge to his voice, which made her want to cry. What was he hiding? 'And, as it happens, she just turned up this evening. I wasn't expecting her.'

'Really?' Sarah asked, even though she knew by persisting with this, it could only end in tears. *Her* tears. The evening was unravelling at breakneck speed. But all she could see was that smug expression on Adeline's face as she had left. A look of triumph. 'I see.'

'I don't think you do, Sarah. You're jumping to ridiculous conclusions. If you must know, I mentioned to her the other night that while I was in France, I had read a few books by Léo Malet. I really enjoyed his detective stories. Unfortunately, it is impossible to get his books here right now. As it turns out, he's one of her favourite authors, too. Adeline said she had a copy of *120 Rue de la Gare* that she could lend me. I was delighted. It is one I haven't read. Look, if you don't believe me, there it is.' He pointed to a book on the table. The cover was striking; the dust jacket was a gory red and the front illustration was of two shady-looking characters, one holding a gun, trained on the other.

Sarah picked up the novel and flipped through the pages, unseeing, as she tried to compose her tumbling emotions. Her hands were shaking. They had never argued like this before. But she spotted '*imprimé à Paris*' on an inside page. Even with no French, she could guess what it meant. The book was French alright. Could he be telling the truth?

'I didn't know you could read French,' she said at last, desperately trying to keep her voice calm. Was he right? Had she jumped to a conclusion based on nothing other than a mischievous smile?

Still frowning, Tony sat down at the table, his index finger tapping the surface. Sarah realised he was as agitated as she was.

'I taught myself. I needed to improve my basic French for the job with SOE. Some of the Resistance had no English, which made communication difficult, which is tricky when you are handling explosives.' He paused before throwing her a glance laced with irritation. 'Besides, there wasn't much else to do in rural France, but read.' His glare intensified. 'Or did you think I was out seducing women every night?'

'I didn't before tonight, but now I'm not so sure,' she said, her fists clenched at her sides. 'I thought after all this time that I could trust you.' Her voice wavered.

An angry colour crept into his face. 'That is utter nonsense, and you know it! You are jumping to conclusions.'

'Oh, come on, Tony. You can't be that naïve. Adeline is up to mischief. She monopolised you the other night, then inveigled a nightcap from you and shows up here to drop off a book? Surely you can see how blatant that is? The clubs and bars are full of "Yank Hunters" like her; you know that. We've often joked about it at The Savoy.'

He threw his hands in the air. 'Sarah! What has gotten into you this evening? I don't understand. You are usually so fair-minded.'

'I don't trust her,' she blurted out. His deflecting comment spoke volumes. 'You can't deny she was flirting with you.'

'She flirts with all men; it's a habit, and it's meaningless. Come on, Sarah; you have come across her type before. If you don't like her, why did you insist on bringing her along on Saturday? It doesn't make sense. Anyway, I might remind you, it was *you* who asked *me* to be nice to her.'

That stung. 'Within limits,' she snapped back. And now she couldn't help but wonder if he *had* left a trail of broken hearts behind in France.

'For God's sake, Sarah; don't be so childish!' Tony stared at her for a moment. 'There is something you haven't told me. Something about this doesn't feel right. Why are you so invested in what this woman does or who she sees? Why hunt her down late in the evening to do a bit of translation? In fact, now I think of it, why would a journalist work as a translator for MI5 at all?'

'I didn't hunt her down. I didn't know she was *here*,' she replied between gritted teeth. 'As to her relationship or otherwise with MI5, I won't answer that—'

'I knew it!' he interrupted. 'That journalism tale is a front.'

Sarah sighed; he was far too insightful. 'No, it isn't. She is a journalist. Inviting her along on Saturday was an impulse and one which I now deeply regret. She was a bit lost, said she was missing home *and* her boyfriend. You do know she has one?' she asked, glaring across at him.

Tony sucked in a breath as anger and possibly hurt flashed in his eyes. 'It's late and I'm tired. I don't need this kind of nonsense from you, of all people, Sarah.'

That hurt. 'Perhaps if I knew where this relationship of ours was heading, I'd feel more secure,' she said, her voice trembling with anger. 'Every time I bring up the future, you change the subject.'

Tony closed his eyes briefly. 'There is too much uncertainty, Sarah. My time in France has taught me that. Do you know how many times I thought that was it? That my luck had run out? You learn to take it one day at a time. Live your life as best you can. Plans are for fools.' He stared down at the floor for a moment as if trying to compose himself. 'I've seen too many couples rush into marriage. Getting hitched for all the wrong reasons. It results in a bloody mess when the poor sod gets killed.'

Bubbles of anger rose in Sarah's throat. He was happy to sleep with her, but it appeared nothing more. 'So, you are saying you don't believe we have a future?'

'Right now, I don't know. The war—'

'I'm tired of hearing that excuse, Tony. We can't even plan a few days away together without you getting jittery.'

'That's unfair. You have no idea of my workload.'

'Nor you mine!'

'I don't know why you are harping on about that trip. And as for the future, I'm not ready to talk about possibilities, not when I have the realities of this goddamn war to contend with.'

'That's a mighty convenient attitude, Tony.'

'I'm trying to be honest!'

'Really? If I hadn't called tonight, would you have told me about Adeline's visit, the flirting, the nightcap?' Tony looked away; his jaw clenched. Sarah's stomach flipped – there was her answer. But the devil inside her kept her pushing. 'You weren't exactly discouraging her attentions.'

Again, he didn't respond.

'Now I am left wondering if we have a future at all.'

When he met her gaze, his eyes were full of sadness. 'Perhaps we don't.'

Each word was like a dagger in her heart. Sarah gasped for air, sick to her stomach. How could she have been so blind? All along, he had seen her as convenient and undemanding. An easy fit for his transient life.

Dispensable.

It was then she noticed the suitcase out in the hallway. It couldn't be worse timing. 'Are you going away again?' The words almost choked her.

With a shrug he said: 'Yeah, first thing in the morning. Most likely, I'll be away for a couple of months.' Tony gazed at her coldly, as if she were a stranger, a trace of a frown marring his handsome face. 'Perhaps it's for the best, Sarah. I think we need some time apart.'

Cold rage coursed through her. 'I couldn't agree more,' she countered, before rushing towards the door and slamming it hard in her wake.

13

29th March 1944, Paddington, London

Half an hour later, Sarah had almost reached home. Still reeling, she could barely recall the journey from Tony's flat. Had they really split up? Several times she had had to stop, unable to comprehend how their argument had escalated so quickly. But how could she not be angry, walking into such a scene? Then an image of Adeline, smugness personified, ignited another wave of pure anger.

Suddenly, an overwhelming desire to confront Adeline was foremost in her mind, and she came to a stop. Ten minutes would bring her to Sale Place. But what would that achieve? It would only give Adeline the satisfaction of knowing she had rattled her. No. As much as she longed to challenge her, more rational thoughts took hold. She still had to work with the woman and the job was far more important than any personal issues. Damn! It would have been so satisfying to have it out with her.

But there had already been too many occasions in the past when her reactions had been uncontrolled. Such as the night she broke up with Paul back in Dublin because he wanted to leave Ireland and join the RAF. She had lived to regret those hasty and selfish words for a long time. But tonight, with Tony, had been different. Surely, her anger had been justified? If he truly cared for her, he would have reassured her. Instead, he had insinuated that she was the unreasonable one.

Thank goodness for the Blackout. No one could see her angry tears as she walked along. It was difficult to grasp what had happened. How could their relationship have disintegrated so quickly? Yes, she probably shouldn't have accused him of dallying with Adeline, even if the woman's presence in his home was suspicious. Tony could not know that Adeline wasn't to be trusted. Dropping off a book, though . . . who was she kidding? Sarah wasn't fooled for an instant. Hadn't the woman been hanging off of Tony for most of Saturday night? And Tony hadn't objected to the attention either. What hurt most was that Tony had given up on them far too quickly, even if she had upset him with, in her opinion, legitimate concerns as to his behaviour. But the fact was, she knew Adeline better. Knew the sort of tricks she might play, purely for the fun of it, out of boredom, even.

Blast Adeline! She should have known the woman would try to stir up trouble. And all because her precious Nikolay was stuck in France. It wasn't Sarah's fault he wasn't in London. Only the day before, she had brought the subject up with Jason yet again, and at Adeline's behest. He had told her they had more important things to worry about than Adeline's beau languishing in Paris. He had neither the time nor the resources to deal with it, and Sarah was savvy enough to recognise a lost cause. It was only a pity that Adeline didn't realise how difficult her demand was to fulfil. Jason must have picked up on Sarah's frustration, for he became sympathetic, but his contribution to the problem was to suggest she string Adeline out a bit longer. Easy for him to say.

And now she had mixed feelings, anyway. How could she feel sympathy for Adeline's position after what had occurred this evening?

She had let Adeline get under her skin, but she could hardly have ignored the situation. The jealousy had sprung from nowhere, but surely it was justified. A sense of panic that she was losing him to someone else had brought out her worst fault, something she had been prey to all her life: her dratted temper. But she wasn't made of stone.

Could she forgive him? But how was that possible when their relationship appeared to have only the shallowest of foundations?

As Sarah passed The Crown Pub, not far up the road from her flat, a couple burst out the door, laughing and joking, arm in arm. With them came the sound of revelry from within. Sarah had to stop momentarily, as a sob caught in her throat. She needed to pull herself together. Move on. She shied away from the light that spilled out onto the pavement, afraid someone she knew might spot her. Sarah's stomach churned as she increased her pace. The sanctuary of a darkened bedroom called to her, almost like a beacon.

Two houses away from the flat, Sarah stopped and took a few deep breaths. If Gladys or Martin spotted anything wrong, they would hound her for answers. She couldn't face them. Not yet. With any luck, she could sneak in and go straight to her room and escape any scrutiny or sympathy. She couldn't handle sympathy right now; she'd fall apart completely. By the morning, she might be able to face them and give them the news. She wouldn't be able to keep it a secret for long and certainly not from Judith when she came back at the weekend.

Hopefully, Martin was still out with his class buddies and wouldn't be back until late. Tomorrow was to be the last day of the current module of his course, and on Friday, he was heading home to Hursley.

Sarah sneaked in the front door as quietly as she could. Thankfully, the hallway of the flat was in darkness. Perhaps everyone was out. But as she reached her bedroom, she heard a sob and froze, her hand on the doorknob. It sounded like Gladys. Since the birthday celebrations on Saturday, Gladys had reverted to being moody, snapping at Martin whenever he teased her, as he was inclined to do. All of Sarah's attempts to find out what was wrong had thus far ended in failure.

Another sob came from the direction of the kitchen. Doing her best to compose herself, Sarah slowly headed back down the hall. When she opened the door, she found Gladys sitting at the kitchen table, tears flowing down her cheeks.

'Oh, Glad; whatever is the matter?' Sarah asked, rushing to her side. Gladys had been crying for some time, Sarah reckoned. Her cheeks were an ugly red, and her eyes were red-rimmed and swollen. Probably a mirror image of her own face, Sarah thought grimly. She pulled out the chair and sat beside her. 'Glad? Talk to me.'

Her friend gulped and shook her head. Sarah threw her arm around Gladys's shoulders. The poor girl was trembling. 'Come on, you can tell me.'

Sarah racked her brain. What could cause so much distress? She knew there was little communication between Gladys and her family, even though Glad sent part of her wages to her mother once a month. From what Gladys had told her, poverty was no stranger to their house when she was little, and all of Gladys's siblings had left home young to find work so they could support the family. Sometimes, Sarah thought that was the reason Gladys could be wild at times. Earning a living had given her boundless freedom. Gladys's father was an invalid needing constant care, which her poor mother provided. The previous winter, he had taken a bad turn and had been bedridden since.

'Is it bad news from home? Is your dad worse?' Gladys shook her head. 'Then what is it? Won't you let me help?' Sarah squeezed her shoulder. 'Best mates, aren't we? Through thick and thin.'

'You'll think I'm an idiot.'

'No, never.'

Gladys inhaled deeply before casting her a pleading look. 'Please don't judge me but . . . but it's Alfie Smyth.' Suddenly, she tensed up, her eyes filling. Sarah took her hand and held it tight. After a minute, Gladys calmed down again and continued: 'I know he can't harm me now as he's in hospital, but I can't sleep at night. Ever since . . . you know, he came here and pushed that stupid letter under the door.'

'Glad, you must let the whole thing go. There is no point in dwelling on it,' Sarah replied. 'The poor fellow is getting the treatment he needs. Once he's better, I'm sure he will realise what he did was wrong.'

'I know. It's not that. I don't feel guilty about him ending up in the hospital. It's that I keep thinking maybe he'll get out and come here to get revenge . . .' She trailed off.

'Oh! But that is very unlikely, Glad. He was ill. I doubt he will be released until he is in a better frame of mind. If they thought he was a danger to anyone, he would be kept in the hospital. I'm sure of it.'

This produced a watery smile from Gladys. 'Do you really think so?' Sarah nodded. 'I should have known I could rely on you to talk sense to me. But promise me you won't say anything to Martin, please, Sarah? Or Tony. I don't want them thinking badly of me.'

'They wouldn't, Glad. At least Martin wouldn't. He was only asking me earlier this evening as we were leaving the flat if you were OK. You should go easier on him, Glad. He's a sweet guy. As for Tony, I'm afraid we won't be seeing anything of him for some time.'

'Oh! Why is that?'

'Tony is leaving London tomorrow for work, probably for months and . . . he wants us to spend time apart. I think it might be over.'

Gladys stared at her with her mouth open. 'No way! I don't believe you.'

'It's true.'

And with that, Sarah burst into tears.

14

Judith arrived back from Hursley on Saturday afternoon and Sarah wasn't too surprised to be cornered by her in the kitchen as soon as Gladys had left for work.

'Well, out with it!' Judith said. 'What's wrong with Gladys? And while I'm at it, there is something up with you, too. You look worn out.'

'Oh, thanks,' Sarah replied, with a half-smile. Sarah quickly filled her in on Gladys's anxiety about Alfie. 'I think we underestimated the effect it had on her. But I'm sure all she needs is reassurance.'

'That's a relief. It did cross my mind that he might get out and try more mischief, but as you say, that is unlikely. Ewan says so, at least.'

Sarah managed a smile. 'Did you miss him while you were down in Hursley?'

'Don't be silly! I barely know him.' Judith actually blushed.

'Hmm.' Sarah gave her a quizzical look. 'Will you see him tonight?'

'Perhaps. I haven't decided yet. Now, stop trying to change the subject. What's up with you? What's going on?'

The last few days had been difficult. Sarah had gone about her day in a mechanical way, and despite several late-night chats with Gladys over the teacups, she was still incredibly sad. After so many loved ones lost, she had thought she was inured to this kind of pain, but it was clear your heart could be broken on numerous occasions in a lifetime. So, it was almost a relief to share what had happened with Judith. Gladys had been sympathetic, certainly, but Judith could always be relied upon to give sensible advice. It didn't take long for Sarah to pour out the entire story about the row with Tony.

Judith looked across the table, tears welling up. 'I can hardly believe it! I am shocked, Sarah.' Her cousin shook her head. 'Tony adores you.'

'Not enough, it would seem,' Sarah replied. 'I think he has been using me. A convenient girlfriend while he's here in England. I doubt he was ever serious about us as a couple.'

Judith reached across and grabbed her hand. 'Oh no! You must be devastated.'

'Yes, and a little part of me still can't understand how things escalated so quickly.' Sarah had to pause; afraid she would cry. 'I realise I shouldn't have accused him of cheating based on a hunch, but if you had seen Adeline's smug expression, like the cat who got the cream . . . and his behaviour *was* questionable.'

'I didn't want to say anything, but Martin told me the woman had monopolised Tony at The Embassy on Gladys's birthday. For Martin to notice, well . . . I was concerned. Tony should have behaved better.'

'Oh dear, poor Martin. I probably vented a bit on the way home in the taxi that night, and he got the brunt of it. Gladys had passed out at that stage.'

Judith gave her a sympathetic smile. 'Don't worry about Martin, Sarah. He is used to me moaning in his ear and his only concern is your happiness. Me, too.'

Sarah cradled her teacup in her hands. 'Thank you, but I don't know what to do, Judith. I don't know if it is a temporary break in our relationship or a permanent split. Once he had said those awful words, I was in shock. In fact, I don't think I said a single word to him after that and I barely recall the journey home.'

'You poor thing. But we all say things in the heat of the moment. Perhaps you should reach out to him,' Judith suggested, her eyes full of sympathy. 'Admit you were hasty.'

'But that's just it. I don't think I was.' Judith gave her a look of disbelief. Sarah continued: 'Yes, I was angry with him but justifiably so. There is something else, though, something that has been niggling away at me. Tony and I have been together about two years now, but every time I try to talk about the future, or make plans, he fobs me off. Only recently, we had discussed going on a short holiday to Devon. But when I brought it up again, he made a lame excuse and said he couldn't go.'

'Well, he is busy, I suppose. And you know what some men are like; they don't like—'

'Committing? Yes, I know, but I was hardly suggesting a trip down the aisle! Anyway, if it comes to it, I'm just as busy with work. No, what bothers me is that when we first spoke of it as an idea, he was all for it, and when I brought it up again that night at his flat, his attitude had changed completely.'

'Or you are reading too much into it with the benefit of hindsight?'

'Well, it's academic now, isn't it?' Sarah said. 'He said he could be away for months. There is nothing I can do.'

'And knowing you, you are frustrated,' Judith said.

'Yes, I'm exasperated with myself and him. I'm constantly swinging between anger and hurt. I don't want to believe he would cheat, but I can't stop the doubt creeping in. Judith, I can't sleep. My blasted mind keeps feeding me images of Tony and Adeline together. And what is worse is that I still have to work with the woman.' Sarah shuddered, then rubbed her face with her hands. 'Argh! This is driving me crazy!'

'Come on, be honest. You don't really believe he would deceive you,' Judith replied. 'Who is this Adeline, anyway?'

'A colleague,' Sarah replied with a grimace.

Judith wore a bemused expression. 'A colleague you brought to your best friend's birthday party? There must be more to it than that.'

Sometimes Judith was scarily perceptive. 'Yes, very well; there is. But what I am about to tell you is in the strictest confidence. Even Tony doesn't know the truth about her.'

Judith nodded. 'Don't worry. You can trust me, Sarah. We have been through so much together. You have kept my secret faithfully all these years. If my parents had ever found out about my pregnancy, they would have disowned me.'

'Suspected pregnancy. We will never really know,' Sarah said. 'Anyway, a promise is a promise, and I was only too glad to help you.'

'Thank you. So, tell me about this femme fatale.'

'Right. Well, she is a French spy, and I am her handler. Unfortunately, that involves looking after her, too. Adeline left behind a boyfriend, trapped in Paris, and she misses him terribly and fears for his safety. I felt sorry for her. I thought if I brought her out and introduced her to some people, it would help ease her loneliness.'

'Oh, dear!'

'Yes. Well, instead, she seemed to latch on to Tony. At first, I thought it was because he has fluent French, but as that night at The Embassy progressed, I grew uneasy. The final straw was Tony insisting on accompanying her home. Well, you can imagine how I felt about that.'

'And rightly so!'

'But finding her all cosy at Tony's flat was a shock. Adeline spun some tale about dropping off a book Tony had mentioned he wanted to read.'

Judith sighed. 'A bit weak alright. No wonder you were suspicious.'

'It wasn't just that though. It was the way she behaved. She flirted with him, right in front of me! Then he admitted she had stopped for a nightcap, at his invitation, the night he accompanied her home after Glad's party.'

'Good grief! So, you think she wants Tony for herself?'

'That's the bizarre thing. I don't think she does. Revenge is the only reason I can think of. She wants MI5 to get her blasted boyfriend out of France. The problem is we can't really do it. The French Resistance are the only ones who could, and they are rather busy at present with more important matters to attend to than one stranded Russian.'

'So, you believe she is punishing you for the state of things?'

'I honestly don't know. Maybe she is genuinely interested in Tony. I mean, he is a good-looking man.'

Judith gave her a sad smile. 'That cannot be denied. Oh, Sarah. I'm so sorry. This woman sounds like nothing but trouble. Could you not ask that someone else takes care of her?'

'No. That would be admitting defeat. This responsibility hasn't been given to me lightly, and the operation she is involved in is vital to the war effort. Besides, there is no one else available, so I'm stuck with her.'

'That is unfortunate. But I refuse to believe that Tony has given up on your relationship. He was defensive because he found himself in an awkward situation — you know, with her being there and acting as she did. He knew it didn't look good. When he returns to London, I'm sure he will attempt a reconciliation. I firmly believe that.'

Despite the emptiness in the pit of her stomach, Sarah summoned a smile. 'Perhaps. I must be patient then.'

'Yes! And I know how difficult that will be for you, but I truly believe all will come good. I've seen the way Tony looks at you. And if that isn't love, then I don't know what is.'

15

Jason looked up from his cluttered desk and beckoned Sarah into his office. She often wondered how he got any work done; he was so disorganised. Yet, he was one of the best agents in MI5. Sometimes, she suspected it was his secretary, Miss Wilson, who kept him on the straight and narrow.

'I got your message, sir. Miss Wilson said it was urgent.'

'Yes, well, more unfortunate than urgent, really. Take a seat,' he said, waving towards a chair. Sarah removed the pile of folders from the chair, placed them on the edge of the desk, sat, and waited patiently for him to continue.

'The thing is, it's bad news,' he said. Sarah's stomach flipped as she tensed. Was it something to do with Tony? Had he met with an accident? 'We received a message from Blet— Station X, which is one of our listening stations. The agent you are running? Honey?'

139

'Yes?' She sat forward, giving him her full attention as she released her held breath. Perhaps they were going to dispense with Adeline's services. A joyous thought, and fitting revenge for being the reason she and Tony had split.

'That precious boyfriend of hers was arrested in Paris about a week ago. Looks as though he has been carted off to one of those German camps.' Jason rooted around his desk and pulled a page out from under a folder. 'Yes, here it is: Natzweiler-Struthof. I've never heard of it. A small camp, it appears, from our intelligence reports. The prisoners are made to work in a nearby quarry.' Jason's gaze was grim when he looked across at her. 'Not for the faint-hearted, those places. They barely feed them and work them to death.'

Sarah had heard similar reports about other camps. It was well known the Nazis did not treat POWs well. In fact, they used them as slave labour to build factories, military infrastructure and camps, or to work in mines or quarries to fuel the regime's war effort. As they had an endless supply of captives for the work, they cared little if they lived or died, which violated the Geneva Convention, which stipulated how POWs should be treated. There were even reports of them denying the Red Cross access to the camps.

All of a sudden, she felt sorry for Adeline, but at the same time realised this was going to be a tremendous problem. 'I can't tell her, sir. Adeline would have a meltdown. In fact, I'm certain she'd stop working for us, or worse, blow the whole double cross system in retaliation for us not getting him out on time.'

'I suspected as much.' Jason rubbed at his chin. 'Certainly, you are best placed to make that judgement call. If you think we should keep the knowledge from her, then that's fine by me, but if she finds out at a later date that we kept this from her . . .'

'She'd definitely go off the rails, sir, but I think that is a risk we have to take, at least until after we land in France. All she talks about is when Nikolay will join her here in London.'

'That certainly won't happen now!'

'No, sir.'

'Is she too great a risk? Be honest now, Sarah. Should we pull her? We can always use one of Pfeiffer's fictional agents to take her place.'

'No, I can manage her, sir. But if at any point I feel she is dangerous or might jeopardise our operations, I'll let you know.'

'Thank you. Come and talk to me if there are any problems.' His gaze was unflinching. Did he doubt her abilities?

'Thank you,' she replied firmly.

Jason gave her a flash of a smile before sitting forward and lacing his fingers. 'You would tell me if there was anything else amiss? You haven't seemed yourself these last few days.'

Sarah thought she had disguised her heartache quite well. It was disappointing to think that scatty Jason had noticed something was up. She'd have to buck up. 'It's fine, sir. Personal stuff.' Sarah swallowed hard, alarmed at how close the tears were. 'I won't let it affect my work.'

'Don't fret; it wasn't a reprimand. I'm just concerned. You are one of my best agents and the service needs you more than ever. Very well, off with you.'

Relieved, she said: 'Thank you, sir.'

Sarah made it as far as the door.

'And make sure you keep Honey sweet,' he said with a grin. Sarah did her best not to groan in response.

Since the break-up with Tony, Sarah had put off visiting Adeline. She didn't trust herself or her temper. Every time she thought about that night in his flat, her blood boiled. But she couldn't avoid her forever. It would take a great deal of restraint not to lash out at the woman, but Sarah was determined to be professional. And she did not want to give Adeline a reason to gloat. However, she knew she would be cold with her. How could she not be? Adeline was shrewd enough, so would definitely notice. Sarah would have to brush off any enquiries the other woman made, saying she was snowed under with work. Yes, that would be believable. And what did it matter if Adeline realised the real reason for her coldness? Of course, there was always the possibility that Adeline had visited Tony's flat again and found out he was away. Well, there was some solace in the fact that Adeline could not get her claws into Tony if he was out of London.

As she walked towards Sale Place, she pondered her earlier conversation with Jason. What a turn-up! It would be impossible to rescue Nikolay now. She wondered who had informed on the unfortunate man. Adeline had told her that some of her Resistance friends were hiding him on the outskirts of Paris. One of them must have betrayed him, the poor sod. The question was, would word get back to Adeline? As far as she was aware, Nikolay hadn't been writing back to Adeline, so there was hope she would not become suspicious about his lack of communication in the coming weeks. Still, Sarah wasn't a hundred percent sure that they hadn't been communicating in some way. She would have to wiggle the information out of Adeline somehow.

One thing was certain: she would not allow herself to be lulled into pity again. Anything other than a professional relationship was out of the question and a valuable lesson had been learned. On the positive side, so far, Adeline's messages were proving successful, as they had evidence of the information being passed on to Berlin. That was the beauty of the closed loop system. The risk of Adeline being a mole was remote now, but if she were to learn of Nikolay's plight, that could all change. Sarah's sympathy for Adeline's lonely state had vanished and though it might be heartless to keep Adeline in the dark about Nikolay, it was for the greater good. This news about him, however, did niggle at Sarah's conscience. If something happened to Tony, would she want it kept from her even if they were no longer a couple?

Sarah paused to wait for a break in the traffic where she needed to cross the road. It was then, out of the corner of her eye, that she spotted a woman in a dark-coloured raincoat and scarf, suddenly come to a halt and turn to look into a shop window. It was a suspiciously clumsy move. How odd! Sarah crossed over the road and continued towards Sale Place, but her mind was in a whirl. Had she just spotted a tail? She'd have to lose them before visiting Adeline. She couldn't risk betraying Adeline's location to an enemy agent.

There was only one way to find out. At the next junction, Sarah stopped and waited for a couple of seconds before doing a sudden about-turn and heading back the way she had come, deciding to abort her visit if someone really was following her. Much to Sarah's dismay, the woman was there, walking towards her. Sarah spotted the panic in the woman's face just before she ducked into a shop.

Right! There could be no doubt at all. Someone *was* following her, but why?

* * *

After a restless night, during which many scenarios played out in Sarah's head, she knew she had to get advice. And quickly. The implications of having a tail were troubling. Did she pose a threat to someone? That seemed ludicrous. Or was it a case of a foreign power trying to keep tabs on MI5 agents for their own ends? Most worrying of all; could there be a connection to Adeline?

As soon as she reached work – thankfully, incident free – Sarah put a call through to Ewan Galbraith in Special Branch. He was the only person, bar Tony, she trusted enough to confide in. If she went to Jason with this, he might think she was now a risk and demote her to a less important task – or worse, think her delusional. Neither of those scenarios was appealing. Unfortunately, Ewan wasn't due in until later in the day, so all she could do was leave a message for him. She dared not visit Adeline until this was sorted out.

It was almost five o'clock when Ewan phoned, and they arranged to meet. It was an anxious wait for him in a café just around the corner from St. James's Street. As she sat there, her anxiety grew. Was she being paranoid? The woman who had followed her, whoever she was, had not reappeared, but perhaps someone else had taken up the job; someone more experienced and therefore invisible. Tailing was often undertaken in relays. But why would anyone want to follow *her*? And was it an enemy agent or someone closer to home? The questions kept reverberating in her head. It was all rather unnerving.

At last, Ewan strolled in. She had first met him eighteen months before. At the time, Sarah was a permanent fixture at the Majestic Hotel on the Strand, with the unpleasant job of listening in on calls made by certain guests that MI5 felt were a wee bit loose tongued. As the evidence of Nazi leanings regarding a certain MP had grown, it had fallen to Sarah to pull together a dossier of taped phone conversations to help build a case against him, and to liaise with Special Branch. Ewan had headed up the Special Branch team, who had swooped in to arrest the MP at the crack of dawn. His professionalism, ready humour, and gentlemanly manner had impressed Sarah. If she hadn't been walking out with Tony, she might even have given in to his amorous advances. Ewan had accepted defeat graciously, and they had remained on friendly terms – especially since he was now with Judith. He had been a great help when Gladys had the problem with Alfie Smyth so if anyone could help her now, it was Ewan.

He approached the table with a smile. 'How do, Sarah?' Ewan sat down opposite. 'It's good to see you, but I hope it's nothing too serious. Judith hasn't sent you to give me the old heave-ho?' He smiled as if he were joking, but Sarah detected an undercurrent of anxiety by the worried expression in his eyes.

'Gracious, no! Absolutely not,' she replied.

Ewan's shoulders relaxed. 'Good. How is she? I haven't seen her all week.'

'She's great. Busy at work, you know,' she said. The poor man seemed very unsure of her cousin. She'd have to give Judith a bit of a nudge.

'Well, then, tell old Ewan whatever is the matter?' Before she could answer, he tilted his head and narrowed his gaze. 'You look a tad peaky, if you don't mind me saying. I hope that fellow of yours is treating you well.'

Sarah blushed, but he was the last person she wanted to tell about the break-up, though inevitably Judith would tell him. But for now, the last thing she needed was Ewan being sympathetic. Her nerves were in shreds as it was. 'Everything's fine with us, thanks. It's a work problem I needed to talk to you about.'

He gazed at her above the rim of his cup. 'Ah! That does sound serious.' He cocked a brow. 'Could the dashing Tony not help with this?'

Sarah hurried to answer. 'I'm sure he would, Ewan, but unfortunately, he has been called away with work. He could be away for months. Besides, this is more your area of expertise. I need to sort this out now, before it escalates.'

Ewan reached across and patted her hand. 'I see. Don't worry, Tell me what the problem is.'

'I was on my way to visit someone yesterday when I realised I was being followed,' she said. 'The thing is, I have no idea who the person is or why they were doing it. I had to abandon my plan and go home instead. The location of the person I planned to visit must remain secret.'

'Why not go to your boss about this?' Ewan asked with a frown.

Sarah grimaced into her cup. 'It would feel like failure. I'd like to have more information before I tell him.'

'Do you still feel you have to prove yourself?'

'Sometimes,' she replied.

'That's a shame. Alright, let's be logical about this. Most likely, it's a foreign agent,' Ewan said. 'There have been rumours of a few German agents slipping through our net. If they know where MI5 is based, it makes sense that they would try to follow you guys. I'm sorry, but Jason needs to know.'

Sarah's heart sank. 'What you say is possible, of course. But I'd like to be sure before I speak to him. My only concern is my current operation. I can't go near my agent until this is cleared up. There is, of course, one other possibility . . . It could be the IRA, which is why I wanted to talk to you. After all that happened with my father, well, I wouldn't be the most popular person on the planet with the republicans.' Sarah's voice broke.

Ewan came around the table and sat down beside her. 'Now you have me worried. Have you any reason to suspect them? Have you any evidence that it could be IRA?' Sarah shook her head, now close to tears. 'You are very stressed, and I can see why. But I suspect there is more to this.'

Sarah took a deep breath. 'I'm facing some hostility at work.'

Ewan looked taken aback. 'Why is that? You're jolly good at your job.'

'That's exactly why. I was promoted above some of the men. It didn't go down well. Some hope I will fail. If there was the slightest suspicion I was working with the IRA . . .'

'Crikey, yes! That would be the end of your career.'

'They wouldn't just sack me. They'd deport me!'

Ewan's expression turned grim. 'Yes, they probably would. I understand. Don't worry. I'll put out some feelers. You know how we work; we keep a very close eye on the London IRA cells. If they are up to anything, one of my chaps will know about it.' He lowered his voice even further. 'We have infiltrated their network.'

'Well done!' Sarah replied, suddenly relieved. 'And this can be done discreetly, can't it?'

'You have my word. We have tabs on all the known foreign spies operating in London, too, and many informers who can dish the dirt on any rogue agents. We'll find your tail and give them plenty of discouragement!'

'Thank you, Ewan. I owe you a huge favour for this.'

Ewan chuckled. 'Oh, I think we are even, Sarah. Thanks to you, I've met the woman of my dreams.' He picked up his cup and made a toast. 'To Judith!'

Sarah chuckled softly as they clinked cups. 'You really are smitten, aren't you?'

Ewan winked back at her. 'You could say that!'

16

The next morning, Judith and Sarah were just finishing breakfast when there was a knock on the front door. As neither was expecting a visitor, they exchanged a puzzled glance. With her heart hammering with alarm, yesterday's conversation with Ewan popped into Sarah's head. In fact, she had lain awake most of the night worrying about the identity of her tail.

She jumped up. 'Best I answer it,' she said, shutting the kitchen door behind her. Heart thumping, she stared at the dark shadow on the other side of the glass pane of the front door. Whoever it was, was tall. Probably a man. Sarah frantically scanned the hallway for some kind of weapon. But there was nothing useful to hand. With an exclamation of annoyance, Sarah ducked into the sitting room just as another knock resonated through the flat. She grabbed the poker from the fireplace and dashed back out into the hall.

'Who is it?' she called out, stepping closer to the door.
'It's Ewan!'

Oh, thank God!

Sarah yanked open the door and glared at him. 'You scared the life out of me!'

'Well, that's a lovely way to greet a friend,' he replied, eyeing the poker in her hand. 'Do you usually greet visitors with a blunt instrument?'

'Only thoughtless ones!'

Sarah closed the door behind him just as Judith emerged from the kitchen.

'What's all the fuss?' Judith asked, then blushed when she saw who it was. 'Oh, hello, there!'

'Good morning,' Ewan replied with a grin. 'I hope *you* have a friendlier welcome for me.'

Judith frowned at Sarah, who was trying her best to discreetly get rid of the poker. Judith tut-tutted, shook her head at Sarah, and turned back to Ewan. 'I do indeed. Don't mind her. Come in and have a cuppa.' She glanced at her watch. 'I don't have to leave for another twenty minutes.'

'I'd love to, but I'm afraid I need to have a quick word with the world's worst assassin first.' This he said with a smirk at Sarah.

With a roll of her eyes, Sarah waved towards the sitting room. 'We won't be long, Judith. Keep the tea warm.' As soon as Ewan sat down, Sarah pounced. 'Well?'

'Sit,' he said. 'And try to calm down. I have good news and bad.'

Sarah pulled a face and urged him on with a nod of her head.

'It's definitely not IRA. However, we have drawn a blank on who it *might* be. Nazis or Vichy French were top of my list, but we have been keeping a close eye on the lot of 'em. No one seems to be your likely culprit. That, or they are very good at it, or new to the job, and we haven't any record of them just yet.'

It wasn't terribly reassuring. 'So what do I do?' she asked.

'Stop worrying yourself to death, and talk to Jason,' Ewan said as he rose. He patted her shoulder. 'Do it today. Take precautions when you're out and about. If the tail reappears, let me know.' He turned at the door. 'One last thing. I suggest you don't carry that poker around with you. It gives the wrong impression,' he quipped, then ducked out of the room.

'Fine!' she called after him.

For all his joking, she was still worried. Although it was good to know it wasn't any of her da's old colleagues, it still left a lot of questions. And how long had it been going on for? Days, weeks? Was it pure luck she had noticed when she did? Had she already unwittingly given away Adeline's whereabouts? A cold dread swept over her. Despite disliking the woman, she didn't want her to come to harm. She would have to warn her to be on her guard.

And Ewan was right; she had no choice. She'd have to tell Jason as soon as she got into work this morning. It was not a conversation she wanted to have, but if something happened and she hadn't come clean, she really would be in trouble.

That evening, as Sarah left MI5, the streets were busy, and it was difficult to keep watch, but by the time she had double-backed and eventually reached Sale Place, she was fairly certain she was not being followed. At last, it was safe to visit Adeline without the risk of revealing her location to any foreign agent. Sarah hoped that by noticing the tail, she had scared her off. But still, her nerves were jangling as she reached Adeline's flat.

There was no answer to her knock, so Sarah let herself in. She had met Jason earlier that day to explain the situation with the tail, and even now, she was still smarting from some of his comments. Nevertheless, it was done and although Jason had been concerned that she had not come to him immediately, he was relieved to know she had turned to Galbraith and no one else. However, he could shed no light on why anyone could be following her and echoed Ewan's advice to keep her wits about her. *As if life isn't stressful enough,* she thought, as she took the seat by the window to await her charge.

But where could Adeline be? It was almost six o'clock. Was she working late at *The Gazette*? Or was she out there somewhere, up to no good, contacting German agents and wreaking havoc with Allied plans? Sarah didn't know Adeline well, but she suspected she could play a very dangerous game with MI5 and hardly blink an eye.

But as the minutes ticked by, Sarah's thoughts grew darker. What if Sarah's tail had linked her with Adeline? And what if one of Haas's agents had taken Adeline and was at that moment spiriting her out of England to face his wrath? And all because Sarah had been careless. With a groan, Sarah sprang up from her seat. Should you go and look for her? That was a crazy idea. She needed to relax. There was no point in torturing herself; Adeline was just late.

Restless, she wandered around the flat for a few minutes. Nothing appeared out of place. No giveaways as to the innermost thoughts of the occupant. Sarah sifted through the books and papers stacked on the mantlepiece, but there was nothing obviously suspicious. Sarah peeped inside the bedroom door. An expensive silk negligee lay neatly folded on the pillow. Sarah had to look away quickly. Had Tony seen that particular item of clothing, she wondered. *Oh no; I can't deal with this.* She had to shake off this paranoia or it would drive her mad.

Suddenly, she heard footsteps coming up the stairs, and she rushed back over to the chair at the window just in time to present a serene expression when the door opened.

Adeline pulled up short when she saw Sarah, her hand flying up to her neck. 'Good gracious! You scared me,' she said, but her expression was more wary than frightened. 'Why are you here? Another letter?'

'No. A social call, and to check that everything is alright,' Sarah managed to say in an even tone. She had to fight to contain her true feelings. Every fibre in her body wanted to lash out – wound – now that Adeline was before her.

Adeline treated her to a sardonic glance, but shrugged. 'All is well. Would you like some tea or coffee?'

'Tea, please,' Sarah replied and watched as Adeline put away the groceries she had brought in with her. Perhaps she hadn't been up to more than a shopping trip on her way home from work. Sarah was almost disappointed to have her suspicions disproved. And suddenly she knew she wasn't ready for this confrontation. It was such a bad idea when she wasn't in control of her emotions.

Adeline worked in silence, throwing Sarah the odd glance as she went about making the tea and coffee. 'You look tired,' she remarked.

'It has been a horrible week,' she replied with a great deal of feeling.

Adeline quirked a brow. 'Is that so? How awful for you!'

Sarah took a sip of her tea. Was that a jibe, she wondered. 'I suppose I should thank you.'

'Why is that?'

'For being *so* kind to Tony and giving him that book. You took the trouble to go all that way.'

'Piff! It was nothing,' Adeline replied, her eyes alight, but Sarah wasn't sure what with, and her anger grew.

'On the contrary; it was extremely generous of you. However . . .'

'However?' Adeline asked.

'I do wonder what prompted it.'

Adeline's stare was hostile and sent a chill down Sarah's spine. Then, slowly, she smiled. 'The goodness of my heart, dear Sarah.'

Sarah quickly set down her cup. She was shaking. 'We don't have to like each other, Adeline. Just work together. But understand this: my private life and my friends are off limits. You may play games with whomever you like, but if you intrude into my personal life like that again—'

'You will what?' Adeline scoffed.

Sarah had to clench her hands in her lap, desperate to stay in control. 'I will make your life extremely difficult.' She paused. 'Do we understand each other?'

Adeline nodded slowly, but Sarah doubted her words had had any effect. The woman appeared to be impervious to her threats, a mocking glint in her eye. In that moment, Sarah knew she had to leave.

As Sarah stood, she looked down at Adeline. 'Oh, and one

more thing. It is possible one of Haas's agents is trying to track you down. So do be careful when you're out and about!'

As she scurried down the stairs, Sarah wasn't exactly proud of herself, but there had been a great deal of satisfaction in seeing the momentary terror cross Adeline's face.

17

A few days later, Judith and Sarah had supper together. Gladys was working the late shift and wouldn't be in for hours yet.

As they were doing the washing up, Judith turned to her. 'Right, missy! You've been down in the dumps long enough. Moping won't bring Tony back.'

'I'm not moping,' Sarah objected. 'It's just—'

'Hmm, I know brooding when I see it. Why don't you write to him? Reach out?' Judith asked.

'Why should I? Tony was the one who wanted us to split up, remember?'

Judith threw the dishcloth into the sink and turned to her. 'One of you idiots will have to make the first move.' She shook her head and sighed. 'Stubbornness is all very well, but it's only going to make matters worse. Anyone can see you two are mad about each other, and I suspect he is as miserable as you are.'

'Well, I don't see why I should take advice from *you*,' Sarah said in a huff. 'You won't even give Ewan a decent chance. The man is besotted. You need to be careful; someone else might snap him up.'

'What nonsense you talk! I don't care.'

'I don't believe you,' Sarah spluttered. 'You hang on his every word.'

With a huff, Judith sat down with her back to her. Sarah smiled to herself as she dried the last plate and put it away. She was extremely fond of Ewan and knew he was a decent bloke. Just the kind of fellow Judith needed in her life. Judith had been so wary since the debacle with Gerald that Sarah feared she would never walk out with a man again. One date at most, and that was it, of late. There was always a reason it hadn't worked out, and usually a lame one too, in Sarah's opinion. Well, it wasn't difficult to understand. Hadn't *she* thought the sun had shone out of Tony only for him to let her down and break her heart?

But now, looking at her cousin's hunched shoulders, she could tell she was genuinely confused about her feelings for Ewan.

Sarah pulled out a chair and sat down opposite. 'I'm the last person who wants to see you hurt, but being offhand with the poor man, you risk losing him. For instance, isn't it silly wanting me and Gladys to go with you two to that concert this weekend?'

'I don't see why. I barely know him!'

'Oh, come on! You've already been out with Ewan several times. I think you are safe enough.'

Judith made a face at her. 'I don't want Ewan – or any man, come to think of it – to think he can click his fingers and I'll go anywhere with him. This way it's a group outing as opposed to a date.'

'You're daft!' Sarah exclaimed. 'Ewan's really keen on you.'

Judith turned away, blushing. 'He's OK, I suppose.'

'You are a terrible liar,' Sarah replied with a chuckle. 'He's one of the good guys, Judith. You need to push the memory of Gerald Pascoe from your mind and move on.'

'I have!' Judith objected. 'But there's no harm in being cautious. I'm not going to rush into another relationship. If he's as decent a fellow as you claim, he will be patient.'

'I know how deeply hurt you were. It makes my blood boil to think how Gerald treated you when he thought you were pregnant. He was a total coward. You didn't deserve to be treated like that.'

Judith's sad smile said it all. Sarah suspected, with alarm, that deep down her cousin was still agonising over the man. 'You haven't seen him since he showed his true character, have you?'

'No, no. From what I've heard, he is back with his wife, though it wouldn't surprise me to hear he has someone hidden away as well. God! I'm not proud of myself. But I was blinded by him and lapped up his lies like an idiot. Luckily, our paths haven't crossed in the two years since and I can assure you if they did, I'd ignore him.'

'Good. I'm relieved to hear it. And I do understand. I'm learning the hard way that hearts are extremely fragile.'

Judith sighed; her eyes full of sympathy. 'Has there really been no word from Tony?'

'Nothing at all. I keep telling myself it's because he's busy, but deep down, I suspect it's because he's hurt that I didn't trust him enough.'

'That is possible,' Judith replied. 'But his behaviour was questionable.'

'He didn't see it that way.'

'But you could hardly *not* challenge Tony about that woman. He's a friendly and outgoing man, but from what I have heard from both you and Martin, he showed far too much interest in Adeline. Honestly, I would have tackled him over it too,' Judith replied, her expression fierce. 'In the end, you must decide whether you believe his version of events that night and the night of the party or not. Have you questioned her about it?'

'I challenged her, yes, and I laid down a marker.' Sarah wrinkled her nose. 'Actually, I was a wee bit cruel and frightened her. I was most unprofessional. I regret it now, not least because I still have to work with her. Our work is vital; I can't afford to alienate her. But it's an intolerable position to be in.'

Her cousin sniffed. 'I'm struggling to feel sorry for her. I'm sure she deserved whatever you said after breaking up you and Tony.'

'I'm not normally vindictive but my temper was up, and she was so smug. She doesn't know we are no longer a couple, though, and I didn't enlighten her, I can assure you! What if she goes off chasing him again?'

'Oh, Sarah!'

'Yes, alright, I know that's unlikely. She was just playing games and I know Tony didn't cheat. He just enjoyed the attention, I suppose.'

'You need to know for sure though. You'll have no peace until you do.'

Sarah knew she was right, but her cousin's words were

little consolation. In the end, whether or not it had all been a misunderstanding, it didn't excuse how he had reacted.

Unfortunately, the split was affecting her work, making her short tempered – and look where that had got her on previous occasions. She desperately needed distraction, for that would be the best way to block out the heartache. She had to focus on what was important, her friends and work. Not to mention the identity of her elusive tail . . .

18

15th April 1944, The Comedy Theatre, The West End, London

A few days later, Sarah and Gladys accompanied Judith and Ewan to The Comedy Theatre. Ewan had wangled tickets from a friend to an army variety show being staged to raise funds for the Red Cross. A less than enthusiastic Sarah followed the others down the steps to their seats in the Dress Circle. Glancing at the programme earlier in the bar, she realised she wasn't in the right mood for this performance. She was too preoccupied. The night was to be a mixture of song, dance, and comedy sketches. Sarah only hoped it would be of a better calibre than similar shows she had seen in the past.

Given a choice, she would much rather have gone to see a play or gone to the cinema after the frustrating afternoon she had spent with Adeline. She had been especially challenging today, demanding to know what evidence Sarah had that a German agent was sniffing around. It had taken some time to steer Adeline away from that topic and even more to persuade her to write the required letter. Eventually, Adeline had knuckled down, but all the while she had griped under her breath.

As Sarah had stood to leave, Adeline had once more demanded information about Nikolay. In frustration, Sarah had snapped and told her to take the issue up with Jason. Words Sarah regretted as soon as she was halfway home and had calmed down. Jason would not be pleased to be confronted about the subject by Adeline directly. He expected Sarah to handle the issue, so if Adeline showed up at St. James's Street, it would be a black mark against Sarah. Perhaps Adeline would think better of it, though the way Sarah's luck was running of late, she probably would turn up and kick up a fuss. It was some consolation that, so far, they had kept Nikolay's incarceration from Adeline. But how much longer would they get away with it? Worryingly, there had been no further intelligence about his situation.

At the top of the steps, Gladys turned to Sarah with a grin. 'My, but this is rather grand, isn't it? I've never been to such a fancy theatre.'

'Me, neither, Glad.'

Well, someone is out to impress, Sarah thought, as they followed Ewan to the front of the circle. These can't have been cheap seats, Sarah realised, as she took her place beside Gladys, and sneaked a peek at Judith to see her reaction. Her cousin was wearing a broad smile and looking around her with interest. Ewan caught Sarah's eye and winked. *Cheeky sod!*

As the lights lowered, Sarah sat back in her seat. However, much to her surprise, the first act was a hilarious comedy sketch, swiftly followed by a young private who performed a solo piece on the violin. The young musician was so good he received a standing ovation. The crowd was growing more and more enthusiastic as each act came on, something Sarah put down to both the quality of the performances and the heaving theatre bar before the concert began. Cheering and stamping feet greeted each turn, with a rising level of hilarity and some good-humoured heckling from the audience, punctuating each part of the night. Sarah wondered how the performers put up with it, but they appeared to be immune and rather enjoying themselves. Soon, she wished she were a member of the cast. Although Sarah had joined an amateur theatrical group and taken part in a few different projects, for the last few months, she hadn't had time to go to the weekly rehearsals. As she sat there, taking in the atmosphere, she realised how much she had missed it.

With two swift gins to soften her mood, Sarah was completely relaxed when the opening act began for the second part of the show. But she could hardly believe her eyes when the familiar figure of Field Marshal Montgomery walked onto the stage. How wonderful that he would take time out from his busy life to help such a noble cause. The audience jumped to their feet and erupted in cheers and applause. Thinking he was there to make a speech, Sarah was bewildered when it transpired he was taking part in the sketch.

Puzzled, she leaned across Gladys and tugged Ewan's sleeve. 'How on earth did they persuade him to do that?' she asked.

Ewan grinned back. 'It's not the real Monty; it's an actor, silly.'

'No!' Sarah stared down at the stage as her mind raced. Hands shaking, she pulled the programme out of her bag and gazed at the back page photograph of the impersonator. The real Montgomery was commander of the British Eighth Army, a real hero in the nation's eyes. El Alamein, Sicily and the Italian campaign . . . His successes were the stuff of legend. *Just think of the mischief we could undertake with someone who looked like him,* Sarah thought as an extraordinary idea formed in her head.

★ ★ ★

Early on Monday morning, Sarah made a beeline for Jason's office. Miss Wilson was not to be seen, so Sarah knocked on Jason's door, hoping he was at his desk. She was in luck.

'Come in,' his familiar voice rang out. 'Ah, it's you, Sarah. Any developments on that tail of yours?'

'No, sir. Whoever it was, they haven't appeared since, and I'm being extra cautious when out and about.'

'Well, that's good to know, but stay vigilant,' Jason said with a frown.

'I will, sir.'

'Good. How was your weekend?' Jason asked.

'Couldn't have been better, sir,' Sarah replied, bubbling with impatience. 'You will not believe what I saw on Saturday night!'

Jason showed surprise, but waved her to a seat. 'Do tell.'

'Well, sir. Remember back in January when you put forward a plan to use that actor chap as a decoy for Field Marshal Montgomery? You know, the man who was in the film *Five Graves to Cairo*.'

'Why, yes. Such a shame that didn't work out. It grieved me to shelve Operation Copperhead. I really thought we were on to a good idea. We have used decoys in the past to great effect. Safer to use them sometimes, too, if we feel someone of importance is in danger. Churchill's double fools everyone. But that other fellow was too tall in the end, wasn't he? So, we couldn't use him.'

'Yes, by a good three or four inches, sir, but I think I have found someone else who would be perfect for the role.'

Jason sat forward. 'Have you indeed? Intriguing! Well, spill the beans!'

'His name is William Hastings. He was in the variety show I attended on Saturday night. I swear, sir, I thought it was Monty. Everything about him is right: his voice, looks, even his expressions. The man was good enough to fool me and the audience.' Sarah pulled the show programme from her bag. 'See? His picture is on the back.'

'By Jove; you'd swear it was the man himself,' Jason exclaimed, shaking his head. 'Do you know anything about the chap?'

'A little, sir. After the show, I went backstage and spoke to him. He is a lieutenant stationed up in Leicester in the Army Pay Corps. Seemingly, he has impersonated the general several times in revues and such. Quite famous for it, too, by all accounts. All harmless stuff. Of course, I didn't let on who I was. I thought it best to discuss the possibilities with you first. But as soon as I realised he wasn't the real Monty on stage, I remembered the other man we had planned to use as a decoy and thought this fellow might be worth investigating.'

'And he fooled everyone?' Jason asked. Sarah broke into a grin and nodded. 'Excellent. Well spotted, Sarah. We must get him back to London on some pretext and check him out – surreptitiously, of course, and as quickly as possible. Mind you, he'd have to be pretty good for us to risk using him. It sounds to me as though he is keen to use his resemblance to his advantage. Enjoys the attention too, I dare say.'

'Yes, without a doubt. As a matter of fact, he told me he is constantly asked to play the field marshal for larks. And he's involved in amateur dramatics, sir, and that stage experience might just give him the confidence necessary to carry it off.'

'Indeed. A shrinking violet would be of no use to us.' Sarah could almost see the cogs turning as Jason sat mulling this over. Then he straightened up, all of a sudden. 'Aha! I know what we can do. My friend Peter Agnew works over at Ealing Studios. I'm sure he'd be happy to help us out. We could entice the fellow down for a screen test or some such.'

'Yes! That would be an excellent plan if we could pull it off. And if we didn't think he could do it, he'd be none the wiser.'

'But, my God, if he is as good as you say, we can carry out untold mischief with him.'

'That's exactly what I thought, sir. Would we have any immediate use for him?'

'Well, I'd have to run it by Everleigh, but we had considered sending that other chap to impersonate the field marshal somewhere overseas, possibly Gibraltar or North Africa. With operations scaling up in the coming weeks and months, it might throw Jerry off if they saw Monty swanning about abroad. They do monitor his movements, you know. The Germans are no fools. They both respect and fear him. The important element of this deception would be that the enemy would think an attack on France was unlikely if the field marshal were out of England. As I say, let me discuss it with the boss.'Then, Jason sat frowning for several seconds. 'The thing is, I'm snowed under.' He gave the paperwork on his desk a rueful glance. 'I'd have to leave a lot of the legwork on this to you.'

'I'd love to take it on, sir. It's right up my street.'

'You're into the amateur dramatic stuff, aren't you?'

'Yes, sir,' she replied. 'I'm with the Paddington Players.'

'Then it would appear to be a match made in heaven, as they say.' Jason smiled. 'And the beauty of it is that we can use your agent Honey to send the relevant messages to Haas to tip him off about Monty's whereabouts. He'll lap it up.'

'Yes, that would be ideal,' she replied.

'Good work, Sarah.'

Sarah quit Jason's office and headed back downstairs. If they could trick the Germans using a Monty decoy, the landings in France would be much easier. If Jerry was unprepared, it could save countless Allied lives. And using Adeline in any deception involving the decoy made sense, since Haas trusted her so much.

As she made her way along the corridor, back to her own office, she continued to mull over the situation. There was only one difficulty she could foresee and that was Adeline. Would she co-operate? Since their confrontation over Tony, Adeline's attitude to her MI5 work had deteriorated. She never missed an opportunity to moan whenever Sarah requested a message be sent out or handed her a list of personal notices for *The Gazette*. It was odd, considering Adeline had been the one who had offered her services to MI5 in the first place.

But Sarah was beginning to think Adeline was just contrary by nature. Perhaps she was bored now or disappointed that the role of double agent wasn't quite as glamorous as she had hoped. And yet, Sarah knew one thing for certain about her charge. If Adeline ever found out that Sarah had withheld the news of Nikolay's incarceration from her, all hell would break loose. Sarah wished Jason had delegated Adeline to another handler so that she could work exclusively with Hastings. But of course, he could not. Just her luck they were so desperately short-staffed.

With a sigh, Sarah sat down at her desk and looked around at the familiar walls. It was unfortunate that she still had to work out of the tiny office she had once shared with Tony. She didn't need the constant reminders. Sometimes she imagined she detected a hint of his citrus scent and she often indulged in reliving some of their previous conversations. Stupid, really. And pointless. She doubted he was pining for *her*. Tony's continued silence was devastating, and she hardly needed any further proof that their relationship was over. She swivelled her chair round and stared out the grimy window.

I wonder where he is and what he's up to. And the most treacherous thought of all: *who is he spending his free time with?*

19

26th April 1944, Ealing Studios, Ealing Green, West London

Somehow, Jason persuaded Hastings' commanding officer up in Leicester to release him to attend a screen test at Ealing Studios. What Jason said to the man to achieve this, Sarah did not know, but she guessed it was some tale of a promotional film for the army. All that mattered was that it had worked. Hastings would be in London for two days. Hopefully, it would be enough time to confirm if he could pull it off. Posing as a talent agent was the perfect cover for Sarah until she was sure Hastings could impersonate Monty. Only then could she explain their plan to him and see if he were willing to help.

Sarah arrived at Ealing an hour before the appointed meeting with Hastings so that she could brief Peter Agnew on what they needed. She had spent the last couple of days watching newsreel footage of the field marshal and making notes about his mannerisms and turns of phrase. It wouldn't be enough for Hastings to fool the press; he would have to convince his fellow army officers and any dignitaries he encountered, too.

Agnew had explained what would happen during the screen test and they had agreed that Hastings should recite one of Monty's speeches. With comparable footage of the real Monty making the speech, the screen test would help Sarah decide if Hastings was suitable to take on the role.

Sarah waited patiently in the reception area of the main house at the front of the studio lot. It was rather exciting to be in the place where many of the films she had seen and enjoyed over the years had been made. The walls were adorned with pictures of film stars and movie posters. To kill time, she wandered about, drinking it all in. There was a particularly fine photograph of John Mills next to one of Michael Redgrave and a stunning profile shot of Jane Baxter. It gave her a thrill to think some of her favourite actors had probably walked through those main doors, just as she had done not an hour before. As Sarah moved on, her eye was caught by a poster she hadn't seen before. It was for a film entitled *The Halfway House*. Definitely a film she was keen to see. Perhaps she could persuade Gladys to come along with her at the weekend. Despite all their best efforts, she was still nervous after the incident with Alfie. The poor girl needed some distraction.

As much as she was enjoying herself, Sarah was relieved to see Hastings walk through the door some minutes later. Gasps of recognition from the various people around the reception area brought a smile to Sarah's face. Such a good sign. He obviously fooled everyone; even in mufti, the resemblance to the field marshal was extraordinary.

Sarah stepped forward and held out her hand. 'Thank you for coming all this way, Lieutenant Hastings.'

'Ah, I remember you!' he exclaimed, shaking her hand. 'Sarah Gillespie, isn't it? Saturday night. Why you sly thing; you never said you were a talent agent.'

'Well, I didn't want anyone else to know,' she replied. 'Come along; we must go out to the studio for the test. They are waiting for us.'

'This is exciting, I have to say, Miss Gillespie. By Jove, yes!'

A young lad did a double-take as they walked through and Hastings winked at Sarah. 'Happens a lot, that!' He shook his head. 'Can disconcert at times.'

They continued out through a back door and into a yard. Sarah heard Hastings' indrawn breath as he gazed at the vast buildings with high sloping roofs on the far side. Two men went past, pushing a large piece of scenery on a trolley.

'So, this is where the magic is created,' he murmured, mirroring Sarah's thoughts exactly, as they strolled towards the middle building.

'Are you a film fan, Lieutenant?' Sarah asked with a smile.

'You could say that!'

Sarah knocked on the studio door. 'Could you tell Mr Agnew we are here, please? Miss Gillespie and Lieutenant Hastings,' Sarah said to the young man who greeted them.

'No need, miss. They are all ready for you. This way first, please.'

Sarah and Hastings followed him through a maze of corridors until they reached a door marked 'Wardrobe'.

The assistant opened the door and ushered Hastings inside. 'We won't be a jiff, miss. Need to get the right uniform on 'im.'

Sarah nodded. Five minutes later, Hastings appeared, looking very much the part of Monty. The young lad pushed past. 'Hair and make-up next,' he said. 'Right this way.'

Ten minutes later, and Sarah would have sworn she was standing beside the real Monty.

'I think I can guess what role I am to play,' joked Hastings, brushing his hands down the sleeves of his jacket. 'A propaganda film, I take it. What's the film called?'

Luckily, Sarah had anticipated the question. 'It doesn't have a title yet, some issue with the writers.' Hastings appeared to accept this. 'You are remarkably like him,' Sarah continued with a smile. She turned to their escort. 'I think we are ready now.'

'Follow me,' the young man replied.

The room they entered was a lot smaller than Sarah had expected, but then they hardly needed a full-size studio to do one screen test. A desk and chair had been set up with a window backdrop. Peter Agnew came forward, holding out his hand.

'My goodness, sir, you are like him alright,' Peter said as he shook hands with Hastings. 'I expect you get that all the time.'

'Rather.'

'I'm Peter Agnew and I will be your director for the screen test. Right, well, if you wouldn't mind, we'll start with you sitting at the desk,' Peter said. 'Miss Gillespie, perhaps you'd like to take a seat over there.'

Sarah moved to the side and watched, fascinated. If pushed, she would have admitted to being slightly envious of Hastings. Wouldn't it be wonderful to be tested for an actual movie?

Once Hastings was sitting down, the cameraman and his assistant pulled out a measuring tape and calculated the distance from the desk to the camera. Another fellow swung a microphone on a boom over Hastings' head. Then the cameraman came up to Hastings, holding some sort of meter up to his face. 'Exposure is fine,' he said. 'We're all set, Peter.'

Peter walked over to Hastings and handed him a sheet of paper. 'This is part of one of Monty's speeches to his troops. Why don't you give us your best shot at it?'

'No problem, Mr Agnew,' Hastings replied. He scanned the page quickly before launching into the short speech. As Sarah watched and listened, she was struck by how similar Hastings' performance was to the original. This augured well, indeed.

Once the speech was over, Agnew had Hastings stand up and walk about. Again, Sarah was amazed at how well Hastings performed. It was as if Monty was there in the room with them. It was clear Hastings had studied the field marshal in great detail. And thank God he had! It made Sarah's job all the easier.

'Thank you, Lieutenant Hastings,' Agnew said at last. 'If you wouldn't mind waiting outside for a few minutes?'

'Certainly, and thank you,' Hastings replied with a wink at Sarah as he walked past.

'Unbelievable!' Peter Agnew exclaimed as the door closed. 'You won't find closer than that.'

'No, I don't believe so,' Sarah said, walking over to join him. 'Thank you so much for facilitating this. But could we look at both reels again, just to be absolutely sure?'

★　★　★

An hour later, Sarah sat across from Hastings in a café around the corner from the studio. Thankfully, she had found a quiet table in a corner where their conversation would be private. Of course, she was incredibly tense. This was a huge decision to make on her own. If it went wrong . . .

'This is awfully nice of you, Miss Gillespie,' Hastings said, draining his teacup. 'Gosh, I must admit, I was terribly nervous about the screen test. I mean, it isn't every day such an opportunity arises. Funnily enough, I love acting, always have, but it has only been since the war started that anyone has been interested in hiring me.' Hastings touched his face. 'I guess this is my passport to success.'

'It may well be, Lieutenant,' Sarah replied.

'Please, call me Bill. All my friends do.'

'Thank you, Bill. And I'm Sarah.' Once she was sure no one was listening, she continued: 'I'm afraid I have deceived you a little.'

The light of excitement died in his eyes. Hastings straightened up. 'What? In what way?'

'We brought you to London under false pretences.'

'I don't understand,' he replied, and she felt awful. Hastings sagged in his chair, his disappointment sketched on his features. 'What do you mean by "we"?'

'I'm not a talent agent, Bill. I work for MI5. Military secret service.'

'Good Lord!' He stared down at the table for a few moments, then looked up at her, frowning. 'What would the secret service want with me?'

'Your country needs you, Bill. I know that may sound trite, but it is true. The mission is called Operation

Copperhead and is vital to the war effort. Unfortunately, I can't tell you why, but we want to use you as a decoy for Monty to trick the Germans.'

'As his double?'

'Yes.'

'This is . . . unexpected.' Hastings reached for the teapot and poured out another two cups. His hand shook. 'Would it be dangerous?'

'Probably,' she replied. She had to be honest with him. 'Do you think you could do it? We would, of course, help train you up. The field marshal is agreeable to the plan and is even willing to meet you to assist and answer any questions you might have. It would be an opportunity for you to study him and his ways up close.'

'Me! Meet Monty!'

The light was back in his eyes and Sarah let herself relax. She smiled. 'Yes.'

'Then, I'm in! No question about it.'

'Wonderful. Of course, we must keep this secret. No one, absolutely no one, must know what you are doing. Not your colleagues or your family. My boss will clear your absence with your commanding officer for the duration of your work with us, but even he won't be aware of your mission. We will come up with some plausible excuse for your absence.'

Hastings leaned towards her, all eagerness. 'I say, it will be far more exciting than army payroll. When do I start?'

20

28th April 1944, Sale Place, Paddington, London

A few evenings later, Sarah headed to Adeline's flat. Using the excuse of being busy with the Hastings job, she had been putting the visit off the entire week. Now that time had passed, she had calmed down. Her focus had to be on the job and utilising Adeline in the best way possible for MI5. Jason wanted another letter written, and it had to go out in the post the next day.

Adeline took a while to answer her knock, and when she did so, Sarah was astonished to see the state she was in. The Frenchwoman's face was bright red, her cheeks damp with tears, and her eyes red-rimmed. For a moment, Sarah's stomach clenched. Damn! Had Nikolay's capture been revealed? This was all she needed. With a look of distress and perhaps resignation, Adeline swallowed hard and stepped back to let her in.

'What on earth is wrong, Adeline?' Sarah asked, closing the door. 'What has happened?'

Adeline grabbed a letter from the table and thrust it under her nose. Her hand shook. 'This!'

Sarah put down her bag and glanced at the spidery scrawl on the page. 'I'm sorry, Adeline. I can't read this. Is it in French?'

Adeline snatched the letter back. 'Yes! It arrived today. From Lisbon; from Haas.'

Adeline and Haas corresponded regularly, which was part of the agreed procedure. Why would a letter from him upset Adeline this much? If it was about Nikolay, Sarah knew the woman would be screaming and ranting at her by now, if not tearing her limb from limb. So, if it wasn't something about Nikolay, it couldn't be too bad.

'And what does it say, Adeline? Why has it upset you so much?'

'Haas demands I come to Lisbon. He wants to meet in person and soon.'

This was both astonishing and worrying. Sarah couldn't allow it; it was far too risky. Her thoughts turned to her missing tail. Had they achieved their aim and reported back to Haas that Adeline was working for MI5?

'Why does he want you to go?' she asked, sitting down on the nearest chair, her mind in a whirl. This was disastrous.

'The man does not say, but he included the agreed code word for it. That is all I know,' Adeline said in a shaking voice. 'There is no choice. I must go.'

'No, we can think of some excuse. It's too dangerous, Adeline. It might be a trap.'

Adeline blanched and sat down rather quickly. 'But if I do not go, he will be suspicious. No one says no to Haas.'

'We will have to stall him, then. Perhaps you could say you are too ill to travel?'

'He would not care,' Adeline scoffed.

'Well, you will have to convince him, and no time like the present; I'm here to give you instructions for a new letter for him, anyway.'

Adeline dropped her head into her hands. 'No, no, no! I'm too upset. I cannot do one of those stupid letters.' Then she looked up, her bottom lip trembling. 'Don't you understand? Haas wants to kill me. What other reason could there be?' Suddenly, her features hardened. 'Someone must have betrayed me. It must be one of *your* colleagues.' Adeline pointed at the letter on the table. 'He lures me to Lisbon too soon. It makes little sense unless he wants to deactivate me . . . No, that isn't the word. Eliminate me . . . yes, that's what he wants.'

'No one in MI5 has betrayed you, Adeline,' Sarah replied. But could she be sure? She rushed on. 'Only a handful of people even know of your existence. Why would Haas want you dead? You are giving him what he wants. Perhaps Haas only wants reassurance that you are still loyal.'

Adeline gave her a pained look, then laughed without mirth. 'Haas assumes loyalty, always. You do not know him. He is an evil man. Haas would not drag me to Lisbon unless it was serious.'

Sarah had to concede she was probably right. The summons to Lisbon, so soon after Adeline's arrival and the appearance of Sarah's tail, had a sinister undertone. Clearly, Adeline was spooked by it, but the last thing Sarah needed was for her to bolt and ruin all their plans. She would have to placate Adeline as best she could.

'I can see you fear him, Adeline. I do understand. But we must put him off. The timing could not be worse. Maybe write back and say you cannot get permission to travel.'

'That is impossible. Why do you not listen to me?' Adeline cried. 'I will have to go.'

But MI5 could not let her go alone to face whatever Haas had planned for her. The situation was far too dangerous, the risk of Adeline revealing Allied plans too great. Haas may well have twigged that something wasn't right about Adeline's operation and her life would be in jeopardy if she showed up in Portugal. On the other hand, what if this was pre-arranged and Adeline was acting? If Sarah went to Lisbon with her, she would be extremely vulnerable. And she already harboured doubts about Adeline's trustworthiness. Still, so far, she had co-operated and sent messages they had been able to verify. Perhaps she had read too much into Adeline's flirting with Tony? She would have to put her doubts aside and put the operation first. Surely this would work if they could put aside their personal dislike and kept their relationship professional? But the reality was, Sarah had little choice. Hoping she wouldn't live to regret it; she made a snap decision.

'Very well, Adeline, but you cannot go alone. I will come with you.'

Adeline stared at her, her eyes wide. A tentative smile appeared. 'Do you mean it? You will help me? Oh, thank God!'

'Of course I will help you. You are my responsibility. Obviously, he cannot know I'm with you, but I can shadow you and do my best to ensure you are safe.'

Adeline exhaled slowly. 'I'm relieved. Thank you. He terrifies me.'

'Alright; don't worry.' Adeline looked genuinely reassured, and Sarah's fear that the whole thing was a trap faded.

'Well, there is no time like the present. You can give him the good news and write the letter this evening.' Sarah pulled the message out of her bag and laid the page on the table. 'I'll have to discuss this with my boss, of course, and investigate the best way to get there, but I'm sure we can manage it. Cheer up, Adeline. At least you won't be saying no to Haas.'

'Thank you, Sarah,' Adeline said, her voice cracking. 'I know this is difficult for you. I do not think you like me very much.'

Unfortunately perceptive, Sarah thought, but she waved her hand in dismissal. 'My feelings are irrelevant. This is my job, and you must be protected.' Sarah had almost said, *you are a valuable asset*, but had thought better of it. Adeline might not take kindly to being considered a commodity. Then, to Sarah's surprise, a flash of hurt burned in Adeline's eyes as she stood and turned away. Had the woman wanted an avowal of friendship? Was she totally oblivious to the hurt she had caused with her antics? It would appear so.

'I must fetch my things,' Adeline muttered, and disappeared off into the bedroom. Moments later, she reappeared, clutching the black leather pouch she kept her pills and toothpicks in. Frowning, she looked about the room. 'Now, where did I leave it?'

'Leave what?' Sarah asked.

'The book. The text I use for codes.' Adeline went over to the mantelpiece and rummaged through the items piled upon it. 'I had it only a few days ago.' She swung back to Sarah, ashen faced. 'This is bad. Without it, I cannot use the right code word in my letter. He will know something is wrong.'

'Calm down. It must be here in the flat. Why would anyone take it? What is it called? What does it look like?'

'It has a red cover. It is a French novel. *120 Rue de la Gare,*' she replied.

Sarah froze. That was the novel Adeline had left with Tony that awful night. Why would Adeline give Tony such an important item? A horrible thought struck Sarah. Perhaps she had misread the scene entirely that night. Sarah knew Tony had not believed her story that Adeline was just a journalist. He was far too worldly wise and would have suspected Adeline was a foreign agent. Had Tony tried to poach Adeline for US intelligence? Had he spent that Saturday night at The Embassy assessing Adeline, as opposed to what she had assumed was being over-friendly? It would explain a lot, even if it made her blood run cold. Was Adeline actually working for him now, for US intelligence? This was too much to take in. How would you even begin to unravel such a situation? Jason was the obvious person to talk to, but she cringed at the very thought. He would think she had lost her marbles! No, it was a leap too far. Tony would not risk the damage of poaching another agency's operative from under their noses. And surely, he would not do such a thing to her.

At the same moment, Adeline clutched Sarah's arm. 'All is not lost. Your boyfriend has my other copy of the book. We must get it from him at once.'

Adeline mentioning Tony in that moment made Sarah suck in her breath and stiffen.

Adeline gazed at her with concern. 'What? What is wrong?'

'It's nothing; don't worry. But I'm afraid it will be impossible to get the book from Tony. He is not in London,'

Sarah replied, peeling Adeline's fingers off her arm as a coldness swept over her.

'Do you not have a key to his flat?'

'I do not,' Sarah snapped. Though she wasn't going to explain why or admit to Adeline that her relationship with Tony was over. And that thought made her anger grow. She swivelled around to confront her. 'Why did you really give it to him, Adeline?'

'What?' Adeline would not meet her gaze.

'You heard me. Why did you give Tony that book?'

Adeline shook her head, as though confused. 'I brought two copies with me from France. I was afraid I might lose one.' She sighed. 'And that is exactly what I have done.' Her chin wobbled. 'I'm always losing important things.'

'But why give it to Tony, of all people?'

'Because he said he liked Malet's novels but could not buy them here in London. There was no ulterior motive,' Adeline said, frowning at her.

Could she believe her? It sounded a bit off, but right now, the priority was finding Adeline's copy. 'Alright, the book must be here somewhere,' Sarah said. 'We need to be method-ical. If you search in here, I'll check the bedroom.'

A quick search of Adeline's tidy bedroom gave little away. Yet, Adeline was happy enough for her to be rooting around in her things. Clearly, if she had anything to hide, it was expertly hidden elsewhere. The bedside locker revealed nothing. Sarah got down on her knees and pushed aside the eiderdown on the bed and peeked underneath. Adeline's suitcase was just visible. Sarah pulled it out, then spotted something wedged in close to the wall. It was a book with a red cover.

'I've found it,' she called out.

Adeline dashed in. 'Where was it?'

Sarah smiled up at her, holding up the book. 'Down behind the bed near the wall.'

Adeline grabbed it from her and held it to her chest. '*Mon Dieu!* It must have fallen off the locker. Today I have nothing but shocks.' With her free hand, she helped Sarah to her feet. Once she had dusted herself down, Sarah followed Adeline back into the sitting room.

'I think you had best show me how your system works,' Sarah said, sitting down at the table beside Adeline. 'How do you know which code word to use in your letters?'

Adeline flicked her a nervous look. 'I'm not sure I should tell you . . .'

Irritated, Sarah folded her arms. 'If you want my help in Lisbon, then you had better tell me, and quick.'

With a sigh, Adeline popped a couple of pills into the glass of water. 'You must tell no one.'

'Adeline!' Sarah's temper was fast coming undone.

'Alright! The important codes I have memorised. They insisted on that when I was in Berlin. Also, I must include a code word from this.' She touched the novel, now lying on the table. 'Haas gives me the key in his letters. This points me to a particular page, paragraph, sentence, and word to use. If I do not use the right word, he knows I am compromised.'

'That sounds straightforward enough, but how do you know what the key is?'

Adeline lifted Haas's letter, then let it drift back down. 'It is always the third word on the fourth line of his last letter.' She tapped midway down the page. 'See, the word is "vedette".'

186

So, I must count the letters . . . "V" is the twenty-second letter of the alphabet; so, I go to page twenty-two of the novel. The next letter is "e" . . . that is the fifth paragraph. The letter "d" gives me the sentence – which is the fourth. Then the alphabet number of the last letter of the word gives me the code word.'

'Here that is "e", so it means it is the fifth word in the sentence. Very clever,' Sarah said. 'And of course, it changes every time he writes. Beautifully simple.' Adeline nodded. 'But where do you use the code word in your response?'

'It doesn't matter. Once it makes sense, I fit it in the text, but always in the visible letter, not the secret text. Now, if we are not to be here all night, let me do it.'

'What will you say about Lisbon?' Sarah asked, watching Adeline dip the toothpick into the pill solution.

'I will say that I have to make travel arrangements and will let him know in my next letter.'

'Let's hope he's happy with that,' Sarah said.

'Happy is not a word I would associate with SS-Obergruppenführer Haas,' Adeline replied before she bent her head and began to scratch out her secret message.

21

29th April 1944, MI5, St. James's Street, London

It was first thing Saturday morning, and once again, Sarah sat before Jason with yet another problem. He had winced when she had explained the situation regarding Adeline, and Haas's request she go to Lisbon.

'I'm not happy about this, Sarah. Lisbon is a highly dangerous place. There are a few of our chaps in the embassy, but I don't know how much they could help you if you ran into trouble,' Jason said.

'I know it's not ideal, sir, but she must go. Haas will think her compromised if she doesn't and we would have to stand her down,' Sarah replied. 'I'm sure we don't want to do that with Operation Copperhead imminent and so important.'

'No, indeed, but what if it is a trap? What if he suspects she *has* turned? You would both be in danger. I'm not sure you are experienced enough to handle that kind of situation and I can't afford to lose an agent.'

That took the wind out of her, but she recovered quickly. 'Please let me try, sir. I know the risks, but she is my responsibility, so I cannot let her face this alone. Besides, we need Haas to continue to believe she is a trusted source of information. Hopefully, all he wants is to give her new instructions or merely to reassure himself that Adeline is working for him and no one else.'

Jason blew out his cheeks. 'It all seems unnecessary to me. Still, you are right; she must go. Do you think she can carry it off and convince him?'

'Honestly? I'm not one hundred percent sure. I've told you before how capricious she can be, but if I coach her well, she should come through alright.'

'Very well, but it is with some reluctance that I am giving you permission.'

'I understand, sir, and thank you,' Sarah replied.

'Miss Wilson will organise your transport and visas as quickly as possible. However, you will have to travel by boat. Journalists don't earn enough for plane tickets. If she were to arrive that way, it would only ring alarm bells with Haas. And although you will be on the same boat, you must keep apart. All transport in and out is monitored.' Jason scribbled down a note and handed it to her. 'Contact this chap in Lisbon; Nicholas Webb. His cover is that he works as press attaché to the ambassador, but he is the head of Lisbon Station. Webb will advise you once you hit the ground.'

'Thank you.'

Jason sat back and gazed at her for a moment, his expression serious. Sarah's stomach did a somersault. What could it be now? 'There is something you need to know.' He glanced down at a telegram on his desk, then picked it up. 'I received this earlier.'

Sarah swallowed hard. Telegrams were never good news these days. That was how she had learned of Paul's death. One sentence which had turned her life upside-down. Surely, fate would not be that cruel. *Please let Tony be OK!*

'It's about that chap Nikolay.'

Sarah unclenched her fists and relaxed. 'Oh?'

'It appears he and some others escaped from that camp. Unfortunately, I don't know if they got very far. If they were caught, they would have been shot. Anyway, I have requested more information, but you know how difficult it is to verify these reports.'

Sarah's heart dropped. This was terrible news, and if it got back to Adeline . . . 'He could be dead, then?'

Jason shrugged. 'As I say, we have no more details than that. However, I thought you should know.'

'Thank you, sir.'

This gave her quite a dilemma. It was one thing to keep Nikolay's capture a secret from Adeline, but if the man were dead, should she not tell her the truth? But she couldn't; the risk was too high that Adeline would betray them to Haas. Operation Fortitude would be in tatters and Sarah's career at an end. At that moment, Sarah truly hated how her job constantly tested her morals.

'And what about Hastings? How is he doing?' Jason asked.

The sudden change of topic threw Sarah, and she scrambled to answer. 'Erm, he's been with the team since lunchtime on Thursday. One of Monty's staff put him through his paces yesterday, and they were very pleased with him. However, we have run into one complication.'

Jason's gaze sharpened. 'Oh, what is that?'

'Hastings is missing the tip of one of his fingers. He saw action in the Great War and sustained a shrapnel wound. Unfortunately, I didn't notice it until yesterday.'

'Well, that's definitely a problem, Sarah. Monty has all of his!'

'It may not be, sir. Luckily, Jack McKinnock was there and has volunteered to make a prosthetic finger. If we wrap it in a bandage, Hastings can say it's just an injury. Unfortunately, Monty rarely wears gloves, which would have been a better solution, but hopefully Hastings can get away with it.'

'Hmm, well, I shall go down later myself, and see how he is getting on.' Jason threw her a stern glance. 'So much is riding on this, Sarah. We can't afford to make any mistakes. The slightest detail being off, and we will be rumbled. The Germans *must* believe Monty is in Gibraltar and not in England plotting an attack on the French coast.'

'Don't worry, sir. We have a month to get him word perfect and I will rehearse scenarios with him. Confirmation has been received that he can spend the day with Monty next Thursday. Then it's just a matter of polishing up his act.'

'I'm relying on you to ensure he does. A further request for his role-playing has been submitted. The army wants us to send him on from Gibraltar to Algiers. General Wilson is willing to have him tag along for a day or two. That will give Jerry the impression that something is going to happen on that front.'

'Do you hope the Germans will move troops south, away from the west coast?' Sarah asked.

'That would be ideal, yes. So far, our fake army in Edinburgh has kept a strong garrison of the enemy up in Norway. If we can keep the Germans stretched in France too, it should make life easier for our chaps when we do attack. The last thing we want is another Dunkirk.'

On reaching home, Sarah was delighted to discover Martin chatting away to Judith in the sitting room, having arrived back in town for another module of his training course.

'There's fresh tea in the pot,' Judith greeted her as Sarah stuck her head around the door to say hello. 'Do come and join us.'

'Lovely; I'm parched. I'll be with you in a jiffy,' Sarah replied.

'Gladys told me about that chap who caused all the bother when I was here before. I thought I was reasonably sympathetic, but she bit my head off earlier for bringing it up. I was only trying to give her some advice,' Martin was saying as Sarah went back into the room.

'But don't you see? Gladys doesn't want to lose face,' Sarah said, sitting down. Martin's eyes widened, but he made no comment. Sarah continued: 'Anyway, it's all sorted now, and she is back to her old self.'

Judith smiled. 'Oh yes, she told me off for not washing out my cup this morning.'

'There! That's typical Gladys; ruling the roost,' Sarah said. Then she cleared her throat and threw Judith a knowing glance. 'Have you told Martin about you-know-who yet?'

The colour rushed into Judith's face, and she glared back at her. 'Told him what?'

'About Ewan.'

'Oh, what's this? Ewan who?' Martin said, his gaze flicking between the two of them, alight with curiosity.

'I was going to tell him in my own good time,' Judith said between clenched teeth, before turning to Martin. 'I was just about to mention it. Then again, I suppose *she* hasn't informed you she and Tony are no longer a couple.'

'No, she has not,' Martin replied, eyes popping. 'No one tells me anything, it would appear.'

'Judith is just trying to distract you from her budding romance,' Sarah said, sticking her tongue out at her cousin.

Judith folded her arms and glared at her again before turning to her brother. 'I have gone out on a few dates with a friend of Sarah's. His name is Ewan Galbraith.'

'Ewan's a policeman, and really nice,' Sarah butted in. 'He's the chap who helped us with the Alfie problem. I've known him a while and can vouch for him.'

'Well, now I feel rather redundant. If you have already vetted him, there's nothing for me to do.' Martin grinned at Sarah.

'Thank you, Sarah!' Judith said, her head snapping around. 'You two are so funny, I'm sure, but let me tell you, it's nothing serious, so you can both stop teasing me.'

Martin smiled back at her. 'The lady doth protest too much. Better and better! I'd like to meet this fellow.'

'Get the cut of his jib?' Sarah asked with a grin.

'Exactly!' Martin answered with a wink.

'You'll scare him off!' Judith protested.

'Well, if he's intimidated by me, sister, he ain't worth bothering with,' replied Martin. 'When can I pin him down with my beady eye?'

'As it happens, Ewan will call here later. We are going out this evening,' Judith replied. Then she swivelled around to Sarah. 'Satisfied now?'

'Oh yes, very. Though you have forgotten to mention how much you like him.' Sarah focused on Martin, fully aware of Judith's Medusa-like stare. 'He's a handsome fellow and very attentive.' Sarah nodded towards Judith. 'She goes a bit doolally when he's around.'

'I do not!' Judith sniffed. 'If you must know, I haven't made up my mind about him yet.'

'What a fibber you are!' Sarah laughed. 'I'd say you're thoroughly smitten.'

The response was a cushion flung at her head as Judith marched out of the room. 'I need more tea!'

Martin flinched as the door slammed. 'Is it serious, do you think?'

'I think it might be, but it's only a couple of weeks since they met,' Sarah replied. 'Early days, but I'm hopeful. That Gerald has a lot to answer for.'

'I never met him,' he said.

'Lucky you! Anyway, let's hope Ewan can make her forget. Judith badly needs to trust a man again.'

'Sure. Look, I don't want to pry, but is it true what Judith said about you and Tony?' he asked. 'I have to admit that I'm astonished.'

'Yes, it's true. Tony wants . . . well, I'm not really sure what he wants, but the fact is that we are not an item at present.'

'Ah, Sarah, I'm sorry.'

'Thank you, but perhaps it is just a temporary break. The thing is, I more or less accused him of cheating, though I had good reason.'

Martin sucked in a breath. 'Ooh! He wouldn't have taken that well.'

'No, he didn't.' Sarah filled him in on finding Adeline at his flat.

'That's no surprise. I must admit I didn't take to the woman. A bit too flirtatious for my liking. And I couldn't help but notice she paid him a lot of attention the night of Gladys's party. But I suppose I put it down to drink and high spirits. Though Tony didn't look put out about it. Was rather lapping it up, if I recall. But her turning up at his flat does sound a bit odd, alright.'

There was some comfort in knowing that someone else had noted Adeline's behaviour and that she wasn't as paranoid as she feared. 'Yes, Tony thoroughly enjoyed the attention that night, as you say. Well, the upshot is that he is away somewhere down south, and I don't know when he will be back.'

Another week with no word at all; it didn't look promising.

'Would you like me to contact him? Maybe if I explained how you were feeling and that in the circumstances, it was reasonable; that I, too, noticed Adeline's behaviour . . .'

'Thanks, but I don't think it would help. I tried to explain it to him that night, but he didn't want to listen. If I'm honest, I think a split was inevitable.'

'But why? I thought you two were mad about each other,' Martin said with a frown.

'I love him to bits, but he could never think beyond the war, and that frustrated me.'

Martin gave her a sympathetic smile. 'Tony wouldn't be the first chap terrified of making a commitment.'

196

Sarah shrugged. 'But at some point in a relationship, you have to decide where it is going. It's not like I expected him to propose, just to talk about a possible future together when the war is over. Sorry, it sounds selfish of me when I say it out loud.'

'No, I think you are right. But you have . . . *had* such a great relationship. Goodness, we were all jealous, actually. I can't believe he would want to throw all of that away. It makes little sense to me. Tony is mad about you. Even I can see that.'

As chirpy as she could muster, she said: 'Not mad enough, it would appear. Until Tony comes back, or he contacts me, there is nothing to be done.'

Judith came back into the room while Sarah was speaking and sat down. 'Don't give up hope. Maybe the separation is a good thing. It will give him time to think, to assess how he really feels. That you were so angry about Adeline must show him how much you love him.'

Sarah laughed, but without mirth. 'Or it might have had the opposite effect and made him think I'm one of those possessive women. Also, the screaming harpy thing might have put him off.'

'And what about his stupid male pride? Besides, he can't have been blind to Adeline's behaviour. It is better to stand up for yourself than to be meek and accepting,' Judith said. 'Look where that's got me in the past. We all make mistakes, and in this instance, it was Tony in the wrong. He should have reassured you when he saw how upset you were; instead, he has risked throwing away everything you have together.'

'Write to him. I'm sure his office would forward it,' Martin said.

'But that would be admitting I was mistaken, that I had misconstrued what I saw,' she said with a self-depreciating shrug. 'And I'm not sure I did. I know I shouldn't have lost my temper, but he shouldn't have been so defensive about her presence in his flat.'

Martin grinned. 'Yes. In effect, Tony threw fuel on the fire.' Sarah didn't miss the knowing glance shared by her cousins.

Sarah smarted but smiled despite herself. 'Yes. Alright; I've already admitted I have a stupid temper. Perhaps I'll write to him when I get back.'

'Back from where?' Judith asked. 'Somewhere nice? Did you get some leave at last?'

'No, it's for work and it's out of the country. Sorry, I can't tell you any more than that.'

'Will it be dangerous?' Martin asked, sitting forward, suddenly serious.

'No, no, of course not,' Sarah replied breezily. How she hated to lie, but she didn't want them to worry. And if Aunt Alice and Uncle Tom heard about it, they would be worried sick. Not that the thought of the trip didn't make her stomach churn. Consorting with the enemy, even as an observer, sent shivers through her. Sarah knew from talk at work that Lisbon was a hotbed of spies vying for information and position, often mingling at the same places and events. It all sounded rather bizarre, surreal even. More to the point, was she ready for such a dangerous assignment? She'd had little field experience since the mission with Tony in Wales. And Tony would not be there to guide her; to have her back. This trip would be the greatest test she had faced yet and a mission she had to undertake with a woman she neither liked nor trusted. Worst of all, the latest news on Nikolay wasn't good. How would she feel if someone knew Tony was in trouble and kept it from her? But what choice did she have? To tell Adeline would risk everything. It didn't sit easy with her, but the greater good had to prevail.

22

It was evening when their ship docked. Sarah watched
Adeline walk down the gangway, and soon she had disappeared into the crowd milling about on the brightly lit
dockside. Sarah scanned the city, stretched out before her
as it spread upwards into the hills. How extraordinary it
was to see a city illuminated, bringing home how used she
had become to the misery of blackout. But as a neutral
country, much like Ireland, there was no need for total
darkness here.

President Salazar was adept at keeping Portugal out of
the war, despite pressure from both the Axis and Allied
powers. However, the result was that Lisbon was now a
hotbed of espionage, with agents from both sides cheek by
jowl engaged in conspiracies and subterfuge on a grand
scale. Sarah knew from her briefing with Jason that Portugal's
vast supplies of wolfram – a metal key to strengthening

steel and therefore invaluable to all sides in the war – was Portugal's main negotiating tool. So far, it had helped to keep Portugal out of the conflict, but also increased its financial stability. SIS and MI5 suspected Jerry was using confiscated gold to pay for the wolfram, which only made the officers in Lisbon Station even more determined to expose the transactions. However, the high value put on the metal, especially by the Germans, had led to an underground smuggling operation controlled by German agents based in Lisbon. There was speculation that the metal was being smuggled across the border into Spain, which was, of course, sympathetic to the German cause. Despite English objections to Salazar, the operation was still ongoing and a source of tension between Britain and Portugal. Spies on both sides were up to their necks in skulduggery, each trying to outdo the other in undermining their position, hoping the authorities would expel the other agents. Jason warned Sarah to be careful and to trust no one other than Nicholas Webb and his operatives.

Sarah fixed her gaze on the quay below with its huge cranes and warehouses. It was hard to believe that earlier in the war, when there was a threat of invasion hanging over Portugal, Lisbon Station SOE agents had drawn up plans to destroy as much infrastructure in the country as possible, including the port, to stop a German advance. Thankfully, it hadn't been necessary.

Sarah's gaze travelled along the quay, but there was no longer any sign of Adeline. Losing sight of her wasn't an issue, as even on the boat journey, they had stayed apart. They had had to in case Haas had Adeline under surveillance. The Germans were notorious for bribing the

Portuguese to spy for them as the local population was predominantly poor and easy targets for the intrigues of the Nazis.

By agreement, Adeline would make her way to the hotel and they would meet up there later. Lisbon Station had warned Sarah that the Portuguese secret police – Polícia de Vigilância e de Defesa do Estado, reputedly styled on the Gestapo – watched all disembarking passengers closely. As did the Nazis and MI6. It would almost be comical if it wasn't so scary; all these spies falling over each other. However, it was sensible to be cautious. The PVDE were obsessed with tracking alien spies, and Sarah knew she would be questioned closely when she made it to the customs checkpoint further down the harbour.

Sarah prayed her cover as a reporter here to interview the ambassador would hold. It was the best solution MI5 had come up with to explain her presence in the city, but it also gave her a reason to visit Lisbon Station, which was based in the grounds of the embassy. The following day, Sarah was due to meet Nicholas Webb there. His role on the embassy staff was that of press attaché, which gave them a perfectly good reason to meet. But they could not be seen together in public until that first meeting was conducted to establish her false identity. Sarah's true role had to be kept secret or the entire operation would fail before it had begun. It was not unknown for both sides to whisk away suspected turned agents, most of whom were never seen again.

An even worse situation that might arise would be if Haas detected even a hint of subterfuge on Adeline's part. He would not hesitate to act and Sarah knew that few could withstand Nazi interrogation techniques. Sarah would have to run for her life, and every agent Adeline could identify would be in danger. Luckily, Adeline did not know that Normandy was the proposed landing site for the Allies, but if she were to reveal even some of what she knew, the Germans would soon realise Calais was not the intended destination of any invasion force. Then Jerry would re-group and defend Normandy at full strength, and the Allies would have to defer or come up with a new plan, wasting precious time. It would mean months of planning down the drain, not to mention all the unnecessary deaths due to the delays. Sarah had to push the thoughts from her mind. It was too awful to contemplate. She had to remain focused and, even more importantly, keep Adeline on track.

Adeline's visa stated she was here briefly to visit family, and she had even brought along Haas's last letter as proof she had an uncle in Lisbon. What the PVDE would make of it, Sarah wasn't sure. Hopefully, the alias used by Haas was unknown to them, and Adeline would be let through. Still, Sarah prayed the coaching given to Adeline at St. James's Street would be sufficient. They needed the woman to be unflappable, but Sarah knew only too well it was like Russian roulette when it came to Adeline's moods and behaviour. As a result, Sarah had slept little the last few nights before departure. Adeline's silence on the train journey to Southampton hadn't reassured Sarah much, either.

Sarah waited a further five minutes before she set foot on dry land. She was carrying her small suitcase and a handbag, which hid the fact that her hands were shaking. She followed the other weary-looking travellers to a large building on the quay. There, they had to join a long queue of passengers waiting to be processed. Although it took a good half hour to get through, and someone indeed questioned her at length, Sarah was relieved to be waved towards the exit. MI5's fake documentation had worked. That was the first hurdle overcome.

A line of taxis was waiting by the roadside outside the port. Sarah nabbed one and slipped into the back seat. The taxi pulled away into the city traffic and Sarah allowed herself a moment to relax and take in the sights. Such a pity she would only be here for a few days; the city was so different in architecture to Dublin or London. Her first time setting foot in Europe, too. Unfortunately, not with Tony, as she had always hoped. *Blast it! Why did he have to pop into my head like that?* Her nails pushed into her palms. She had to accept their relationship was over. It did no good to dwell on any of it. But her mind had been treacherous in these last few weeks, dropping memories of him, his voice, and his touch into her head when she least expected it.

What would he make of this mission if he knew of it? Was it time to admit that she had jumped at this chance to prove herself not only to progress her career as a spy, but also to gain Tony's respect? It hardly mattered – how would he hear of it? – and there would be time enough to analyse her motivation when she and Adeline were both safely back in Blighty.

As the taxi climbed towards the Hotel Dora, in the Bairro Alto district, the streets narrowed, with tall buildings towering on either side. The taxi now had to compete with trams as it bumped over the tracks, climbing ever higher into the back streets. Sarah caught glimpses of cafés and bars, hotels, and restaurants. Most striking of all was the number of people out and about at this hour of the evening. The taxi swung onto Rua da Misericordia and continued to ascend before pulling over to the kerb. Sarah paid the cabdriver and stepped out of the taxi, looking about. The buildings were tall, four or five storeys high, with large floor to ceiling windows and metal railings surrounding their balconies. Some buildings were faced with beautiful old tiles; though in places she could see some were broken. There was a neglected feel to the street, too. A hint that for all the liveliness of the city now, the pre-war economy had not been a thriving one.

A couple came out the hotel door in high spirits, and Sarah's attention returned to the building before her. The sign above the entrance proclaimed it to be 'Hotel Dora'. Well, she was here, it was time to play her part. With luck, Adeline had found her way here too, hopefully without mishap. With mixed feelings, Sarah gripped her bag tightly and pushed through the door.

The small reception area was empty but for a young man standing behind the desk. He looked up and smiled in welcome.

'Good evening,' Sarah said, hoping he spoke English.

'Good evening, miss, and welcome to Hotel Dora,' he replied. 'Do you have a reservation?'

'Yes, I do. My name is Miss Butterworth, and I am here for four nights.'

'Ah, yes, miss. Room twelve.' He rummaged around under the desk before placing a pad before her. 'If you could fill in this registration form for me, that would be good. And please, I must see your identity papers and passport.'

'Of course,' she replied, pulling out the required documents. He examined them carefully while she filled in her details on the form. When he turned to get her key from the rack behind the desk, Sarah quickly scanned the forms underneath. Adeline was in room fifteen.

The receptionist took the pad back and handed her the key. 'Thank you, miss. Do you need help with your bags?'

Sarah held up her small bag. 'Thank you, but that won't be necessary.'

He nodded. 'The lift is around the corner, miss, and your room is on the third floor.'

Sarah found her room easily enough. Through habit, she didn't turn on the light when she entered in case the curtains were open. Then she paused and smiled to herself; the precaution was unnecessary here. She flicked the light switch and was pleasantly surprised. The room was large and clean, though scantily furnished with only a bed, and a dresser with a wash bowl and jug. She dropped her bag down on the bedcover and wandered over to the open window, drawn by the sound of traffic and voices. Her training kicked in and she scanned the street below, but there were no suspicious-looking characters lurking in the shadowy doorways. Everything looked innocent enough and somehow, that was more unsettling than if she had seen someone watching the hotel. Perhaps the secret police didn't need to follow people, having the likes of the receptionist below in their pay. She drew the curtains and did a quick sweep of the room, searching for any listening devices. All clear. She glanced at her watch. Hopefully, Adeline was well settled in by now. Sarah ran a brush through her hair and splashed her face before making her way up to the fourth floor.

Adeline answered her door swiftly after one knock, and Sarah wondered if she had been standing beside it, anxiously waiting. She was certainly pale.

'Is everything alright?' Sarah asked.

'Yes. But this was waiting for me,' Adeline said, handing Sarah a note. 'Haas wants to meet me tomorrow morning at Café Chave d'Ouro in Rossio Square. You will come too?'

'Of course,' Sarah replied.

The tension left Adeline's shoulders, and she smiled. 'That is a relief. I must admit I am terrified.'

'There is no need,' Sarah said. 'If you stay calm, everything will be alright. Now, best we go over those possible questions again.' She sat down on the bed and gave her charge a sympathetic look. 'Stop worrying; you will be fine.'

But Adeline hugged herself and paced up and down. 'I wish I knew what he wanted with me.'

So do I! Sarah thought, but she didn't voice her concern. It looked as if Adeline was jumpy enough already. If Adeline lost her nerve, they would be in deep trouble.

'What if he knows I am working for you? You said they were watching me in London.'

'No, no. I was mistaken about that,' Sarah said.

Adeline glared in response. 'Why didn't you tell me? I have been scared.'

'It slipped my mind,' Sarah murmured, not without a little guilt. That situation was far from resolved but there was little point in both of them worrying about it.

Adeline continued to pace. 'Maybe they watch us here.' Then she stopped in front of her, wringing her hands.

'Haas may well have you watched, Adeline, and we have no way of knowing what the local secret police are up to.

We must assume the worst. But we have been careful, and I made sure no one saw me come up here to your room. If we keep our distance from each other, we should be fine.'

'It's easy for you; I'm the one who has to meet him face to face,' Adeline replied. 'If he suspects me, anything could happen. What if he has found out that I was hiding Nikolay for all those months? He will not trust me anymore and all will be lost. Haas is capable of anything.'

Sarah swallowed hard. Perhaps Haas *had* connected Nikolay and Adeline. It all hinged on whether Adeline's Resistance friends had betrayed her. But she could hardly discuss that possibility with Adeline without revealing the bad news about Nikolay. The woman was already in a state.

'You need to calm down. If you are like this with him tomorrow, he will definitely suspect something isn't right. You must act normally with him, as you would have done before, in Paris and Berlin.'

Adeline stopped before her and scowled. 'But I am not a block of stone, like you,' she countered. 'I have emotions. I am afraid.'

The jibe hurt. If only Adeline knew how bad her inner anxiety was. How many unpleasant thoughts she had to push down. The pressure Sarah was under was enormous. Having to come to Lisbon at a crucial time in Hastings' preparations was unfortunate, not to mention the danger coming here posed. The machinations of the players they faced here were obscure. Murky characters, most of them, waiting in the shadows to pounce. And on top of all of this, she had to deal with the realisation that her emotional turmoil hadn't diminished at all. But, if she gave in and admitted how much she missed Tony, she would not be able to carry on. Work helped to block it all out. That was where all her focus had to be.

'When you meet Haas tomorrow, you must be calm and civil,' Sarah said. 'If you show weakness or anxiety, he will pounce on it. He may well be testing you by bringing you here. A man of his experience will know the signs to watch for. It is vital we are professional at all times, if we are to get through this safely.'

Adeline shook her head and sat down with a sigh. 'Yes, I understand the situation only too well. However, I am baffled. Here I am, terrified of this man, and you are so calm. I do not understand you, Sarah Gillespie.'

It was on the tip of Sarah's tongue to agree with her.

23

7th May 1944, Café Chave d'Ouro, Rossio, Lisbon

It was a beautiful morning. Sarah jumped down from the yellow tram on reaching Rossio Square and glanced at her watch. She had plenty of time to reach the café and decide where best to sit to ensure she could observe Adeline and Haas undetected. As she strolled along the square, Sarah enjoyed the warmth of the sun on her face. If only she were here as a tourist, for she had caught glimpses of quaint narrow streets during the journey from the hotel. Maybe when the war was over, she could come back and explore the city properly.

Soon, she spotted the grand entrance of the café and headed across the square. Inside, it was buzzing with people; it was obviously a popular spot on a Sunday morning. Perhaps the locals came here after church as everyone appeared to be in their best clothes. Sarah gazed around the enormous room, and up to a mezzanine floor. When a waiter approached her, she indicated she wished to sit up there. Once she had ordered her coffee, she pulled a book from her bag. Now, all she had to do was wait. Was she conspicuous, sitting on her own? Hopefully not.

Having studied photographs of Haas, she recognised him immediately when he entered the café. He was even more striking in person. Gaunt about the face, with the rigid bearing of a military man, Haas was an intimidating sight. From his file, she knew him to be in his late fifties with quite the army record and a reputation that would give one sleepless nights if one dwelt on it for long. It wasn't hard to believe he had shot one of his own.

Whatever he barked at the waiter had the man scurrying away. Totally at his ease, Haas beckoned over another man, more formally dressed than the waiters, who Sarah guessed must be the manager. After a brief discussion, Haas was shown to a table on the ground floor, close to the entrance. Was that so that he would spot Adeline straight away, or was it a clever exit strategy in case of unforeseen circumstances? Surely, such a man had a price on his head. Sarah would have to ask Webb about the failed attempts on Haas's life, when she met him later. Suddenly glad she didn't have to deal with him, Sarah looked away and kept her nose in her book.

It was almost twenty minutes later when Adeline strolled into the café, looking every inch a Parisian lady. On spotting her, Haas jumped to his feet. Adeline waved away the waiter who had rushed up to her and made her way to Haas. They greeted each other in the French fashion, then sat down. So far, so good. As luck would have it, Adeline was facing in Sarah's direction so she could just about read her expressions. Things looked to be friendly so far.

It was difficult to stay inconspicuous, seated alone, and Sarah knew she could not watch the couple continuously; it might draw the wrong kind of attention. Jason had warned her that all the bars and cafés were full of either the Portuguese secret police, their spies, or German agents. It was even possible they had followed her from the hotel, even though she had double backed twice to shake off anyone who might be following her. After a few minutes, she took another peek downstairs. Adeline looked calm and was nodding at Haas. And suddenly, Sarah was proud of her. It looked as if the interview was going well. But it was so frustrating to be at a distance. Sarah longed to know what they were talking about. Would Adeline tell her the truth when she debriefed her back at the hotel? All Sarah could do was order another coffee and do her best to be patient.

At last, Haas summoned a waiter and paid the bill. Sarah was relieved to see them both stand and prepare to leave. Perhaps all was well and there was no danger; the meeting purely to discuss procedure or to reassure Haas that Adeline was still under his control. Gradually, the tension left Sarah's body. She had not dared to hope things would go as smoothly as this. But suddenly Haas bent down and said something into Adeline's ear, his hand gripping her upper arm. Even from a distance, Sarah could tell the colour drained from Adeline's face. Sarah's stomach clenched in alarm. This didn't bode well at all.

Once Sarah reckoned Haas was at a safe distance, she followed Adeline out onto the square. A second later, and she would have missed seeing Adeline hop onto a tram. It was the same number tram Sarah had taken to get to the square from the hotel. It was safe to assume Adeline was headed back to Rua da Misericordia. Sarah hung back, pretending to look at a shop window. As much as she longed to know what was going on, she had to take precautions. Reflected in the window, she spotted a well-built, blond-haired man in a trilby hat, run up at the last minute and jump onto Adeline's tram just as it was about to pull away. She had seen him in the café earlier. Could he be following Adeline for Haas? At least she knew what he looked like and could keep an eye out for him again. If he was lurking outside the hotel when she got back, it would confirm her suspicions.

It almost killed her to wait and hear what Haas had said to Adeline, but it was an hour later before Sarah reached their hotel. Sure enough, the blond man was standing opposite the building, smoking a cigarette, as casual as you please. Keeping her gaze averted, Sarah entered Hotel Dora, praying she had not come to his notice.

As she put the key into the door of her room, she heard footsteps coming from the stairwell at the end of the hallway. Nervously, she waited, her grip on the door handle. Was she about to be ambushed?

Next thing, Adeline's head popped around the corner.

Relieved, and with her heart pounding, Sarah pushed open her door. 'Hurry! Get in!'

Adeline hastened past her and collapsed onto the bed. 'I thought you would never get back.'

'Shh!' Sarah replied, checking both ways in the corridor before finally closing her room door. 'We must be careful.' She took off her jacket and hung it up on the hook on

214

the back of the door. 'Now, tell me all. What did he say to you and, most importantly, what does he want?'

'Oh, Sarah. It was horrible. He was curt and correct, which is what I always expect from him, but . . .'

'But?' Sarah prompted.

'I think you are right. He suspects something isn't right. He grilled me about all those troop movement reports I sent for you. Wanted to know exactly how I came across the information.'

'Yes, but we were prepared for that,' Sarah replied.

'Yes, yes, and I think I persuaded him. I hoped that would be all, but then as we were about to leave, he said he needed me to do something for him.'

'Uh-oh, what?'

'There is an Englishman by the name of Carter who lives out in Estoril. Haas says he haunts the casino there.' Adeline frowned down at her hands, clenched in her lap. 'He wants me to go out there and to befriend this man.'

'Why?'

'Haas believes Carter is involved in helping prisoners of war escape from the German camps in France. Haas wants me to find out where the man hides these men before they board the ships or planes for England. He believes it is somewhere here in the city.'

Sarah sat down beside Adeline and blew out a long breath. 'Damn!'

'I know. This is not good. I do not like the idea, but what choice do I have? I must try.'

'Yes, we have no choice, but somehow, we must warn the man involved. If he is smuggling POWs back to England, we don't want to endanger that operation.'

'I don't see how we can warn him,' Adeline said with a bewildered expression.

'But don't you see, if Haas is correct about the smuggling, Carter is on our side, and Lisbon Station will be involved and know him. They may even be working with him. I'm due to meet the head of the station at the embassy in about an hour. I'll discuss it with him; he'll know the best course of action for us to take.'

This seemed to appease Adeline. 'What do I do now?' she asked.

Sarah jumped up and grabbed her jacket. 'Don't worry. Go back to your room once the coast is clear and stay out of sight. I'll be back as soon as I can.' Sarah turned, her hand on the door. 'By the way, you do have a tail.'

'What?' Adeline stared at her.

Sarah laughed. 'Sorry! It's an expression. There is a man following you. I spotted him getting on your tram when you were leaving the square. Blond hair, black trilby. He's probably one of Haas's men, but we expected that. He's outside on the street. Whatever you do, don't get caught looking out your window for him.'

'Wonderful!' Adeline exclaimed, jumping to her feet with a grimace. 'Just wonderful.'

24

7th May 1944, The British Embassy, Rua de São Domingos, Lisbon

The embassy on Rua de São Domingos was housed in the Palácio de Porto Corvo, and only a twenty-minute journey by tram. It was a beautifully proportioned structure, about halfway down the steep street. In the distance, at the bottom of the road, Sarah could glimpse the ocean sparkling in the afternoon sun. Tempting as it might be to explore the area, she had work to do. Sarah presented her identification papers at the main door and was escorted to a waiting room. But it was unlike any waiting room she had seen before, with its ornate plasterwork, and painted ceiling from which hung an enormous chandelier. French doors led outside to a manicured garden.

She had barely sat down when those doors swung open, and a dapper, red-haired man breezed in.

'Sarah Gillespie?' he asked, coming towards her with an outstretched hand.

'Yes.' They shook hands.

'Excellent. I'm Nick Webb. Glad you found us alright. Come along with me. My office is far more comfortable for us to have our little chat.' He linked her arm and steered her back out the doors, through the garden to another building. 'It's nice and quiet here today, being a Sunday. Is your hotel to your liking? We try to use different ones each time we have one of our lot over. Don't want Jerry to know where our chaps are.'

Nick stopped at an unmarked door and pushed it open. 'Here we are. Take a seat. I've ordered tea. Or would you prefer coffee?'

Sarah was thinking she'd never get a word in. 'Tea is perfect, sir, thank you.'

Nick sat down beside her on the ornate sofa and smiled. 'Welcome to Lisbon Station.'

Sarah glanced around the room. 'Thank you, sir. It's certainly different to St. James's Street.'

Nick grinned back at her. 'Yes, better weather, too. So, tell me, do you think an hour would be sufficient for you to stay here? The ambassador is in residence today, so if anyone is snooping around, your presence here to interview him will look legitimate. I dare say London will pop an article in one of the papers, just for the fun of it. They do like to close the loop on these things.'

'Yes, thank you, that should be long enough.' She pulled a wad of pages out of her bag. 'I've already prepared some notes, which I can peruse on my way back to the hotel on the tram, in case anyone is following me.'

'By Jove! That's clever of you. Ah, here's the tea. Shall I be mother?'

A young girl left the tray down on the table in front of them, smiled at Sarah, and nodded to Nick before slipping back out the door.

'My secretary, Doris,' Nick said, pouring Sarah a cup. 'Bright as a button, she is. The service could do with more like her. Sugar?'

'No, thanks.'

'Well, has your lady met up with Haas yet?'

Sarah suspected he already knew and probably had a detailed report of the meeting sitting on his desk across the room. 'Yes, at a café in Rossio this morning.'

'Any difficulties?' he asked, his gaze steady.

'Yes, I'm afraid so.' Sarah placed her cup and saucer down on the table and turned to him. 'My girl is in a bit of a quandary. Haas has given her an assignment.'

'Has he indeed? I'm intrigued. What does he want her to do?'

Sarah filled him in.

'Hmm, I suspected they knew about Carter. That is unfortunate. This evening, you say?'

'Yes. She is to befriend him and then wheedle the information out of him. Haas didn't exactly say how she was to do it, but I think we can both guess.'

'Is she an attractive lady?'

'She is, and French to boot.'

'Ah-ha, poor old Carter would certainly be responsive!' Then Nick shook his head. 'Not the most original way to gather intelligence, but you would be surprised how often it works.'

'Should we warn Mr Carter?' Sarah asked.

'What? Oh, yes. Do you know, I think we can use this to our advantage. We can lead Jerry to the location and then we will know who *they* are, perhaps even neutralise them.'

This was said with a great deal of satisfaction. Sarah wasn't quite sure she liked his meaning, but Lisbon was his affair. Her only concern was Adeline.

'Sir, it's important for us to maintain Adeline's credentials with Haas. It is vital she passes critical but false information to him in the next few weeks. We can't afford for her cover to be revealed.'

'Don't worry. We can instruct Carter to give her some tempting nuggets. Last night, we got a few chaps out on a flight to Bristol. The house we have been using lately is empty now, so it would be safe enough to reveal that address. We will ensure there is some evidence of their stay left behind, which should satisfy Haas and keep your girl in his good books. Losing the location doesn't pose us much difficulty. Alternative locations in the city are easy to find. No more than the hotels, we try not to utilise the same place too often if we can help it.'

'That's a relief, sir. Thank you. May I tell her to go ahead?'

Yes, I'll get a message to Carter straight away. He's a good sport and will play along.'

'What's his background?'

'Carter is an ex-pat and has been living here for some time. At the beginning of the war, he came to us keen to help out. Rich as Croesus and a jolly useful fellow, actually. To most, he is merely a useless playboy, but he joined SOE as soon as it was set up.'

'The Resistance and SOE in France have been scooping

up escaped POWs. Carter has them picked up by his company trucks, which then travel down through Spain and here to Lisbon. Blast Haas! I wonder how he figured out Carter's involvement. Just a pity we will have to stop using him for a while.' Nick sighed. 'It's a constant headache, you know. We expose some of the Jerry agents and then they retaliate in kind. Just as well the crew here enjoy the challenge of ducking and diving.'

'Should I go to Estoril with her, sir?'

'No. Don't risk it. You are bound to be tailed leaving here and once you have been connected to the embassy, they will follow you until you leave the country. Suspicious blighters, the lot of 'em!'

'Who do you think it will be, sir? The Germans or the Portuguese PVDE?'

'Probably the local secret police. Fancy themselves as spy catchers,' Nick said with a wide grin. However, it didn't give Sarah much comfort. 'Why the anxious look? Let her go. Trust her to do a good job and report back when she's done,' he said.

'It's just that Adeline is unpredictable.'

'Do you doubt her loyalty?' Nick asked with a frown. 'Perhaps we should not risk letting her loose in Estoril?'

'No, she is loyal. If you saw how terrified she is of Haas, you would understand. That fear is genuine.'

'That doesn't surprise me. He has quite a reputation,' Nick said with a shake of his head. 'I could tell you some tales about that blighter.'

'I have heard some disturbing things about him already, sir. However, I believe her fear would be absent if Adeline were truly working for him. In fact, for the first time since

I've started working with her, I am confident she is actually on our side. It's more that she can be temperamental on occasion. Tiresome stuff, but I can handle it.'

'I don't envy her. Haas is SS, as you probably know.' Sarah nodded. 'We have pretty good intelligence that he was involved in the transport of Jews to some of the camps in Germany and Austria. Not a man you want to cross.'

'She knows that,' Sarah replied.

'Good. You don't want her to walk into anything unprepared. And when does she report back to Haas again?'

'Tuesday afternoon at a bar in Baixa.'

'Gosh, he isn't giving her much time.'

'That concerns me, too, sir. Still, if Carter is playing along, anyone watching them will think she is succeeding.'

'Let us hope so. Well, it looks like you will be free this evening. Fancy a spot of dinner?'

'Would it not look odd, sir?' Sarah asked, slightly taken aback, even though Nick had been openly eyeing her up.

'Not at all. I'm press attaché and you're a journalist. I rather think it would be odd if we didn't have some social interaction. I know a nice little place close to your hotel. Would seven-thirty suit you?'

'Yes, certainly, and thank you, sir.'

'Oh please, call me Nick.' Again, the rather friendly grin. 'We don't stand on ceremony here.' At least she wouldn't have to spend the evening alone at the hotel, worrying about Adeline.

'I gather it's a small community, sir . . . Nick. Do all the spies know each other? It must be strange.' Sarah was intrigued and curious. It all sounded like something out of a movie.

'Yes. Gosh, the number of times I've sat on a tram with a blasted Jerry sitting across from me. We all frequent the same bars and clubs too. Dashed awkward sometimes. You want to give the blighters a good thrashing, but it wouldn't be the done thing in public.'

'I'd heard that MI6 had attempted to liquidate Haas,' Sarah probed.

'Well, between you and me, they made a hash of it. Someone blabbed,' Nick replied.

'Did they find out who?'

'Yes, though what happened to him I'm not sure. As you can imagine, there wasn't much sympathy for the chap in the service.'

'I can imagine. But on a day-to-day basis, what do you do when you do come face to face with one of the German agents?' she asked.

'I stare right through him, and he does the same,' Nick replied with a grin. 'With the PVDE everywhere, you can't react. If we annoy the local secret police, we could find ourselves on the first flight out, back to Blighty.' He waved his hand and looked about the room. 'Would you want to leave this behind for the dreariness of London?' His gaze came back to rest on her. 'I don't suppose you'd fancy transferring here for the duration? I've heard nothing but good things about you from Jason and we could do with some fresh blood.'

Taken aback, Sarah finally managed: 'I'm . . . flattered, sir, but I'd have to think about that.'

Nick smiled in response as he picked up the teapot. 'Make sure you do. More tea before you go?'

25

7th May 1944, Hotel Dora, Rua da Misericordia, Lisbon

Adeline stalled in her packing and looked across at Sarah, her features frozen in horror. 'What do you mean you are not coming to Estoril? You are joking, but it is not funny. We are a team.' She gave a dry laugh and tossed her head. 'You must come.'

'No, Adeline. You need to understand the seriousness of our situation. Haas mustn't know I am here, not just to ensure my safety, but yours, too. Do you wish to disappear into the bowels of the German embassy, never to be seen again? I certainly don't!'

'No, of course not, but it will not happen if you are there to protect me.'

'That's impossible, Adeline. You are already under surveillance by his man, and I am reliably informed that I am being followed by the Portuguese secret police.'

'Who said this?' Adeline scoffed.

'The head of the British secret service station here in Lisbon. He'd hardly make it up!'

Adeline made a face. 'I do not like this place. It is full of spies.'

Sarah spluttered with laughter. 'Which is exactly what we are!'

'Yes, but we have honour,' Adeline replied, perfectly serious. 'These foreigners are nasty.'

With a sigh, Sarah sat down on the other side of the bed. 'Adeline, I know what I am asking of you is dangerous, but if I am seen at Estoril in your company, either − or even both our tails − will soon realise what is going on. So far, we have been lucky. As it is, every time there is a knock on my hotel room door, I almost panic. I wouldn't be surprised if the hotel staff were in the pay of either the police or enemy agents. And that is why this specific mission can only be completed by you, on your own.'

'Oh no! I refuse.'

'Adeline, please be reasonable.'

Her nostrils flared, her eyes flashing a warning. 'Always, I am reasonable, but you promised before we left England that you would protect me. I would not have agreed to come if you had not.' Adeline wagged a finger at her. 'This man, Carter, might be a trap. Perhaps he really works for Haas, and they are testing me. My mutilated body will be found and then you will be sorry!'

'God, Adeline! Why the dramatics? Carter is on *our* side. He works for . . . well, I can't tell you exactly, but he is one of us. A message has been sent to him and he will expect you to turn up. All you need to do is to play along and go through the motions. Carter will give you the information Haas wants. It won't be an issue. You must trust us.'

'Do you think I have survived this long by trusting people? You are a fool, Sarah.' Adeline pushed the lid of her case closed and sat down on the bed and folded her arms, her shoulders hunched. 'I will not go without you. There is nothing you can say that will change my mind.'

'But if you don't do as Haas asks—'

'Yes! It will be the end for all of us. But I will not be . . . what is the expression . . . cannon food?'

'Fodder!'

'Pah!' Adeline exclaimed.

Sarah was both impressed by the spy's audaciousness but also deeply frustrated. Adeline was constantly resisting direction. But Sarah had no comeback. The woman was right. If Adeline didn't complete the mission for Haas, it would make him suspicious of her. If he investigated deeply enough, he might discover who Sarah was. They would be vulnerable, especially so far from home. Damn! She'd have to make the best of it and go.

'Very well, Adeline. I'm not happy about this, but I will go to Estoril on the understanding that you do exactly as I tell you.'

Adeline's response was a smile of triumph.

Sarah stood. She would now have to cancel the dinner date with Nick. But had she given in too easily? Too late for regrets now. Sarah paused at the door of Adeline's room. 'I must leave a message for my colleague from the embassy down at reception. Finish your packing.'

'Oh, yes, I am sorry you are missing a boring work dinner.' Adeline smirked. 'But there will be a host of sophisticated rich men at the casino at Estoril. Even in Paris, we heard about the place. I am eager to see it for myself.'

If Sarah didn't know better, she would say Adeline was positively ecstatic at the prospect. She, however, had to concentrate on practicalities. 'We will have to travel by train but on different ones, obviously. The same for our accommodation. We cannot risk being seen together. Be ready to leave in an hour.'

'But we cannot go this evening,' Adeline announced.

Taking a deep breath, Sarah turned back into the room. 'Why?'

'We will need better clothes to carry this off. The casino is home to the elite and royalty. I cannot act my part without the proper clothes and if you are to be there too, you will need something better than what I have seen you in so far.'

Sarah didn't miss the dig at her clothing choices, but in a world of rationing, few had options for being fashionable. 'Adeline, you cannot be serious. Where are we going to get new clothes? And more to the point, who will pay?' Sarah asked through gritted teeth. Her patience was running out.

Adeline cocked her head. 'Ah! Haas insisted on giving me funds.' She reached for her handbag and pulled out a wad of money. Sarah could only stare. 'You see, I can look after our interests as well as you. We cannot travel until the morning. First thing, after breakfast, I will go out and get dresses for us. I can guess your size. So, now you do not have to cancel your boring dinner.' Adeline waved her hand in dismissal as she reopened her suitcase.

Not trusting herself to speak, Sarah left.

An hour later, as she tramped down the stairs to meet Webb, it was some consolation that Adeline hadn't argued about staying at a different hotel at Estoril. A minor concession on the woman's part, but Sarah was grateful for it. She had expected another tiresome argument. Sometimes, she suspected Adeline acted as she did to drive her crazy. But much more of this stress and she would be a nervous wreck.

★　★　★

Early the following afternoon, as the packed train pulled out of Lisbon bound for Estoril, Sarah allowed herself to relax a little. What a bizarre assignment this was turning out to be. Adeline was even more of a nightmare than before, and she had not thought that possible. Sometimes, Sarah was mystified by her behaviour and what her motivation really was. Why did she always kick back and resist direction? Adeline had approached MI5, asking to work for them, and yet she always acted as if she was doing them an enormous favour. Did she not realise the authorities could just as easily have had her incarcerated or worse? There were days when Sarah regretted recruiting her to the service. If this all blew up, it would all be down to her. If MI5's activities were revealed to the Nazis, the Allied forces would be going straight into a trap, and countless lives would be lost. Yet she had no one to confide in and no one would believe her if she told them how extraordinarily complicated her life had become. Well, perhaps Tony would, having been through many perilous assignments with the SOE while in France. But he was out of reach.

What are you like, girl? Sarah sighed. It was dangerous to let herself think about him. *I must stop torturing myself*, she thought, while pulling a well-handled photograph from her purse, the one of Tony in his white naval uniform. The one that always made her smile, recalling how embarrassed he was when he had given it to her and how delighted she had been to receive it. It had taken ages to persuade him. It was touching, sometimes, how sensitive he could be. Behind the tough exterior, he was a real softy. At least she had thought so then, but his behaviour that night they split up . . . it had certainly shown a different side to him. A hardness she had almost forgotten he could employ. Their first meeting had left her reeling; he had been so obnoxious and deeply distrustful. Then, as they had grown closer, that hard outer shell had gradually disappeared.

So why had he acted the way he did the night they split up? Deep down, she knew he hadn't had a fling with Adeline. It was almost as if he had been waiting for an excuse to ditch her and she had provided him with it when her temper got the better of her. Why had he not been honest with her if he had had doubts? Instead, he had left her feeling she had been the one in the wrong. One thing Sarah did know for sure; it was going to take a long time to get over him.

Now Sarah cringed at her own weakness. It had been a stupid impulse to bring his photo to Portugal, but she couldn't help herself. If she were found with it, it would raise some awkward questions. Should she scrunch it up into a ball and chuck it out the window of the train? No. *To hell with it*, she'd take the risk, for she couldn't bear to part with it, not now, when it was all she had left of him. With one last look, she tucked the photograph back into her bag. It took a few moments to regain her equilibrium, so Sarah stared out the window, but the passing landscape was blurred by her tears.

26

8th May 1944, Estoril, Portugal

An hour later, the train pulled into Estoril. Once outside the station, Sarah consulted the directions given to her by Nick at dinner the previous evening. He had tried to dissuade her from going, but in the end, had agreed she had little choice. Nick recommended a small hotel in the town but advised, for the sake of appearances, that Adeline should be booked into the Hotel Palácio, close to the casino, and the haunt of the well-to-do. With the funds provided by Haas, Adeline could afford it. Besides, Sarah didn't expect any objections from Adeline, for she knew it would suit her to a T. Adeline's upper-class background was such an advantage. She could blend into such places, whereas Sarah would struggle with the niceties.

As she walked along the promenade, Sarah looked down at the beautiful stretch of golden beach with delight. It all seemed so normal. Lots of people were in the water and the sound of children's laughter did her heart good. Even at a distance, Sarah could tell the swimmers were enjoying themselves immensely, so she reckoned the water was lovely and warm. Nick had mentioned that the Praia do Tamariz was extremely popular, even this early in the season. At the far end of the beach was a fine castellated building, and at the rear of the beach, close to the walkway, was a row of changing huts covered in striped fabric. What a lovely idea, Sarah thought. At home, back in Ireland, there were no such things as changing facilities. One wiggled in and out of one's clothes behind the spartan modesty of a large towel, if one was lucky. Then you raced into the icy water until you turned blue, and your teeth chattered so hard you thought they would break. It had always been a competition between her and Maura to see who could last the longest in the freezing water. A competition Sarah invariably lost. However, the sea here looked very inviting, and Sarah wished she had had the foresight to bring a bathing costume. She smiled to herself; not exactly standard spy kit, swimsuits, but perhaps they should be. Maybe she could come back here later and take a paddle. It would kill some time before she had to go to the casino.

Sarah's hotel was easy enough to find, and it was a relief to plonk her case down on the single bed upon reaching her room. So far, so good. Except she was now sure that someone *was* following her. A small, dark-haired fellow in cloth cap and ill-fitting trousers, who she had seen on the train, had peeked in the door of the hotel as she waited for her key at reception. Their eyes had met, and he had turned away first, before walking past. Suspecting she was being tailed was one thing, knowing it for certain left her perturbed. Sarah's nerves kicked in and she almost abandoned any thought of going back down to the coast for a quick paddle. But to an observer, wouldn't it be odd if she didn't? Surely anyone coming to Estoril would indulge in two things: the beach and the casino. Right, she would lead her tail a merry dance and head down to the waterfront straight away.

Now, was he there, waiting? Through the net curtain, she spotted him leaning against the wall of a building on the opposite side of the street. He wasn't even trying to be subtle. Speculating who he might be was pointless, but, hopefully, he was PVDE and not one of Haas's men. Best she pretended he wasn't there. If she tried to give him the slip, it would only make him suspicious, and the last thing she needed was to come to the attention of anyone hostile. Sarah took a deep breath, determined to keep her head. *You can do this.*

A few hours later, Sarah returned from the beach in a cheerful mood. As she crossed the reception area, she spotted a small, shady courtyard out back. She would grab her book and sit out there and read, a pleasant way to spend the last few spare hours before tonight's assignment. Back in her room, Sarah flipped open her case and rummaged for her book. However, at the bottom was the dress Adeline had bought for her that morning. Adeline had been running late for her train, and had raced into her room, shoved a large package in brown paper at her before flying back out the door again. Sarah hadn't even had time to see it, never mind try it on. She had pushed it into the case, hoping Adeline had chosen wisely. But what if it didn't fit? She'd have to try it on now, just to be sure.

A little impatient, Sarah tore off the brown paper, then stopped, her eyes glued to the contents. Well, this looked interesting. The dress was wrapped in white tissue paper. This was an expensive item, for sure. Taking her time, she carefully peeled the tissue away. Then gasped. Sarah held up the dress, thrilled as the fabric revealed itself in a whoosh of silk. The sleeveless, floor-length gown had a fitted bodice, which was ruched at the sides. The colour, much to her delight, was royal blue, her favourite shade. Was that a lucky guess on Adeline's part? Nervous she would crease it, she cradled it up against her body. She had never owned anything as fabulous as this. Then she spotted another small item at the bottom of the package. To her astonishment, it was a silver wrap, a perfect accessory for the ensemble. With some reluctance, she had to admit that Adeline had admirable taste. She slipped out of her clothes and stepped into the dress. It fitted perfectly.

With the gown on, Sarah climbed up onto the bed. *How on earth did Adeline get this so right?* Sarah wondered, as she twisted this way and that, trying to get a good view of the dress in the small mirror on the dressing table. Adeline could so easily have chosen something unsuitable, ugly even. Was it an olive branch for being such a pain in the neck? Sarah chuckled to herself. Well, whatever had prompted it, she was grateful. And the girls back in London would be so envious when they saw this! Suddenly, feeling a lot more confident, Sarah slid off the bed, removed the garment, and hung it up in the wardrobe. Sarah couldn't help but wonder what fabulous outfit her partner in crime would turn up in tonight, but she knew for certain the casino patrons were in for a treat.

★   ★   ★

It was almost eight o'clock in the evening when Sarah entered the casino. By agreement, Adeline was to wait until eight-thirty to give Sarah time to find a suitable observation spot. Sarah was nervous, feeling such an imposter as she mingled with the slow-moving crowd strolling down the hallway towards the noisy bar. How Judith and Gladys would envy her if they could see who she was rubbing shoulders with tonight. This was no ordinary group. The men were in dress suits with white shirts and dickie bows, the ladies in long evening attire and dripping with diamonds. Amidst so much glitz, Sarah was grateful that Adeline had been savvy enough to know they needed to dress the part. Nothing in her own wardrobe would have been good enough.

Then she entered the bar. What a room! It was fabulous, and it took a lot of self-control not to gasp. The bar area was in the art deco style, with a mirrored back wall with shelves containing the largest array of alcoholic drinks Sarah had ever seen. Even The American Bar in The Savoy could not compete with it. She took in the ornate chandeliers hanging from the ceiling, which cast a soft glow to the wood-panelled room. Most of the clientele were milling around the bar area, where dapper barmen were mixing cocktails. A row of high stools graced the front of the bar, all of which were occupied by glamorous young women and a cluster of gentlemen stood around, deep in conversation. But she couldn't risk being swamped by the crowd; she'd have to find somewhere else. Luckily, there were small groupings of chairs and tables scattered about, providing intimate niches for those more inclined to privacy. One of the smaller tables, directly opposite the entrance, would give her a better view of Adeline's arrival and the evening's subsequent proceedings.

Sarah noticed a few curious glances in her direction, but whether it was because she was alone or her appearance wasn't up to scratch, she wasn't sure. But it only made her more determined to carry it off. Nick had told her the place was haunted by the monied and the displaced, who sought sanctuary in neutral Portugal. It was all a bit intimidating, to be mingling with such people, however, all she had to do was try to blend in and watch out for Adeline. She had a description of Carter from Nick, but no one she saw in the room at present matched it. Hopefully, he would appear soon, or it would be a wasted evening. Head held high, she made her way to the table and sat down. But no sooner had she taken her seat before a waiter appeared, asking for her order. Sarah requested a G&T and settled down to wait. There was little else to do until Adeline showed up but observe the crowd.

Just as the waiter returned with her drink, a debonair young man detached himself from the group at the bar and, drink in hand, sauntered over. 'Well, well, I do believe that is an Irish accent I just heard. Would I be correct? May I join you?' he asked. 'I'm a Dub, myself.'

Sarah smiled up at him, taking in the typical Irish pale complexion and dark hair, said to result from a certain armada being wrecked off the west coast of Ireland many moons ago. 'Of course.' This was perfect. She would no longer be conspicuous by sitting alone.

'Dave O'Connell,' he introduced himself as he sat down.

'Laura Butterworth,' replied Sarah, as they shook hands. 'Nice to meet you, Mr O'Connell.'

'And you, and please, you must call me Dave.' Then he threw her a mischievous look. 'You must be waiting for someone,' he said, 'for I cannot believe such a lovely creature would be alone.'

His compliment made her squirm a little, but she glued a smile on her face. 'Yes, my friends should be along a little later.'

'I am glad to hear it, but . . . perhaps you would like some company until then?' he asked, a twinkle in his eye.

'Thank you. I don't like to drink alone,' Sarah said.

'Of course. It can give the wrong impression. Especially in a place like this.'

'Exactly.'

'So, Laura, what part of Dublin are you from?'

'North Strand, and you?'

'Raheny! But that is only a few miles away. What a coincidence!' Then he gave her a sympathetic look. 'Shame about what happened down there. Were you affected by the bombing?'

'Unfortunately, yes. Our house was destroyed.' Sarah hoped her tone would dissuade him from probing any further. The memory of that night was still raw, even all these years later.

'Ah, now, that's awful. It was a shocking business.' He took a sip of his drink. 'Them damned Nazis, eh?'

'Yes. I'm not a fan.'

O'Connell went up in her estimation by changing the subject. 'So, tell me, what brings a glamorous young lady such as yourself to Estoril?'

'An acquaintance recommended it. I'm only in Lisbon for a few days on business and he thought I would enjoy a trip out here. He was right. It is a lovely place. Unfortunately, I won't be here long enough to explore it properly.'

'Here on business, I see. Might I ask what you do?'

'Nothing very exciting, I assure you. I'm a journalist with *The Gazette*. My editor arranged for me to interview the British ambassador.'

'Ah, yes. I have met Sir Ronald myself. Here, in fact.'

Sarah's heart dropped. She hadn't met the ambassador; only seen some photographs of him. What if this fellow twigged it or Sir Ronald turned up and she didn't recognise him? Now *she* needed to change the subject. 'I take it you are a regular here, Dave?'

'Indeed, yes. I come here as often as I can get away. Normally, I am based in Madrid, but luckily, I have business interests here. I always stay at the Hotel Palácio, it's a home from home and so convenient for popping in here.'

'I've heard it is very lovely, but unfortunately I could not get a room there on such short notice,' Sarah remarked.

'That is a shame. It is far superior to anywhere else. If you ever come back, drop my name at the front desk and they will look after you,' he said with an oily smile. 'I assume you will try your luck at the tables tonight?'

'Oh dear, it is best I confess I am a complete novice,' Sarah said with a self-depreciating smile. 'I've never gambled in my life.'

'Then it would be my pleasure to show you the ropes,' he replied.

'That is very kind of you.' Sarah almost panicked, for she had little money on her and who goes to a casino with empty pockets?

The clock above the bar only read eight-fifteen. *Please Adeline, don't be late.*

'Would you like another drink?' Dave asked as he rose, 'What's your poison?'

'Gin please,' she said.

As he walked away to the bar, Sarah wondered how tricky it would be to extricate herself from this situation. Adeline would expect her to be close by and in sight, not gallivanting in the gaming room. Still, a small part of Sarah thought, *what the heck? I shouldn't be here at all.*

Just as Dave reappeared, Sarah suddenly felt uneasy, as though someone were watching her. Next thing, she spotted him. Her tail. Well, it was hardly surprising that he would have followed her here. However, the fact that he was now smartly dressed, which could only be to mingle unnoticed among such illustrious clientele, showed a great deal of fore-thought. Sarah stiffened. Or could someone have told him she would be here? But who could have betrayed her? Adeline? Nick? The implications of that notion were enormous.

Sarah barely heard Dave speak as he put her glass down on the table. 'Thank you,' she managed, as a cold hard knot formed in the pit of her stomach.

27

8th May 1944, Estoril Casino, Portugal

A quarter of an hour later, Sarah was witness to Adeline's grand entrance. And it was as dramatic as she had anticipated. Draped in a stunning emerald-green dress, which showed her figure to perfection, in she waltzed. Sarah could not look directly at her or acknowledge her in any way, but she could tell from the swivelling heads of the gentlemen present that Adeline's entrance had caused a stir. Soon the Frenchwoman was swallowed up in a sea of admirers. Sarah was sure Adeline was enjoying every minute, despite her reason for being here. Dave's eyes flickered, noting the newcomer with interest before he turned his attention back to Sarah and continued their conversation.

At this stage, Sarah was convinced the charming Dave was a spy. His probing questions intermingled with some strong flirtation were enough to convince her he was no ordinary businessman. He was sounding her out. Though who he worked for, she wasn't sure. It hardly mattered. It was enough that she should be on her guard and take care what she revealed. However, he fulfilled a purpose for now. Thankfully, he didn't seem to be in a hurry to get to the gaming tables, and Sarah relaxed while monitoring Adeline as best she could.

The swarm of gentlemen surrounding Adeline thinned out, and for one brief moment their eyes met. At least now Adeline would be reassured, Sarah thought. *I'm here; I've done my bit*. Adeline didn't react, much to Sarah's relief, but continued to chat to a tall blond-haired man Sarah had not spotted before. However, he matched Carter's description perfectly. To be fair to Adeline, that was fast work, even though Carter was expecting her. If their luck held, Haas's men, who were no doubt present, would see this and report back to their spymaster in a positive light. All that was needed was for Adeline to keep calm and act the femme fatale for all to see. With a twinge of disappointment, Sarah realised her job for the night was done; she could leave. Tempting though it might be to stay with Dave and have a flutter in the gaming room, she knew it was likely to become a messy situation when the evening drew to its inevitable conclusion. That would be too much for her bruised heart to deal with. Tony might have rejected her, but her feelings for him were still too strong to contemplate what she would regard as a betrayal.

Sarah pulled her attention back to Dave; he had just mentioned The Azores.

'Rather clever of Salazar, don't you think? He's always playing off one side against the other. Now that it looks like the Allies may win, he's willing to help them and give them access. It's not that long ago he was selling wolfram to the Germans.'

Distracted by Adeline's antics – she was now hanging on Carter's arm and flashing him seductive smiles, almost in front of where they were sitting – Sarah muttered: 'Is that so? I don't know much about it.'

Dave's eyebrows shot up. Too late, Sarah realised her mistake. If she were a proper journalist here to interview the ambassador, she would be well versed in Salazar's decisions and the background to them.

'A pity,' Dave replied, his gaze narrowed. 'I find it all terribly fascinating. The regime here is very interesting.'

'Indeed, it is. I look forward to hearing more about the situation and its implications from Sir Ronald,' she said. It was a lame response, but the best she could do under pressure. Sarah could feel the heat moving up her neck. How could she have been so careless? Such a stupid faux pas; she needed to recover, and quickly. But she needed time to think. A trip to the ladies seemed the best course of action. 'Would you excuse me for a few minutes, Dave?' she said, rising from her seat.

'Not at all. Hurry back!' Dave stood and smiled his suave but entirely false smile. Sarah felt his gaze on her as she pushed her way through the ever-increasing crowd entering the bar. The temptation to leave now was strong, but she had to hold her nerve. If she fled, it would only confirm Dave's suspicions and could lead to all sorts of problems, depending on who he worked for. Once she regained her perspective and composure, she would return to Dave and hope some charm might divert disaster.

Across the hallway, Sarah spotted a sign for the ladies' room and followed the arrows to a secluded corridor. It was a relief to find the bathroom empty. She braced herself against the washstand and took a few deep breaths. But her doubts rushed back in. Maybe she should bolt and go back to Lisbon immediately? Contact London? She raised her head and stared at the sophisticated stranger staring back at her in the mirror. *Why am I panicking like this? I must not act on impulse. I can handle this.*

Once she had used the facilities, she sat down at a dressing table. Slowly, she powdered her nose while wondering if she stalled in here long enough, would O'Connell get the hint and seek new prey? Perhaps he wouldn't blow her cover. What conceivable motive could he have, anyway? If he had disappeared when she went back to the bar, she could escape back to her hotel, leaving Adeline to complete the task at hand. Adeline was playing her part to perfection, and hardly needed Sarah to be present.

Ten minutes crawled by. Impatient now, Sarah put away her make-up and, with one last check in the mirror, headed for the door. But as soon as she opened it, and saw the two men waiting for her, Sarah knew she was in trouble. One man she recognised as her tail, the other she had not noticed before. The first man stepped forward.

'Miss, you must come now,' he said with a steady and unfriendly gaze. His English was stilted with an accent she guessed was Portuguese. *They must be PVDE,* she thought with some relief. *At least they aren't German.* But what did they want with her? Was there any point in trying to make a run for it? There were few people about who she could approach for help. Besides, two against one were odds she didn't fancy. Hadn't she been trained for this kind of situation? *Stick to your story, girl, and you will be fine.* But if she came across as prepared and calm, would it not indicate that she probably was a spy? She needed to make the fuss an innocent person in this predicament *would* make.

Sarah straightened up, inhaling deeply. 'How dare you accost me like this! I will not go anywhere with you. Who are you?' she demanded loudly.

'We are police,' the man said, taking a step closer.

'What do you want with me? I have done nothing wrong,' Sarah cried. 'I am a British citizen, you know. You can't order me about.'

The man exchanged a look with his companion, then shrugged. 'No matter. You must come with us.'

Sarah stood her ground. 'This is ridiculous. What have I done? There must be a misunderstanding of some sort.'

A muscle twitched in his cheek. 'Visitors who violate our laws must answer to us.'

'What laws? I don't understand,' she said. From the corner of her eye, she spotted Adeline approach from the bar area, then suddenly come to a halt. Quickly, she swivelled and disappeared back around the corner. So much for help from that quarter, Sarah thought, then relented. At least Adeline had had the sense to not get involved. There was no point in both of them being carted off.

'You must come to the station,' the man said, grabbing her arm none too gently. Before she could object, however, he frog-marched her down the corridor towards a door, which was standing open to the outside. Sarah eventually found her voice and objected loudly, but was ignored. They continued around the outside of the building, heading towards a car park. As they passed along the terrace, Dave O'Connell raised his glass to her from the doorway.

Sarah threw him a look of disgust. *The rotten bastard; he was responsible for this.*

When they reached the car park, an engine fired up and a sleek car pulled in to the kerb.

'Please,' the tail said, indicating the back seat with a flick of his wrist.

'Where are you taking me?' she demanded.

The man exchanged a look of frustration with his companion. 'To the local station.'

'But I don't want to go with you,' she tried once more.

With a heavy sigh, the man pointed to the rear seat and continued to stare at her. Bluster wasn't going to work on him, Sarah realised. And she suspected he was carrying a gun. She couldn't push him too far. She'd just have to wait and see what was at the end of this car journey. Not a little nervous, she slid into the back seat. The tail got in beside her. The door slammed, and the car accelerated away.

Sarah stared out the window, doing her best to remember the route, but soon they had travelled too far for her to recall it with any great clarity. However, she was sure they had not left Estoril. Her fear had been that they would take her to Lisbon or somewhere else further afield.

28

8th May 1944, A PVDE Station, Estoril, Portugal

The car stopped halfway up a side street. From the little Sarah could see, it was a commercial district; the street deserted. They hurried her out of the vehicle and through a doorway before she could discover more than that. Now, her tail had a hold of her arm again and pulled her along a dark passageway until they came to a battered door. With a 'wait here', he pushed her inside, and she heard a key turn in the lock. So much for Portuguese hospitality, she thought with a wry smile, *and here I am all dressed up and ready to socialise!* She turned around and surveyed the room, her good humour dissolving rapidly. A sharper contrast to the casino's plush interior would be hard to find. The paint was peeling off the unadorned walls, the floorboards were bare and dirty, and the only furniture was a table and two chairs. There was no window to the outside. It was an interrogation room, if she wasn't mistaken, and she suddenly had flashbacks to her training.

Momentarily, she was overcome with panic. What if they didn't believe her cover story? If they figured out who she was and connected her to Adeline, they might both be imprisoned or expelled. Both scenarios would come to Haas's attention and the game would be up. The scariest thought was that no one knew where she was unless Adeline had somehow followed them. That was highly unlikely. Sarah pulled out a chair and sat down, clasped her hands together on the table, and prepared to play the waiting game as a disgruntled British citizen.

But time to think wasn't always a good thing. There was still the burning question of how the tail knew she was going to the casino. But perhaps it had been a lucky guess on his part? After all, most people who came to Estoril frequented the gaming rooms. Besides, her gut feeling was that Adeline would not betray her, despite their prickly relationship. Nick, however, was an unknown quantity, but what possible motive could he have had to reveal her identity unless he was in the pay of the Nazis?

Half an hour passed, and Sarah began to wonder what was going on. But when the door eventually opened, the two men who had brought her to the station stepped inside the room. The man who had been her tail held a clipboard. The other just stared at her for several minutes. Sarah returned his gaze as steadily as she could manage, but she felt very uneasy. Why was he looking at her like that? Suddenly, she felt vulnerable, and not a little ridiculous sitting there in her fancy clothes. How should she react? But then the second man turned his back on her and spoke rapidly to the other man in Portuguese. It sounded like he was barking out orders of some kind. She had a very bad feeling about this situation, and she was at such a disadvantage not knowing the language. But all that happened was that her tail wrote his notes rapidly, gave her a quick glance and left the room. The second man turned back to her and then, with one last lingering look, he followed his companion out of the room.

What on earth had that been about? She wondered, doing her best to slow her heart rate.

Over the next hour or so, Sarah heard voices and footsteps outside in the corridor. She guessed she was being left to stew to soften her up for whatever was coming next. Well, she was made of sterner stuff! Staying calm was vital, so she recited her times tables. How the nuns would have been proud!

However, Sarah had only reached the nine times tables when she was interrupted by the next man to enter the room. This fellow was in uniform, mid-fifties at least, with heavy features and a hard stare. Sarah held his gaze despite her stomach doing a few somersaults as he took the seat opposite.

The man said nothing but made a show of taking a sheet of paper from his pocket. It was placed on the table before he swivelled it around for her to see. It was her Estoril hotel registration. 'You are this Laura Butterworth?' he growled after a few seconds of continuous eye contact. How thorough! No doubt her room had been searched as well.

'Yes. Why did your men bring me here?' she asked in reply. 'This is outrageous!'

He ignored this. 'Why are you in Portugal?'

Sarah sat back and folded her arms. 'I'm a British journalist and *The Gazette* newspaper commissioned an interview with the British ambassador. As far as I am aware, that is not illegal.' The officer maintained his stare, so she rambled on. 'And, I can tell you, I don't appreciate being treated like this. I shall make a complaint to the British embassy. The press attaché there, Nicholas Webb, can verify all of this for you,' she said, waving at the page on the table. 'I was at the embassy on Sunday and spoke to both him and Sir Ronald.'

The policeman tapped the hotel registration sheet. 'But why come here to Estoril? What business do you have here?'

'None. Mr Webb suggested I visit to see the sights and try my luck at the tables. However, if I had known this was the treatment I would receive, I wouldn't have bothered.'

The man grunted. She knew well he didn't believe her. '*Who* did you contact here?' he asked.

'No one,' she replied with an exaggerated sigh.

'You were seen in the company of an Irishman by the name of David O'Connell. He is known to us. What did you discuss, please?'

Sarah huffed. 'Honestly, sir, this is ridiculous! I don't know the man. He approached *me* in the casino bar and bought me a drink. I'd never met him before, but I have to say he was a charming and friendly chap, and very knowledgeable about your country, by the way.' Her interrogator's expression didn't change, and briefly she wondered if his English was good enough to understand what she was saying. But she ploughed on nevertheless. 'We had a pleasant chat about places to see and he offered to accompany me to the gaming room. What

250

is so sinister about that? I don't understand what all the fuss is about.' She added a glare for good measure.

'The man is a spy,' he snapped.

Sarah sat forward, eyes wide. 'Really? How extraordinary! I wish I'd known. I've never met a spy before,' she said, holding his gaze.

The man blinked at her, then rose abruptly. 'We will check all of this.' He grabbed the sheet of paper, turned on his heel, and left.

Sarah sighed with relief as she heard the key turn in the lock, certain she had planted some doubt in the policeman's mind.

Now, all she had to do was hope Nick would come to the rescue when he heard of her predicament. If he didn't show, she'd have her answer as to who might have betrayed her.

⋆ ⋆ ⋆

A sleep-deprived and hungry Sarah was relieved to see Nick Webb walk into the interrogation room early the next morning. He didn't look pleased, and she could hardly blame him. He was a busy man. The last thing he needed was to be dragged to Estoril to rescue her. But at least it put her mind at ease about him. Her interrogator from the night before strolled in after Nick. The officer didn't look happy either, and if she hadn't felt so wretched, she probably would have laughed at the absurdity of the whole situation.

'Miss Butterworth,' Nick greeted her, unsmiling.

'Mr Webb,' she replied, unable to keep the weariness from her tone. 'I am delighted to see you. Perhaps you can make this man see sense. I'm being held here against my will. Is this how journalists are treated in this country?'

The policeman quirked a brow but remained silent. Nick turned to the officer, then back to her. 'A misunderstanding, Miss Butterworth. All sorted now. Sub-Intendent Paredes has agreed to release you into my care.'

Sarah shot the police officer a glare. 'That is very kind of him, however, as I have done nothing wrong, I rather think I am owed an apology.'

Nick's answering look said, 'don't push it', but she was annoyed. Besides, a truly innocent person would be indignant at the treatment she had received. Not even a glass of water had appeared or the offer of a bed for the night. All she had managed was about two hours' sleep, resting her head on her arms on the table. Nick had been correct when he had warned her the PVDE was more styled on the Gestapo than any police force she had encountered before. Still, she had to be grateful. If she had been picked up by the Germans, lack of sleep would have been the least of her worries.

Paredes shrugged. 'I do my job. Be thankful you are free to go and do yours.'

Nick cleared his throat. 'If you are ready, Miss Butterworth, let us not delay. I'm sure you are eager to return to Lisbon.'

Sarah rose and came around the table. Nick turned and headed for the door. As she passed Paredes, Sarah paused. 'I shall make an official complaint, you know.' But Paredes stood, impassive.

'Miss Butterworth!' Nick exclaimed from the doorway between gritted teeth. 'The car is waiting.'

29

9th May 1944, Estoril, Portugal

'Well!' Nick said, as he ground the gears and pulled away from the pavement. 'You've certainly been busy. How on earth did you end up on the wrong side of the secret police? I thought I had warned you to be careful. These people don't play games, Sarah.'

'That's unfair, sir, and I'm sorry you got dragged into it, but I suspect a fellow Irishman by the name of Dave O'Connell, whom I met at the casino last night, made an allegation against me.'

'Why would he do that?'

'Mischief,' she replied, unwilling to tell him of her faux pas.

'Yes, I can believe it of Dave. We know him well. Charming rogue, but don't be fooled by him. Quite a dangerous fellow.'

'That I had figured out, sir, trust me. So, who is he?'

'A spy for hire with uncertain loyalties. We're never quite sure who he is working for.'

'Ah! That explains it.'

As they drove along, Sarah thought it might be better to come clean. After a minute or two of silence, she said: 'I'm afraid I made a stupid error in front of him. I was distracted when I spotted my tail in the bar at the casino and dropped a careless remark. He picked up on it immediately. I did try to retrieve the situation, but he was too smart.'

Nick's head snapped around and he glared at her. 'You need to be more circumspect. This could have ended differently.'

'I know.' Another uncomfortable silence followed. Sarah was mad at herself. When word of her brush with the PVDE reached Jason, everything she had done to prove herself would lie in shreds. Not to mention the risk to the Allied operations in preparation for landing in France. Sarah flinched at the thought. Now even more fed-up, she asked: 'I take it Dave is an informer as well?'

'Yes. Sells information to the highest bidder. How else do you think he can afford to spend so much time at the tables? I suppose we were lucky it wasn't the Germans he tipped off.'

Sarah had to bite down on her lip. Really, she had acted like an amateur. 'Hmm, yes. That would have been a very different experience. Do they actually snatch people off the street?' she asked.

'Not too often. They have to be careful not to tread on the PVDE's toes, much like ourselves. Your agent . . . what's her name?'

'Adeline – have you seen her?' Sarah asked, fearing more bad news.

'No. She's your problem. I came straight on my white charger to rescue *you*.'

Nick's light-hearted response helped raise her bruised spirits a little, and she could answer in kind. 'Oh, thank you, sir knight. Much obliged, I'm sure!'

Nick dipped his head and kept his eyes on the road. 'Did she turn up at the casino as planned?'

'She did and caused quite a stir. When I left, she was well on her way to getting into Carter's good books, if not his bed! However, she witnessed the PVDE taking me away. I only hope she stuck to the plan and didn't panic.'

'We will know when we get back to Lisbon.' Nick made a face at her, but then broke into a smile. 'Don't be hard on yourself. All things considered, you handled that fairly well, really. Paredes wasn't quite sure about you and probably suspected you're one of my agents, but he had no proof. However, the sooner you and your charge leave the country, the better. Paredes could pull you in again if he receives more negative intelligence about you.'

'I hope not! Anyway, we are scheduled to leave on the boat tomorrow evening,' Sarah replied. 'Adeline is due to meet Haas this afternoon to give him the information she gathered from her encounter with Carter. Hopefully, that should be the end of it.' With a sigh, she continued: 'I'll be only too glad to finish this assignment and go home. I have to admit, I'm a nervous wreck!'

Nick parked up outside her hotel. 'That's understandable. Right! Go and grab your things and let's get you back to Lisbon.' He nodded at a car which drove past slowly, then parked further up the street. 'It's what the PVDE would expect. They followed us from the station.'

As she got out of the car, Sarah sighed. 'Persistent blighters, aren't they?'

'You have no idea.'

She leaned back in the door. 'What about Adeline? Should I check on her before we leave?'

Nick shook his head and waved his hand at the PVDE car. 'You can't risk it. We must hope she didn't panic when she saw you taken away last night. Hopefully, she completed her task . . . She knows she cannot risk being seen with you. Surely the arrangement was that she would travel back separately first thing this morning?'

'Yes, of course,' Sarah replied.

He looked at his watch. 'Well then, she should be on the train back to Lisbon by now.'

Sarah slowly climbed the stairs to her hotel room in Lisbon, longing to lie down, but as she unlocked the door, she thought it best to check if Adeline was back. However, there was no response to her knock at Adeline's door. As she went back to her own room, she realised Adeline might have gone straight from the train to the meeting with Haas. Sarah checked the time. Haas and Adeline were due to meet in twenty minutes. She really should go and observe but as far as Adeline was concerned, Sarah was likely still in custody, which suited her just fine. Besides, she was fed up with all the handholding. The woman needed to stand on her own two feet. With a sigh of relief, she removed her now crumpled gown, splashed her face and put on some fresh clothes. With a yawn, she sank down on the bed. A short nap would do her the world of good.

★ ★ ★

Sarah awoke to screaming and ranting. Heart thumping, she scrambled to her feet. Someone was pounding on the door. Suddenly afraid, she stood unsure what to do. Could it be the PVDE or some of Haas's men? But it was a female voice.

'*Laisse-moi entrer!* Sarah, let me in!' the familiar voice cried. It was Adeline! And she was hysterical. Sarah wrenched the door open, and the Frenchwoman practically fell inside. The hotel receptionist appeared in the hallway, out of breath from running up the stairs.

'What is going on?' he demanded, peering into Sarah's room at Adeline, who was still remonstrating. 'Do you know this woman? This is not acceptable behaviour in this hotel.' He pointed at Adeline. 'She is disturbing the other guests. If she is your friend, you must make her stop or you must leave.'

Sarah glared back at him. 'I don't know her, sir, but if the lady is distressed, I will help her.'

'Please, or she must go,' he replied before walking off.

Sarah slammed the door shut and turned to face Adeline. But before she could say anything Adeline cried: '*Mon Dieu!* You have betrayed me!' Arms flailing, she lunged at her.

Shocked, Sarah raised her arms to fend her off. Adeline was like a woman possessed; her eyes wild. Now she was ranting in French, her voice guttural. Sarah didn't need a translator to know something was terribly wrong. Adeline was both furious and deeply distressed. Then Sarah recognised one word amongst the tirade: Nikolay. And she was filled with dread.

'Adeline, stop screaming at me!' Sarah shouted, pushing her away once more. 'I don't want to hurt you, but if you keep this up, I will. I don't understand. What has happened? What has this to do with Nikolay?'

The mention of his name caused Adeline to freeze.

Breathing heavily, Adeline stood glaring at Sarah, as if preparing for another verbal and physical assault. Sarah had to defuse the situation quickly.

'Sit down at once!' she demanded, staring at her, hands on hips. For a second, Adeline's stare was full of hatred. Next minute, the fire in her eyes died, and she had crumpled down onto the bed, sobbing.

What on earth?

'Adeline, I cannot help you if I do not know what is wrong,' Sarah said, more gently, but the sobbing continued. Sarah sat down close to her. 'Did you meet Haas? What has happened to Nikolay?'

Adeline lifted her head from her hands briefly, desolation in her eyes. 'Nikolay was in one of those vile camps. He led an escape attempt but was caught. They shot him. He is dead!' Adeline groaned as if in pain.

'I'm so sorry.'

'I will be . . . sick,' Adeline replied, jumping up and running to the wash bowl.

As Adeline retched, Sarah's mind was whirling. Nikolay dead! The poor man. This was awful, but not totally unexpected. But how had Haas connected Nikolay to Adeline? What was Haas's reason for revealing the news to her? Was it just to be cruel?

Adeline sat back down beside her, and Sarah's heart went out to her. 'This is terrible news.'

Adeline stiffened. 'But you knew he was dead. You lied! All of you. You said you were trying to get him out of France, so you must have known he'd been captured!'

'No! You must believe me; I didn't know.' Sarah put her arm around her shoulder, but Adeline shook her off.

'Don't! You are no friend to me!'

'Adeline, you must believe me. I was in an impossible situation.'

'Huh!'

Sarah desperately tried to defuse the situation. 'Perhaps consider the possibility that Haas may have lied to you. The man is nasty enough.'

Adeline's chin clenched. 'Lie? Like you did? No, he did not lie. He took great pleasure in giving me all the details.' She swallowed hard several times, and Sarah guessed she was fighting for control. At last, Adeline asked the question Sarah dreaded most: 'Did you know Nikolay was in that camp?'

She had to be honest. 'I'm sorry, yes, I did, but no more than that.'

Adeline shook her head, clearly bewildered. 'How could you keep that from me?'

'I had no choice,' Sarah whispered, feeling rotten.

'But there is always a choice! If our situations had been reversed, I would have told you. How could you be so callous?' Adeline asked, and Sarah squirmed. Yes, she had lied, but for the greater good. What a foul and wretched situation this was. Having to choose between telling Adeline the truth and Operation Fortitude had posed a moral dilemma. Perhaps she should have considered the issue in more depth, but it was done, and regrets were futile.

'I can only be honest with you now, Adeline. If I had to do the same again, I would, and I know how awful that is. You must believe I wasn't happy about it, but I feared you would react badly and jeopardise all we had worked for. I couldn't risk that. Too many lives depend on our work. What we are doing could change the course of the war, shorten it by years.'

Vernier threw her a nasty look and shook her head. 'How easy you justify yourself! Well, let me tell you, the only life I cared about was Nikolay's.' Then she turned away, hunching her shoulders as if drawing herself inwards to drown in her grief.

Sarah feared she was losing her and panicked. She needed to know what the outcome of the meeting had been. Now, all that mattered was damage limitation. Had the woman fallen apart in front of Haas and let something slip? Then guilt swept over Sarah. By pursuing this, she was hurting Adeline even more, but their safety now depended on how Adeline had responded to Haas.

'How did you react when Haas told you, Adeline?' Sarah asked gently after several minutes of silence.

'I walked away. I could not bear to be near him any longer,' Adeline sneered. 'Much like I feel now, sitting here beside you.'

Her words stung. 'I don't blame you for feeling that way,' Sarah said. 'I truly wish things could have been different.'

Adeline arched a brow, disbelief written all over her face, but she remained silent.

'Did he say anything else before you left?' Sarah asked.

'He had said enough. The bastard just laughed at me.'

'I'm so sorry; what a horrible thing to do. Your heart is broken, I can tell. But I don't understand why Haas told you, or how he knew Nikolay was your boyfriend.'

'Someone betrayed Nikolay, someone I had trusted to keep him safe.'

'But it might not have been like that. Perhaps your Resistance friends were captured and tortured. They would not have had much choice but to reveal his whereabouts and your connection to him.'

The Frenchwoman's expression grew fierce. 'They should have resisted. Then Nikolay would not be dead. I will find out. Whoever betrayed us will pay a heavy price.'

Sarah shivered at her words but understood. In her shoes, she would feel the same. Hadn't that been her motivation when she joined MI5? Seeking revenge for the deaths of her loved ones?

'I'm afraid they are probably already dead,' Sarah replied. 'When did he tell you about Nikolay? Before or after you give him the information from Carter?'

Adeline treated her to a waspish glare, and hissed into her face: 'Don't worry, I told him where Carter hides those POWs. I did your dirty work. That's all you care about, isn't it?' Sarah started to object, but Adeline cut across her: 'Leave me be. We are finished. I will no longer work for you British. You don't deserve my help.' An angry colour crept into Adeline's face as she turned her head aside, rigid with anger once more.

Sarah struggled to see how she was going to put this right. This was a disaster. Adeline might bring down the double cross network in retaliation. How could she calm her down? Her efforts so far only appeared to be making the situation worse.

'Please, Adeline. I'm sorry we let Nikolay down, but we really need your help,' Sarah said.

Adeline stiffened, then swung around and slapped Sarah's face. Momentarily stunned, Sarah could only stare at her.

Adeline hissed into her face once more: 'If you really cared, you would have told me the truth. I will tell Haas everything, do you hear? I will bring down your dirty little network, piece by piece, and make you pay!'

30

9th May 1944, Hotel Dora, Rua da Misericordia, Lisbon

Adeline refused to talk any more. Eventually, she fell asleep, curled up on Sarah's bed like a child. Such a sad sight, Sarah thought. Nikolay's death had crushed her. But what on earth was she to do now? Sarah's greatest fear was that Adeline had already let something slip in front of Haas and he was ready to pounce. Despite her nerves being in shreds, she had to keep her head. Having considered her options, she was convinced she needed help as quickly as possible: this wasn't a situation she could handle on her own. A quick exit from Portugal was the only solution.

After double checking that Adeline was sound asleep, she slipped out of the room and down to reception. A young woman was behind the desk, not the irate man from earlier, however, he must have told his replacement about Adeline's behaviour.

'Is the lady better?' she demanded as soon as she spotted Sarah approaching the desk.

'Yes, the poor woman. It appears she received some terrible news. Most unfortunate, but I have managed to calm her down. I will help her; you need not concern yourself. In fact, that's why I'm here. I need to contact a friend. May I use a telephone, please?' Sarah asked.

The receptionist pointed to a booth tucked away down a corridor behind the reception area. 'You may use that one, miss.'

Sarah pulled over the door of the booth and allowed herself the luxury of a deep breath. This would not be an easy conversation, but she had no choice. Hopefully, Nick Webb would help. Again.

Once the embassy accepted the call, Nick was put through straight away.

'Sarah! I wasn't expecting to hear from you so soon. What can I do for you? Are you languishing in a prison again, by any chance?' He laughed.

'Eh, no, but I do have a rather large problem.' She quickly explained about Adeline, half expecting him to blow a fuse.

'We need to get you out tonight, then,' he replied, suddenly all business. 'Leave it with me. Wait in your room and keep her quiet.' He hung up.

Sarah stared at the receiver. The man was rapidly becoming her favourite human being.

Slowly, Sarah climbed the stairs back to her room. Although her senses were jangling, she felt a lot calmer now, having spoken to Nick. Nevertheless, she braced herself before opening the door. *Please, no more drama!* Hopefully, Adeline was still asleep.

But a shock awaited Sarah as she opened the door. The bed was empty. Adeline was gone! Sarah took a couple of steps into the room, alarm rising in her throat. *Where could she be?*

Sarah dashed back out into the hallway and ran along the corridor to the bathroom. It was empty. Maybe Adeline had gone back to her room? She raced up the stairs only to find the door of Adeline's room standing open, the room unoccupied. Sarah stumbled over to the bed and collapsed onto it. *What on earth am I to do? Where could Adeline be?* Sarah stiffened with her arms by her sides as she was overwhelmed by pure panic.

Was Adeline carrying out her threat to tell Haas everything? Was that where she had gone? She couldn't follow her to the German embassy; that would be suicide. Sarah's cover was probably already blown. The consequences of that, for both of them, were all too dire to contemplate. Feeling helpless, Sarah trembled, on the verge of tears. This assignment was a complete nightmare. Now all she could do was wait for the fallout to descend.

It was the worst hour and a half of Sarah's life. Back in her own room she paced, she tried to sit it out, then paced again, in a limbo of indecision. Her only hope was that Nick was on his way. Perhaps he could get her out of Portugal before Haas's agents arrived. All the stories she had ever heard about Haas played out in her mind, leaving her nauseous with dread.

When Sarah heard footsteps approach, she backed away from the door. *Was this it? Was this how her life would end?*

The door opened.

To her utter consternation, it was Adeline who stood in the doorway, her demeanour wretched. They faced each other in silence for several moments.

'What have you done?' Sarah asked at last, as Adeline stepped into the room.

With a strange smile, Adeline walked past her and sat down on the bed, facing the window, her back to Sarah.

'*Adeline*?' Sarah cried out. 'Have you betrayed me?'

Silence.

At that moment, the door flew open once more. Sarah spun round and almost wept with relief. It was Nick. Sarah hurried him back out the door and closed it behind her.

'What's going on?' Nick asked. 'What's happened now?'

'While I was phoning you, she slipped out of the hotel. She has only just returned, but I don't know where she went or what she has done. I've tried to get through to her, but she refuses to speak.'

'Goddamn it!' Nick ran a shaking hand over his forehead. It was then Sarah noticed another man standing a little apart, holding a bag. Beside him was a wheelchair.

'What are we going to do?' Sarah asked Nick.

'Get you both out of the country as quickly as possible,' Nick replied. He nodded to the other man. 'This is Dr Rubenstein.'

Sarah was confused. 'What—?'

Nick patted her arm. 'I'll explain later. Let me talk to her.'

Sarah followed Nick back into her room. Adeline hadn't moved an inch. Nick walked around the bed to face her, but Adeline glared up at him. From behind her, Sarah threw

Nick a questioning glance, but he did not respond. Instead, he held out his hand to the Frenchwoman.

'I'm Nick Webb, British embassy. I'm delighted to meet you, Mademoiselle Vernier.' Adeline looked at him as if he were mad, but eventually shook his hand. 'The thing is, mademoiselle, I need to know where you have been this afternoon. Did you go to the German embassy by any chance?'

Adeline swung her head around and glared at Sarah. For a moment there was triumph in her eyes, but then she looked away. 'No. I did not.' Sarah's relief was short-lived, however, as Adeline looked up at Nick and said: 'Yet!'

'Ah, now, mademoiselle, I'm sure you realise that if you reveal certain matters to the Nazis, you will also be exposing your own duplicity. You would have to admit to Haas that you have betrayed him,' Nick said this quietly, but there was no mistaking the undertone of threat.

'I don't care!' answered Adeline, hunching her shoulders. 'My life has no meaning without my Nikolay.' But somehow Sarah knew Adeline was saving face; she was far too intelligent. No doubt she had stormed off intending to do her worst but soon realised the implications for herself. However, they weren't out of the woods yet.

'Yes, I understand. It is a great tragedy.' Nick turned to the other man, who had followed them into the room. 'And that is why I have brought along my friend, Dr Rubenstein. He's a jolly nice fellow. Looks after the ambassador, don't you know? Sarah told me you were terribly distressed. We can't have that, Adeline. May I call you Adeline? You are an important member of the team, and we always look after our own. Ain't that so, Sarah?'

Sarah nodded, wondering where on earth this was going. But to her amazement, Nick's words seemed to work. A tentative half-smile appeared, and Adeline shook hands with the doctor.

'I'm sure Dr Rubenstein can help. Perhaps give you something to help with your distress?' Nick said.

'Indeed, I can, Mr Webb.' Rubenstein smiled down at Adeline. 'Nothing easier, young lady.'

Sarah didn't know what was going on and decided to let Nick do the talking. At least Adeline was paying attention.

'No, I want nothing,' Adeline said, shooting Sarah a glance laced with venom.

'Now, Mademoiselle Vernier, it is simply a sedative to help you sleep,' Rubenstein said, sitting down on the bed beside her. He had a gentle smile. 'I understand that you have received some very sad news about your friend. It is only right that you are upset. And Sarah, here, is very concerned about you. A good night's sleep will help, and, in the morning, you will feel better able to cope.'

Sarah held her breath. Suddenly, Adeline's shoulders slumped. She sighed. 'Very well. I would welcome the oblivion of sleep.'

Sarah shot Nick a thankful look, but he would not meet her gaze. Instead, he beamed down at Adeline. 'That's the ticket.'

The doctor, if he actually was one, administered an injection into Adeline's arm. 'Now, my dear young lady, lie back against the pillows and you will soon be asleep.' He patted her arm, then rose to address Nick. 'It will soon take effect.'

For a few minutes, all three stood watching Adeline. Eventually, her breathing slowed to a steady rhythm, and she closed her eyes. *Respite at last*, Sarah thought, *at least for a while*. Nick gestured towards the hallway, and they followed him outside, leaving the door ajar.

'What have you given her, doctor?' Sarah asked, suddenly concerned. Could Nick's idea of helping be to neutralise Adeline permanently?

'There is no need to be alarmed. It's a sedative, miss, and quite harmless,' he replied before speaking to Nick. 'I'll be off, then.'

Nick shook his hand, thanked him, and bade him farewell. As the doctor disappeared down the stairs, Nick turned to Sarah. 'It was lucky he agreed to help out at such short notice.'

'Yes, but is it really a sedative? Is he really a doctor?' Sarah asked.

Nick looked baffled by her questions. 'Of course. Don't you trust me?'

It was on the tip of her tongue to say *probably not*. After all, she had learned the hard way that war made people do the most awful things. But she pasted a smile on her face. 'I do, sir. It's just all happening so fast. Adeline is vital to our current operation, and her wellbeing is my responsibility. It is imperative I get her home as quickly as possible. But what if she did contact Haas?'

Nick sighed. 'She didn't. You can be damn sure if she had, his men would have been here by now and you and your French friend would be checking out the facilities of the basement of the German embassy.'

Sarah gulped. 'Yes, I suppose you're right.'

'Look, Sarah, we don't have much time. This is the best solution. We can't risk the lady waking up and having a meltdown here or at the airport. Run along to her room and pack up her stuff. Then do the same for your own. We have a car waiting to take you straight to the airport.'

'Alright,' Sarah said, then paused, peering in at the now sleeping Adeline. 'She will be OK, won't she? I do feel responsible for her.'

Nick gave her a grim smile in response. 'Yes, she'll have a nasty headache when she comes round, but she will be fine.'

Sarah glanced at the wheelchair. 'I assume that is for her?'

Nick sighed with impatience. 'Yes, lucky I thought of it and could borrow one. We can get her downstairs in the lift easily enough.'

'And what about the hotel staff? Won't they think it's all a bit odd? They might report it to the PVDE.'

'Sarah, relax! We have it all under control. When we arrived, I told the receptionist that we were from the hospital and here to collect Adeline. I don't think the young woman will question it and the money I slipped her will keep her silent on the topic, at least for now. Where's Adeline's room?' he asked.

Sarah nodded towards the floor above.

'Right! Stop asking questions and get going.' Nick pushed her towards the stairs. 'Your flight leaves in two hours.'

31

9th May 1944, Portela Airport, Lisbon

The next couple of hours had a surreal quality for Sarah. In the car, Nick had produced a bottle of brandy and had proceeded to sprinkle some of it on Adeline's clothes. Sarah watched on in horror.

'Don't you see? If she smells of alcohol, they are more likely to believe our story,' he said, looking rather pleased with himself.

'Yes, sir,' Sarah replied, then fixed her gaze on the view beyond the car window. This was one trip she would not forget in a hurry.

Once at Portela Airport, Nick and his driver gently removed the still unconscious Adeline from the car and lowered her back into the wheelchair. Nick then pushed it into the terminal, Sarah close behind. With a wide-brimmed hat and dark glasses, they had done their best to ensure Adeline was difficult to identify, as Haas's men were known to hang around the terminal watching the comings and goings. However, there were still curious stares from the airport staff and other passengers. Sarah was sure they would be challenged at any moment, and her anxiety grew. As they joined the queue for check-in, Sarah spotted several police standing close behind the desk. They were checking and stamping the passports of all the passengers. Sarah's nerves ramped up another notch.

'Sir?' she whispered. 'Could they stop us from leaving?'

'Relax,' Nick whispered.

'You've done this before?' she asked, thinking she'd never be used to this kind of stress.

Nick licked his lips and grinned. 'Perhaps.' She wondered if he was the one who put escaped POWs onto flights. If so, he was an old hand at this game.

When Nick was asked about Adeline's condition by the British Overseas Airways Corporation lady at the desk, he smiled and said as cool as you please: 'Mademoiselle Vernier hates flying. I'm afraid she had a few too many drinks to calm her nerves. However, I can assure you she won't be any trouble during the flight.' Then he turned to Sarah. 'Miss Butterworth is travelling with her and will take care of her. Isn't that so, Laura?'

'Oh yes, I'm sorry, this always happens. She's terrified, you see.'

The attendant didn't look impressed but processed their tickets. Then the woman passed Sarah and Adeline's passports to one of the policemen, who took his time examining them. To Sarah's consternation, he walked off and disappeared into an office, still holding the passports.

'Hold your nerve,' Nick murmured.

Another few nail-biting minutes ticked by before the police officer reappeared. As he approached the desk, he nodded slowly to a colleague.

'Remove glasses, please,' the policeman demanded, pointing to Adeline.

Nick slipped the glasses off. The officer held the passport photo next to Adeline's face, then recoiled, coughing. The whiff of brandy was quite strong, Sarah had to admit. Then the officer shook his head and grunted. He seemed satisfied, and Sarah could breathe once more. With that, the other policeman stamped both passports and handed them back. As soon as they were clear of the desk, Nick and Sarah exchanged looks of relief.

They walked towards the exit, which led out to the apron, Nick still pushing the wheelchair. 'It has been an interesting few days, Sarah Gillespie,' he said. 'Give me a good deal of warning if you decide to visit again; that way I can be out of the country!'

Sarah could only grimace and reply: 'Sorry, sir.'

'Never mind, I'm only teasing. You have plenty of guts, my girl. This one hasn't given you an easy time of it,' he said, nodding at Adeline. 'There's many who would have abandoned her to her fate.'

The idea horrified her. 'Oh, no. I couldn't have done that! As much as she has tested me to my limit, we were always in this together.' Sarah chuckled. 'But yes, I will admit every day with Adeline is a test of one's nerves and resolve.'

Nick threw his head back and guffawed. 'Give me nasty Germans any day over a volatile Frenchwoman! Far more straightforward.' When they reached the exit, Nick stopped. 'I can't go any further with you, I'm afraid. Will you be alright from here? That's your plane, just over there. Take good care of your charge. Let's hope that sedative lasts.'

Sarah shook his hand. 'Gosh, yes! Thank you so much for your help, sir. And again, I apologise for being such a nuisance, but I couldn't have managed this on my own.'

The words seemed inadequate, but Nick gave her one of his crooked smiles. 'It's all part of the job,' he replied. 'Now, don't worry. The attendants will help her on board, and I have wired ahead to HQ. Someone will meet you at Bristol and accompany you back to London.' Then he reached into his pocket and pulled out a box. 'If you have any further trouble, you can give her this.' He handed over the box.

'What is it?' she asked.

'More of the sedative.'

'But I don't know how to administer it,' she replied, almost in a panic. 'I've never given an injection in my life.'

'You shouldn't need to. Worst case, you may need it on the train journey back to London, but you will have help from another agent at that stage. Try not to worry. It's a fallback, that's all.'

'You've thought of everything. Thank you, sir!'

The plane's engine started, and Nick had to raise his voice. 'Until we meet again,' he said, squeezing her hand. Then he winked as he waved her off. 'Keep in touch.'

Sarah stood aside as two airport staff manoeuvred the unconscious Adeline up the steps and onto the plane. From their expressions, Sarah knew they smelled the brandy. Even the flight attendant wrinkled her nose and gave Sarah a curious look. Sarah shrugged and repeated the falsehood of Adeline's fear of flying. But Sarah's embarrassment grew as several passengers had to move seats so that Adeline could be placed in the front row. Sarah did her best to ignore the comments of *disgraceful,* and *what is the world coming to.* If only there had been a less awkward way to get Adeline out of danger and home.

Sarah thanked the men for their help, then took the seat beside her sleeping charge, keeping her head lowered. At least they were on the plane and would soon be in the air. Sarah let herself relax as she watched the flight attendants prepare for take-off. What luck that Nick had been willing to help, for she would have struggled otherwise. However, she was worried about the report he would send back to HQ. The whole sorry mess was down to her.

Suddenly, a figure appeared in the still open doorway of the aircraft. A hush fell over the passengers, and Sarah wasn't surprised. To her dismay, the newcomer's uniform was similar to that worn by Paredes, the PVDE officer in Estoril. Her heart rate shot up and a trickle of sweat crept down her back. She kept her eyes lowered, hoping she was invisible; her gaze fixed on his shoes, mere feet away in front of her. What did he want? Were they about to be hauled off the plane? Was this a routine check, or had someone at the terminal tipped off the secret police about a suspicious passenger? The treacherous thought of denying knowledge of Adeline turned her stomach. *I can't take much more of this,* she thought with a gulp. Of course, for all she knew, Nick might have placed some escaped POWs on the flight as well. Something the Portuguese secret police would not be too pleased about, nor Haas's men, who were known to monitor the airport building for that exact reason.

An attendant stepped up to the PVDE officer, and they conversed briefly in hushed tones. Sarah strained to hear what they said, but to no avail. Just as suddenly, the man turned and left, and the flight attendant closed the door of the aircraft. As her breathing calmed, Sarah longed for a stiff drink and barely heard the instructions being given by the crew for take-off. By God, she'd have some tales to tell from this trip when the war was over!

Not that the danger was over yet, and as the plane slowly began to move, Sarah's heart rate rocketed once more. She had never flown before. What would it be like? Then she recalled that only a year before, the Luftwaffe had shot down the actor Leslie Howard's flight from Lisbon over the Bay of Biscay. Since then, in fact, the flights on this route only took place at night. The craft sped up and the lights of the terminal building blurred as they raced past. Sarah squeezed her eyes shut and gripped her hands tightly in her lap. Beside her, Adeline stirred and muttered 'Nikolay', then fell back into oblivion. For a moment, Sarah wished she, too, had been sedated.

Five hours later, their plane landed at Whitechurch Airport in Bristol. Much to Sarah's relief, the flight had been uneventful, and Adeline had remained silent, despite the noise of the engines and a few intervals of turbulence that Sarah had endured with alarm.

The flight attendant told Sarah she would have to wait until all the other people on board had disembarked before help would arrive. Again, she had to endure curious and disparaging glances from the other passengers as they shuffled past and down the steps. And on slept Adeline.

'Well, hello there!' a familiar voice greeted her about ten minutes later. It was Jack McKinnock, an agent she knew well as she was working with him on the Hastings project.

'Thank God!' Sarah exclaimed, jumping to her feet. 'Am I glad to see you!'

Jack squeezed her arm and looked down at Adeline 'So, we need to get sleeping beauty here back to London.'

'Yes, please.'

'No problem. Lisbon Station gave us the details.' Jack threw her a curious glance. 'You alright?'

'Yes, but I'm suffering from lack of sleep. It's been all go. Have we a car?'

Jack shook his head. 'Only as far as the train station, I'm afraid. I was able to negotiate a spot for us on a troop train. Sorry, doubt you'll get much sleep on that. Right! You go ahead of me, and I'll carry her down the steps.'

Sarah waited on the tarmac as Jack make his way down with Adeline rather gingerly, then held the wheelchair as he lowered Adeline into it. Ten minutes later, they were on their way to Temple Meads train station.

The train was packed with American troops just off a ship at Bristol Docks, but somehow Jack had obtained a compartment by pleading they were accompanying an ill passenger. So far, their luck had held, and Adeline remained oblivious to the world. Jack gently laid her down on the seat, and Sarah covered her with her own coat. The box containing the extra sedative was safely in Sarah's bag, but she really didn't want to have to resort to it. She showed it to Jack and explained why Nick had given her an additional dose.

'Gosh,' he said. 'You don't really think she'll have a meltdown?'

'I'd say it's jolly likely. She's already given me a few anxious moments back at the hotel in Lisbon.' But perhaps Jack's presence would inhibit Adeline's hysterics when she eventually came round.

In the meantime, knowing Adeline was bound to wake up at some stage, Sarah took the opportunity to fill Jack in on the entire trip to Lisbon. Jack was an old hand, but he whistled when she told him of her run-in with the PVDE and their hasty exit from the hotel. All the while, Sarah kept half an eye on the sleeping form laid out on the seat opposite.

Of course, it was too good to be true. Only an hour out of Bristol and Adeline's eyes snapped open. Sarah met her gaze, nerves jangling. Adeline struggled to sit up, but when Sarah moved to help her, Adeline snarled, holding up both hands. 'Stay away!' Then her eyes swung around and rested on Jack. 'And who are you?' she demanded.

'This is Jack, Adeline. A colleague. One of us,' Sarah replied.

'Hello, Mademoiselle Vernier,' Jack piped up. 'Nice to meet you.'

Adeline stared back at them both as if they were deranged. 'I'm not one of you. Not anymore.' She pulled the blackout blind towards her and peered outside. 'Where are we?'

'Heading back to London. You're safe, now. Haas cannot harm you,' Sarah said, hoping this would placate her. Adeline's colour was rising rapidly. Not a good sign.

'I did not agree to this!' Adeline shouted back before jumping up. 'You tricked me into coming back to England. I wanted to go to France.'

Sarah exchanged a quick glance with Jack. 'Adeline, we were in extreme danger. France would have been impossible, you know that. We had to leave Lisbon immediately. You were distraught and in no condition to decide and I was worried that Haas was going to come looking for you.'

'Huh! You were afraid I'd expose you.' All of a sudden, Adeline clutched her temple. 'Argh, my head! What did that man give me?' She slumped back down onto the seat. 'You drugged me! I should never have trusted you.'

'Sarah had no choice,' Jack said. 'Your safety—'

'The truth . . .' Adeline gasped, a shiver running through her. 'I deserved the truth, not this rough-shod treatment.'

'You're right; you did,' Sarah replied. 'I'm sorry, but I couldn't risk Haas finding us. I know you are distressed, but too much is riding on our mission. I could not risk exposing our work.'

Adeline threw her head back and laughed, but it was a hollow sound. 'Always you lie with such ease. And in the end, I had to get the truth about Nikolay from a German.' A strange expression settled on her face, and she wrapped her arms around her body. 'Oh, my precious Nikolay!' Adeline rocked back and forth for several minutes.

Sarah couldn't think straight anymore as her lack of sleep caught up with her. In despair, she glanced at Jack. He raised a brow in question, but she didn't know what to do. Jack didn't look like he did either, his gaze wary as he watched Adeline.

Then suddenly, Adeline stiffened. Sarah could hear her own heart pounding, her instincts telling her they had reached a crisis. But it was still a shock when Adeline suddenly lunged at her and grabbed her by the neck. They struggled for several moments, but Sarah couldn't shake her off as Adeline's entire weight bore down on top of her. Sarah was vaguely aware of Jack jumping to his feet. Then suddenly, Adeline gasped, loosened her grip and fell to the floor. Jack stood looking down at her, then back at Sarah, an empty syringe in his hand.

'You OK? What a tigress!' he said before bending down and lifting Adeline's prostrate form back onto the seat. 'Have to say I'm glad she's not my responsibility,' he added, rather unhelpfully, in Sarah's opinion.

Sarah sat back in her seat, rubbing her neck. She couldn't stop shaking. Jack was right. That was the reaction of a wounded soul. But could she really blame Adeline? The woman felt betrayed. Would she not react in the same way if she found out that Tony had been shot?

32

11th May 1944, Hyde Park, London

It was two days since Sarah had returned from Lisbon. Adeline was now a patient in a small private nursing home, organised discreetly by MI5. The doctors' reports were not encouraging. Adeline's mental state was extremely fragile and she barely communicated. Instead, her focus appeared to be inward, her grief consuming her.

To add to Sarah's woes, Jason was not pleased when he heard her report of what had transpired in Lisbon and Estoril. Sarah knew Nick would already have reported on her exploits to him, but she still had to go through a tough interview. Jason made it clear he was displeased, and she had left the meeting crestfallen. After all her hard work, a moment's lapse had almost undone her with the Portuguese secret police, and leaving Adeline unattended could have resulted in disaster, even death. But if Sarah had learned one thing in the past three years, it was that determination was her strength. Now, she had to throw herself into her work with renewed focus.

On her way home that evening, Sarah was still mulling over the situation with Adeline. She had to find a way to break through the barrier of Adeline's grief. Hadn't there been a moment of friendship in Lisbon? Could she use that to get through to her? As she waited to cross the road, she glanced across to the opposite pavement.

No way! Not again! Her elusive tail was back.

They locked gazes and Sarah caught the look of panic in the woman's eyes before she turned and hurried away back down the other street. Seconds later, Sarah had crossed the road and caught sight of the woman's distinctive head-scarf in the distance. The woman was striding quickly; she was going to lose her again. Sarah broke into a run. She pushed through the oncoming pedestrians, desperately trying to keep her prey in view. And just as she thought she was gaining on her, her tail hopped on a bus just as it pulled away from the stop.

As the bus passed Sarah, she saw the woman was taking her seat. She gave Sarah a little wave and settled back with a smile. Fuming, all Sarah could do was watch the vehicle drive away.

Gladys was waiting for Sarah when she got in from work that evening. Throughout dinner, her friend appeared to be distracted and Sarah could sense she was bursting to tell her something. So, when Gladys suggested a walk down to Hyde Park, she agreed. Soon, she was glad she had accepted.

It was a warm evening for May and lots of people were taking advantage of the fine weather. Sarah welcomed the distraction, and soon her problems with Adeline, that cheeky tail, and the worry that Hastings might fluff his assignment drifted away.

Gladys kept up a steady chatter about all manner of things as they walked towards Marble Arch, and Sarah was beginning to think she had been mistaken.

Then, out of the blue, Gladys asked: 'Have you heard from Tony?'

Sarah had been trying hard not to think about him. Adeline's situation had resonated with her far too much. It was not as bad for her, of course, as Tony wasn't dead, but the heartache was similar. She still missed him terribly. Sarah kept her eyes straight ahead and her tone even. 'No, not a word.'

'Isn't that odd?' Gladys replied, giving her an anxious glance.

'I don't see why. I'm sure he is extremely busy. Besides, he wanted time apart, and he must have meant it. At this stage, I don't expect to hear from him again.'

'Stupid man! I wish I could give him a good shake! He has hurt you so deeply.' Gladys paused and touched her arm. 'You still love him, though, don't you? I know you do your best to hide it, but I can tell how sad you are.'

'Yes, I do love him, but I don't think there is much hope of a reconciliation at this stage. He has probably forgotten all about me or found someone else.'

'Nonsense, girl. He's mad about *you*,' Gladys said, shaking her head.

'Then why no contact? No, Glad, I'm sure it's over. I must accept that.' Feeling a lump in her throat, she desperately needed to move the conversation on. 'How is work?'

'Same as ever.'

They walked along but Sarah could sense that Gladys's tension was back. Sarah had to give her time. She'd tell her eventually what was up.

'It's lovely walking along here. It was a great idea to get out of the flat and get some fresh air.'

Gladys remained silent, almost as if she hadn't heard her. A couple passed them, hand-in-hand, both in uniform.

Then Gladys cleared her throat. 'Actually, something happened while you were away, Sarah. Something I want to tell you about.'

Sarah paused and gave her an encouraging look. For once, Gladys appeared hesitant. Sarah was intrigued. 'Go on.'

'Well, remember I told you I was nervous that Alfie Smyth might show up at the flat again?'

'Yes?'

'Thing is . . . he did!'

'No!' Sarah exclaimed. 'The nerve of him!' She clutched Gladys's arm. 'What happened?'

'It was last Sunday, when you were away. Luckily, Martin was in the flat that evening, listening to the radio in the sitting room. I guess he heard the raised voices. Heard me telling Alfie to get lost. Next thing I knew, Martin had rushed out into the hall.' Gladys's eyes sparkled. 'Oh, Sarah, you should have seen him. You know we don't normally see eye to eye, but wow, he really was wonderful. As soon as Alfie saw Martin, he started shouting at me. Accused me of cheating on him with Martin!'

'Oh my God!' Sarah exclaimed. 'Then what happened?'

'Alfie lunged at Martin. It was all a bit of a blur as they scuffled, but seconds later, Alfie was sprawled on the floor clutching his face, blood streaming from his nose. Martin had landed a mean right-hook! As soon as Alfie managed to get to his feet, Martin grabbed him by the arm, and booted him out the front door.'

'Oh, my! Well, I am delighted Martin was there to help, and that you came to no harm. You must have been terrified.'

'I was. Especially after what he did to you.' Gladys shook her head. 'I know the man isn't well, but he shouldn't have been discharged if he's still doolally. He's a danger to the public.'

'Absolutely! I hope you contacted Ewan.'

'Didn't have to. He arrived with Judith shortly afterwards. Said he'd sort it.'

'That's a relief. Unfortunately, I'd imagine there are many like Alfie. Men who have seen terrible things or suffered appalling injuries. We can have no idea how awful combat must be. Their lives are changed forever. Some are affected mentally and there's no coming back from it.'

Gladys nodded. 'I suppose so. Even my brothers won't say much, and I know they have been to hell and back. My mother tries to keep busy, and God knows my dad's situation is distracting enough, but she is terrified something dreadful will happen to Graham and Sid. I also worry about them.'

Sarah squeezed her arm. 'Of course you do, but they have made it this far. Hopefully, the fighting will end soon.'

Gladys gave her a look full of curiosity. 'Do you know something?'

Sarah rushed to cover her tracks. 'No, of course not. How could I? But most people think Germany is struggling. It might be the beginning of the end.'

Gladys gnawed her bottom lip, then smiled. 'Wouldn't it be something? What would peace even look like? It's hard to remember what normal was like.'

'Better than this. That's for sure,' Sarah replied.

Gladys had a dreamy look. 'Imagine . . . No rationing. Chocolate. Stockings. Make-up!'

Sarah laughed. 'Oh yes, the essentials! Do you know what I miss most? Butter. Loads of it, melting into your toast.'

'Oh, God, yes!'

They walked along, each lost in their thoughts. 'Speaking of pleasant things, what about your love life?' Sarah asked. 'It's unlike you to be without a fella for long. Do you have your eye on anyone at the moment?'

To Sarah's utter amazement, Gladys blushed. 'Well, actually, now that you mention it, there is someone.'

Sarah stopped and turned to her. 'Oh Glad, I'm so happy for you. Where did you meet him? What's his name? Tell me all about him.'

'Eh, you already know all about him. In fact, you know him far better than I do.'

It took Sarah a moment. 'Oh my goodness! It's Martin, isn't it?

'Ha-ha! It is, yes!'

'I want to know *everything*,' Sarah urged.

They walked on again, along the shaded North Carriage Drive, under the trees. 'Well, it was the night after the run-in with Alfie in the flat. Judith was out and we were alone. I got quite upset, and Martin was very

286

sweet about it. We talked a lot. It turns out we like a lot of the same things.'

'And?'

'Then, on the night before he was going home, he asked me out to the cinema.' Gladys shrugged, then grinned. 'That was it.'

Sarah grinned back. 'I'm delighted. Two of my favourite people.' She linked Gladys's arm and squeezed it. 'I will have such fun teasing him about it. To think you were always bickering. It goes to show you never can tell.'

'Yes, well, no one was more surprised than me. But he was so kind, and he was good enough to listen to my guilty rants.'

'Martin is one of the good guys. You know how much I value him. He's like a big brother to me, really.'

'I know. And I see his value now,' Gladys replied with a grin. 'I just wish I'd seen it sooner.'

Later that evening, alone in her room, Sarah sat brush in hand at her dressing table. The news about Martin and Gladys was wonderful and so unexpected. So many times, she had to listen to Martin giving out about Gladys and her ways, or Gladys complaining about how bossy and judgemental Martin could be. Martin was a sly old thing; he must have had a *grá* for Gladys for ages. After all Gladys had been through of late, she was delighted to see her so happy. Judith also appeared to be getting along very well with Ewan. They hardly ever saw her now, bar at breakfast.

Sarah didn't like to wallow – it wasn't in her nature – but her friends' happiness threw her own situation into stark relief. Only a few months ago, she had been as happy as Judith and Gladys were at present. Sarah placed the brush down on the dressing table and frowned. The talk with Gladys had churned up her feelings for Tony, which she thought she had successfully repressed. Now, they were flooding back. Tony's silence was killing her, but her pride would not let her make the first move. Despite loving him, she was still angry and disappointed. What had changed between them? Had he felt trapped because she had wanted to discuss the future, or had her novelty worn off?

Or was it as she had feared that night? That she had been merely an easy fit for his life right now. Someone to sleep with but not love deeply enough to want something more permanent. No, that was unfair. She might not know him very well, but she knew his affection had been genuine. So, what was behind his reaction that night in his flat? Had there been someone else all along? Perhaps at home in Illinois. A girl waiting for Lieutenant Tony Anderson to come home to a hero's welcome. Maybe there had been promises made, which had to be kept, and he just couldn't bring himself to tell her the truth.

Blast! Sarah squeezed her eyes shut. *Keep busy. Keep moving forward.* But it was proving difficult. Since her return from Lisbon, she frequently had nightmares in which Tony was injured or killed in action. She would wake up gasping for air, sobbing even. Why was she having those awful dreams? Was it the stress of those few days in Portugal? Or a deep fear of losing Tony without a chance for a reconciliation? Perhaps it was seeing Adeline so distressed over Nikolay?

She turned her mind to Adeline. *I wonder what she is doing now,* Sarah thought, as a vision of her in her hospital room, sitting at the window and staring at nothing, popped into her head. Sarah remembered her own grief after Maura was killed. That emptiness that you were certain would never leave you. Yes, she could empathise with Adeline's state of mind.

What a horrible mess it all was. It was difficult not to feel guilty about Nikolay, because Sarah knew MI5 had made little or no effort to extract him from France. And Adeline was right, she *had* lied. A lie of omission, but it was still a lie, and she would regret it for a long time. Essentially, it had boiled down to sacrificing one life in the hope of saving thousands. But what right did MI5 have to play God? And what right had Sarah Gillespie to conspire with them? The years of working in the secret service had rubbed off on her and not in a good way. What kind of person had she become?

I don't recognise who you are anymore, Sarah Gillespie.

33

16th May 1944, St. Mary's Nursing Home, London

Sarah didn't have high hopes that Adeline would recover from the shock of Nikolay's death any time soon. The news had completely unhinged her. Sarah was torn. She wanted to help Adeline as she felt some sympathy for her situation, but she was terrified the woman would carry out her threats and ruin everything. They had all worked so hard to ensure Operation Fortitude would be successful and with Operation Copperhead, using Hastings as a decoy Monty, probably only weeks away, MI5 desperately needed Adeline to be in communication with Haas.

Of paramount importance was persuading Adeline to resume her vital work. Sarah had some misgivings, for she knew the poor woman was inconsolable, but thousands of lives depended on what would transpire in the weeks ahead – possibly even Tony's – and Adeline was an integral part of the plan. With a great deal of guilt, Sarah continued to visit Adeline every day in the hope she could talk her round, and every day she went back to the office disappointed and frustrated.

A week after the hasty exit from Lisbon, Sarah paid one of her visits to the nursing home. As she walked past the small office, she nodded to the nurse and enquired after Adeline. Unfortunately, like every day before, the nurse didn't have good news. Feeling despondent, Sarah headed to Adeline's room. Due to her distressed state, Adeline was in a private room where she wouldn't disturb the other patients. Bracing herself, Sarah paused before the door of Adeline's room. In her hand was a small bunch of flowers from the garden of her flat. She had no idea what they were, but she had spotted them when leaving that morning and thought they might brighten up the hospital room. However, she suspected it would take more than a few blooms to cheer Adeline up. *We are in miracle needed territory*, Sarah thought dolefully, as she knocked.

There was no answer, so Sarah opened the door as softly as she could in case Adeline was asleep. However, Adeline was sitting out on a chair, staring out the window. At least she was out of bed. That had to be a good sign.

'Adeline?' No response. Sarah walked over and placed her hand on her shoulder. 'Adeline, how are you today?'

Adeline sighed and slowly raised her head to look at her. Her eyes were red-rimmed, her face deadly pale. 'The same. Because I am here.'

'You need to rest, Adeline, and it's nice and quiet here. Look! I thought these might cheer you up,' Sarah said with forced brightness, showing her the flowers. 'I'll put them in a vase.' Sarah could feel Adeline's gaze on her as she popped the flowers into the glass vase on the bedside locker. Sarah turned, expecting to catch a glare, but Adeline's expression was completely blank. That was more disconcerting.

'Perhaps you could ask the nurse to give them some water?' Sarah suggested, but Adeline did not respond. With the ghost of a shrug, she turned away and continued to gaze out the window.

Sarah's heart sank. She was floundering, but somehow she had to get through to her.

Sarah sat down on the bed and collected her thoughts. 'Adeline, I have asked my boss to see what he can find out about what happened to Nikolay. It might help you come to terms with his passing.'

Adeline's head snapped round. 'You knew about that camp and didn't tell me. I don't trust you.'

'We heard a rumour about his arrest, which we could not confirm. We must rely on bits and pieces of information coming out of France from the Resistance. Sometimes the information is unreliable, or we cannot make sense of it, and we didn't want to upset you unduly. Please believe me, we didn't know he was dead.'

Adeline scowled. 'Everything is lies and manipulation with you British.'

Sarah could hardly argue with that, but she had to re-direct the woman's anger. 'I'm not always happy about what I am asked to do, but I signed up for this job so I could make a difference. I'm not always privy to the bigger picture, but I do know there are things happening now that will shape the course of the war, and your work is vital as part of that. It could save countless lives. What better way for you to get revenge for Nikolay's murder?'

'Huh! Don't worry; those responsible will pay. As soon as I escape this place,' Adeline scowled, 'I will contact Haas and tell him the truth.'

A wave of weariness swept over Sarah. 'But why? That doesn't make sense.'

'Because he is the only one I can trust. *He* told me the truth about Nikolay; you did not!'

'You're not thinking straight. Haas is your enemy. He sent you here to spy, to help Germany win the war. All he is doing is using you for his own ends,' Sarah replied.

'Just like you!'

'Adeline, you came to us and offered to help us. Don't forget that.'

'But you reneged on our deal. You didn't even try to get Nikolay out.' Adeline almost spat the words at her.

'I am really sorry about Nikolay, and I wish we had got him to safety, but I was honest with you from the start. I told you it would be extremely difficult. Be reasonable. We cannot control what is happening in an occupied country. You said yourself, someone you trusted, someone who had promised to hide and protect Nikolay, must have betrayed him, either willingly or not. The *Nazis* took him. They put him in that camp and when he tried to flee, they shot him. It is the Germans, not us, who deserve to be punished. We have a common enemy. Working with *us* will get you your revenge. We may even be able to liberate France.'

Adeline didn't respond. Instead, she bent her head and stared down at her hands in her lap. They were clasped so tightly her knuckles were devoid of colour.

Had Sarah said enough to convince her to take up the reins once more? She wasn't sure.

It took several minutes, but then, with a shaky breath, Adeline raised her head. 'Perhaps.'

Sarah dared to hope. It was a start; she might be able to retrieve something from the mess. She could leave Adeline now, knowing she would mull over what she had said.

She reached across and squeezed her hand. 'Thank you, Adeline. I'll leave you in peace,' Sarah said, getting to her feet. 'Is there anything you need? I will call in to see you again tomorrow.'

Adeline shook her head and turned away to stare out the window once more.

'Well, Sarah, what news?' Jason asked as she came into his office a few hours later. 'How is the patient?'

'No great change, sir. But I think I have managed to sow the seed of revenge. If she sees Haas as the enemy again, I believe she will co-operate.'

Jason sat back and crossed his arms. 'What a mess and it couldn't be worse timing.'

Sarah fidgeted with discomfort. 'Yes, sir.'

'Let us hope she comes round to the idea quickly. Our plans are moving forward rapidly. With Hastings' training going so well, we will send him to Gibraltar at the end of the month. It will be leaked as an official visit to the governor. If Jerry sees him there, they will think any invasion is weeks away. As you know, we also intend to send him on to Algiers, where he will make several public appearances with General Wilson. That should hopefully misdirect the Germans into thinking an attack will come from North Africa into Southern France.'

'Might I ask when the actual invasion is going to happen?'

'I'm sorry, that is classified, but I can tell you it is imminent. While you were in Lisbon, the chaps put Hastings through his paces many times. We believe he is sufficiently prepared. Naturally, he is nervous, knowing so much rides on this trip, but he has worked hard on the accent and Monty's mannerisms. His dedication to the role has impressed me.'

'I agree, sir. I was with him yesterday and thought he was marvellous. Today we plan to go through more of the dos and don'ts, but essentially, he is ready.'

'Don't forget, it's those little details that will convince people.' Jason chuckled. 'The boys were telling me that Hastings was very aggrieved to learn that Monty neither drinks nor smokes.'

'A small sacrifice, I'm sure, in the scheme of things. So, what part will Adeline play in this, sir?'

'A very important role indeed. Her letters to Haas will help enormously,' he replied. 'We will have one of Pfeiffer's fake agents corroborate what she sends. That will be something along the lines of a report that says Monty has been spotted at RAF Northolt boarding a plane. We will let the message go out via radio once Hastings is on his way to Gibraltar.'

'What exactly do you want in the first message from Adeline?' Sarah asked, pulling out pen and paper.

'Hold off for now. I'm not completely sure yet, but my idea was for her to tell him that she had overheard other journalists at *The Gazette* discussing a forthcoming trip accompanying Monty to Gibraltar. Haas knows she would not be part of the press corps, but he might believe she had heard others discuss the trip.'

'So, the first letter would be dangling the bait. And how soon would we need to send it?'

'We can probably wait a few days, but the first one will have to go by the beginning of next week. You'll have to pull out all the stops to get that damn woman to co-operate.'

It didn't give Sarah much time to work on Adeline, but she would have to try. 'Very well, sir. I'll give her another few days to rest up and have a good think, then I'll broach it.'

34

19th May 1944, Sale Place, Paddington, London

A few days later, the doctors were happy to discharge Adeline back into Sarah's care. Delighted at her progress, Sarah escorted Adeline from the hospital back to the flat in a taxi. However, Adeline sat beside her in silence, which put Sarah on edge. Was she truly better, or was this just a ruse to get out of the hospital? Might she bolt at the first opportunity?

A few days had certainly made a difference. There was some colour back in Adeline's cheeks, and although she was subdued when she had spoken earlier, she had talked sense. Most important of all, there had been no more threats to betray MI5. Sarah wondered if she could have recovered so quickly. What had changed? Sarah could only hope that her attempt to redirect Adeline's anger and lust for revenge had worked because Adeline's renewed energy, if channelled correctly, could help them achieve a satisfactory result. And if Operation Copperhead *was* a success, it could spell the beginning of the end of this awful war. However, Adeline had made one demand. She wanted Sarah to move in with her for a while.

The car drew up to the kerb and Adeline hopped out. Sarah paid the cabbie and when she joined Adeline on the pavement, she found her staring up at the building, seemingly hesitant to enter.

Sarah was puzzled and touched her arm. 'Are you alright?'

'Yes,' she replied with a shake of her shoulders. 'Sorry. A shiver went through me . . . it's nothing.'

'It's chilly out here. Let's get inside,' Sarah said, 'then I can get settled in.'

At first, Sarah had been reluctant to agree to the arrangement, but as she thought about it, it made sense. Adeline was still recovering, and MI5 needed her to be fully operational in the weeks ahead. If that meant Sarah had to sleep on a chair in Adeline's flat, so be it. She had hoped to persuade Mr Cartwright to give her the top-floor flat, but when she enquired, she learned it had been let out already.

As it happened, Mr Cartwright was in the hallway as they entered. The landlord nodded to them both and held out a bunch of letters to Adeline. 'Post for you, miss,' he said.

Adeline took the handful of letters and headed up the stairs without a word. It still irritated Sarah the way Adeline treated the man, so she leaned over the banister. 'Hello, how are you, Mr Cartwright?'

Cartwright's eyes followed Adeline. 'Fine, thanks, miss. She alright, then?'

'Mademoiselle Vernier is doing well,' Sarah replied. But she waited while Adeline unlocked the door of her flat before turning back to him and lowering her voice. 'I'm going to stay for a few days in the flat with her, but could you keep an eye on her when I'm not here? She's had a tough time of it.'

Cartwright scrunched up his nose. 'She don't like me much. I barely get a hello out of her, but as it's you asking . . . I will.'

'Thank you. Who's the new tenant? Are they here yet?'

'No. Some bloke or other, dunno yet. He ain't moving in till next week,' he said.

'OK, thanks,' Sarah replied with a smile before scurrying up the stairs.

Adeline was standing at the table, the bunch of letters in her hand. With a grunt, she plucked one out and held it up. Her voice shook. 'I'd guess this is from Haas.'

'That's a relief,' Sarah said, setting her bag down on the floor. 'I was afraid our rapid exit might have drawn the wrong kind of attention. It's timely, too.'

'Don't tell me; you want me to write a letter.' Adeline plonked down into the armchair and crossed her slender legs. 'You don't waste any time.'

'I'd much rather not bother you, but the thing is we need this letter to go out immediately.' Sarah sat down at the table. 'Look, I'm going to trust you with some top-secret information. What we need you to do in the next couple of weeks could change the course of the war. Even free France. It is a tremendous responsibility, Adeline, but also an opportunity for you to avenge Nikolay's death and see your country free again.'

Adeline arched a brow but made no comment.

'We want you to tell Haas that you have heard a rumour that Field Marshal Montgomery will visit Gibraltar next weekend.'

Adeline uncrossed her legs and sat forward, her mask of ennui falling away. 'Is it true?'

'Yes, absolutely,' Sarah replied.

'But why do you want Haas to know? Is this not dangerous? They will try to kill the man.'

'That is unlikely. They know he is well protected. Besides, he will be on British soil. No, the object is to confuse them. You see, we need to distract them.'

Adeline narrowed her eyes. 'Distract them from something else, something big?'

'Yes.'

'And this something big will help win the war?'

Sarah licked her lips, hoping this strategy of making Adeline feel important was going to work. 'I dare say it will.'

Adeline mulled it over, then slowly nodded. 'Very well. If this helps to free my country, I will write this, but how do I explain how I know about it?'

'Perhaps you have overheard colleagues discuss the trip at *The Gazette*.'

Adeline broke into a smile. 'Ah yes. That is possible.'

'Why not get your equipment and we can go over what you need to say?'

Adeline went into the bedroom, returning moments later with her leather pouch and that damned French novel. Sarah watched Adeline as she set up.

'I'm ready, but first I must find the code word,' Adeline murmured, running her finger down Haas's letter. 'Line four . . . third word . . . *périple*.'

'What does that mean?' Sarah asked.

'Journey. He asked if I had a pleasant journey home.' Adeline quirked her lip as she opened *120 Rue de la Gare*.

'Page sixteen, fifth paragraph, eighteenth word.' Adeline looked up and grinned. 'Casino!'

'*What*?' Sarah jumped in her seat. 'Do you think he knows about me? Has he guessed who you are really working for?'

'No! I don't see how he could,' Adeline said with a frown. 'I think it is a joke aimed at me and my stupid mission with that Carter man.'

'Perhaps,' Sarah replied, slumping back against the seat. Could such a man as Haas have a sense of humour? It seemed unlikely. Her stomach churned because she didn't like coincidences. 'How will you include it?'

Adeline threw her a smug look. 'It is easy. In the covering letter, I will mention my trip to Estoril and how I won at the tables.' Something seemed to amuse her, and she shrugged. 'You are – what is the word in English – *paranoïaque?*'

'Paranoid, perhaps? Oh, yes, I think it goes with this job.'

Putting her pen down, Adeline gazed at her. 'Do you think if we had met before the war, that we could have been friends?'

'I . . . I'm not sure, Adeline. What put that into your head?' Sarah asked, slightly uncomfortable.

'I don't know. I can never decide whether I like you,' Adeline replied. Sarah smiled at her honesty as Adeline continued: 'When we first met in Scotland, you were so official and cross.'

'And I thought you were superficial and dangerous.'

'Piff! How stupid!'

Sarah laughed. 'Yes. Well, if I'm honest, I think we both know the answer is no; it is unlikely we would have been friends.' Sarah tilted her head. 'But what we have been through

303

lately has brought us closer together. Someday, hopefully soon, this damn war will be over and life and normal relationships can resume.'

'I hope so,' Adeline said with a sigh. 'But what will you do after the war?'

'Right now, I have no idea. I might go back to Ireland for a while. I have family in Cork and Galway. Cousins I've never met. I've never been that bothered about them, but the war has made me realise how important family can be.'

'What about Tony?' Adeline asked with a frown. 'Will he go with you?'

'Unlikely. I imagine he will return home to America when the fighting is over. Besides, we are no longer a couple.'

Adeline's fine brows rose. 'Ah! I'm sorry. Though I did wonder. You looked so sad at times and never mentioned him. You should have told me.'

Now, weeks later, Sarah knew she could not really blame Adeline for her and Tony's break-up. If their relationship had been strong enough, they could have laughed off that whole sorry episode. However, Sarah was still surprised to hear the sympathy in Adeline's voice; she sounded sincere. Perhaps their exploits together had formed a bond that she hadn't even noticed. Friendship with this woman wasn't quite the anathema it had once been. And suddenly, Sarah was disconcerted. She swallowed a few times before asking: 'And you? What will you do?'

'I will go home to France. To my old flat, my old job. But first I will find Nikolay's grave and grieve for him.' Then her expression hardened. 'Also, I will find out what happened and see if justice is possible.'

The way Adeline said this gave Sarah a shiver.

'Then I will try to make a new life,' Adeline continued, a slight wobble in her voice. 'It will not be easy . . . for any of us.'

A lump formed in Sarah's throat. She reached across and squeezed Adeline's hand. 'I hope it is a good new life, Adeline. You deserve it after all you have been through.'

Then the most extraordinary thing. Adeline got up and went into the bedroom. When she returned, she handed Sarah a battered photograph, her hand shaking. 'This is Nikolay.'

Sarah sat up straight and studied the picture of the man who had caused so much trouble and heartache for the woman before her. She had expected handsome, but Nikolay was more striking than handsome, with strong features and dark, almost wild eyes below a large forehead. Sarah welled up as she handed the precious photo back to Adeline. 'Thank you for showing me, for sharing something so personal. It means a lot.'

'It's all I have left,' Adeline said, putting the photo away. 'I will never forgive the Germans for this. Somehow, I will make them pay.'

'You will.' Sarah nodded towards the empty page on the table. 'If it is any comfort, what you are doing now, for us, for the Allies, will also make them pay.'

Adeline pushed out her bottom lip and muttered. 'I really hope so, or Nikolay's death will have been in vain.'

35

23rd May 1944, MI5, St. James's Street, London

Sarah watched as Hastings was put through his paces yet again. The man looked exhausted. But just before the signal to begin, he took a deep breath, his shoulders went back, and a determined expression settled on his features. Sarah felt a rush of pride; not misplaced, she believed; after all, they had worked so hard together to ensure this operation would succeed.

At the signal from Jason, Hastings stepped out of the imaginary plane and walked across the room to where several MI5 officers were playing military and government officials. The men saluted.

'Good morning, gentlemen,' Hastings said, returning the salute with aplomb. 'Where's Foley?'

One man stepped forward and escorted him to the mock car. This time, Hastings sat in the correct seat; left side, at the back. Monty was a man of routine. The slightest variation and someone could suspect something wasn't right.

'Excellent,' Jason said, rising to his feet. 'Well done, Hastings. That was perfect. Thanks everyone. We might do one more run-through on Friday.'

Hastings beamed but Sarah could tell he was extremely nervous, his forehead shining with perspiration. Hopefully, it would be warm in Gibraltar on Saturday when he arrived, which would disguise any sign of sweating with nerves. It was imperative he looked calm and self-assured.

As Sarah and Jason walked back along the corridor towards the stairs, Jason turned to her. 'I believe Operation Copperhead will be a success. You've done an excellent job with Hastings.'

'Thank you, sir,' she replied, greatly relieved. 'But it was a team effort. I won't be happy until it is over, and we have confirmation that Jerry has misconstrued the reason for the visit.'

'I think it is safe to assume that the wires to Berlin will be hopping,' Jason replied with a grin. 'If you come back to my office, I'll give you the wording for the next message to our friend Haas.'

'That's great, sir. As it happens, Adeline received a letter from him this morning. She said he is keen to hear more about Monty's trip. I brought it along, as I thought you might like to see it.'

'I say, yes, indeed.' Jason gave her a conspiratorial look. 'If only he knew we were reading his letters. He'd be furious!'

'I doubt he would be pleased,' she replied cheekily. 'Not a man one would like to upset.'

'At least Lisbon Station got one over on him regarding that Carter chap. By all accounts, Jerry turned up at the address Adeline gave Haas and tore the place asunder, looking for our escaped POWs.'

'It's a relief that worked out, sir, or Haas might have twigged something wasn't right about Adeline,' Sarah said. 'As it was, he wondered why she had left the country so quickly. He asked about it in his last letter. Adeline pleaded shock and upset at the news about Nikolay.'

Jason looked grim. 'Which was true.'

'He appears to have accepted it,' Sarah answered. They walked past Miss Wilson, who nodded to them both but carried on typing.

'Take a pew,' Jason said, as he sat down at his desk.

Sarah pulled the letter from her bag and handed it over.

Jason skimmed through it, translating the French into English for her benefit.

'That's a relief, sir. Adeline did translate it but—'

'You're never one hundred percent sure you can trust her?' Jason asked.

'Yes, is that awful of me, after all she has been through? The irony is that we have become friends of a sort, but I guess my training will always kick in.'

'As it should. A wise agent trusts no one. Still, we can agree that Agent Honey has done a good job. Now, we need her to confirm the rumour she put in the last letter. Tell him Monty is due in at midday on Saturday and that he will visit the governor, et cetera. The letter must go in this evening's post, though, to ensure he gets it in time.'

Sarah checked her watch. 'Don't worry; I'll go straight to Sale Place, sir. It's almost six-thirty; Adeline should be back from *The Gazette* by now.'

'Excellent. It is vital Haas knows about the trip details, for I'm sure Berlin is anxious to know more. I will see you on Friday as I must head off to Kent for a couple of days. We can speak again then.'

'Yes, sir.' Sarah turned at the door. 'Have a safe trip.'

Half an hour later, as Sarah drew closer to Sale Place, she noticed more activity than usual. People were hurrying past, their expressions grim. Then an ambulance passed her at high speed. An acrid smell hung in the air – smoke, if she wasn't mistaken. Sarah increased her pace, her heart thumping, and when she turned the corner into Sale Place, she came up short. The way was blocked and a special constable manned the barrier across the road. But that wasn't what made her blood run cold. Dirty black smoke rose from what was left of several houses . . . and one of them was Cartwright's.

Oh, my God! Adeline!

'I'm sorry, miss, you must move along now. No access until further notice,' the constable said, coming over to her.

Sarah stared at him. 'You don't understand, my friend . . . One of those houses is where I am living at present. I must find her.' Her voice rose in panic.

'Sorry, miss, but it's not safe. The heavy rescue lads are in there now.' He pointed to a sign which said '*Danger: Unexploded Bomb!*'

'No, please. I must make sure she is alright,' Sarah cried, fumbling in her bag for her ID. She flashed it at him.

He quirked his mouth. 'I don't know, miss. My orders are to keep everyone back. There could be another bomb.'

'Please.' Sarah could see he was weakening. 'I won't get in the way. I promise.'

'But it's the risk, miss. If anything happened to you—'

'I take full responsibility,' Sarah said as she slid around the barrier. 'Who's in charge?'

With reluctance, the constable pointed to a burly man in dungarees and a steel helmet. 'Peter Cuttle is the foreman.'

Sarah was almost choking on the thick black smoke as she approached the leader of the rescue crew. But as she reached him, he roared: 'Silence!'

The men, scattered amongst the rubble, froze, and a young lad rushed over to the crane that had pulled up minutes earlier, and turned off the engine. No one moved.

Cuttle shouted out: 'Can anybody hear me?'

Sarah strained her ears, hoping. Then one man on the mountain of rubble called out. 'There's tapping, Pete. Coming from over there; I'm sure of it.'

'Right. Get digging again, lads,' Cuttle called out. Then he swung around and stared at Sarah. 'Who the hell are you? You can't come in here.' Sarah showed him her ID. 'I don't care who you are, you can't stay. Too dangerous.'

'I've been staying there,' she said, pointing to where she thought Cartwright's house had stood. 'I'm sure my friend was in that house.'

His expression softened slightly. 'I see. I'm sorry, love, but you will just have to wait. And hope. Stand well back and let us get on with it.'

'But do you know what happened?' Sarah asked.

'A crew were clearing out the old bombed out site. We reckon there was an unexploded bomb in the basement, which the original clear-up crew missed,' he answered, keeping his eyes on his men's progress.

'And they set it off? How awful.'

'Far too bloody common.'

'When did it happen?' she asked.

'About an hour ago. So, I have five men from that crew missing, plus whoever was in the buildings on either side.' He turned and gave her a brief glance. 'Any idea who would have been in your building?'

'As far as I know, Mr Cartwright, the owner, an elderly man, and my friend, Adeline Vernier, who would have been in the first-floor flat. The other flat on the top floor would have been empty.'

Cuttle nodded. 'Thanks, that 'elps,' he said with a wave of his hand towards the far pavement. 'You can stand over there.'

A shout came from the pile of rubble, and Cuttle scrambled over to join his men. Sarah's mind was a whirl. Could Adeline have been spared? Perhaps she was still at *The Gazette,* working late. But it was past seven o'clock now, and Adeline was normally home by six. There was a high probability she was in the flat at the time of the explosion. *Please God, let her be OK.*

Sarah stood, feeling helpless, as the workmen dragged bricks and timber away. Another shout went up and a couple of the men standing at the top of the pile kneeled. Now, they were removing pieces of debris as gently as they could, forming a chain. Sarah reckoned they had found someone. And then it hit her. The memory of that night back in Dublin in '41, when No. 18 imploded, trapping her in the rubble and killing Maura, who had been only feet away when the bomb struck. Sarah wrapped her arms around her body, trying to stop the trembling. Darkness encroached on her vision and the tears flowed unchecked.

312

'Excuse me, miss,' a man said. 'We need to get closer with this.' The man and his colleague were holding a stretcher.

'Sorry,' she replied, taking a quivering breath as she stood back to let them through. As she watched them approach the desolation, an overwhelming sense of helplessness swept over her. Her heart was palpitating wildly. She wanted to help, desperately, but it was as if her limbs had turned to lead.

Cuttle yelled over at the two stretcher bearers. 'Come on, lads, we have a casualty here.'

Sarah watched as they carefully lifted someone out and placed them on the stretcher. But whoever it was, was covered in dust and debris and was unmoving. One of the stretcher bearers felt for a pulse and, to Sarah's dismay, shook his head. *Please don't let it be Adeline*, she prayed. From where she stood, it was impossible to tell if it was a man or a woman. As the stretcher bearers made their way back, they had to negotiate the unstable mound as best they could. Cuttle was close behind. As soon as they were clear of the danger, they headed straight for the ambulance, parked up on the other side of the road. Sarah ran over.

'Do you know him?' Cuttle asked. 'Poor blighter. Hopefully, it was quick.'

Sarah looked down at Cartwright's bloodied face and pushed down on a sob. 'Yes, it's Mr Cartwright.'

Cuttle gently touched her shoulder. 'Sorry, miss. OK, lads, make a note of his name and take him to the morgue.'

36

As the hours dragged by and it grew dark, the rescue crew had to train large lamps on the rubble so they could continue to work. Sarah thought the men were marvellous. Gritted determination could be read on each of their faces, despite the mammoth task confronting them. They would dig until they were sure they had found everyone. Eventually, all five missing men from the clear-up crew were dug out. Each of them was dead, leaving Sarah to fear the worst. What hope was there that Adeline could have survived when they did not?

It was well past ten o'clock that evening when Adeline was pulled from the remains of Cartwright's house. Sarah had almost given up hope. But although her injuries looked terrible and she was unconscious, she was still breathing, and that was all that mattered. There was hope.

A short ride in the ambulance brought them to St. Mary's Hospital. Sarah waited out in the corridor as a doctor assessed Adeline's injuries. He seemed to take forever, and her anxiety grew. Eventually, the doctor appeared in the doorway. His weary gaze came to rest on Sarah.

'You are this lady's friend, I understand?' he said.

'Yes, doctor. How is she? Will she be alright?' Sarah asked.

'Mademoiselle Vernier has sustained some serious injuries. Broken ribs, several fractures in her right leg and lots of cuts and bruises, not to mention a nasty gash to her head, which will need stitches. What worries me most is that she is still unconscious.'

'But she will survive?' Sarah held her breath.

'I'm sorry, but it's probably too early to say. There could be internal injuries we haven't discovered yet. However, she was lucky. She must have been trapped in a pocket of the rubble. I understand none of the others involved were lucky enough to survive.'

'Six others perished; so yes, she was extremely lucky. May I see her before I go?'

'Not this evening. Once we have a cast on her leg, we will move her to a ward for observation. You may be able to see her tomorrow if she regains consciousness. Call back then.'

Sarah was disappointed but understood. 'I will. Thank you, doctor. If her condition should deteriorate during the night, could someone get a message to me?' The doctor nodded and waited while she wrote her address and telephone number. He pocketed the note and Sarah hoped he would remember it, for he looked dead on his feet.

'Thank you. And if she should regain consciousness, please tell her that Sarah was asking after her,' she said. He acknowledged this with a nod, then slipped back into the room where Adeline was being treated and closed the door.

Suddenly exhausted, Sarah leaned against the wall. Her head pounded so much she could hardly think. Perhaps she should wait? Yet there was little she could do for Adeline but pray, and that she could do just as well at home. She had to trust the medical staff would do their best for Adeline. Suddenly she longed to see her friends for some comfort. Witnessing the aftermath of the explosion had triggered some awful memories. Her emotions were jumbled, and she couldn't think straight. All she could focus on was home and bed. At least it was only a short walk back to the flat.

As she made her way to the exit, Sarah spotted a bathroom and ducked inside. Having used the facilities, she splashed her face with cold water to remove the smut from the fire from her forehead and cheek. Unfortunately, her clothes were also soiled by soot and dirt and would need a good wash. At least it was dark, and no one would notice. But as she rummaged in her bag for a handkerchief to dry her face, her heart almost stopped. A piece of paper, the one given to her by Jason only hours before, was sticking out of her bag. The one with the instructions for the urgent letter to Haas.

Aghast, Sarah froze. *Oh, no! I completely forgot!* It must go out in the post this evening if it is to reach Haas on time. Hastings was due to fly to Gibraltar on Saturday and today was Tuesday. Sarah felt the bitter taste of panic in her mouth. What on earth was she going to do? Adeline was in no fit state to speak, let alone write.

Calm down, girl! It's going to be OK. Just think! Alright. I will have to write it except, of course, I have no blooming French!
Sarah gripped the edge of the basin, breathing in and

out as a cold sweat formed on her skin, her blouse sticking to her back. *Jason! He could write it; he is fluent in French.* But she didn't know where he lived. Then she remembered he had left for Kent as she was leaving the office earlier. There was also the small matter of access to Adeline's equipment. Not to mention Haas's last letter, which would contain the code word required to complete a new one.

Sarah groaned aloud and an elderly lady entering the bathroom treated her to a side-eye look. Sarah pasted a smile on her face, curbing a powerful urge to curse. The situation couldn't be any worse. She'd have to go back to Sale Place and see if she could find any of the things she needed. Maybe she'd be lucky enough to find some of her own belongings. Not that there was much, only a few clothes. *Oh, you stupid girl; that's daft!* She couldn't crawl through what was left of those houses in the dark; she'd never find what she required. The workmen might still be there too. How would she explain any of it? Besides which, it would be highly dangerous.

'Well, sod it!' Sarah exclaimed.

The lady in the cubicle harrumphed her displeasure.

What the hell was she to do? Sarah then remembered she had left Haas's letter with Jason and almost cried with relief. How fortunate was that? Perhaps it was still on his desk. Sarah raced out of the door. It was vital she retrieved it now. Time was running out.

The taxi dropped Sarah off outside MI5. She had never been in the building this late in the evening and only hoped that the night porter would let her in. The man who eventually answered her ring at the door was unknown to her, and Sarah almost panicked. Would he deny her entry? Sarah produced her ID and held it up to the glass for him to see. After he squinted at it for a minute, he nodded and unlocked the door. The man surveyed her with raised brows, and she knew bravado was her best bet.

'It's urgent. I need to collect something from my office,' Sarah said. 'I won't be a tick.' She raced off up the stairs before he could offer to accompany her. She had to avoid awkward questions. After all, how could she explain searching her boss's office this late at night?

With a churning stomach, Sarah checked the blackout blind was down before she flicked the light on in Jason's office. She really shouldn't be here, but it was an emergency, after all. He'd understand when she'd tell him the whole sorry story on Friday. As she swivelled around to tackle the desk, she let fly some choice expletives. The desk was completely bare. Miss Wilson must have used Jason's absence to do a huge clean-up. Cursing Miss Wilson's dedication to duty, Sarah pulled out and looked through the desk drawers, praying the secretary had put the letter somewhere close to hand. On the point of giving up, she found it by chance, sticking out of the corner of a folder entitled *Operation Copperhead* in the bottom drawer. Sarah said a swift prayer of thanks to whoever was the patron saint of spies, stuffed the letter into her bag and fled back down the stairs.

But now what? she pondered, as she walked down St. James's Street. It was hopeless. Without that stupid novel to give her the code word, she was stuck. She stalled, frowning into the darkness, desperately trying to think of a solution.

She didn't have Pyramidon either, but she could improvise; there were other methods, and she could explain that away in the letter. The real sticking point was her total lack of French and the darn book now buried under what remained of Adeline's flat.

Think Sarah! Think! And then it dawned on her, there *was* another copy – at Tony's! It was a long shot, but she had nothing to lose. But what if Tony had taken the novel with him? The consequences of that possibility made her groan aloud. But she had to check and hope that luck was on her side, just as it had been for Haas's letter. Sarah hailed an oncoming taxi and jumped in.

When Sarah reached the newsagent below Tony's flat, she spotted the owner still inside, tidying up. Perhaps her luck really was turning! Sarah tapped on the door and waved. Mr Emsley noticed her and opened up.

'Good evening, Sarah,' Mr Emsley said, letting her in. 'You're lucky to catch me here. I'm doing my monthly stock check. It's good to see you. I haven't seen you in a while. What brings you here so late?' Then he glanced at her clothes and his eyes popped. 'Good Lord! What happened to you?'

'Oh, I was helping out with a rescue operation. It's only dirt. Nothing serious.'

'That's a relief. What can I do for you?' he asked.

'Oh, well, you see, I'd like to borrow the key to Tony's flat. I need to retrieve something for work, which I left behind. Silly me! Sorry to bother you, but with him away . . .'

Emsley frowned. 'Didn't you know he's back?'

'What?' She gasped. *Oh, no!*

'Didn't he get in touch?' he asked. 'I must say I'm surprised, but perhaps it is another one of his fleeting visits. There's been plenty of them of late. Well, ain't he a dark horse?'

'Nothing more certain, Mr Emsley. Are you sure he's here? Did you see him?' she asked.

'Well, no, I didn't see him, but I heard him pottering about up there only a few minutes ago. Why don't you go on up?' Emsley winked at her. 'Nothing like a reunion, eh?'

Flummoxed, Sarah nodded and turned to walk away. She was numb. Tony had been back in London but hadn't contacted her. That told her everything she needed to know. She froze, her hand on the door handle. A horrible ache had settled in her tummy and the throbbing in her head showed little sign of abating. If Tony *was* in, how could she explain her presence without looking a total idiot or revealing MI5's top-secret operation? Of course, he would know some of the detail but how much would Everleigh want her to reveal? She had no idea.

'Was there anything else you wanted, Sarah?' Emsley called out to her.

The trick was to keep calm; think logically. Sarah turned and walked back to the counter. 'Actually, there is something I need. Sorry, Mr Emsley, I'm a bit scatty tonight. I'll take a box of matches, please.' At least she could use one for the invisible ink message she'd have to attempt to write.

Sarah paid and left the shop, cursing under her breath. It really wasn't her day. The last thing she wanted was an awkward conversation with Tony and yet she didn't have a choice. The letter had to be written, somehow, so she needed the book. Steeling herself for the inevitable confrontation, she stood at the bottom of the stairs leading up to the flat, trepidation coursing through her veins.

You have faced far worse, Sarah Gillespie, you'll just have to brazen this out.

37

23rd May 1944, Tony Anderson's Flat, Paddington, London

The door opened. Although Sarah had thought she had mentally prepared, seeing Tony was like receiving an electric shock. Sadly, it was obvious from his reaction that she was the last person he had expected to knock on his door. How cruel of fate to bring her here and throw them together once more. A jumble of sensations hit Sarah as she stood there. However, her predominant feeling was one of embarrassment, and it took every ounce of courage not to bolt. She tried to read his expression, but, other than a raised brow, it was hard to tell what Tony was thinking. However, one thing was clear: the man was exhausted, with dark shadows under his eyes, and an unusual pallor. But despite that, he was as attractive as ever and her impulse was to hug him and soothe away his weariness as she had done so many times before. But of course she could not. That relationship was in the past.

As guilt, regret and not a little self-loathing battled in her pounding head, Tony's gaze swept her up and down. 'Good God, Sarah! What on earth happened to you? Were you in an accident?'

Unfortunately, the power of speech was proving elusive and all she could do was shake her head. Sarah knew she was on the verge of tears and fought hard to keep them in check. All she could do was stare at him like an idiot. But before she had recovered her equilibrium sufficiently to say something sensible, Tony had grabbed her hand and pulled her over the threshold, kicking the door shut.

Then he stalled, frowning down at her. 'Is that smoke?' he asked, sniffing the surrounding air. 'Where have you been?'

Sarah knew if she were to survive this awkward meeting, she needed to stay calm and keep her focus on getting that book. No personal stuff. If she succumbed to tears now, they might never stop. But to Sarah's consternation, Tony continued to stare at her with deep concern, and she knew she was undone. It was going to be difficult to carry this encounter off with aplomb. Why couldn't she speak? The words, as soon as they formed in her mind, dissolved on her tongue.

With a sigh, he said: 'Right. Obviously, you are in need of a strong drink.' He pushed her along into the sitting room and towards the sofa. 'Sit.'

As Sarah watched him pour a glass of whisky, a sudden calmness descended. The shock of seeing him again was now over and she could concentrate on the job in hand.

You are in control, Sarah. Don't let the sight of him, as wonderful as it is, distract you.

However, when she reached out to accept the drink, her hand shook. Thankfully, he didn't comment, though she knew he had noticed by his sudden frown. Instead, he sat down at the table and waited.

Eventually, he ran out of patience. 'Sarah, why are you here? How did you know I was back in London?'

'That's just it, I didn't know,' she replied, taking a gulp of whisky, then coughed as it hit the back of her throat.

'I don't understand.'

'It wasn't my intention to bother you. I only came here to . . . I need to borrow the paperback Adeline gave you,' she said at last in a rush. 'Do you still have it? Is it here?'

Tony's gaze hardened, and he glanced up at the clock on the wall. 'You came all this way to borrow a novel at eleven-thirty at night? What's the urgency? And you still haven't explained the state of your clothes. There's soot on your coat and smears of it on your face and neck.'

Sarah's hand strayed to the scar on her neck and her fingers slid along the ridge of skin, the only physical reminder of her injuries from the bomb in North Strand. It was a habit she thought she had grown out of. Struggling for words, she took another sip of the whisky, then put the glass down.

She glanced down at her clothes. 'It doesn't matter. I'm not hurt. I was involved in a rescue operation, but only as a bystander. I don't want to detain you. Please, may I have the book? Then I will leave you in peace. I'm sorry, I know it's late, but I must have . . . It's urgent.' She almost cringed. How had it come to this? She was being rude and abrupt. It was like her mind was shrouded in fog and she was seeing herself from a distance.

To Sarah's dismay, a flicker of annoyance flared in his eyes. 'I see. Sure. Whatever.' Tony rose and left the room, returning a few minutes later with the book in his hand. 'This one, I assume?' he asked, holding it out to her, the gory red cover flashing before her eyes.

But when she tried to take it, his grip on the book remained firm. 'An explanation would be nice.' But it was his expression that undid her. There was anger there, yes, but also worry.

Suddenly, it was as if she had hit a wall. 'Oh, God!' She dropped her head in her hands and the floodgates opened.

'What the hell, Sarah?' Tony dropped to his knees in front of her and gently lifted her head, his hand cradling her chin. His gaze bored into her, demanding an explanation. 'Come on, don't cry. Whatever is wrong, it can't be that bad.'

'Oh, but it is!' She hiccupped.

Gently, he wiped away a tear and when his arms went around her, she was too overwhelmed to resist. His hug almost took her breath away. 'Tell me what's wrong, please. I can't bear to see you like this,' Tony muttered into her hair. 'Let me help, even if it's only for old times' sake.'

The reminder of how things stood between them only worsened her suffering. Sarah tried to pull away. 'I don't . . . I can't ask you. I must deal with this myself.'

'In your present state, I'd guess that's unlikely. Look, if this is to do with your job, I'd remind you that, despite our personal differences, we are on the same side. I cannot and will not ignore your distress. If I can help, why not let me? At least, tell me what is going on. I've been around the block a few times, you know that; I might be able to suggest a solution.' Then he grimaced. 'Sorry, this floor is

326

killing my knees.' Tony scrambled up to sit beside her, capturing her hand in his as he did so. 'Come on, out with it!'

His touch brought back memories she had suppressed these last few weeks. Lovely memories of lying in his arms, the world held at bay. Safe, comfortable, and loved. How she had missed their intimacy. He still cared, that was obvious, but could she read more into it than that? No, she wasn't thinking straight. What had transpired at Sale Place had triggered visions of her own experience of being buried in rubble, leaving her unable to focus. But her reactions were too much to deal with tonight. There were more important matters, such as what the hell she was going to do about the letter to Haas. If it didn't go out, Operation Copperhead might fail. Jason had forgiven her for the Lisbon fiasco, but if she didn't get that message out on time, he would be livid, and the Germans might miss the whole show they'd been planning for months. Before she knew it, she would be back to eavesdropping on hotel guests for the rest of the war, and rightly so.

'Sarah?' Tony squeezed her hand. '*What* is it? Please tell me.'

It wasn't easy to admit to being an idiot, but Sarah realised he was her only hope. With Jason away, she needed someone to help her get that letter to Haas. She would have to swallow her pride and ask Tony. There was a risk that Jason would not be happy that she had used someone outside the firm, but under the circumstances, she had little choice. The greater good – wasn't that what she had spouted at Adeline? – was all that mattered. That letter had to be in the post by morning.

Sarah drew a deep breath and turned to him, barely able to meet his gaze. 'You must believe me. I didn't come here to involve you. I just wanted the novel Adeline gave you.'

This seemed to confuse him. 'But you didn't know I was here. How did you intend to get into the flat? By breaking in?' He sounded incredulous.

'No! Well, not if I could avoid it.'

'How else could you have avoided it?'

There was an angry edge to his voice, and she didn't like his expression much either. But she had come this far, and she had to be honest. 'I hoped to persuade Mr Emsley to let me in. My plan was to tell him I'd left something up here on a previous visit. But I suppose if he hadn't been in the shop or in his own flat, I might have had to force my way in . . .'

'Brazen!'

Sarah felt the colour rise in her cheeks. It was awful to have to admit what she had intended. If he was cross about it, he probably wouldn't help her, but instead send her packing. And he would be right to do so.

'You're right, of course, and I know it's horrible, but I had no choice. So many lives depend on what I must do. Adeline's copy of the novel is . . . unavailable, and I need it for reference. I'm running out of time and the book is a vital part of what I need to do.'

'OK, let us overlook the potential breaking and entering,' he said with a quirk of his lips. 'What is so goddamn urgent?'

'I probably shouldn't tell you.'

'*Sarah!* If you want my help . . .'

She could hear the frustration in his voice. 'OK. First, I need to explain about Adeline.' A shadow flitted across

his features, and Sarah rushed to reassure him. 'Not about
. . . that night when we . . . You see, you were right. Although
Adeline is a journalist, that is also her cover. She *is* working
for MI5. As a double agent.'

Tony whistled. 'I suspected as much.'

'I guessed you did. But there is more. I'm her handler.'

'Ah! That I had *not* guessed.'

'Adeline has been drip-feeding information to her German
handler for us since she arrived. He is based in Lisbon.'

'Not SS-Obergruppenführer Haas, by any chance?'

'Yes. Sorry, of course you know of him,' she replied,
seeing the distaste cross Tony's face. 'Anyway, this evening,
the lodging where Adeline was living was destroyed in an
explosion. The derelict site beside the house contained an
unexploded bomb, which was set off by a clear-up crew
late this afternoon.' Sarah looked down at the dirt on her
skirt and tried in vain to rub away the worst of the smudges
as she tried to stem another wave of distress.

Tony's grip on her hand tightened. 'Were you there when
it happened? Are you hurt? Is that why you are in such a
state?'

'No, no, I'm fine. I wasn't there at the time, though I
have been living with her these last few days . . . It's a long
story. Anyhow, I arrived after it happened, just in time to
witness the rescue operation. Unfortunately, I didn't know
where she was. I kept hoping she was still at the newspaper
offices. Then, an hour or so ago, they dug her out, still alive.'

'Good Lord! Was she badly injured?'

'Yes, she was unconscious when she was pulled out. She
looked ghastly, Tony. It was a miracle she survived.' Sarah
paused a moment, in danger of bursting into tears again.

'Hopefully, she will make a full recovery, however, her indis-position poses an enormous problem for us – for me. Adeline was to send out a letter to Haas and it must be posted this evening or early in the morning, to ensure the success of an operation we are undertaking abroad. I need the book. Luckily, I remembered she had given you a copy, so I came here from the hospital, as I knew there was little point in looking for Adeline's copy in what's left of the house.'

Tony pursed his lips. 'I see. So, you plan to write this letter yourself.'

'That's another problem, I'm afraid. If it were in English, yes, I could write it, but they correspond in French.'

'Ah!' Tony glanced at the novel in her lap. 'I take it that book is the source of her codes? That's why you need it?'

Sarah nodded. 'Yes. Haas's letters direct her to the next code word to use.' She tapped the cover of the book. 'So, I have access to the key and know how to find the correct code word but—'

Tony released her hand with a disappointed expression. 'But you can't write a letter in French. I see.'

This was awful. Now, he would think she had only turned up to use him. Which was kind of true in a way, except, of course, she didn't know he would be here. *What a mess!*

'I hate to ask, but Jason is away for the next few days, and he is the only other person I know who knows French . . .'

Tony gave her a sad smile. 'Well, Irish, your luck is in. I'm due to go back to Southampton first thing tomorrow. A day later, and I would not have been in a position to help.'

Sarah's heart soared. He *was* going to help her. Now she could stop panicking. What would she have done otherwise?

330

It was lowering to realise how close to failure she had sailed.

But Tony stood, an odd expression on his face. 'Let's hope my French hasn't deserted me. You best tell me what you want written and hopefully I can translate it correctly. I should have some writing paper in the bedroom.' Then he paused halfway across the room and looked back at Sarah, a crease between his brows. 'But I don't know how to imitate her style of handwriting. He'll know straight away it isn't from her. Do you have one of her letters on you so I could try to copy her?'

'No, but I may have a solution to that. Let's tell Haas part of the truth: that she *has* been injured in an explosion which destroyed her flat, but of course not saying what her actual injuries are. We can say she sustained a broken arm, which has forced her to use her left hand to write.'

'That's plausible,' Tony replied with a smile and a nod. 'And inspired.'

Sarah gave him a self-depreciating smile. 'Thank you. At least part of my brain appears to be working this evening.'

'Mmm.'

She rushed on: 'The letter doesn't have to be long. Adeline always keeps the secret part short and to the point, and the cover letter could explain about the accident. The explosion also helps us in another way.'

'And what's that?' he asked.

'Adeline usually uses Pyramidon to make an invisible ink solution. Her tablets are buried somewhere in Sale Place and there's no chemist open at this time of night. She'd need to use an alternative. Isn't milk a viable substitute? I'm sure I've heard it mentioned somewhere.'

Tony nodded. 'It is.'

'Do you have any?'

'I do.'

Sarah exhaled slowly. 'That's a relief. I'm not up to hunting down milk at this hour of the night,' she replied.

'OK. Give me a minute,' he said, hurrying out the door.

Sarah sat back, almost dizzy with relief. *Thank you, God! Perhaps I can salvage something from this disaster of an evening.* Their relationship might still be in tatters, but Tony was magnanimous enough to help her. Sarah pulled Haas's letter from her bag, searching out the third word on the fourth line in readiness.

Tony soon appeared, waving a sheet of writing paper and a bottle of milk. 'Let's get started, Irish.'

The next three-quarters of an hour were intense. Tony worked in silent concentration, frequently consulting his French-English dictionary. He spoke only to check some detail or other with Sarah. As Sarah watched him work, the whisky and the stress of the evening took its toll, and she became drowsy. Several times, she wondered if she were, in fact, only dreaming. Sarah glanced around the flat, her eyes drinking in the familiar. This was the last place she ever expected to see the inside of again. How ironic that work should bring them together, yet again, however briefly.

At last, Tony held up the letter. 'It's done. Do you have a stamp?'

'Yes. Here.' She handed it to him. 'Thank you. I don't know how I will ever repay you.'

'You'd do the same for me if our roles were reversed.'

'Yes, but still, I'm really sorry. Besides the fact that you look as though you are out on your feet, I know the last thing you needed tonight was me dumping my problems on you.'

Tony made a face. 'Work has been hectic. I've been travelling up and down the south coast for weeks. Preparations . . .' Tony stalled, and colour rushed into his face.

'It's OK, Tony. You're not being indiscreet. I know all about Operation Fortitude and a little about Operation Overlord. I hope your involvement, whatever it might be . . . That you stay safe. Now, I'll bid you good night and let you get to bed,' she said, rising to her feet.

'Oh, don't be daft. Stay put. Now that you're here, we really ought to talk things over.'

Consternation left her breathless. 'It's late and I've already wasted enough of your time . . .' She knew she wasn't up to that kind of conversation right now. Even if her brain were fully awake and functioning, it would be challenging.

'Sarah, I'm not sure when I will be back in London. Please, stay a while longer. It's important we discuss what happened.'

Her stomach did a tiny somersault. Perhaps he was correct. There might not be another opportunity. What if something happened to him in the months ahead? She would regret not trying. 'Yes, sorry, you're right,' Sarah replied. She owed him that much, although she was anxious about the conversation to come. She did not know what to expect, and the last thing she wanted was for them to argue again. Opening up old wounds would do neither of them any good.

However, Tony's answering smile suggested he was relieved.

'Great. I'll pop down and put this in the post-box on the next street. I won't be long.'

Sarah sat back down on the sofa to await his return. Closing her eyes, she rested her head against the cushions and wiggled out of her shoes. *Just a few minutes' rest to prepare myself.*

Before long, she was fast asleep.

38

24th May 1944, Tony Anderson's Flat, Paddington, London

The bang of a door closing intruded into Sarah's dream. Still half asleep, she stretched and slowly sat up. *Ouch!* Now she was fully awake. Pain shot through the side of her neck, but she rubbed at the crick, to no avail. Then snatches of the dream taunted her as it faded away. Bother! Her sleep had been fitful, she realised, and those dreams had been dark. Haas and Adeline had featured prominently, and she had been back in that interrogation room in Estoril, pleading her innocence to an impervious Jason. How odd!

Sarah shook off the remnants of her nightmare as best she could. There was a horrible taste in her mouth, and she recalled drinking whisky and feeling wretched. As she looked around the flat, the previous evening's events came rushing back. Adeline, the hospital, and coming here and finding Tony. *Oh, no!* It was embarrassing, the whole sorry episode, and then, after all that, she had fallen asleep on the poor man's sofa. Sarah closed her eyes in frustration, tears not far off. Whatever hope of a reconciliation there might have been was surely gone now. She had used him unashamedly. Worse still, the silence of the flat suggested he had already left.

Discarding the blanket Tony must have put over her, she padded across the room to check. Softly, she opened the door to his bedroom and peered in, just in case he was still there. But the room was empty, the bed made. Then she recalled he had said he was leaving for Southampton early in the morning.

Bitter disappointment as well as embarrassment. Not your finest hour, Sarah!

Any chance of apologising to Tony was gone. He hadn't mentioned when he might return to London. And what if he thought she was pretending to be asleep last night, to avoid that chat he so badly wanted?

With a sigh, Sarah struggled into her shoes, feeling wretched. Then she checked her watch. If she hurried, she would have time to get back to the flat and change her clothes before work. No. She'd go to the hospital first, then work. With a bit of luck, there might be good news about Adeline. She might even be able to see her. Sarah took one last look around Tony's flat, feeling filled with sadness. She'd probably never see it again. So many happy memories within those four walls. In that moment she knew she would need to engage some strong internal resources to move on.

But as she passed a mirror in the hallway, she saw herself and squirmed. *Good God, no wonder Tony was astonished at my appearance.* She peered at her image more closely and almost laughed in despair. Well, there wasn't much she could do about it, only a hot bath and washing her hair would sort it out. Still, she couldn't walk the streets looking like something from a refugee camp, with her short hair standing up in spikes like that. A quick comb through would have to suffice. She dropped her bag onto the table below the mirror and rummaged in it for her comb. It was then she noticed an envelope propped up on the table. It was addressed to her in Tony's scrawl. What on earth? Sarah snatched it up in disbelief and held it to her chest, her heart hammering with hope. Then she tore it open, all her plans forgotten.

Sarah,

This isn't easy, but as I sit here watching you sleep, I know I might not have another chance to say what I feel. No one knows what lies ahead, and I must face the fact that many of us may not survive. The battles to come will be bloody because Jerry will fight to the bitter end. So, I don't want to leave you without at least trying to make amends.

I'm a simple guy and sometimes the words don't come out right. Maybe it was fate that I was here tonight, and you came by. I don't know, but I will not question it. I will rejoice in it.

Sarah's heart did a little flip of delight.

Yes. I was mad at you that night when Adeline was here. I'll admit it. Mad and hurt that you didn't trust me. However, as I have cooled off in the long and painful weeks since, I have realised I have to make an effort to understand what happened from your point of view, if there is to be any chance for us. Now, I can see how my behaviour and Adeline's could have been misunderstood, and I did little to put her off. Yes, she did flirt with me, and I admit I enjoyed it, but I was fully aware that her boyfriend was in the background. That night at the club, he was pretty much all she talked about. Anyhow, that's a feeble excuse.

I hope you can forgive my stupid impulse to be defensive and please know that was all it was. A gut reaction with little or no logic to it. I was exhausted that night, having pulled an all-nighter at the office the previous evening. Not that that is an excuse. I'm not perfect, Sarah, far from it. I find this emotional stuff tough to talk about, but I guess you know that already. You're a smart cookie, as my mom would say.

I, on the other hand, appear to be an idiot. I was well aware of how frustrated you were becoming with me. I treated our relationship lightly, not because I don't care, but because I care too much. I have seen so many people die these last few years that it seemed ridiculous to even think about the future. Whenever you tried to talk about it, I panicked.

In my clumsy way, I'm trying to say I regret my hasty words. The last few weeks have been hell. In the few free hours I've had, my thoughts were firmly fixed on you. And full of regret, too. It's awful to admit, but my damn pride would not let me write to you or phone. I should have, I know. But as I have already mentioned, I'm an idiot.

Seeing you tonight was a shock, I'll admit it, but I guess my old friend fate was in my corner, rooting for me. And who am I to argue with him? Of course, my timing is awful. I am truly sorry I must leave London again so soon. But, as you know only too well, we are not masters of our own lives at present. Merely pawns in this God-awful war!

I have lost count of the number of times since Fishguard that I have been on the point of telling you how I really feel. So, yes, I'm admitting when it comes to this stuff, I'm a coward. I hope, then, it's not too late to tell you I love you. Seeing you tonight has made *the world feel right again. Like finding the last piece of a jigsaw puzzle and it clicks smoothly into place. I do see a future for us, Sarah, but I also know that you may no longer want one with me.*

I guess I'm rambling on a bit, so I best get to the point. I will do my best to be back in London next Tuesday. If you aren't still mad at me, meet me at The American Bar on Tuesday night and let's talk this out. On the other hand, if you don't show, I'll understand and accept your decision.

Yours, in hope, Tony.

Two shocked faces stared at Sarah when she entered the kitchen back at the flat. She'd almost forgotten she looked and probably smelled like a vagrant, but having read Tony's letter several times before she left his flat, her appearance had ceased to matter. But then, that's what declarations of love do to you, she thought. She was grinning like an idiot, too. She couldn't help it. Tony had said he loved her and that they had a future. That was precious and wonderful, and right now, nothing else mattered.

With a worried expression, Judith sprang up from the table and rushed to her side. 'What happened to you?' she cried, clutching her arm.

Sarah shook her head, then pointed at the teapot in the middle of the table. 'Anything left in that? I'm parched.' Then she sighed and leaned her head on Judith's shoulder. 'Oh dear, so much has happened. Honestly, I don't know where to start.' Judith put an arm around her shoulder and guided her to the nearest chair.

Gladys poured her a cup and pushed it in front of her as she sat down. 'Perhaps start with why you look like that? Or is it a new fashion we haven't heard about?'

'Ha-ha!' Sarah replied, gulping down the hot tea. Suddenly aware of the tense silence, Sarah looked across at her friends and tried to reassure them with a smile. It probably looked more like a grimace, though. Now that she was sitting down, she was shattered. Probably a reaction to everything that had happened since the previous afternoon.

'Well, are you going to explain?' asked Judith, now beginning to look cross.

Sarah's eye fell on Gladys's plate. 'Sorry, Judith, but I'm starving. Do you want that toast, Gladys? I haven't eaten since lunchtime yesterday.'

'Here,' her friend said, handing it over. 'Can't have you starving to death.'

Judith sat back and sighed. 'I'm glad to see you, though, frankly, dismayed at the state you are in. But we weren't expecting you for a few days. I thought you were going to stay with that woman – what's her name – until next week?'

'Adeline,' Gladys supplied, making a face, then adding in a dramatic voice: 'The femme fatale.'

'Poor Adeline,' Sarah said with a sigh.

'What? Why?' exclaimed Gladys. 'Didn't she try to steal Tony from you? I thought you couldn't stand her.'

'It's complicated, Gladys. All that nonsense about Tony? I think she was punishing me for something else which, unfortunately, I cannot tell you about; she wasn't really interested in him.' Both the girls looked confused. 'It's too difficult to explain right now. But yes, my plan was to stay with her,' Sarah replied, rubbing her face with her hands. 'The thing is, there was an accident yesterday evening and Adeline was badly injured. An unexploded bomb in a site next door was disturbed and blew up.' She pulled at her dirty jacket. 'It destroyed the flat. I ended up as a bystander to the rescue operation.'

'Oh no!' Judith's hand flew up to her mouth. 'The poor woman! Is she badly hurt?'

'It killed quite a few people, but she was lucky; they got her out, but I won't know for sure how bad things are until I go back to the hospital this morning.'

'Were you in the flat when it happened?' Gladys asked, her eyes wide.

'No. The explosion occurred before I got there.'

'So, were you at the hospital all night with her? You must be exhausted,' Judith said.

'Ah! No. The thing is . . . gosh, I can't really tell you why, but I ended up at Tony's.'

Gladys and Judith exchanged a look of confusion.

'Tony's flat?' Gladys grinned at her. 'You sly old thing!' Then she spluttered: 'Please tell me you didn't turn up at his place looking like that? Oh, my God, Sarah, what were you thinking? Or did you do it on purpose, so he'd feel sorry for you? How clever! Did you kiss and make up? Did you?' she gushed.

Sarah held up her hand at the barrage of questions, laughing. 'Steady, Gladys. Firstly, I didn't know he was there. I went to his flat to pick up something I needed.'

'And?' the girls said in unison.

'And . . . as it turned out, Tony was there and was able to help me with an urgent work problem. That's it.' The girls' faces dropped, and they exchanged a disappointed glance. Sarah hurried on: 'Tony had to leave early this morning, but he will be back next week. We are meeting up on Tuesday night for a chat. Maybe, just maybe, there is a chance we will make up.'

Grins all round.

'That's wonderful,' Judith said, tearing up. 'I knew things would work out.'

'I said maybe, Judith.' But her cousin simply grinned back at her.

'Sooo, you stayed the night at Tony's . . .' Gladys then said, eyes narrowed.

'I don't know what you are implying, Glad. I slept – well, tried to sleep – on his sofa,' Sarah replied.

'Ho-ho, that's a good one!' Gladys laughed as she stood. 'Do you really expect us to believe that? You are such a chancer!'

'It's true!' Sarah protested.

Gladys just shook her head. 'Right, I'm off. Some of us have important jobs to do.' But she squeezed Sarah's shoulder as she passed. 'Glad you're OK.' Then she wrinkled her nose. 'But I suggest you have a wash before you go to work. And you can tell me what really happened at his flat, later, if you wish to spare Judith's blushes.'

Sarah gave her a dirty look, but then ruined it by grinning. '*Goodbye*, Gladys!'

Judith's eyes followed Gladys out to the hallway. 'Will you get back together?' she asked Sarah, gently. 'Please say you will. If you and Tony's relationship can't survive this wretched war, there is no hope for the rest of us.'

When Sarah reached Adeline's ward in St. Mary's, a curtain was pulled around her bed. Much to her frustration, Sarah could hear the murmur of voices coming from inside, but not what they were saying. Worried, she hovered close by.

A nurse approached. 'Hello. Are you here to see Mademoiselle Vernier? The doctors are with her at present, but they shouldn't be too much longer, miss.'

'Thank you. How did she get through the night?'

'Are you family?' the nurse asked.

'No. She has no family here in England. I'm a friend and a colleague,' Sarah replied. She touched the nurse's arm. 'Please, I'm anxious about her.'

The nurse leaned in closer and lowered her voice. 'She is still unconscious, and she barely moved all night. I think it is too early to say. I'm sorry.'

Sarah frowned. 'Is it serious? Should I be worried?'

The nurse gave her an anxious look. 'It's not my place to say. You must speak to her doctor. There is a waiting room outside. I could ask him to come and see you there, if you wish? It's more private.'

'Yes, thanks. That would be great.'

It was an anxious wait for news, and Sarah oscillated between hope and despair. The fact the nurse was so reluctant to tell her anything might be because the news was bad. Or perhaps it was because Sarah was only a friend and not family. All she could do was wait, watching the clock on the wall.

About ten minutes later, the same doctor from the night before appeared in the doorway of the waiting room. 'Sorry, I don't recall your name,' he said. 'We spoke yesterday evening.' He shook her hand. 'I'm Dr Murphy.'

'Yes, we did have a brief chat. I'm Miss Gillespie; a friend of Mademoiselle Vernier. I'm the nearest thing to family she has in England. How is she doing? Is there any improvement in her condition?'

'Please, Miss Gillespie,' he waved to a chair, 'sit down.'

The doctor's face gave nothing away and Sarah's anxiety ratcheted up once more. 'Please, is she going to be alright?' she asked.

'To be honest, we don't know yet. I am concerned about her head wound, in particular. These kinds of injuries can be tricky to assess. There could be bleeding on her brain, but we have no way of knowing the extent of it and if it has done any damage.'

Sarah's heart sank. 'That doesn't sound good. Would it be possible for me to see her, even for a few minutes?'

'Yes, of course. Look, it's best I warn you; she has extensive bruising and swelling to her face,' he said.

'I understand, thank you. I'm just so glad she's alive.'

'She was lucky. Crush injuries can be fatal,' he replied.

Despite the warning, the doctor's words didn't adequately prepare Sarah for the sight of Adeline lying so still, half her head swaddled in a large bandage. Her face was so swollen that Sarah would not have recognised her if she'd passed her on the street.

'Oh, Adeline, I'm so sorry this happened to you,' she whispered.

Sarah picked up Adeline's hand and pressed it, feeling entirely helpless. After all they had been through – the dangers, the risks they had taken on that trip to Lisbon, even managing to escape the clutches of the Portuguese secret police and the Nazis together – for it to end this way, in an accident, broke Sarah's heart. The bond of friendship had formed little by little, and sitting here with Adeline now, Sarah was reluctant to let it go.

39

To say the journey out to RAF Northolt was tense would be an understatement. Sarah was in the back seat, Hastings in the front passenger seat, with Jason driving in silence. It was hard to say who was the most nervous. It was ridiculously early, but Sarah was alert, her stomach roiling as they drove out of London. Operation Copperhead was about to begin. All her hard work and Adeline's efforts were about to pay off. At least they would if Hastings held his nerve. Had they been foolish to trust in his abilities? Sitting behind him, it was obvious he was rigid with nerves, and she had to restrain the urge to pat his shoulder and comfort him. There was no going back now. Everyone was ready and the governor and his staff were expecting Hastings to land and reach the embassy by mid-morning.

Sarah's meeting with Jason the previous day at St. James's Street had been uncomfortable. Having to explain her late-night ransacking of his desk and the reason for it had led to an intense discussion. However, in the end, Jason understood, and even went so far as to praise her presence of mind, though she suspected he was still displeased. She had left his office greatly relieved and then spent the rest of the day with Hastings, drilling him in what he would have to do and say when he reached Gibraltar.

Unfortunately, they had no way of knowing if the letter written by Tony had reached Haas. The wires had been frustratingly quiet, much to Jason's unease. But Sarah was sure there would be enough hoo-ha to signal Hastings' arrival in any case. It wasn't every day that a field marshal visited the territory. It was bound to be widespread news within hours. MI5 suspected that many of the local population were in the pocket of the Nazis, so the plan was for the plane to circle the airfield for some time, to ensure anyone watching would register its arrival and be curious about the passengers.

'Now, Hastings, you do remember who everyone is? These people know Monty well. They must not suspect you are an imposter,' Jason said.

'Yes, sir.' Hastings' answer was firm, much to Sarah's relief.

'What's the governor's name?' Jason shot at him; his expression fierce.

'Governor Eastwood, sir.'

Sarah simmered in silence. This would not help the man's nerves at all. Hastings needed his confidence bolstered, not smashed. However, to say so would earn her a tongue-lashing from Jason later.

'And who will meet you off the plane?' Jason asked.

'Major Foley. I'm to ask for him immediately after I

land, and he will escort me to the governor's residence,' Hastings replied.

Jason sniffed. 'Good.'

Sarah kept her gaze fixed out the window, wishing the day was over. She hoped to visit St. Mary's when she got back to town. The doctor was still cagey about giving any prognosis, but Sarah was determined to keep positive.

As the car passed through the security check at the gates of RAF Northolt, the guards did double-takes of Hastings.

'They recognise him, sir,' Sarah piped up. 'That's a good start.'

'We need to convince more than a couple of Tommies, Sarah,' Jason replied. Sarah would have rolled her eyes, only she feared he would catch her in the rear-view mirror.

Jason swung the car around a large building, following the directions given to him at the gate. Ahead was a single plane on the apron. As they pulled up close to it, they saw the pilot climb the steps. Jason, leaning on the steering wheel, peered out at the airplane for several minutes, and Sarah wondered what was going through his head. Eventually, he turned to Hastings. 'Right, Hastings, this is it. Best of luck, old chap.'

The men shook hands.

'Thank you, sir, and thank you for the opportunity to serve my country in this way.'

To Sarah's surprise, Jason looked a little embarrassed as he cleared his throat. 'Not at all.'

Hastings twisted around in his seat and spoke to Sarah. 'Thank you, Miss Gillespie. I won't let you down.'

'I know you won't,' she replied. 'Come on, I'll see you as far as the plane.' Sarah hopped out and walked over to the aircraft, Hastings beside her.

'You'll be fine, Hastings,' she said, keeping her voice low. 'Sorry if Jason spooked you in the car, but there is a lot riding on this mission.' Sarah hoped she wasn't compounding Hastings' nerves, but if her dealings with Adeline had shown her anything, it was that honesty was always the better option.

'No, it's fine. I understand. Of course, I don't know why, but I do know this wee venture is important.' Hastings gnawed at his upper lip. 'I will do my very best. I want this to be a success as much as you.'

'I know that,' Sarah said, wishing she could squeeze his arm to reassure him, but to be seen to do so would look very peculiar.

Just then, a young officer approached, then saluted. 'May I take your bag, Field Marshal?'

Hastings handed it over. 'Thank you, son.' He watched the man climb the steps and onto the plane, then Hastings turned to Sarah, his eyes twinkling. 'They really believe I'm him.'

'Why wouldn't they? You're really convincing,' Sarah replied, holding out her hand. She whispered: 'Remember everything we have told you and you will be fine. Best of luck, and I'll see you for your debrief when you get back from Algiers.'

They knew there would not be any news until later that day, so Jason dropped Sarah off at St. Mary's. On entering the ward, Sarah was astonished to see Adeline sitting up in bed. And Adeline had a visitor: Mr McKensie, her editor from *The Gazette*. An enormous bouquet rested on the locker beside Adeline's bed. Sarah held back, but Adeline spotted her and beckoned her over.

'You remember Miss Gillespie, Edward,' Adeline said.

'Of course,' he replied.

Sarah noted the first-name terms and grinned at Adeline, who pretended not to notice.

Mr McKensie jumped up and shook hands with Sarah. 'A pleasure,' he gushed. Then he turned and gazed at Adeline. 'Isn't it marvellous how well she is doing after all she has been through? How well she looks.'

'It is, indeed,' Sarah replied, trying not to smile. The man was obviously smitten, for Adeline still looked battered, her face inflamed, and her bruises were turning an ugly yellowy-brown . . . and that was just the part of her face that was visible. The other half was still covered in a large bandage.

'Well, I'm sure you ladies have lots to talk about,' McKensie said. 'I'll pop back in a few days to see how you are doing, my dear. And you are not to worry. Your job will still be there when you are ready to return to us.'

'Thank you, Edward,' Adeline cooed and waved him off, queen-like.

'Good afternoon,' Sarah said with a grin. 'I'm delighted to see you are awake at last. You really scared us. It was touch and go for a while, you know.'

Adeline tried to smile. 'It wasn't deliberate!'

'Of course not!' Sarah replied, squeezing her hand. 'I brought you some newspapers and some chocolate in the hope that you were awake.' She glanced at the flowers. 'Somehow they seem inadequate compared to those.'

'Nonsense!' Adeline exclaimed. 'And chocolate! Where on earth did you get it?'

'It helps to have an American boyfriend,' Sarah replied. 'I have a secret stash of it in my flat.'

'Thank the Lord! I have such a sweet tooth.' Then her gaze narrowed. 'Boyfriend? As in Tony? Ah! You are back together?'

'Possibly . . . probably. Funnily enough, you could say it's down to you,' Sarah replied with a smile.

Adeline winced as she tried to get more comfortable. 'Tell me. I want to know all the details.'

Sarah explained about the urgent letter to Haas and going to Tony's apartment to retrieve *120 Rue de la Gare*.

'Oh, that is wonderful. It is fate. Though, of course, I am sorry I could not help with the letter,' Adeline said.

'It was hardly your fault. I'm just glad you survived. Now all you must worry about is getting better.'

Adeline sighed. 'But all my lovely things. They are lost forever.'

'Perhaps not. I've asked the clean-up crew to keep anything undamaged they find. You never know, they may come across some of your belongings.'

'I am foolish. I am alive, and must be grateful,' Adeline said, but her voice held sadness. 'But my only photograph of Nikolay . . .'

'Oh, gosh, yes. That's awful. But you never know; they might find it.'

'You mean well, Sarah, but I am a realist.' With a sigh, Adeline continued: 'At least I still have my memories. No one can take those away.'

A tightness formed in Sarah's throat, and they sat in silence for several minutes.

'I was thinking, Adeline. When they are ready to discharge you, would you like to stay with me and my friends? Maybe until you get back on your feet. Of course, MI5 will source new accommodation for you, but I thought . . .'

Tears filled Adeline's eyes, and she wiped them away with the back of her hand. 'Thank you. I would like this, but . . .'

'Yes?'

'There is something you must know. I have reached the conclusion I do not want to work for you anymore. It's not personal,' she lowered her voice, 'but I dislike the spy business.'

Sarah grinned at her. 'Do you know there are days when I feel exactly the same? Don't worry, I completely understand. Give yourself time to recover, then make your decision. Besides, it sounds like *The Gazette* wants to keep you on. In the meantime, I will speak to my boss. You have helped us enormously in the past few months. And, if the present operation is a success, I think you will have more than fulfilled your obligations.'

'Thank you. But when will you know if it has worked?' Adeline asked in a whisper.

Sarah peered at her watch and grimaced. 'In a couple of hours.'

It was six o'clock when Sarah reached MI5 and headed for Jason's office. When she entered, he was sitting at his desk staring into space, his expression blank. *This doesn't augur well*, she thought, and braced herself for potential disaster. Was the news in already? Had Hastings messed up?

'Any reports yet, sir?' she asked as she approached, half fearing his answer.

Jason waved her to a seat. 'Other than to say he arrived safely – and that was from our chaps – there's been nothing. Has Adeline's condition changed?'

'Good news there, sir. She is awake, sitting up and talking. Mind you, she still looks appallingly battered. Her face is swollen and bruised, and her leg is in plaster.'

'Did you speak to her doctor?'

'Yes, briefly. He's happy with her progress so far, but it is still early days,' she replied. 'Sir, I think her recovery will be slow. She won't be able to work for us again for some time. Will that be a problem? Do we need to keep communicating with Haas?'

Jason gave her a sharp glance. 'Possibly. That is a shame. Despite all the drama, she has proven useful to us.'

This wasn't what she wanted to hear now that Adeline was talking about retiring, but perhaps she would change her mind when she felt better. 'I could always ask Lieutenant Anderson to write another letter for us while Adeline is indisposed. I'm sure he would be willing,' Sarah said.

'Hmm. It was all very well to use him in an emergency – and, obviously, we are extremely grateful to him for helping us out of that particular difficulty – but no, if anything crops up and we need to send one while she is still in hospital, if she will agree to supply me with the codes, I can write it.'

'I see,' Sarah replied.

'Haas believes her indisposed temporarily, does he not?'

'Yes. Tony told him to send all correspondence to the hospital for now. We may even get a reaction to Operation Copperhead from him in his next letter.'

'Good thinking. Bring the letters to me so I can monitor the situation.' This made Sarah smart. Did he not trust her to do her job? Jason drummed his fingers on the desk, deep in thought. Then he looked up, frowning. 'Well, I suppose we can reactivate her when she has recovered. I would like to keep that channel open, if possible, no matter how we achieve that. We have a long way to go yet to win this war. Keep me informed of her progress.'

'I will, sir. There is one thing . . . When she is discharged, she will have nowhere to go. I was going to suggest she come and stay with me for a while.'

Jason raised a brow at this. 'That is a little unconventional, and unnecessary. I'm sure we can find somewhere for her.'

'I know, sir, but I feel guilty. Keeping her in the dark about her boyfriend didn't sit easy with me.'

'Nor I, but the job and winning this war must always take precedence. I thought at this stage you would have come to terms with that.'

Sarah didn't miss the rebuke and resented it. 'I have, but that doesn't mean I have to like it.'

Whatever Jason was about to say next was interrupted by Miss Wilson putting her head around the door. 'Call from Station X, sir,' she called out. Sarah's pulse shot up. This would be it; confirmation that the Germans thought Monty was in Gibraltar.

'About time!' Jason picked up the phone and barked into the receiver: 'Well?' For several gut-wrenching minutes, he listened intently. Sarah would have given anything to be privy to what was being said.

At last, Jason ended the call and hung up. He stared at her, deadpan, for what felt like an eternity. Then, he broke into a grin. 'Well done, Sarah. They intercepted a message from Haas in Lisbon followed by another from a known informer based in Spain, both notifying the High Command in Berlin that Monty is in Gibraltar.'

Sarah exhaled slowly. 'Thank God!'

'Let us hope they misconstrue it as we wish. Later this evening, Hastings will fly on to Algiers, which should get Jerry even more excited. However, I'll rest easier when I hear of German divisions being sent to the south of France to bolster defences there. It will make it much easier for our chaps to get a foothold once they land further north.'

'I take it we plan to invade soon?' she asked.

'I can't give you details, but yes, it will be very soon.'

40

30th May 1944, The American Bar, The Savoy Hotel, London

Sarah stood in the shadow of the doorway, suddenly hesitant. Across the room at the bar, Tony sat, his drink untouched before him. She stood and watched him for a few minutes, during which he checked his watch twice. Was it possible he was more nervous than she? A difficult conversation probably lay ahead. One she had rehearsed over and over as she lay awake the last few nights, trying to figure out what was best. For him *and* for her. But somehow, she knew she would end up here tonight, eager to see him, yet terrified what the outcome might be.

Did she really know him? was the question she had grappled with for the last few days. Sadly, *not well enough* was the conclusion she had reached. If he couldn't open up to her this evening, share something of his innermost feelings, she would have to walk away. But could she? Tony wasn't perfect. He had his faults, but so had she; buckets

355

of them. Sometimes Tony drove her crazy, but he often said the same of her. The question was: did she love him deeply enough? Their separation had been unbearable at times, heart-breaking even, but she had survived it. And yet, she was drawn to him, inexorably. So, if any kind of commitment were to be made tonight, she had to be sure.

She loved him but had never said the words. Even though she had been tempted, fear of rejection had always held her back. The irony of him saying them first, albeit in a letter, wasn't lost on her. Perhaps she was the one who was afraid of commitment. And that, perhaps, was a result of losing so many loved ones since the war began. But the thought of living the rest of her life afraid of loving or being loved was too awful to contemplate.

A conversation with Gladys the night before had helped. And with Gladys's final words on the subject ringing in her ears – 'life's too short; if you love him, take a risk' – Sarah stepped out of the shadows and headed for the bar.

Tony stood when he spotted her, and she felt the heat rise in her neck and into her cheeks. He looked so anxious that she smiled, despite the tangle of emotions making her slightly light-headed. She was pleased to see the tension leave his shoulders, and when she was within reach, he took her hand and bent down to kiss her cheek.

'It's good to see you, Sarah. Let's find somewhere more private,' he said, keeping a hold of her hand and leading her across the room to an empty table. 'Thanks for coming,' he said as they took their seats opposite each other. 'I was afraid . . . I wouldn't have blamed you for not showing up.'

A waiter appeared and Tony ordered her usual tipple, never taking his eyes off her. Once the man had drifted off, he continued: 'If nothing else, I wanted the chance to apologise in person.'

'There's no need, Tony. You have already. If anything, I owe *you* an apology. I let jealousy blind me that night in your flat. I should have trusted you, brushed the whole situation with Adeline off with a laugh. Instead, I lost my temper. It's my biggest failing, if you haven't figured that out yet.'

'And I overreacted,' he said. 'It wasn't our finest hour.'

'That's for sure!' Sarah exclaimed. Tony didn't smile as she expected, merely nodded. It was unsettling to see him so solemn and ill at ease.

'Neither of us are perfect. Just human. Doing our best.' Tony sighed, frowning down at his drink. 'I guess what I'm trying to say is that you deserve to be treated better.' She started to object, but he held up his hand. 'No. Hear me out, please. It has taken these weeks without you to realise that my feelings were far deeper than I had let myself believe.' He looked up then. 'I'm sorry, it's not my intention to hurt you. I just want to be completely honest because I realise now I should have been more open with you.'

Sarah struggled to fight back her tears. This was what she had hoped for. At last, he was opening up, not hiding behind the brash words and devil-may-care attitude he liked to show the world.

The waiter appeared and left Sarah's drink on the table. Tony snatched up his glass and took a gulp before he continued. 'So, while I was away, I had decided that our break should be permanent. Then you could move on and find someone better.'

Sarah's heart dropped, and she squeaked: 'Oh! No!'

But Tony gave her a roguish grin. 'But then you turned up at my door last week and suddenly I thought maybe it's not too late to start over. That there might still be a chance for us. Although you were all business, I detected something, a glimmer of hope. But when I got back to the flat, you were asleep. To be honest, I was gutted. Our chance to talk things over was gone, and I knew there was little possibility of us having time in the morning as I had to leave at the crack of dawn to catch my train.'

'You should have woken me,' Sarah said. 'I wouldn't have minded.'

'No, I couldn't disturb you after the rotten day you'd had. You were exhausted and stressed to the point of breaking.'

'Hence your letter.'

'Yes, I didn't want to leave without at least trying.' He flinched all of a sudden. 'I'm sure it was badly written. I hardly knew what I was writing, but I knew I had to try to win you back.' He cleared his throat. 'Did you burn it?' he said with a half-smile.

'No. I will *treasure* it, always,' she said, reaching across and squeezing his hand.

Tony captured her hand and held on to it, gazing at her as if willing himself to believe her. 'You will? Does that mean . . . are you sure?'

But before Sarah could answer, she gasped. Who had walked in the door of the bar but the woman who had tailed her weeks before! Even more astounding, the woman nodded to Tony as she walked past.

Sarah whipped around. 'You know her?'

'Yes, she works at the US embassy. Why?'

'But . . . she was following me. I had Special Branch trying to find out who she was.'

Tony's colour rose. 'Ah! Well, the thing is . . . I asked her to keep an eye on you.'

'You *what?*'

'I was concerned, Sarah. After you told me about having to tackle that chap that was bothering Gladys, and then you went all secretive on me about your work, I was afraid you were in danger, and I knew I would be out of London . . .'

Sarah stared at him in disbelief. Should she be angry or delighted he cared enough to do something so damned stupid?

'But Tony, she really worried me. I didn't know who she was. I thought she was an enemy agent or an IRA operative out for revenge.'

Tony grimaced. 'Sorry, I didn't really think it through. I was just so worried about you, and you were never meant to spot her!'

Sarah smiled, seeing him so contrite. 'I suppose I should be flattered that you cared enough to do that.' Then she slapped the back of his hand. 'But don't do it again.'

'I won't,' he said with a sheepish grin in reply.

'Well, if we are going to confess all, I need to tell you something, too,' she said. 'When we first got together, my motives were purely selfish. I was hurt, and I was grieving for my father. His death was devastating. I had never felt so alone in my entire life. At the time, I was convinced I would go mad. Da's death had left me adrift. To make matters worse, it wasn't long after I'd lost Paul as well. I truly believed that anyone I loved would die, too.'

'Ah, Sarah, you should have explained how you were feeling,' he said. 'I'd have done my best to reassure you.'

'But that's just it. I couldn't tell you or anyone else. Saying it would admit I was crazy, and I desperately wanted you to think well of me. So, it wasn't the most honest of starts for us and I'm sorry. You deserved better than that.' Sarah paused, trying to gauge his reaction. Tony's gaze was steady, but she couldn't read him.

'Tony, those few days in Fishguard are a blur now, and I'm not trying to belittle what happened. I wanted it as much as you. You were there when I needed a shoulder to cry on and I clung to you like a drowning woman. If I'm being honest, I'm not even sure if I liked you much then. It was purely a physical need for comfort. You always seemed so strong and sure, and I wanted some of that to rub off on me.'

At last, he spoke. 'I think you're wrong, Sarah. It wasn't simply physical. There was something else there, too. There was a spark between us from that very first day we met. I certainly felt it, though I did my best to ignore it.'

Sarah exhaled slowly. 'I'm glad you failed.'

Tony grinned back at her. 'So am I! But so what if it was purely physical in the beginning? It's not surprising considering we didn't have the best of starts.'

'No, we did not! With you accusing me of being an IRA informer on our very first day working together.'

'Sorry,' he said, rather sheepishly. 'But you must admit, it was an odd partnership. Sometimes, I think Everleigh set us up deliberately to see the sparks fly. Wily old goat!'

'You could be right; he can be devious at times. But the suspicion wasn't only on your side, Tony. I didn't trust you, either. It was only when you intervened in Clara Mazet's assassination attempt on de Gaulle that I was absolutely sure of you. Before that, I suspected you were keeping secrets from me. After all, you let me believe Clara was your girlfriend.'

'All in the line of duty, as you know,' he said.

'Yes, but I was in the dark at the time. I thought you had cheated on her with me. That left me feeling guilty, and I thought you were rotten for doing it.'

'It was a messy business, alright,' he replied with a scowl. 'This job makes you do things . . . And I intended to tell you the truth about her at the time, but it was never the right moment. It was only after the de Gaulle incident that I *could* tell you.' He looked at her, his expression grave. 'Didn't you believe me?'

'Yes, I did, of course. It all made sense. But then you had to go to France just as our relationship got off the ground. While you were away, I built you up into my ideal man.' Tony looked surprised, but she ploughed on. 'When you came back, I was overjoyed. But I quickly realised you were not this unrealistic ideal I had created in my head. To add to my frustration, the real you always seemed to be out of reach.'

'What do you mean?' He sounded perplexed.

'You rarely speak of your family or the life you left behind in the States. I want to know everything about you, but there have been times when I have felt like I hardly know anything about you.'

Tony sighed. 'I'm sorry; it isn't deliberate. The fact is, my relationship with my parents is strained. I already told you my father wanted me to stay on the farm, but I hightailed it to enlist in the Navy as soon as I was of age. I wanted adventure and freedom, as most young men do. My mother didn't take it well, either. After I left, their marriage went through a rocky patch and my father blamed me for that.'

'But that's totally unreasonable!'

'Yep! Not that he'd see it that way.' Suddenly, he looked sad. 'It was never my intention to freeze you out. Honestly, Sarah, it's dull stuff. But if you want to know, I'll gladly give you the whole kit and kaboodle. But I warn you, it's likely to put you to sleep.'

'I'll take the risk,' she replied with a smile.

For a little while, they sat holding hands and Sarah finally relaxed, appreciating Tony's more mellow mood. Gone was the man who hid behind the brash, joking demeanour. At last, he had opened up. Sarah listened as he spoke about his childhood and life on the farm as a young man, working alongside his father. That was when the trouble had started. Tony hated every minute of it, bored with the monotony of farm life. Only his sister Lily was sympathetic. Sarah quickly realised his strongest bond was with her. Lily, too, had left home at the earliest opportunity and now lived in New York. As soon as the war was over, he planned to visit her there, and he wanted Sarah to come with him.

'Of course! I'd love to. Now, you see?' Sarah said. 'I didn't actually fall asleep.' But there was one more thing Sarah wanted to know. Perhaps, in his present mood, he would be willing to tell her.

'But you know, speaking of sleep . . . what causes those bad dreams you have? I hate to see you so distressed,' she said.

'That *is* difficult to talk about. It's stuff that happened in France and is best forgotten.'

'But maybe if you talked about it, it might help. It might stop the nightmares,' she coaxed. 'Please. Something bad must have happened.'

'It did.' Tony swallowed hard.

'Tell me about it, please,' she said gently.

A sad smile played briefly on his lips. 'OK . . . I was working with a small team of French Resistance. The work was risky and dangerous, but my God, those people were the bravest I've ever met. Nothing seemed to daunt them. Our job was to destroy railway lines to make Jerry's life as difficult as we could. Lightning strike stuff. Quick in, lay the explosives, and hightail it back out. We were successful, too. We caused a lot of chaos. Then, one night, we were ambushed. Someone had tipped the Germans off. Antoine and I managed to escape. It was a close-run thing for us, but a local farmer hid us in his barn. Saved our sorry skins, but two of the women weren't as lucky. Got caught.' Tony stopped and sipped his drink, his gaze a million miles away. With a sucked in breath, he continued: 'They were taken to Rouen. A couple of days later, Antoine and I followed. Foolishly, we thought we might be able to get them out.'

'And?'

It took several moments before Tony could speak. 'Maria and Sabine were shot in the main square. In cold blood. Just stood them up against a wall in front of half the inhabitants and . . . They like to do that, to make an example of anyone they catch, to deter co-operation with the Resistance.'

'And you witnessed it? The executions?' she asked.

Tony nodded. 'And it wasn't the first time I had seen

something like that, but it was different because I knew those women. Had worked with them. Knew their families, shared their food.'

'How do you cope with that?' Sarah asked, aghast.

'You don't. Not really. It's there in your head, but you must keep moving and inflicting as much destruction as you can. You hope what you are doing, when you succeed, will make their sacrifice worth it. But it doesn't. It just doesn't. We spent months trying to find out who had betrayed us, but we never found them. Maybe it's as well. I'd have torn them limb from limb. Then I had to move south to work with a different group. I never saw Antoine again. I've no idea if he is alive or dead.'

'Is that why you were so reluctant to leave SOE and come back here?'

He didn't answer straight away. 'Kinda. I missed you, of course, but I felt I was deserting them. They are still fighting on while I swan about England in my cushy safe job.'

'But your work is vital, Tony,' she replied.

'Perhaps, but I'm more of a hands-on kinda guy, I guess. Sitting around in an office doesn't suit me. I'd much rather be blowing up Jerry transports.'

'I suppose I can understand that, though I must admit I found fieldwork challenging. Still, nothing as horrible happened to me. I'm not surprised you have nightmares,' Sarah said. 'I did suspect it was something like that. Thanks for telling me. I know it wasn't easy.'

Tony gave her a crooked smile before polishing off his drink. 'Let's not mention it again. It's still quite raw.'

'Sure. I guess we both have a lot in our past to deal with, things that shape our decisions and reactions without our even realising it. Da's betrayal is always to the forefront of my mind. I think that's why, when I found Adeline in your flat, I faltered. Found myself floundering in jealousy and doubt and a good deal of anger. It's as if I expect betrayal from everyone. But I should have trusted you, Tony, and I didn't. I'm sorry.'

'It's OK,' he said. 'I understand. I didn't help matters, either. I bitterly regret that night.'

'As do I,' she answered.

'But if we hadn't argued, we would have continued the way we were. You dissatisfied and increasingly frustrated with me, and me oblivious to what I was letting slip away. It was only a matter of time before we would have drifted apart.'

Sarah mulled over his words. He was right, she realised, and it terrified her. 'Can we prevent that from happening? Because I don't think I could bear it.'

Tony straightened; his eyes lighting up. 'Do you mean that? You still want a future that includes me?'

For a minute she was lost in his gaze, but then whispered: 'Yes, of course I do.'

Tony moved closer. 'Well, that's excellent! Because I feel the same way.'

Sarah raised her hand and cradled his cheek. 'I can't imagine my future without you. And I should have told you ages ago that I love you.'

Tony swallowed hard several times. 'And I, you.' Then he kissed her.

Eventually, Sarah pulled away. 'People will stare.'

'Let 'em. I don't care,' he said, swooping in once more. Then, to her surprise, he sat back and wiggled his brows. 'Wait! I have something for you.' He rummaged in his jacket pocket and took out a small square box. 'Open that,' he said with a grin, before slipping down on one knee. 'Marry me, Sarah!'

Half-laughing, she scolded him. 'Get up, Tony! Now, everyone *is* staring.' But then Sarah flipped open the lid. 'Oh, Lord! It's a Claddagh ring! How wonderful!'

Tony cleared his throat. 'And?'

'Oh, sorry,' she replied with a giggle. 'Yes, yes, I will. And thank you, the ring is lovely.'

Tony insisted on putting it on her finger, the heart facing towards her fingertips. The people at the tables close-by clapped, and one man called out 'good luck'.

Sarah stared at her ring finger. 'Ah, you've done your research.'

'Yes. The jeweller was most adamant about the correct position of the heart.' Tony got up off his knees and sat down, but he looked a little sad.

'What's wrong? You're not having regrets already, are you?' she asked.

'No! Don't be daft.' Tony shifted uneasily. 'The thing is, it will have to be a long engagement. I must go back to Southampton tomorrow and I may be away for some time.'

Sarah laid her head on his shoulder. 'Don't worry, I understand and I can wait. I know something major is about to happen. We have been working towards it for months. I don't expect you to tell me the details, but is it the big push we have been hoping for? France?' she whispered.

Tony nodded and squeezed her hand. 'Darling Sarah, all I *can* say is we are about to find out if God is on our side.'

The End

Acknowledgements

I have been incredibly lucky, for I grew up in a house where books were king and trips to the library were a weekly occurrence. However, it was my father's love of history which resonated with me the most, and although I devoured crime novels as a teenager, historical fiction has always been my 'go-to' when choosing what to read. It's no surprise, I suppose, that I have ended up writing historical mysteries and crime!

And my luck has continued in having such a supportive family and group of friends. To Conor, my husband, and my children, Stephen, Hazel and Adam, thanks for putting up with the rushed dinners, un-ironed laundry, and general scattiness! Becoming a full-time writer is daunting and would not have been possible without the encouragement and support of family, friends and work colleagues who urged me to take the leap. Two years on, I am happy to say I have no regrets.

I would like to take the opportunity to thank one incredibly special lady, Thérèse Coen, my agent. The Sarah Gillespie books are the result of her suggestion that I write a WW2 novel with an Irish perspective. For your continued support, guidance, and hard work, I am extremely grateful. A big thank you to all the team at Hardman & Swainson and Susanna Lea & Associates, London. You guys are the best. No book is worth writing without a few baddies! My brother-in-law, Dave O'Connell, was keen to feature as one and I was happy to oblige. Thanks Dave!

Producing a novel is a collaborative process, and I have been fortunate to have wonderful editors, copyeditors, proof-readers, and graphic designers working on this series. Thanks to you all, and in particular, thanks to Elisha Lundin, my editor, who is a joy to work with. To all the team at Avon Books UK and HarperCollins, thanks so much.

I am extremely grateful to have such loyal readers. For those of you who take the time to leave reviews, please know that I appreciate them beyond words. To the amazing book bloggers, book tour hosts and reviewers who have hosted me and my books over the years – thank you.

Last, but certainly not least, I am incredibly lucky to have a network of writer friends who keep me motivated, especially Sharon Thompson, Valerie Keogh, Jenny O'Brien, Fiona Cooke, Brook Allen and Tonya Murphy Mitchell. Special thanks to the members of the Historical Novel Society, RNA and Society of Authors Irish Chapters, and all the gang at the Coffee Pot Book Club.

Go raibh míle maith agat!

A life changing moment. A heartbreaking choice. A dangerous mission . . .

A gripping story that explores a deadly tangle of love and espionage in war-torn Britain, perfect for fans of Pam Jenoff, Kate Quinn and Kate Furnivall.

Available in all good bookstores now.

When working for the British Secret Service, Sarah Gillespie can trust no one, not even her closest friends . . .

A heartbreaking and completely addictive page-turner about one woman's bravery in World War Two Britain.

Available in all good bookstores now.